Elle...
Radio News and has wri...

she was employed as an economist at ...
She has lived and studied in Russia, France, ...
Spain, Italy and Britain. She is fluent in French and Spanish
and has a Master's degree in International Relations from The
Johns Hopkins University School of Advanced International
Studies and a Bachelor's degree in Political Science from The
Catholic University of America.

... ow *Nights* is her first novel. She lives in Oak Hill,
Virginia with her husband and three sons and is currently
...ing on her second novel.

Moscow Nights

by

Ellen Crosby

PIATKUS

For more information on other books published by Piatkus, visit our website at www.piatkus.co.uk

Copyright © 2000 by Ellen Crosby

First published in Great Britain in 2000 by
Judy Piatkus (Publishers) Ltd of
5 Windmill Street, London W1T 2JA
email:info@piatkus.co.uk

This edition published 2001

The moral right of the author has been asserted

A catalogue record for this book is available from the British Library

ISBN 0 7499 3210 4

Set in Times by
Action Publishing Technology Ltd, Gloucester

Printed and bound in Great Britain by
Mackays of Chatham, plc, Chatham, Kent

For André

Author's Note

The principal characters in this book are pure fiction, completely conceived in my imagination. The setting – Moscow, USSR – could be said to be fictitious as well, for the Soviet Union no longer exists and Moscow in the twenty-first century is vastly different from the city where I lived in the waning years of Communist rule. Those who knew Moscow in those days will, I hope, forgive the few liberties I took with geography and some of the arcane details of life in that fascinating place. However, the historical events and figures I describe are as real as I can make them, with the exception of Baron Caspar von Müller whose existence and connection with the fate of the Amber Room are entirely invented.

I owe thanks to my publisher, Judy Piatkus, and to my editors, Gillian Green and Lynn Curtis, of Piatkus Books. My agent, Mary Bruton, has been ever-generous with sound advice and friendship; there when I need her despite the time difference between the US and UK. Thanks to my husband, André de Nesnera, for showing me Russia through his eyes and for enduring faith. Lastly, a profound debt of thanks to Cathy Brannon whose friendship, blue pencil, sympathetic ear, and a place to stay when I return to London have meant more than I can say.

September, 1989

'In Russia, everything is a mystery but nothing is a secret'
– Mme de Staël

Chapter One

I stepped off the airplane into a black and white movie of a place I thought only existed before I was born. Through the plane window I had watched immeasurable empty spaces and faraway horizons grow steadily bleaker until finally, on arriving, the colour was bleached from everything around me. I had come nearly five thousand miles on this late-September day to a faded landscape where sour smells choked my first breath and seeped through my clothing into my skin. I reckoned the psychological distance I had travelled needed to be measured in light years.

I walked through a set of double doors where an adolescent boy with acne and a military uniform watched me the way a guard watches prisoners returning to their cells. Then I followed signs down narrow glass-walled corridors feeling like a rat in a maze.

A different alphabet, but I could read the words. I wonder why that surprised me.

I must have stopped walking to stare because suddenly a guard standing sentry along the way caught my eye and jerked his head. I knew what he meant. Every cop in the world does that when you're loitering some place you're not supposed to be. Move along, now.

So I moved.

Why on earth did I think I'd be able to act like this was just another city? Another assignment, just like all the others. Who was I kidding?

This place was my mother's home. But after she died, I had been told to erase that fact and every remembered story from my mind, until the memories were bleached white and clean as old bone.

I walked down a flight of stairs and found the queue for passport control. The room was dimly lit, like a cave, guarded by more military uniforms. In the washed out yellow light their grey-green jackets and trousers blended into the dark walls so they disappeared like chameleons and watched from the shadows. One of them vaporized next to me and indicated that I should present my documents to the passport officer.

Yet another adolescent with acne and a uniform that looked as if it had been borrowed from his father. He sat, carved in stone, behind smoky glass and watched as I slid my papers toward him under the glass window. The lower part of the window was opaque so I couldn't see what he was doing, but obviously he had opened my passport. He looked up and stared. I hate it when they look at you like that. Who looks like their passport photo anyway, or even wants to? My hair was different. And, okay, older. Well, aren't we all? No makeup. And dead tired. But it was still definitely me.

His head kept bobbing up and down as if a hidden puppeteer was pulling strings to make him move. I clasped my hands together and found they were wet. This was crazy. I had absolutely nothing to be nervous about. So what if he was scrutinizing me like I was a fugitive on the run and now he'd caught me?

Finally I had to look away. Above my head was a copper-coloured mirror, tilted at a forty-five degree angle. So I did what any woman does, confronted with a mirror. I started arranging my hair, which looked pretty disastrous after a bad night's sleep in a cramped airline seat. I was pulling my fingers through a twisted strand of auburn hair that had turned the colour of liquid fire in the copper reflection when I knew for sure.

Someone was watching me on the other side of the mirror.

I looked away for a second time and, on cue, the telephone in the cubicle rang. The teenager in front of me said something into it and then he stamped my passport and my visa. He kept right on stamping papers, at least another six or eight documents. Things I hadn't given him. I stood on tiptoe but I wasn't tall enough to see past the opaque glass.

4

What kind of file did they have on me already? I'd never been here before.

He shoved my passport and visa back to me underneath the glass. I heard a loud click as he pressed a button unlocking the gate next to me. I had been processed.

Time to go deeper into the labyrinth and rescue my suitcases.

It was another hour before a customs officer made important slashes across my customs declaration after sucking my bags into a clunky X-ray machine that looked like it ought to be tested for leaking radiation. That was all. They were finished with me and I was free to leave the nowhere land of the airport, the nebulous in-between place that was neither where I'd come from nor where I was going.

I walked toward the wall in front of me as a set of double doors slid open, spilling me into the main terminal and a mass of humanity waiting on the other side. A sign said 'Welcome to Moscow'. The long trip and the time difference were making me feel numb and lightheaded. With a hiss the doors closed behind me.

My connection to the real world was severed.

David Manning, one of the correspondents from our Moscow bureau, rescued me from an onslaught of people who pushed and gawked like they were looking at an animal in a zoo. A familiar face. It should have been a welcome sight in this sea of shoving strangers, but it wasn't.

Anyway, the look in his eyes said it all. He was suffering. The bosses in New York had sent him a kid to do a grownup's job. And then there was that other thing. The 'I-hope-you're-not-the-same-bimbo-you-were-in-New-York' look of forbearance.

Some day that mountain peak he sat on all by himself was going to crumble beneath him and he'd be like the rest of us mere mortals. If the man ever pricked his finger, I bet motor oil would ooze out instead of blood.

I stared at him longer than I should have, though. He looked terrible, like he'd come straight to the airport after a month-long hike through the Siberian wilderness. His photo in the rogues' gallery of pinups that hung outside the newsroom in New York showed a good-looking man, probably late-thirties, with neatly groomed dark hair and features that

5

said 1940s matinée idol, strong and clean. The person in front of me was Grizzly Adams' cousin. He'd pulled his hair, now well streaked with grey, into an untidy ponytail and his eyes were bruised-looking and bloodshot. He hadn't seen a razor in a while which only made him look more haggard.

He'd aged ten years in two.

But he was looking me over as well, and I can't say I came off any better than he did. My hand went instinctively to my hair, which I knew looked like I'd styled it with an electric mixer. Frankly, I didn't look any more like my glamorous newsroom mugshot than he did, but any resemblance between me and the fantasy my photo conjured up was purely accidental. I think I was in the middle of telling the receptionist that yes, please, I'd love a cup of coffee when the photographer snapped it. My mouth was slightly open and my eyes, usually the colour of pale jade, had become exotically, almost glitteringly, emerald-coloured. I guess it's because I'm a hopeless caffeine addict. Talk to me about coffee and I apparently look like I've been discussing something vaguely erotic. My hair was riotous, but then it always is. I forgot an umbrella and got caught in a downpour on the way to the studio. I remember looking in the mirror and thinking a paper bag over my head would be an improvement.

Surprisingly, the photo made me look like one of those late night television babes on the 'call me, big guy' ads. Stan, my boss in New York and one of those rare men who wouldn't look up if a naked *Playboy* centrefold wandered past his desk, astonished me by absolutely loving this sex-kitten picture. Don't ask me why but I let him use it as my official press photo instead of choosing one of the staid, more professional poses where I looked like the kind of person you could believe in if you were serious about your news. The real me, normal and ordinary-looking. I have to say, though, that I regret that flirty picture was taken after I'd already gotten my passport – the one I'd just presented to that prepubescent soldier, with the photo that looked like I'd been preserved in formaldehyde.

Manning reached over and grabbed my luggage trolley. 'Keep your hands on your bag. This place is full of pickpockets.' He moved toward the exit and said, 'Yuri's waiting outside with one of the cars. He would have come in to help, but the car would have been stolen.'

I watched his retreating back as he steered my luggage expertly through the maze of people. Still the same friendly guy I remembered from New York. Not one to waste time on trivialities like 'Hi, welcome to Moscow' or 'How was your trip?'

I guess we were going to pick up our relationship where we'd left off in the States.

I had to struggle to follow the swath he had cut through the crowd because it immediately surged around me so I was swept along like a cork bobbing on the tide. I lost sight of him as though he'd disappeared into a black hole.

'Taxi? Taxi?' A stranger with a glittering gold and silver smile and breath that would have stopped a charging elephant in its tracks stood, practically on top of me, so close I thought he was going to kiss me. Unshaven and wearing a red and white striped cap with a pompom on it. One of Santa's elves run amok. I stepped back and stopped breathing.

'*Nyet* taxi.' Manning rematerialized by my side and grabbed my elbow. He pulled me along with him and said in my ear, 'Whatever you do, don't get into a taxi alone. Especially the ones that cruise around Sheremetyevo Airport. There have been tourists who were robbed and beaten by guys who showed up here, claiming to be taxi drivers. They drive you out to the countryside, strip you, and do it there.'

'I won't.' And no more complaining about the outrageous fares the cabbies at JFK charge, either.

It felt like someone was pulling the scenery past me too quickly and I needed to run to stay in the picture. We walked through an automatic door into a black cloud of exhaust fumes.

'David?'

'What?'

A large, dirty blue and white bus was parked directly in front of us. The driver had backed up so that the bus was overhanging most of the sidewalk in front of the main door, forcing us to manoeuvre single-file through the congealed pedestrian traffic.

'How's Ian?' I had to shout it over his shoulder into his ear

7

so he could hear me above the din of angry voices and hostile car horns. The bus belched more black smoke into my face. I coughed and waved it away. Manning seemed immune to it.

He half-turned and shouted back at me, 'Let's get out of here first.' He caught my arm and dragged me past the bus. He scanned the crowd. 'Damn. Yuri was right here. The *militsia* must have made him move when the bus showed up.' He pushed the luggage trolley toward me. 'Stay here. And don't let go of that cart or someone will walk off with it. I'll go find Yuri.'

He left before I could tell him I had no plans to go exploring. I clung to the cart and ignored the stares.

'Claire!'

Manning returned, from somewhere behind the bus. 'Yuri's coming. He'll be here as soon as the bus moves.'

'Right.'

'Look, about Ian . . .' He was staring intently at a spot near my left shoulder.

There are moments when you know with absolute clarity that something is about to happen that will change your life forever, derail it so there is no going back to the way it was before.

Like now.

I was tired and vulnerable and overwhelmed. I did not want to hear this.

'What is it?'

'He's dead.' It sounded like Manning was apologizing. 'The hospital phoned just before I left to come get you. We've got to go there now. They want me to sign some papers before they'll release the body.'

I heard his voice through the roaring of the bus as it pulled away. Except the roaring didn't stop after the bus left. I said faintly, 'That's not possible.'

Ian, the man I had once lived with and still loved, had never been ill a day in his life. He couldn't be dead. I couldn't have lost him to this drab, threadbare city where time ran backwards until it got stuck in a place the rest of the world had left behind.

When Stan had told me Ian was in a coma in a Moscow hospital, I didn't believe him at first. Then he said I was going

8

to Moscow to fill in until Ian got better. He figured I would want to be with Ian anyway.

He'd given me barely enough time to throw a few things in a suitcase and, presto, here I was. The company's travel agent nearly had a coronary trying to get me a visa on such short notice. As it was, it didn't arrive until I was practically on my way out the door to Kennedy.

'He died this morning . . . I'm sorry.' Manning was watching me and I could see he was worried I might come unglued right here in front of him and then he would have to deal with it. The messiness of a woman bursting into tears and all that.

He worried for nothing. I was too shocked to cry. At least right now. Too stunned to do anything except stand there, glassy-eyed and speechless, waiting for him to take it all back and tell me he hadn't meant it. That it was all a bad joke and he was sorry he made it up.

But no, instead he was tugging at my arm, trying to uproot me from the sidewalk, helping me walk unsteadily to where a midnight blue Volvo station wagon had pulled up to the kerb. A dark, slender man whose silver-grey hair did not go with his youthful face waited for us. 'This is Yuri,' Manning said, 'one of our drivers.'

Yuri murmured a greeting in Russian. I think I responded. Manning opened the car door and I slid across the back seat. He slid in beside me. Behind us, Yuri was arranging my suit-cases in the boot. He slammed the door and the noise made me jump. Then he got into the car and pulled out into the clogged airport traffic attempting to funnel into narrow exit lanes.

I turned to stare out the window so they could not see my face. I bit my tongue so hard it hurt and concentrated on looking at the scenery. It became blurry almost immediately.

Dammit.

I fished in the pocket of my blazer. Why, I don't know. I never carry tissues or extra change for a pay phone or anything utilitarian like that. But just now, there was no way I was going to ask Manning, who had all the compassion of a Marine drill sergeant, if he had a tissue so I could wipe my eyes.

The silence in the car became even more hauntingly quiet.

9

He knew. Yuri knew, too.

Mercifully they said nothing.

After a while we got to the edge of the airport and its sea of impatient, congested vehicles. The road opened up and became a multi-lane highway. Yuri deftly shifted the Volvo from one lane to the other, weaving past slower moving Russian cars and trucks. The highway was full of military vehicles and cars that looked old and worn out, with windshields cracked like giant spider webs. A filthy dump truck carrying a mountain of pale green cabbages and spewing fumes from its tailpipe bounced and jolted in front of us, occasionally spilling cabbages on to the road. A khaki-covered jeep carrying a group of young soldiers drove past us. I saw their vacant-eyed faces as they stared out the back window. A bunch of scared kids. Across the rear door of the jeep the word '*lyudi*' had been painted. 'People.' Like they had to explain it.

Ian, who had been my lover, my mentor, my dearest friend, was lying cold and alone in a hospital somewhere in this godforsaken place where they wrote 'people' across the back of a truck carrying kids playing soldiers.

I cleared my throat. 'What did he die of?' My voice was reasonably steady.

Yuri finally overtook the dump truck and we sprinted past the jeep.

'They don't know.'

I was stunned. 'What do you mean, they don't know? They have to know. Maybe he's not even dead. Are they sure about that?'

Manning's look would have frozen mercury. 'When you've been here a while you'll understand.'

I know a put down when I hear one and that was a put down. Coming from Mr Congeniality only made it more irritating. 'I have no intention of being here for a while,' I snapped. I wasn't too worried about hurting his feelings since he obviously didn't have any.

Besides, where did he get the idea that I was staying?

Maybe he thought I had asked to be exiled here.

Not too likely.

The only reason I came was Ian. I would have walked

10

across hot coals barefoot for him. Even now, even when my life was falling apart in New York and leaving town was only going to make things worse. Make it look like I was running away.

A little problem between me and the bank. If I didn't give them their money – soon – they were going to take my house. The one I'd grown up in. My heart and soul were in that house. I couldn't lose it.

Of course I didn't dare tell Stan any of this when he ordered me to pack my bags and get to Moscow. A personal life must never interfere with our sacred mission to be where the story is. It didn't help, either, that the company was in the middle of yet another budget crisis. The big bosses were once again looking for ways to 'cut the fat'. A nifty little euphemism for getting rid of a few more bodies. So saying I didn't want to go to Moscow would be a dumb thing to do, under the circumstances.

Which left me begging Aaron, my lawyer, to do whatever it took to buy me a little more time with that nice bank. Two weeks, tops. Then I promised I'd be back and we could straighten everything out.

'You obviously don't understand where you are,' Manning was speaking with that grating know-it-all superiority, hauling me back to reality in the rear seat of the Volvo, 'or you'd realize that in this country you can't so much as find a bandage or an aspirin. The pharmacies are empty, a joke. There's nothing. They re-use condoms. Wash 'em out and dry 'em. Did you know that?'

The mental image of a clothesline full of recycled condoms blowing in the wind reduced me to silence.

I said, finally, 'Does Susan know?'

'Susan?'

'Ian's sister. She's his next-of-kin. His parents are dead.'

'Ah, no. Not yet. I think New York is trying to find her.' He shifted in his seat so he was turned towards his own window, his back towards me. I took it as a hint our conversation was over. Fine by me.

I never understood why Ian liked Manning, but he did. Ian said they got along just fine, but then Ian got along with everybody, however quirky or weird they were. I always figured it

11

was more professional respect than personal rapport, especially given Manning's sunshiny personality. Ian had told me once he thought Manning wrote like a poet. When Ian said something like that, it was as if God had handed it down on a stone tablet. Ian had a Pulitzer; he knew what he was talking about.

We were approaching the city now and I was no longer exhausted but somewhere in that witless jetlagged state between wakefulness and sleep that felt like swimming under water with my clothes on. We swept down wide boulevards in slow-motion unreality.

Ahead rows of dark grey boxes sat on a flat, lighter grey skyline. The glacial silence in the car continued as the boxes slowly grew larger until they dominated the view like high-rise sentries on either side of us. They were ugly and graceless, products of an architecture of gigantism, meant to destroy all sense of human scale. Their only distinguishing feature was the absence of any distinguishing feature. No colour, no pretty garden out front, no special details, just a grim, overwhelming sameness. We passed what looked like a large sports stadium, then Yuri turned left and pulled into a parking lot.

In front of us was a box, like the other boxes, except that this building was low and much smaller. It was depressing-looking and dirty. 'Why are we stopping here?' I asked.

'This is the hospital.'

'You're joking?'

'It's a special hospital for high-ranking Communist Party members and foreigners,' Manning said, getting out of the car.

I followed him. 'Good God! Where does everybody else go?'

He looked at me the way you look at merchandise in a store when you're not sure if you want to buy it. 'Maybe it wasn't such a good idea to bring you here. Maybe you should wait in the car,' he said.

No way.

I hadn't really thought about what it would do to me to see Ian, lying dead in a morgue in this dump of a hospital on the dark side of the moon, but there was no chance Manning was going in there alone.

'Don't be ridiculous. I'm coming with you,' I said. I swept past him and started toward the steps of the hospital.

He loped past me and held the door.

I stared straight ahead, ignoring him, but as I walked through the doorway he leaned over and said roughly in my ear, 'I meant it, Claire. I shouldn't have brought you. You don't want to do this.'

I acted like I hadn't heard him.

He was right, though. I didn't want to do this.

Chapter Two

Inside, the hospital was as bad as it was outside. Actually, it was worse. The place smelled of the mustiness of stale air and sour, unwashed bodies overlaid with the stink of cheap cigarettes. I caught my breath and wondered if this was the smell of Moscow and if I would ever get used to it.

A woman with a helmet of iron-coloured hair sat behind a reception desk. Manning walked over to her and set the battered backpack he was carrying next to her desk. 'I am David Manning,' he announced, 'we've come to sign papers to release the body of Ian Kendall who died here this morning.' His Russian was quite good.

Wait until he heard mine. Three years of college Russian gone rusty from lack of use. On my job application I'd whimsically described myself as 'fairly fluent'. The first time I had to carry on a proper conversation they'd find me out. Under the best of circumstances, I probably had the linguistic abilities of an eight year old.

The woman glared at both of us. Her voice matched her hair. 'Is this his wife?' She hooked a thumb in my direction like I was the coat rack or something.

'I'm a friend,' I said. I suppose I didn't mean to make it sound like a threat, even if it came out that way. Manning laid a warning hand on my arm.

It didn't matter. She steamrollered on, speaking only to him. 'And you are not a relative, *gaspodin*?'

Manning shook his head. 'Mr Kendall was my colleague. We worked together.'

She shrugged with the weary disdain of a petty official and

14

said unctuously, 'Only family may sign the documents.' She looked down at some papers on her desk, having dispensed with us.

I set my hand down and it happened to land on top of her papers. 'He has no family in Moscow.'

Manning reached for my hand and folded it in both of his, like a vice. 'Mr Kendall's family is in America,' he said pleasantly, as though we were all good friends. 'They are very distressed and grieving deeply over their loss. I'm sure you understand.'

'It is not possible . . .'

'Mr Kendall's family has asked me to present you with something as a token of their appreciation if you would be so kind as to allow us to take care of this matter on their behalf,' he continued. 'Perhaps there is some place more private?'

The bribe had been as subtle as a ton of bricks. She would surely be insulted and throw us out. He was a fool to assume she was so venal and easily manipulated. But she was already murmuring, 'Yes, of course. I will take you to the morgue immediately. Please follow me.'

Manning grabbed my elbow and said violently in my ear, 'Don't say another word. I'll handle this.'

I yanked my elbow free. 'Stop treating me like a child.'

'Stop acting like one.'

He dropped my arm and strode ahead to catch up with the Russian woman. I trailed behind, nursing my arm and my dignity.

I've never been inside a prison, but I know it would look like this place. Every door we came to was locked. On both sides. So we had to stop each time and wait while the woman unlocked the door and then locked it again on the other side. By the third door the sound of the metal tumblers clicking into place was giving me the creeps.

Were they trying to keep people in or out?

We were now in what apparently was one of the wards. The corridor was filthy, littered with bloody bandages and cigarette butts, and the place smelled foul, of sickness. Bare bulbs dangling from electrical wires cast pathetic circles of pale light on the floor. Everything else was shadows and gloom. As for the patients, they were left lying on stretchers on the concrete floor, end-to-end along both walls, for the entire length of the corridor. Not a nurse or doctor in sight. And silence. Awful, chilling silence. Then someone on one of the stretchers moaned and a hand plucked at my ankle as I walked by. I would have tripped if Manning hadn't grabbed me.

'Watch your step.'

I nodded because otherwise I was going to throw up if I opened my mouth to answer him. We walked past a row of interior windows where you could see into rooms beyond. More bodies, one to a room, lying still as statues on thin cots. That was it. Nothing else in the room. And the faces were always turned to the wall. Other than having that crummy bed to lie on, I couldn't see that they were any better off than the inmates in the corridor. So we kept playing hopscotch over silent bodies as we moved down the hall.

It seemed when we'd walked through those locked doors, we'd entered some bizarre Dickensian time warp, gone back to the days of primitive medicine when illness meant unbearable pain and suffering. Anyone who left here better off than when they arrived only did so because they clung grimly to a desire to get out.

The locks were definitely to keep people in.

We walked down two flights of stairs. The air felt distinctly cooler and smelled of damp, but at least the revolting smells from the wards were gone. Instead there was a cloying odour of chemicals, like the smell in high school biology labs when you had to dissect frogs or sheep's eyes or baby pigs.

We came to another locked door. The last one. On the other side a small man with a grey handlebar moustache and stooped shoulders sat at a desk, doing nothing. He looked up when we entered.

'Anatoly Nicolaievich, these people have come to sign documents for the body of the American, Ian Kendall,' the woman said.

'Only family members may do that.'

I'd heard that before.

Manning launched into his speech. Cue the bribe. 'We bring a token of appreciation from Mr Kendall's family in America who has asked us to take care of this matter for them.'

16

The magic door opened at once. 'I see. First, then, you must identify the body.'

'Of course.' Manning's voice was dry and tight. He was perspiring, too, though the room was quite cool. He turned to me and said in that same tense voice, 'I really think you should wait here.'

Forget it. If he could do this, so could I. Although his face was now the colour of chalk, and he was beginning to look as though he might pass out at any moment.

'Maybe you're the one who should wait outside. You don't look well, David.'

For some reason that upset him. He said coldly, 'I'm fine. Have it your way. We'll both go.'

Anatoly Nicolaievich and the woman were watching our little drama. I don't think language was any barrier. They didn't miss a thing. Then the woman coughed, a fake polite cough. 'I must return to my post.'

Manning stared at her as if he didn't know what she meant.

'Your backpack,' I hissed.

'Oh. Sure. Right.' He slid the backpack off his shoulder and set it down on the desk. When he unzipped it, I saw the two bottles of Scotch. He handed one to the woman and set the other on the desk. 'Thank you for your help.'

The woman held the Scotch as if she were cradling a baby. 'I will leave you now.' She looked triumphant, having just cashed in on Ian's death and won the jackpot. She walked across the room, but in the doorway stopped and turned around. 'I'm sorry about your friend,' she said, and suddenly her voice grew soft and you might have thought she actually cared. 'I'm sure he was a good man.'

Then she left.

There was a sound of metal scraping metal as Anatoly Nicolaievich opened his desk drawer. He set his bottle of Scotch inside and said, 'Follow me.' He picked up a key ring with a single large key on it, like the one to the dungeon of a castle.

The morgue was a square room with a high ceiling and dingy white-tiled floors and walls. Fluorescent lights suspended from the stained acoustical tile ceiling turned my skin pale and artificial. A row of pipes ran the length of one wall, but condensation had obviously corroded them and there

17

were rivulets of dried rust running down the wall. A battered antique typewriter sat on a small table next to a glass cabinet filled with bottles of dark, viscous-looking liquids in greens and browns. There were several fragile-seeming trolleys in the middle of the room, their surfaces heavily soiled with stains I didn't want to examine too closely. A sign in Russian said 'No Smoking' next to a loudly ticking wall clock. Each time the minute hand leapt forward, it first moved back infinitesimally. Along the far wall was a line of compartments that looked like rows of refrigerator doors.

'Now let's see,' Anatoly Nicolaievich was saying, 'Kendall, Kendall ... he's here somewhere.' He counted down and across the rows, pointing a nicotine-stained finger at each compartment like he was working out clues in an over-sized crossword puzzle. 'Ah!'

He opened a door in the top row in the middle of the wall. 'I'll just get him for you,' he said, as though he were going to produce Ian, alive and well, before us.

He wheeled one of the metal trolleys over to the compart-ment and positioned it in front of the door. 'Here he is.' He tugged on a body bag inside the compartment, trying to slide Ian's body out. But the bag had been only loosely covering him, tucked around like a blanket. It fluttered to the ground, leaving him stuck inside the compartment.

'Give me a hand, then,' Anatoly Nicolaievich said impa-tiently. 'We've got to get him out of there.'

I saw Manning swallow hard and then he walked over to the other side of the compartment.

'On three,' Anatoly Nicolaievich said. 'One ... two ... three.'

Manning probably didn't have too much experience in pulling dead bodies out of morgue refrigerators and maybe Anatoly Nicolaievich, a tiny grey cricket of a man who looked like he might blow away in a strong wind, miscalculated how large Ian had been and how much force it would take to free him from his cubby hole. His body came out with such momentum that Manning stumbled and accidentally kicked the trolley away from its position in front of them.

'Claire, grab it!' he shouted. I could see he'd lost his balance and Ian was slipping out of his arms.

I leapt forward and shoved the trolley toward them, but I was too forceful. It crashed into the wall of refrigerator doors and bounced off again, like a ball ricocheting in a pinball machine.

'Get it! Get it!'

'Quickly, quickly, we are losing him!'

They were hollering at me at the same time, in English and Russian. I did as I was told again, but this time I held the trolley in place. That's when I realized Ian's body, naked as the day he was born, was stained a horrible, violent purple underneath. One of my hands brushed his feet. They felt like ice cubes.

I had seen Ian naked before, of course.

But not like this.

Watching them wrestle with him like they were landing a large, dead fish was unbearable. I closed my eyes but still I heard them, panting and grunting. I didn't want to remember him this way. Not Ian who had lived like there were no second chances, so do it all while you can, don't miss out on anything. *Carpe diem* and all that. He would do anything on a whim, take any dare, make any bet.

It was fun at first and I loved him, as deeply, madly and intensely as he loved me, but he was burning through life so fast ... too fast for me. I wanted to slow it down, smell the roses, watch a sunset, fall asleep in a meadow of wildflowers, run on a beach ... do nothing, sometimes. Surely it didn't always have to be crash and burn.

I was the one who moved out, insisting he keep our apartment. Otherwise I was afraid he'd end up living out of his car or camped at our friends' places, like a gypsy. Then he took the job in Moscow. The night before he left, he came over to my new place with champagne and Russian caviare and fed me in bed by candlelight. He told me that he thought it would be easier to get over me if he were on the other side of the world. When I woke up the next morning, he was gone.

I didn't see him for nearly two years. Then five weeks ago he came home to be with me for Kathleen's funeral. Kathleen Brennan was my father's mother, the great lady who raised me after my parents' accident. When she died, I called Ian in Moscow and asked him to come. I didn't know who else to ask.

That was the last time I'd seen him . . . until now.

Manning and Anatoly Nicolaievich finally laid Ian's body properly on the trolley. There were two enormous dark stains under Manning's arms and he looked like he'd just stepped out of a sauna. The back of his red plaid flannel shirt clung to him like a second skin. I could see the contours of his muscles. He was built lean and hard, like Ian had been. He wiped his forearm across his face and looked up. Our eyes met, purely by accident, then we each looked away.

He reached for the identification tag that had been tied around Ian's ankle. 'Right. That's Ian Kendall. You know it and we know it.' His voice was curt. 'Now tell me why he's been turned into a block of ice?'

Anatoly Nicolaievich shrugged. 'We cannot control the temperature so precisely. Our equipment is poor. Be grateful it is not too warm. You would have green flies . . . and maggots. It has happened before.'

He spoke in a breezily appraising manner, as though we were in an abattoir instead of a morgue, discussing hygienic conditions for slaughtered meat. Now I really was going to throw up. I put my hand over my mouth.

Manning grabbed my elbow. 'Why don't you wait in the other room.'

It wasn't a question. 'We can't leave him here like this,' I said.

'I know, I know.' He started to propel me toward the door. 'We haven't had time to book a flight yet. There's no place to take him . . . no coffin . . .'

I cut him off. 'He is *not* staying here. He's coming with us!' It was, of course, a completely ridiculous thing to say under the circumstances. But I was jetlagged and upset. Okay, scared, too. This place was sinister enough to make you wonder if they practised necromancy after dark, or God knows what else.

'Oh, sure. Why didn't I think of that? How about you take his arms and I'll take his legs? We can throw him naked in the back of the Volvo with your luggage . . . are you nuts? There's *nothing* we can do today.' Manning turned to Anatoly Nicolaievich. 'We're through here. Let's get him back in his . . . let's finish here and get on with signing the papers.'

I left the room.

20

I could still hear them, though, and the sounds were worse torture than if I had stayed to watch. Especially the sound of a metal door being slammed shut.

The end of everything.

When Manning and Anatoly Nicolaievich came back into the little anteroom, I was sitting in a chair by the door. I didn't look up.

Then there was the quiet rustling of papers and the scratching noise of a pen as Manning signed all the documents. It took forever. Manning said he would contact Anatoly Nicolaievich as soon as he could make arrangements to take Ian to Sheremetyevo.

'Claire, are you ready?'

I nodded and stood up.

Anatoly Nicolaievich took us to an exit down the corridor from his office. 'I'm sorry about your friend,' he said. 'A death from complication of the cookies is tragic, especially in one so young.'

Manning looked startled. 'What are you talking about?'

'The cause of death,' Anatoly Nicolaievich said. 'It was on the hospital death certificate that you just signed. Our doctors have confirmed it ... now I must get back to my post. Good afternoon.'

He closed the door, practically in our faces. We heard the key turn in the lock.

Just in case one of the bodies tried to escape from the morgue, probably.

I turned to Manning. 'Do you mind telling me what that was all about? What was he talking about ... *cookies*? Ian died of a sweet tooth?'

Manning squinted at me. 'He didn't say cookies, Claire. He said 'liver'. Ian died of liver failure. The word for liver is *'pyehchyehn'*. The word for cookies is *'pyeechyehnyah'*. I thought you were supposed to be fluent in Russian.'

That did it.

'Yeah, well, fine, I'm not perfect like you are, okay? But I'll tell you this, I *never* would have signed something I didn't read first. The first time we were told anything about the cause of Ian's death was two milliseconds before we got the door slammed in our faces. How very compassionate. Where

21

do these people do their sensitivity training – Lubyanka Prison? How could you let him get away with that?' I spoke with the punch-drunk attitude of the sleep-deprived, a semi-mindless state that confers absolute authority uncontaminated by rational thought or knowledge. I had reached the point of no longer caring about anything. Besides, Manning and I had been drawing the battle lines for the last hour.

'Listen, sweetheart, this isn't America. Do you think I had any choice in there? They'll do an autopsy in the States. What I signed is irrelevant.' It was pretty hard to miss the sarcasm, even in my somnambulant condition.

'Is that so? Thanks for telling me. Unless, of course, his body has decomposed so badly by then that it's no longer possible. Or maybe you weren't thinking that far ahead.'

By now, we were both hollering at each other. Anatoly Nicolaievich had let us out of the hospital into what was probably the staff parking lot. We were surrounded by small, dusty Russian cars. Yuri and the Volvo were nowhere in sight. I heard a window open above us. We had an audience.

Manning didn't seem to care. He was as coldly cutting as he'd been in the morgue. Just like the time we had our big blow-up in the newsroom in New York.

'You just don't get it, do you? You think you can show up here and act like you're still in New York. I told them not to send me some pampered little correspondent who needed a babysitter. Especially one who doesn't speak Russian. Look, if this place is too much for you, maybe you should catch the next plane home.' He turned and began walking away from me.

'You think I asked to come here?' I screeched after him. 'I got *sent* here! The only reason I could possibly want to be in this godforsaken dump is to be with Ian and now he's dead. And you know what? Now I'm *glad* I came. At least Ian had someone with him at the end who cared about him. You didn't even care enough to find out why he died until that wonderful humanitarian mentioned it in passing before he slammed the door.'

Manning stopped walking and turned around to face me. The air between us was practically vibrating. He'd hit a nerve with that crack about needing a babysitter. And my Russian.

Who did he think he was, anyway? Edward R. Murrow? 'I had no idea you and that man were going to shove him around like a piece of meat in a butcher's shop,' I said, and made sure he heard the contempt in my voice. 'Do you think any of those people in there gave a damn about Ian? They cared more for their stupid bottle of Scotch than they did about him ... and you're no better. You're as big a hypocrite as they are. Catch a plane yourself, back to the real world – unless you're afraid to. You've been here too long.'

He looked absolutely stunned, as though I'd slapped him hard across the face. Then he said, 'You can go to hell.' He turned on his heel as though I were the dirt under it and strode to the car where Yuri was waiting. I followed him like a sleep-walker a few seconds later and we drove into Moscow as though each other didn't exist.

I stared out of the car window and watched the overwhelming shabbiness of the city as the modern boxlike bunkers gave way to the crumbling elegance of Neo-Classical architecture and the streets became more built up. We passed a sign that said 'Zoopark' and after a moment the Moscow River, lead-coloured and serpentine, came into view. Across the river was a fantastically tiered building of turrets and gingerbread, a monstrous ochre wedding cake. It looked like a place where the Prince of Darkness would live.

'That's your hotel,' Manning said abruptly.

'What?' I sat up.

'The Ukraine Hotel. You're staying there.'

'Stan told me I was staying in Ian's apartment.'

'I moved in when he got sick. You've got my old suite at the Ukraine. You're not going to be here that long anyway.'

You're telling me, sweetheart, I thought. Aloud I said as calmly as I could, 'Where's the office?'

'Down the street. About a fifteen-minute walk. I did it every day.'

I ignored that.

Yuri pulled into the parking lot in front of the hotel and stopped the car. He got out and began taking my bags out of the back, setting them on the sidewalk.

'I'll help you get those inside,' Manning said. There was the thinnest veneer of civility on his words.

'No need. Yuri can help me.'

'This is a hotel for foreigners. Yuri can't get past the front door.' He summoned a porter who bustled over, pushing a rickety cart. 'Sure you don't want any help?' He rocked back and forth on his heels.

The temperature between us was hovering near absolute zero. 'I'm sure I can manage.'

'Suit yourself. I put some food and bottled water in your refrigerator. Don't drink the tap water or you'll get giardia. It's a nasty little parasite, very debilitating. The food in the dining room teeters between inedible and merely revolting. I always cooked on the hot plate. It's in a box under the desk.' He paused. Advantage, Manning.

'Right.' Deuce.

'And don't forget to tip the porter with a pack of cigarettes. You did bring cigarettes like I told you to?'

I fished in my purse and found the pack of Marlboros. 'Good,' he said. 'I'll send a car to pick you up at nine tomorrow morning. By the way, the phone in your room rings incessantly. All hours of the night and day. Take it off the hook if you're too tired tonight.'

'Sure thing.'

'Fine.' He was staring at his feet as though they were new acquisitions. There was obviously something else. I waited. Then he looked up. 'There's something you ought to know, and I might as well be the one to tell you. New York's probably going to ask you about it anyway, since you and Ian were close.'

'Ask me about what?' I watched him and felt the same way I had at the airport, when he'd told me Ian was dead. Like a speeding train was headed straight for me and I was wearing cement overshoes.

Manning looked over his shoulder. I followed his gaze. He was looking at Yuri who was standing on the far side of the car, smoking a cigarette. Yuri was out of earshot but Manning stepped closer to me and dropped his voice anyway. One thing about Manning, he didn't beat around the bush. 'There's some money missing from the bureau.'

I don't know what I was expecting, but it wasn't that. It took a second before I realized that Manning was probably not talking about loose change. And then, a heartbeat later, I understood the rest of it. Ian, who was constantly overdrawn when we'd lived together, who had so many credit cards he could have made a deck of playing cards out of them, had been the Moscow bureau chief. He had been responsible for the office budget.

'How much?'

'Fifty thousand.'

'Fifty thousand *dollars*?'

He nodded.

I already knew what he was going to say, but I asked anyway. 'Do you think it's an accounting error?'

'No. It's cash that's gone, not some bookkeeping thing. We usually keep about a hundred thousand in the office safe. It saves a lot of hassle paying bills and when we need money to travel. There's only one bank in the Soviet Union that handles foreign accounts and half the time they tell you they can't find the money that's been wired to your account. Anyway, there's only thirty thousand in the safe now. And receipts for another twenty. Which leaves fifty thousand unaccounted for.'

I looked over at Yuri and watched him finish off his cigarette and throw it to the ground. 'Does Stan know yet?'

'I only found out about it myself when I checked the safe this morning. Then I started going over the books. They're a mess.' During this whole conversation he had completely avoided looking at me.

'You think Ian had something to do with it, don't you?'

He shrugged. 'I can't exactly ask him now, can I?'

'Ian is not a thief.' I realized as soon as I said it that I was still talking about him in the present tense. I saw Manning's eyelids flicker. He realized it, too. I snapped, 'Careless, maybe, but not dishonest. Do you have any proof?'

Now he looked me straight in the eye. 'Ian was the only one in the office with access to the safe, Claire. So if he didn't take it, then who did?'

'Maybe you did and now you're trying to put the blame on Ian,' I said, 'conveniently, now that he's dead. But of course you're going to tell New York that he stole it, aren't you?'

'You're way out of line,' he said, and now the battle lines between us really were entrenched. 'I was an idiot to think you might be able to help me.' He opened the car door. 'Don't discuss this with anybody.'

I called after him, 'Who am I going to tell? The porter?'

'I think you'd better get some sleep. You're obviously overwrought. My mistake to have discussed this with you in your present state. Or at all, for that matter.' He slid into the car, slamming the door in my face. Game, set, and match.

My bags had disappeared long ago. The porter didn't even know who I was.

Which Russian had said that above the gates of Moscow there should be a sign: 'Abandon intelligence all ye who enter here'? Dostoevsky? Gogol? I watched the blue station wagon disappear out of the parking lot.

Pushkin. My mother's favourite poet. If Pushkin were standing here right now, he'd say the exact same thing again, I know he would. Whisper it in my ear.

I started up the steps of the enormous ziggurat looming over me, eyes fixed straight ahead, pretending not to see the hard stares of the scruffy-looking crowd milling around the entrance. The two massive front doors were shut. I shoved against one of them until it flew open, and stumbled in the unexpected gloom of the small entryway. Then I groped my way toward a second set of double doors and went inside the Wizard's Disney castle.

Chapter Three

A woman with a clown-red mouth and blonde cotton-candy hair leapt out at me from behind a battered wooden desk as I stepped out of the elevator on the eleventh floor of the Ukraine Hotel. 'Mees Brennan.' Her eye makeup looked like it had been painted by a road-marking gang.

I was startled as much by the fact that she knew my name as by her appearance. 'Yes?'

She smiled, showing uneven, stained teeth, the bottom ones smeared faintly with red lipstick. 'I will take you to your room,' she said. 'Please, your key.'

They had given it to me downstairs. It was a large old-fashioned key, the kind that unlocked old trunks or rusty gates. I reached out to give it to her.

She caught my hand. 'Do you wear varnish?'

'What?'

'Varnish ... varnish.' She wobbled back to her desk on stiletto heels and waved a nearly empty bottle of red nail polish. 'Nail varnish.'

Scotch. Cigarettes. Now nail polish. 'No, I don't.'

She was not deterred. 'It is very difficult for us to get here ...'

I was too tired to be diplomatic with someone who applied makeup with a gardening trowel and was unsubtly pressuring me to become her new supplier thirty seconds after we met. 'I'm sorry to hear that. Could I see my room, please?'

Her eyes narrowed into two congealed black lines. 'Of course. Follow me.'

Her skirt and turtleneck moulded a once-shapely figure that

had become lumpy and solid. I could see the contours of undergarments taut against her bulk as she swayed down a dim, fusty hallway of high ceilings and heavy wooden doors. The floorboards creaked underneath a threadbare oriental carpet runner. Dust motes, caught in the slatted golden light of a window at the end of the corridor, sifted to the ground.

She stopped at a door in the middle of the hall, put my key in the lock and turned it. She muttered something under her breath, withdrew the key, and opened the door. She walked into the room and I followed her.

He was standing with his back to us, on tiptoe, his head in the freezer of an oversized refrigerator that stood next to the sofa. We were in a large living room with heavily carved furniture covered in faded sepia floral-print fabric that had come straight from a grandmother's attic. My companion let him have it in high-pitched, rapid-fire Russian.

He backed himself out of the freezer, calm as anything, and turned around, wringing hands that were red from the cold. 'I came to get what's mine, so stop fussing, Lydia,' he said in Russian. He smiled at me like this sort of laissez-faire room swapping went on all the time. 'Didn't expect you so soon.' He'd switched to English. 'Your freezer works better than mine. I like my vodka icy cold.' He smiled again and looked me over with the brazenly proprietary air of an owner surveying a prize animal at the county fair.

'Really?' Lucky me. The coldest freezer on the eleventh floor.

'Absolutely. You can get ill if you drink it at room temperature.' He sounded faintly amused.

'I see.' To my left was a set of open double doors leading to the bedroom. My suitcases were there, next to a narrow bed with a claret-coloured bedspread on it. Hopefully we weren't going to share the bed, too. 'I'm sorry, but I'm very tired. It's been a long day. If you'll excuse me, I'd like to go to bed now.'

Lydia took the hint at once, wishing me a curt *'spokoiny nochi'* as she left, but the vodka connoisseur stayed where he was. English, probably in his fifties, short with greying hair combed carefully to hide incipient baldness, thick horn-rimmed glasses, big ears, pear-shaped and puckish, the ruddy cheeks of a serious drinker, wearing a green and brown checked suit that might once have been dapper but now looked slept in.

After the woman left, he said, 'She's all right, Lydia is. When you get to know her. The friendliest of the lot.'

'Of the lot?'

'The *dejournayas*. Our minders.' He winked at me like we were conspirators. 'You can't slip off anywhere without someone knowing it. They watch us.'

He said it casually, but he was watching me, too. I kept my face neutral before this stranger who made himself at home in my hotel room and stared as though he could see me without my clothes on. 'Look, I'm very tired . . .'

'David told me about Ian, Claire. I'm so sorry. I know you've come straight from the hospital, love. I thought you might need a drink.' Up until that moment I'd been thinking that this garden gnome who acted like he was God's gift to women couldn't be for real, but all of a sudden he dropped the act and now he was dead serious. His eyes were kind and I could see the sympathy in them.

My voice wasn't too steady. 'Yes, please.'

'Then fetch two tumblers from the bathroom, my dear, and I'll get the vodka. It's stuck to the freezer. I was trying to prise it loose when you came in.' He reached up and put a hand on my shoulder, steering me towards the bedroom. 'It's just through there.'

I fled the room. The bathroom was on the other side of the bedroom. When I turned on the light, cockroaches scuttled into the greyish-pink tilework.

'Have you eaten?' he asked when I came back with the two glasses. I set them on a large circular dining table that was in the middle of the living room. There were straight-backed chairs on either side of the table.

'I had lunch over Poland.' I pulled out one of the chairs and sat down.

He looked startled, then laughed. 'Well then, it's been a while. You really ought to eat something first. Vodka on an empty stomach will make you drunk in no time.'

'I know.' I must have said it too forcefully because he looked at me, sharp-eyed and perceptive, over the top of his glasses, like some genial leprechaun, except for those probing eyes. I said, to deflect his gaze, 'Maybe you should tell me your name?'

'Nigel Bradford.' He splashed a generous amount of clear, viscous liquid into the tooth glasses. 'You know how to drink this stuff?'

'All at once.'

He reached across the table and clinked his glass against mine. 'To Ian. 'The good die first . . .''

'Ian,' I said, shaky again, and gulped the fiery cold down my throat.

Nigel poured me another. 'When was the last time you spoke to him?' He asked it casually, gently, but I heard the extra beat at the end of the question.

'Before he got sick.'

'And everything was okay?' He clinked my glass again. '*Na sdorovye*. Your health.'

We drank. 'What do you mean . . . okay?'

'Just that. I mean, his illness was sudden, don't you think?'

'The hospital told us he died of liver failure.' I thumped my glass on the table. 'Obviously they haven't a clue what they're talking about. Ian is as healthy as a horse. There's nothing wrong with his liver . . . was . . . nothing wrong, I mean.' I couldn't keep talking about him in the present tense like this. I bit my lip.

Nigel raised his eyebrows above his glasses, two furry caterpillars. 'Liver? Are you sure that's what they said?'

I wasn't about to admit to Nigel that I'd thought they'd said Ian died of an overdose of cookies. So I nodded and said, 'They said "*pyehchyehn*".'

'I find that hard to believe.'

'So do I. But after seeing that place, I wonder if they've even heard about the discovery of penicillin.'

We were having another round. 'They've heard about it. They just haven't got it. Poverty isn't the same as ignorance, you know.'

Nigel said it quietly, but I still heard the reproach. 'I'm sorry, that was probably very rude. But that hospital was like something out of Dickens. We had to step over patients lying on the floor and when we got to the morgue . . . it was filthy. Then Ian . . . his body was frozen like a block of ice.' I

30

knocked back the vodka without waiting for him this time and closed my eyes.

When I opened them, Nigel was watching me. 'I'm sorry. Terribly insensitive of me to talk about this when you've had such an awful shock. Drink up, love. This will help. ' He poured another shot and pushed the glass in front of me. Then he added, 'So he didn't say anything to you?'

I cupped my hands around the glass, but I didn't drink. Already the vodka was seeping into my brain, having a lethally confusing effect on my thoughts. 'About what?'

He said, slowly and patiently, 'What was wrong with Ian. You brought it up.'

'Did I?' I'd thought he did.

He looked at me assessingly as if trying to decide if I was drunk or just being obtuse. 'Yes, you did. I thought these last few weeks that he seemed . . . perturbed.'

'And why do you think I would know what perturbed him?' I sat up straight in my chair, sucked in my breath, and tried to fix both eyes on him.

'Well, because. He talked about you constantly. Especially recently. Now, after seeing you, I understand why.'

Wherever this conversation was going I didn't like it. Nigel clinked his glass against mine and stared into my eyes. I raised my glass and stared right back at him while we drank.

'If Ian didn't die of liver failure, then what did he die of?' I asked with the excessive precision of early-stage inebriation.

He shook his head. 'I don't know. But you knew him better than anyone, so I thought you might have an idea.'

Now how did he know that? When Ian came back to New York for Kathleen's funeral, he'd told me he was finally over me. Friends, not lovers. That he'd even started seeing someone new. So what had happened in the five weeks since he'd left New York and come back to Moscow? Before he got sick, that is. We'd talked a few times on the phone, erratically, since he always seemed to be on the road and the only time he could make or get an international call was when he was in Moscow. But there was nothing unusual when we talked. He never hinted that something was bothering him, or even that he was pining for me unduly. Like I said, he'd told me he had a new girlfriend.

Unless, of course, Nigel was getting at something that had to do with the fifty thousand dollars Ian might temporarily have borrowed from the office budget. That is, if he'd borrowed it at all. Even if he were on the verge of bankruptcy, which he usually was, Ian would never pinch money to pay off his debts. Besides, knowing his squirrelly bookkeeping, the money was probably right there under Manning's nose and he just hadn't figured out where to find it. But Nigel couldn't have known about that, could he, because Manning had said he'd only discovered today that the money was missing.

So what exactly was Nigel talking about?

He was watching me with those laser eyes of his and I'm sure he saw the gears whirring around in my tired, confused little brain. But he said nothing, so neither did I. Instead he poured me another shot of vodka. I didn't bother to protest. We drank without speaking. The edges of the room had receded. Everything seemed otherworldly. 'How did you get in here?' I could hardly concentrate but knew I needed to change the subject.

'The maid. She was in tidying up and forgot to lock the door. I live down the hall.'

'Live?'

'Moscow hasn't enough flats to accommodate all the foreigners who come here to work. So you end up living in a hotel.'

'Oh.' The furniture softened, colours swirled. My tongue felt thick as a plank. 'What do you do? I mean, what is your work?'

'Journalist. Same as you. Freelance, mostly, though I work fairly steadily for *Today's World*.'

'What's that?' I didn't mean to sound so abrupt but my mind was becoming disconnected from my mouth.

'Soap opera journalism. A perennial fascination with the weird and wonderful.' He smiled and knocked back another shot of vodka with practised efficiency. It seemed to have no effect on him at all. 'Pays well. Far better than the serious stuff.'

I think I mumbled something inane, although what I don't remember, and then Nigel said something about getting me off to bed. Whether I managed on my own or whether he led me

32

there, I have no recollection. I passed out from exhaustion, grief, and five wickedly potent shots of vodka.

There was a loud banging somewhere at the end of the tunnel. It wouldn't go away and then I remembered. Moscow. I was in Moscow. In a hotel room. I rolled over and nearly fell out of the narrow bed. I reached for my alarm clock. Eight a.m. I sat up and a lightning bolt ricocheted through the back of my head. I was wearing the clothes I had on yesterday; in fact, the ones I'd been wearing since I left New York. I ran my tongue over my teeth and tasted fur. A shower would help considerably. The pounding continued.

Someone was knocking at my door. And they weren't going away until I answered. I got out of bed and walked through the dim, unfamiliar suite while more lightning bolts shot through my head.

She was tiny, like a child, wearing a faded print smock and a cherry red scarf that covered her hair. She was holding a rag and a can of what looked like powdered cleanser. 'I am here to clean your room,' she announced in Russian. Her tone of voice said she wasn't asking for permission.

Well, okay, this wasn't the New York Hilton and it was already clear I wasn't going to be treated like royalty here. Still, this was my room.

'It's not convenient,' I said. 'Come back later.' I started to close the door.

'*Nyet*. Now.' She slipped past me, quick as a flash. Little Red Riding Hood with an attitude, sashaying down the corridor to my bathroom. I heard the sound of running water a moment later.

I guess the shower could wait. Maybe I should have breakfast first.

I walked back into the bedroom and sat on the bed. I looked down at my pillow and saw the mascara streaks on it. I touched the pillowcase. It was still damp. I don't remember how long I cried. I turned the pillow over and looked across the room at a three-way mirror on the dressing table. I squinted at it in the dingy, viscous light and three pale strangers with smudged, puffy eyes stared back, all of them in badly wrinkled clothes, looking forlorn and remote.

I got up and walked over to the window, shoving aside the heavy claret-coloured curtain so the room had less of a bordello air about it. A barge stirred a muddy wake as it slid down the Moscow River. Across the river, a flag snapped above the truncated clock tower of a large, white, official-looking building. It was severely modern, a multi-storeyed elliptical structure of white marble with hundreds of tiny windows set atop a much broader horseshoe-shaped base. There was a gold emblem over the doorway and the numbers on the clock showed that it was just past eight o'clock. I had an hour to get ready.

I walked into the living room and put the phone back on the hook. Had I taken it out of the cradle last night or did Nigel do that? Our two empty vodka glasses were still on the table but the bottle was gone.

The room was fixed up so it was possible to live here in a quaint, bohemian sort of way. Besides the sofa, there were two lumpy armchairs in different floral patterns of brown and gold surrounding a ring-stained coffee table. A glass-fronted armoire held chipped dishes and a few glasses. There was an old television and, in the corner, a desk with an old-fashioned telephone. The enormous refrigerator next to the sofa looked like it began life before I did. The scuffed wood floor was warped in front of it and there was a suspicious damp stain by the door.

I opened the refrigerator and found milk and a box labelled in a language I didn't recognize. Juice, obviously, judging by the pictures of dancing oranges on it. There was also butter and a jar of blackcurrant jam. In the armoire there was a loaf of black bread and a jar of instant coffee. I pulled the hotplate out from under the desk and plugged it into the only electrical outlet in the room, behind the desk. I found a saucepan next to the television and was getting ready to reassert myself in the bathroom so I could get water for my coffee when I remembered that Manning had told me not to drink the tap water. There was a box containing half a dozen bottles of mineral water next to the refrigerator. I opened one and poured some into the saucepan.

The coffee tasted burnt, but the black bread was dense and pungent, smelling vaguely of beer. I slabbed at least half an inch of butter and jam on three thick pieces and ate like I hadn't seen food for days, which wasn't too far from the truth. The last meal I'd eaten was airline food.

I was still eating when my cleaning lady whirled into the doorway to deliver her departing ultimatum. 'I am Zoya,' she said in Russian. 'I take care of these rooms. The man here before you, the American. You work for the same business.'

Clearly a woman who never asked questions. I nodded.

'Your friend took care of me.'

You didn't have to be a rocket scientist to get her meaning. Cigarettes. Makeup. A pack of gum. In return, she would do what the hotel paid her to do.

Ian had told me about the pervasiveness of *blat* in Russia, what a tentacle-like chokehold the bribes and wheeling-dealing had on every aspect of life here. He wasn't kidding. He also said it wasn't an option whether you played along or not. She held all the cards. Given a choice between a self-righteous refusal to be intimidated and no soap or toilet paper, I'd say it was pretty clear which way I was going to go. '*Kharasho.* Of course.' I stood up. 'I have to get ready for work.'

She probably didn't care if I wanted to turn cartwheels. We understood each other. Zoya blew out of the room the same way she'd come, slamming the door behind her.

I ran over and locked it, then peeled off my slept-in clothes on my way to the bathroom. It reeked of bleach, which didn't seem to bother the cockroaches. I saw one scuttle into a hole by the bathtub. The water was tepid. I checked for more cockroaches before stepping on to a threadbare towel that passed as a bath mat. In the living room the telephone rang.

I ran for it, wrapped in a towel, and pushed my dripping hair out of the way as I picked up the phone. It was Manning.

'You're going to have to get over here on your own this morning. I need the driver who was going to pick you up. I just found out there's a flight that can take Ian to New York today. I'm leaving for the hospital right now.' Not yesterday's deep-freeze, but still chilly.

'You said it was only fifteen minutes away so I expect I can cope.' I adjusted my bath towel and watched rivulets of water run down my breasts. The gold clock on the tower across the river showed eight-thirty. 'Just tell me where it is.'

He gave me directions to Number 7/4 Kutuzovsky Prospekt and disconnected before I could ask him anything. I hung up. It wasn't going to break my heart that Mr Personality wouldn't be in the office this morning. Lucky we weren't going to have a permanent working relationship.

Number 7/4 Kutuzovsky Prospekt was a dirty, dun-coloured warren of buildings sprawled around a sunken paved parking lot crammed with cars parked in all available nooks and crannies, like rows of crooked teeth. I walked past a tiny tin shack at the entrance to the parking lot. A man in a military uniform came out and stared at me. I looked at the paper on which I'd scribbled the address Manning gave me. 'Korpus 3, entrance 5, flat 17'. Korpus 3 meant building three so I counted from the outside of the parking lot and headed for the third building. It was wrong, but the building next to it was the one I wanted. I checked signs in Roman numerals above the doors, looking for the fifth entrance, until a man throwing a pail of dirty water over a mud-coloured car finally directed me to the small graffiti-covered doorway tucked into a corner.

There was no sign outside the elevator indicating which flat was on which floor. I stepped inside and pulled a chain-link door shut. Someone had burned holes through the third and fourth floor buttons, clear through to the wiring, so you couldn't push them. I did some calculating and pressed the button marked five. With a jerk, the elevator climbed slowly.

The fifth floor was, of course, not the right one. I ran down a narrow marble stairway that spiralled around the elevator shaft until I got to the third floor. An International Press Service sign hung on a battered door. I opened the door and nearly knocked over a coat rack heaped with a mountain of jackets. Stacked cartons of bottled water took up the rest of the cramped foyer. Good thing I'd been so tentative about opening that door. The way those cartons were stacked, I could have knocked something over if I'd decided to sweep in and make a big entrance. I don't suppose anyone would have been too thrilled if I'd flooded the place on my first day.

Across the hall, a man and a woman sat at a Formica table in a small, windowless room, smoking and talking, an ashtray and a haze of smoke between them. They stared at me and I felt, as I had yesterday, like a caged animal being observed at the zoo. So I murmured 'good morning' in Russian. They answered and continued staring.

The office was quiet. If I turned right, it looked like I'd be in the kitchen. So I turned left and walked down the hallway into a large room. Annabel Kandinsky stood at a desk heaped with papers, shoving a tape recorder into a scuffed canvas bag, puffing on a cigarette clenched between her teeth. She looked up as I walked in and took the cigarette out of her mouth.

We hadn't known each other too well back in New York, but I didn't remember her looking so old and tired then as she did now. She looked worn out, like Manning did. She had pulled her peroxided hair into a ponytail on top of her head so bleached curls cascaded down around dark roots. She looked like a poodle in need of a trim. Not a speck of makeup, either, which only accentuated her weariness. I remembered her in New York as someone who'd always dressed theatrically, wearing clothes no one else would be caught dead in and carrying it off with a kind of careless, avant-garde chic that really gave her style. I'd look ridiculous if I dressed like that. She'd looked terrific. Now she looked downright frumpy and unkempt in a frizzy electric pink sweater with orange pompoms on it, a floor-length gauzy black and white polka dot skirt, and burgundy gaucho boots.

She smiled self-consciously, like she knew what I was thinking. Then she walked over and bent down, kissing the air next to my ear, the New York version of a hug. 'Claire! It's great to see you, hon!' She squeezed my shoulder. 'It must of been *hell* for you yesterday, kiddo. Right off the plane, then David schleps you *straight* to the hospital. I've been thinking about you ever since you got here. God ... Ian. I mean, who can *believe* it?'

She shoved the cigarette, which had burned into a long ash, back into her mouth. I'd forgotten about that accent. Pure Brooklyn. The ash dropped on to an orange pompom and she swiped at it absently. It left a grey streak. 'Oh, *jeez*! I gotta quit smoking. But this place ... I *swear* ... are you all right?'

'Sure. I'm fine. Just fine.' I thought I was all cried out after last night. 'It's jetlag.'

Annabel was watching me. 'Go ahead and bawl, Claire,' she said, 'you'll feel better. Trust me.'

'I'm all right.' I looked around the room at the tired shabbiness and clutter, the same seedy neglect that permeated my hotel room and the hospital. Except the hospital was worse, a hundred times worse. Ian had died in a place that seemed to have no humanity, without anyone by his side who knew or cared about him.

The tears slid down my face and I couldn't stop them. Annabel, bless her, came over and put her arms around me until I managed to pull myself together. Afterwards she walked over to a windowsill and got a couple of tissues from a box next to a dead plant. She gave one to me, then used the other to swipe at her own eyes. 'Welcome to the country God created when he had a hangover.'

She wadded up her tissue and threw it in the trash. Then she fished under the rubble on her desk and pulled out a pack of cigarettes. She held it out to me.

'No, thanks.'

She lit up another cigarette and blew out a vicious cloud of smoke. 'David said it was pretty awful at the morgue yesterday. What happened?'

I didn't know how much Manning had told her: about Ian being frozen solid or about nearly dropping him or about our argument, screamed for the benefit of all Moscow, in the hospital parking lot. 'You don't want to know.' My voice sounded ragged.

She nodded. 'I've been there, hon. That place is your *worst* nightmare.'

'You went to the hospital?'

She puffed on her cigarette. 'A bunch of us were taking turns staying by Ian's bedside. We had to bribe the staff, of course. But, *jeez*, for the right price those guys would have let Attila the *Hun* stay with him. You could get away with *murder* and no one would say "boo". I was there Sunday afternoon. He was ... well, getting worse. He was thirsty like, I don't know ... like he'd just crossed the Sahara Desert or something. It was *weird*.' She pulled an overflowing ashtray over and tapped her cigarette ash into it. 'I had some bottled water so I kept giving him something to drink. But you could see he was getting worse. Nick ... you don't know him ... he came after me. But he said the hospital staff wouldn't let him stay. They told him no more visitors so he had to leave. I guess it was only a few hours before Ian ...' She stopped and looked at the ceiling. Then blew a perfect smoke ring.

I walked over to the windowsill and started picking dead leaves off the plant. If I picked them all off, there'd be nothing but the stalk left. So I left three of the least droopy leaves and asked, with my back to her, 'Do you think he suffered?'

'I'm afraid so,' she said gently. 'He was in a lot of pain in the end.'

I turned around. 'How did it happen?'

She shrugged. 'Beats me. He'd been travelling ... he was in Smolensk. He got back to Moscow last ... Wednesday, I think it was. He came by here to dump his equipment, but he looked absolutely *exhausted*. Really pale. David told him we could handle everything and to go home and go to bed.'

'How did he sound?'

'He said he thought he might have picked up some kind of bug. His stomach was bothering him. Here you always gotta worry about food poisoning, you know? He was tired, too, but who isn't in this town? And the usual trip bellyaching, of course. You live on beer and black bread for breakfast, lunch and dinner, something's alive inside your mattress, and some- body ought to torch the hotel it's so bad. But then he didn't show up for work on Thursday and you know that's not Ian. I wanted to run downstairs to his apartment and check if he was okay, but David said maybe he was sleeping and why didn't we give him a break. But when he didn't show up by lunchtime even David was worried.' She glanced over at me. 'You sure you want me to tell you all this?'

'Yes.'

'Well, okay.' She hesitated then said, 'He was lying on the floor next to the front door. He was dressed like he was coming to work. We ... don't know how long he'd been lying there. God, Claire, I am so *sorry*. David felt like *hell*. You know, maybe if we'd gotten to him sooner ... Anyway, David carried him in his arms to one of the office cars and drove him to the hospital. I think he's been torturing himself ever since.'

I closed my eyes. No wonder Manning had acted the way he

39

did when we were in the morgue yesterday. He'd never said a word, though. 'They said he died of liver failure,' I said.

Annabel snorted. '*Jeez*, Claire! They'll say anything. What do you expect from people who get their medical diplomas inside a box of breakfast cereal, for God's sake? My Uncle Sol the plumber knows more about medicine.' She stabbed out her cigarette. 'Do you know they waited six hours before they told us he was dead? Six hours! What a bunch of *schmucks*! When you've been here a while you'll see that human life is worth *zilch* in this place.' The cigarette was out but she continued grinding it into the ashtray until it was shredded into tiny flakes.

I watched her. 'I don't plan to be here that long. I only came to fill in until Ian got better. I'm going back to New York.'

Annabel walked over to another desk across the room and picked up a piece of paper. 'I guess David didn't tell you about this.'

It was a telex from New York. I knew what it said before I read it. I was to stay in Moscow 'indefinitely' until they decided who would take Ian's place. Carole Martin would take over my assignments while I was in Russia.

Great. Just great. How was I going to explain all this to Aaron and the bank? I couldn't stall them forever. As for Carole Martin, she'd been angling for my job for the past eighteen months. Now Stan had given it to her on a platter. When I finally got back to New York, it would probably take surgery to get her out of my chair and unclench her fingers from my Rolodex filled with all my carefully cultivated contacts.

I looked out the window at the grey, weatherless day and wondered, absurdly, how long before it turned cold and the lightweight clothes I'd brought would be completely inadequate. Ian told me it could snow in Moscow as early as the middle of October.

That was in two weeks.

'You don't look so thrilled,' Annabel said.

A major understatement. 'I didn't expect this.' I shrugged. 'I'll call Stan and find out what's going on. How long he thinks I'm going to be here.'

She looked at a row of clocks along one of the walls. 'He's in bed.'

I looked at the clock with a New York placard underneath it. It was still last night in New York. 'Oh. Right.'

I heard the front door bang and a moment later a woman's voice machine-gunned questions in Russian. The replies from the other room were muted. 'That's Larisa,' Annabel said. 'She runs this place.'

Ian had told me about Larisa. He said she had the grace and elegance of Pavlova overlaid with the despotic control of Rasputin. She walked into the room, a lovely Russian princess with raven hair swept up gracefully in a chignon. I saw what he meant about Pavlova.

'You are Claire.' She came to me and held out her hand. 'I am Larisa Shebanova. I hope you are settled at the Ukraine?'

'Yes. Thank you.' I figured she expected me to shake her bejewelled hand rather than kiss it and wondered where she had acquired her English boarding school accent. She smelled faintly of lavender.

'You have had breakfast? Yes? Well, then, you must have some tea. I shall get Tanya to make you tea. This dreadful news has been a shock for us all ... you poor child.' She looked at my blotchy face and shook her head.

After she'd left for the kitchen Annabel said under her breath, 'Stay on her good side and she'll get you the keys to the Kremlin, if you want them. If you cross her, she won't do diddly. Which you need like a hole in the head in this place, let me tell you.'

'What do I have to do?'

'Don't step out of line. Anyway, I think she likes you.'

'What makes you think so?'

'The *tea*.'

'Tanya will come soon with the tea.' Larisa must have tiptoed back into the room.

We both jumped. 'Thank you,' I said. Hopefully she hadn't overheard us.

'Not at all.' Her expression was perfectly bland. She walked over to a desk in the centre of the room and pulled off a fringed shawl. She draped it over the back of the chair. 'Where's David?'

41

'Gone to the airport,' Annabel said. 'With Ian.'

Like he was leaving on a trip, instead of in a coffin.

The woman who'd stared at me through the smoke haze when I arrived came into the room carrying a tray with three glasses of tea set in delicate silver filigree holders.

'This is Tanya,' Larisa said. 'She is our cook.'

Tanya put milk and sugar in my tea and served me butter cookies as though I were the Queen of England. I thought of the canteen in the New York office and the coffee machine that occasionally forgot the plastic cup when it shot out the coffee.

'You are half-past,' Tanya said immediately. Definitely not a good thing to be, whatever it was, judging by her tone of voice. She was round and apple-cheeked, a pretty, feminine little bit of a thing with the kind of shrewd, stiletto gaze that could bore a hole right through you. Sugar and spice wrapped around steel.

'Pardon?'

'Half-past.' She reached over and pinched my cheek. 'You must to eat. Otherwise, you are being eel. You are too theen.' She set the plate of butter cookies on the desk next to me. 'You are eating these, so no more half-past. All.'

I got one more up and down look, the kind you give live-stock that needs fattening up before the slaughter, then she left the room. I bit aggressively into a butter cookie.

'She's got that look in her eye,' Annabel said. 'You better not say you're on a *diet,* Claire. It's like waving a red flag in front of a *bull* with Tanya around.' She set down her tea and walked to her desk. She picked up an opaque jar, opened it and shook out a handful of large white pills. 'Anybody want one?'

Larisa shook her head.

'Claire?'

They were too big to be aspirins. 'Tranquillizers?'

'Multi-vitamins.' She threw a couple in her mouth and washed them down with a mouthful of tea.

'Thanks. I think I'll pass.'

'Suit yourself. You don't want to get run down while you're here. If you get sick you can end up feeling like the walking dead . . .' Annabel stopped abruptly. After a moment she said, 'I guess that was a dumb thing to say, considering.' She picked up her equipment bag and hoisted it over her shoulder. 'I'm going to the Foreign Ministry for a briefing, Larisa.' She suddenly sounded weary. She patted my arm as she walked by and a moment later I heard the front door close.

Larisa lit up a cigarette and blew out the match with a sharp, exasperated breath. 'Come,' she said, standing. 'We must get you settled. You shall take the desk at the back of the room while you are here.'

I looked at the desk she meant. 'Is it Ian's?'

'I'm sorry, but it is the only place.'

'I really don't think . . .'

'I would not insist if there were somewhere else. Ian won't need it now. We are all practically sitting on top of each other in this small office as it is.' Her tone said she expected unquestioning obedience.

'But his things are still . . .'

'My *dear*.'

I was definitely not her dear, judging by the way she said it. I could feel the scales tilt as I started to slip out of her good graces. In fact, I could very well be moving into the she-won't-do-diddly zone Annabel warned me about.

'I'm sorry but I really can't . . .'

'Very well,' she snapped. 'I shall have the desk cleared. In the meantime . . .' she gestured to a worn leather sofa along the far wall '. . . you can sit there.'

She started back to her own desk. 'My dear,' she said again as she sat down, 'this is *not* New York.'

No kidding.

A few minutes ago I'd had tea and sympathy. Now you'd think I was behaving like the office prima donna, told to go sit in the corner. I looked at Ian's desk with its mile-high clutter, then at the old sofa.

'I've changed my mind,' I said. 'I'll clear it.'

I swept my hand to encompass the mountain of papers and files heaped on Ian's desk as I spoke. If I'd been looking at what I was doing, I probably wouldn't have whacked the huge sheaf of file folders that fell off the desk and hit the floor. Papers slid everywhere.

I think Larisa had been on the verge of saying something

43

conciliatory, but now she looked like a mother who just discovered her child colouring the walls. She stubbed out her cigarette and stood up.

I waved a hand at her, but this time I made sure to avoid taking out more of Ian's Mount Everest heap of paperwork. 'Don't bother. I'll clean it up. I knocked it over.'

She started to say something again but the phone interrupted. I knelt on the floor and listened to her trilling the scales in gushy Russian, begging a favour, something for the office it seemed, and, by the sound of it, getting what she wanted. So I picked up strewn papers and files, reading the subject labels as I went along. Soviet agriculture. Soviet economy. Orthodox Church.

Fortunately, most of Ian's papers hadn't come separated from their subject folders, so I just slid everything back into place. I picked up the last folder, which had slipped almost entirely under the desk. No label but a big circular stain in the middle where Ian had placed a cup of coffee or a glass of water. His drink coaster. I dumped the folder in the trash, but then I saw papers slide out so I retrieved it.

Good thing I did. Most of the other folders contained news stories or press releases but this one had several pages of hand-written notes. It was strange seeing Ian's handwriting, knowing he was dead now. I fingered the papers as though I could get close to him again by touching something he had touched. The date on the top paper was from last week. Right before he got sick. The rest of the writing was Ian's usual chicken scratch, indecipherable fragments of sentences, probably an interview or telephone conversation, and some doodles in the margins. I flipped through the other papers. There was a photocopied biography of Marshal Georgy Zhukov. I skimmed it. It was from an encyclopaedia, the compressed facts of Zhukov's life. The most decorated soldier in Soviet history. The architect of the Red Army victory of the Battle of Stalingrad during World War II, a turning point for the Allies of the war on the Eastern Front. After the war Stalin exiled him into insignificance in one of his jealous fits. Later Khruschev rehabilitated him, then there was another fall from grace. It was only after his death that Zhukov was recognized as a true national hero.

People like that had always fascinated Ian. He admired anybody who was a maverick or a bit of a rebel. I slid the biography back into the folder. This file would have to be something for Ian's book. When he was in New York for Kathleen's funeral, he'd told me he'd been doing research for a book on the Russian front during World War II. He'd even landed a contract with a small publisher in London. These were probably his notes.

On the inside back cover of the folder Ian had scribbled Zhukov's name. Next to it he'd written another name: Harold Miller. He'd connected the two with arrows pointing in both directions and put stars and exclamation marks around them. Maybe Harold Miller was a historian who knew a lot about Zhukov. Or maybe he was Ian's publisher. Below Miller's name Ian had written something else.

'Call at noon. Tuesday September 26. Money.'

It would be too bizarre to expect that Ian was referring to the money that was missing from the safe. The cash Manning was so sure Ian had taken. Than again, why not? Maybe, by some fluke, Harold Miller, whoever he was, knew something about it and there was a perfectly logical harmless explanation for what had happened to the money.

I looked at Ian's wall calendar. The twenty-sixth was today. And it was now precisely 10:45 a.m. If Harold Miller didn't know Ian was dead, either he'd call at noon, if he was the one who was supposed to call, or else he might call later to see why Ian hadn't kept a pre-arranged telephone date.

Either way, we might clear up the mystery of the missing cash and put Manning back in his place. I still couldn't believe he'd actually accused Ian of petty theft. Ian was as straight as an arrow.

In retrospect, it was a good thing I'd come to Moscow. Otherwise, there'd be no one to stop Manning from throwing Ian to the wolves.

The man had no soul.

Ian didn't steal the money.

I'd bet my life on it.

Chapter Four

I spent the rest of the morning cleaning Ian's desk. The phone never rang, so maybe it was Ian who was supposed to call Harold Miller, not the other way around. Either way, there was no call from Miller. I looked through Ian's Rolodex, but there was no card with his name on it. Nothing filed under either 'M' or 'H'. I knew Ian well enough to look in both places. Just finding his Rolodex was a challenge since his desk was a complete hodgepodge, heaped with the debris of unopened mail, press releases, office memos, wire copy. It was the desk of someone in the middle of working, someone who'd planned to return to finish the unfinished projects. The vague, peppery scent of his pipe tobacco still permeated the papers and the fabric of his beat-up chair, haunting me with its aching familiarity. A couple of times I actually looked up, half-expecting him to be standing over me, scolding me for touching his precious papers, wreaking havoc with his highly organized filing system.

His trashcan was now nearly filled with junk mail and old press releases. I was still a long way from finding the surface of his desk.

'Claire, it is time to go.'

I looked over and saw Larisa standing by her chair, winding her shawl around her shoulders.

'Where?'

'To the Kremlin. David left a message that if you got your press accreditation today you should attend the session of the Congress of People's Deputies. I just received a call from the Foreign Ministry that your pass will be waiting at the Press

Centre.' She picked up an expensive-looking leather bag. 'Come. Yuri is waiting for us downstairs. David said you could take his equipment bag since he is at the airport.'

I pushed Ian's papers into a pile and reached for my blazer.

'Do you have warmer clothes?' Larisa asked as we clattered down the marble staircase that spiralled around the elevator shaft.

'I have a raincoat.'

She clicked her tongue. 'That will not be enough. Soon the cold weather will come.'

I followed her outside. The temperature had dropped since this morning. When I'd left New York two days ago it was still Indian summer and the days were full of golden sunshine and the kind of distilled, pellucid light that made trees and buildings shimmer against sharp blue skies. Here the light breeze felt distinctly autumnal and the sky was the colour of dull pewter. I shivered.

Yuri was not waiting for us at the car. At least I thought it wasn't Yuri. This man was tall and skinny as a stringbean and dressed in a much-worn leather jacket and jeans.

'This is Yuri Karpov,' Larisa said, introducing us.

He took a toothpick out of his mouth and said, '*Ochen priyatna.*'

I smiled and said hello. 'I thought the driver who picked me up at Sheremetyvo was named Yuri?' I whispered to Larisa as we got into the back seat and waited for Yuri to take his place in front.

'That is Yuri Sokolov,' Larisa said. 'They are both Yuri.'

The drive to the Press Centre took us past the Ukraine Hotel, then briefly along the embankment of the Moscow River. We passed another building that was a double for the Ukraine.

'It is the Foreign Ministry building,' Larisa said, reading my mind. 'Stalin built seven such castle-like buildings in Moscow. One is your hotel. Another is Moscow State University. Moscow was once supposed to be the third Rome. Seven buildings for the Seven Hills of Rome . . . now they are called Stalin's Follies. You cannot miss them on our skyline.'

The Press Centre, however, was a low, boxy modern building of concrete and glass, as aesthetically pleasing as a bunker. Larisa said my pass was supposed to be at the guard's desk at the front door and ordered Yuri, in staccato Russian, to fetch it and make it quick. He loped across the parking lot like there was all the time in the world, emerging a few seconds later with an envelope. He handed it to Larisa when he got back in the car. She informed him tersely that all men, himself in particular, were worthless swine, then opened the envelope like one of the presenters on Oscar night.

'Ah, yes. Excellent.' She beamed at me and handed me the laminated photo ID card.

It was not excellent. It was as bad as my passport photo. I had to use one of those do-it-yourself photo machines because I couldn't find my press photos anywhere. The day had been sweltering, a real New York end-of-summer scorcher, so my hair co-operated like it always did in that kind of humidity. I looked like I was wearing a fright wig. I'd pulled an all-nighter at work so my eyes were two slits with bruises under them. I rubbed my finger over the photograph and my name, written in Cyrillic. Whoever had issued this card had changed me from 'Claire' to 'Clara'.

'This pass is only valid for a month,' Larisa said, tapping her finger by a date in the lower right-hand corner. 'You will need to get it renewed.'

I nodded, but said nothing. No point making waves by telling her I didn't plan to be in Moscow that long. Despite what Stan said.

We were driving through the older part of Moscow, passing buildings whose pastel sherbet colours and Neo-Classical architecture gave the city a softer, faded grace.

Suddenly Larisa said softly, 'Look over there. The Kremlin. Your first view.'

As many times as I had seen photographs, I was still unprepared for the fairy-tale sight of the gold-domed churches with their filigree crosses and the ancient turreted towers and walls which glittered, brilliant and jewel-like, against the sombre sky. We were in sight of the river once again. Yuri turned down a road that ran along the embankment on one side and, on the other, the red-brick crenellated walls of the Kremlin with their graceful swallow-tailed design, surrounding a kingdom of churches, palaces and towers with ruby red stars atop them that turned slowly in the wind. I recognized the vivid, swirled colours of the faceted domes of St Basil's Cathedral, like fantastic spiky pineapples ahead of us.

'We are at the back of Red Square,' Larisa said, 'We go to the Great Kremlin Palace and it is simplest if we enter by Spasskaya Bashnya. The Saviour's Tower. I'm sure you will recognize it. Yuri can wait there with the car.'

He parked at the end of a crooked row of Volvos, Mercedes and battered Russian cars lined against the outside wall of the Kremlin. Around us other drivers leaned against their cars, waiting and smoking. A few had drifted into small groups. Someone next to a black Mercedes called Yuri's name. As he handed me Manning's equipment bag, Larisa said something sharp to him again. He saluted irreverently and swaggered off to join his friend.

I thought I heard Larisa mutter 'swine' again as we started up the cobblestone hill. It was noon precisely because as we were walking, the gold and black clock above the Saviour's Gate chimed the hour, drowning out all other noises. Larisa was right; I did recognize the tower with its ogee-shaped porticoes, turrets, and pinnacles outlined in white like an exuberantly decorated confectionery creation. In the distance was the angular profile of Lenin's dark red and black granite mausoleum, its receding tiers resembling a collection of child's building blocks piled up in a short, stubby tower.

We reached the edge of Red Square. It was more grandiose and imposing than I'd expected it to be. The few people who walked there seemed diminished and insignificant in so much space. The windswept distance to the other side felt vast. It was not a place of laughter and outdoor cafés and children playing games. Instead, it seemed austere and vaguely forbidding, the perfect dramatic stage for events manipulated from the other side of the wall by leaders who, like the Great Oz, needed a splendid setting to remind their subjects and themselves of their omnipotence.

'What is that place that looks like a palace?' I asked Larisa, pointing to a liver-red building across from us, on the far side of the square.

'It is the Historical Museum. And on the right is GUM. You know GUM? Our big department store?' She pronounced it 'goom'. I nodded. What in Russia was not big? She pulled me along. 'Come. We must go inside the Kremlin. Another time you shall come back and see everything properly ... I shall arrange a tour for you.'

We were stopped at the gate by guards who checked our credentials. My bag was searched and one of the guards gestured for me to turn on my tape recorder. 'They check for explosives,' Larisa murmured. Then they let us pass and we walked through the tower and entered the citadel of the Kremlin.

There are places where the past leaves no traces or whispers. The memories of those who made its history fade and disappear, to be coloured and overwritten by the demands and events of the present. The Kremlin was not such a place. Its violent, turbulent history pervaded everywhere I looked, sending shivers down my spine. Russia's Tsars and Tsarinas had walked and ruled, loved and hated here, but actually it was Lenin, the man responsible for frog-marching his country backward to its current anachronistic time warp, who leapt at me from the shadows of a copse of oak and fir trees. He half-sat on a bronze seat, an enormous man wrapped in a flowing overcoat, restlessly ponderous like an animal who has been held against its will and intends to bolt at the first available opportunity.

'That is Tainitsky Garden,' Larisa said, waving at the statue of Lenin. 'And you know, of course, the cathedrals ... the Cathedral of the Archangel, the Cathedral of the Annunciation, the Cathedral of the Dormition... come. Another time, another time you shall see them. Here is where we go now ... the Great Kremlin Palace.'

The Palace was an enormous classical building of intricately carved white stone cornices, pilasters and windows etched sharply against walls of clear, brilliant yellow. The colour seemed incongruous, almost gaily Mediterranean, contrasting with the severe red brick walls and the fragile-looking white and gold churches. Larisa said it used to be the Tsars' residence and had more than seven hundred rooms.

We entered a large white marble foyer where we were searched again and our credentials re-checked. For all its exterior splendour, inside the building was shabby and tired-looking, the walls redolent of the mingled smells of musty age, stale tobacco and sour body odour. The enormous lobby was overrun with people, milling like guests at a cocktail party, talking in small groups and smoking.

'I think there is a problem,' Larisa said. 'All the journalists are here, not in the press gallery. Wait, I shall find out what has happened.'

I leaned against a pillar and waited.

'You're new.'

'Pardon?'

American, wearing a dandyish striped button down shirt, cashmere sweater knotted around the neck, and jeans. Jeans that were ironed, with proper creases. He was watching me with the look of one of those men who rate women from one to ten and instantly discard the low numbers. He took off a pair of gold wire-rimmed glasses and began to polish them on the sleeve of his beautiful sweater. Salt and pepper hair, craggily good-looking in a weatherbeaten way, but the deep crow's feet around his eyes said he was older than the way he dressed. Rich, maybe. Playboy, definitely.

'I said, "you're new". With International Press Service.'

I said coolly, 'Now who told you that?' Nothing puts me off faster than a guy who acts like you're lucky he's deigned to talk to you.

He looked amused. 'You don't have the brain-dead look of near exhaustion the rest of us have, so you must be fresh meat. Anyway, this is Moscow. The Sovs put us in a gilded cage so they can keep an eye on us. Or should I say, a gilded goldfish bowl?' He raised his eyebrows and grinned, enjoying his own wit. I think he'd told that little joke before. 'As a result, everyone knows everyone and everything about them, too. Saves a lot of time and useless questions.' He put his glasses back on and adjusted them. 'Hugh Davis, AP.'

'Claire Brennan. But you probably already know that.'

He laughed. 'No.' He flipped open his reporter's notebook and wrote something on a page. He tore it out and waved it at me. 'My numbers. Give me a call any time.'

And you'll do what? I smiled an icicle smile that said he should get lost, but I took the paper. 'Thanks.' The newest vestal virgin in town, just off the plane from the States. He didn't waste any time.

51

I'd misjudged him, though, because all of a sudden the Lothario act dried up and he said shrewdly, 'I've been here a long time. It can get pretty depressing and lonely sometimes. I know my way around this place and my Russian's not too bad. All I meant was, if I can help you with anything, feel free to give me a call. We all try to help each other out. Everyone needs a friend sometimes, Claire. And we all miss Ian. He was a good man.'

He said it smilingly, but there was no mistaking his tone. Served me right for treating him like a teenager with overactive hormones. He'd only been trying to be friendly. 'Your offer's very kind,' I said. 'I mean it.'

He squeezed my shoulder sympathetically. 'I know you do,' he said. 'You poor kid, you've been through hell since you got here, haven't you?'

'Hugh!'

She was dark-haired, slender, and incredibly beautiful. Hugh looked up and any foolish ideas I'd had moments earlier that he was interested in me were completely dispelled when I saw the way he looked at her. She seemed oblivious to the fact that every head turned to watch as she threaded her way toward us, artlessly graceful and utterly stunning. I saw Hugh's smooth machismo disintegrate.

'I've been trying to find you,' she said in a reproachful voice. 'They're abandoning the Congress for the rest of the day after that brawl.' She smiled at me. She had absolutely perfect teeth. 'Oh, hello.'

She looked at Hugh, waiting for him to introduce us, but he had clearly forgotten my existence entirely. 'I'm Claire Brennan, with International Press Service.'

She held out her hand. 'How do you do? Victoria Nobary with CBS.'

I should have recognized her at once. Her picture had been splashed all over news-stands in New York just before I left. She was on the cover of one of the big fashion magazines, looking impossibly ravishing in the middle of some backwater, pretending to do her stand-up. Flawless makeup in a steamy jungle, cool and unruffled in chic clothes, another glamorous day at work where it looked like her biggest worry was potentially breaking a fingernail while pushing the record button on the tape recorder.

Victoria and I shook hands and Hugh woke up. 'Sorry. Claire just got here,' he said to Victoria. 'What were you saying about the Congress?'

'That it's over for the day. We can leave now.' Her voice was low and faintly musical, different from the gung-ho person I'd seen on television.

'You don't mean they were physically fighting?' I asked. Around us, everyone started to drift toward the main door.

She nodded. 'Someone threw a punch after the last vote. No one understood what was going on. The "noes" should have voted "yes" and the "yeses" should have voted "no". By the time they figured it out, the winners insisted they'd won fair and square.'

'Does this kind of thing happen often?'

Hugh shrugged. 'The Sovs don't exactly have a historical tradition of parliamentary debate, do they? I think they're still working on technique.'

Victoria interrupted him. 'What about Ian?'

Her tone was sharp.

Hugh slipped his arm around her waist. 'Victoria was with Ian the night before he collapsed,' he said to me. His eyes held mine and then I got it.

Ian and Victoria. He'd have been an idiot not to fall for her. She was a goddess.

'Oh.' Did Hugh mean 'with him' like they had dinner together or 'with him' like they were sleeping together?

'So I was wondering what plans had been made?' Victoria said. Her voice shook slightly.

When Ian had told me he had a new girlfriend, he never mentioned she was drop-dead supermodel gorgeous. And I guess I was probably figuring that this new relationship was just drinks or dinner with someone who, okay, let's face it, was an also-ran second-place substitute for me. How was it I ever thought I was irreplaceable? Particularly when I was the one who ended things between us.

It's just that he must have said, at least a million times, that he would never get over me. But, hey, big surprise. He got over me. Life moves on. I should be glad he found someone so . . . spectacular.

53

I tried to keep my voice neutral. 'He ... his body, that is ... is being flown to New York today. David Manning went to the airport to arrange it this morning.'

She nodded.

'You were with him in Smolensk, then?' I asked. Why couldn't I just drop it?

'Not this trip. He went there on his own this time. He wanted to do some more research for a book he was writing. We decided to get together when he got back.'

Oh. We.

'So when was the last time you saw him?' I sounded like his mother. Or maybe even like a cranky ex-girlfriend. This was really none of my business.

Victoria said calmly, 'I spent Wednesday night at his place after he got back to Moscow. He wasn't feeling too well. I left at five to do a standup for our overnight news show. I didn't have the heart to wake him. I wish I had.' She swallowed and looked at me steadily.

She'd figured out who I was. Ian obviously hadn't told her, or if he had, he'd minimized what he chose to reveal, just as he'd done with me.

Hugh took my elbow with one hand and Victoria's with the other. 'Come on,' he said. 'Let's get out of here.' I could tell by the pressure of his grip on my arm that he'd figured it all out, too.

When we got outside, Victoria said, 'I'm having a dinner party at my place Friday night. Sort of a memorial dinner for Ian. Hugh's coming and a few other people who were Ian's close friends. I think you should come, too.'

It was a charitable and gracious invitation. She didn't need to include me.

'Thanks for asking,' I said. 'I'd like to come.'

'Good.' Like Hugh, she scribbled her address and phone number on a piece of paper. She handed it to me. 'See you then.'

They left together. Hugh's arm was draped protectively around Victoria's shoulders. It looked like he was already starting to make his move, fill the hole in her life left by Ian's death.

Who could blame him?

She was perfect.

Larisa found me then. 'So,' she said, 'we can go. It's finished for today.'

'I need to write something about that debate,' I said. 'I ought to talk to someone who can tell me why they were arguing, what the debate was about.'

Larisa patted her purse. 'I have this information,' she said. 'In English. David explained to me that you do not speak Russian so you will not understand.'

The rat. He didn't waste any time undermining me, did he? 'Of course I speak Russian.'

She arched perfectly shaped eyebrows. 'He said you do not.'

We were walking by the statue of Lenin in Tainitsky Garden again. The crowd had thinned out. That's when I saw him.

Or thought I did.

Why would he be in Moscow?

It was probably just someone who looked like him. How odd that I should think of him after all these years.

'So how much do you understand?'

'About what?'

'I said, how much Russian do you understand?'

Philip Robinson had barely known I existed, even though I was one of his research assistants when I was a student at Harvard. I hadn't thought of him for years. The man who had so many women throwing themselves at his feet it was a miracle he got to work everyday without tripping over someone.

'Claire? Is something wrong? You look as though you're not well.'

I jerked my gaze away from Philip, or the man I thought was Philip, and refocused on Larisa. 'No. Nothing. I'm fine. And my Russian is . . . fine. I'm just out of practice.'

'You must practise then.'

'Yes.'

A magnetic force pulled my gaze back to the statue of Lenin. There was no one there but Lenin himself.

Philip, if that's who it was, had disappeared.

When we got back to the office, Larisa gave me the keys to Ian's car. She said I needed transportation of my own so I could get around the city. I stared at the keyring. A silver horseshoe on a silver chain.

I'd given him that keyring.

Ian's desk. Ian's friends. Now his car.

I was slowly slipping deeper into his life, like quicksand.

Later the tall Yuri took me out to the parking lot and showed me the car. It was a small two-door Volvo, probably white underneath the mud. He told me the odometer was stuck and the petrol gauge unreliable. Apparently Ian had run out of petrol several times when he'd forgotten how far he'd driven since the last time he'd filled up and the gauge showed there was still some in the tank.

'You must have benzine always,' Yuri said, pulling a toothpick out of his mouth and stabbing it in the air for emphasis, 'or else you stop. Like Ian.'

'Maybe I could get these things fixed,' I said hopefully, 'if you can recommend a garage?'

He leaned against one of the front fenders and shook his head. 'Moscow garages are no good. The mechanics are crooks. They take good parts, give you bad parts.'

Surely he was pulling my leg? 'You mean, the mechanics at the garage swap parts?'

'What is "swap"?'

'Switch. Change.'

'*Da*. They swap.' He reinserted the toothpick.

'So how do I get the car fixed?'

He smiled with the innocence of an angel. 'My friends, the *ribiata*. My . . . buddies. They are okay guys. The *ribiata* fix your car and it is okay.'

'So . . . where, exactly, will the *ribiata* get parts for my car?'

'They know people.'

Of course. 'Is this legal?'

He shrugged. 'You are not in Moscow too much time so you do not understand. It is '*na lyeva*".'

Ian had told me about '*na lyeva*.' It meant literally 'on the left' and was the slang expression for doing something under the table. Anything of consequence happened '*na lyeva*.'

'If you want, you can order parts from Helsinki,' he continued, 'they come in two weeks, maybe three. Then you pay

56

duty. Then you wait to go to the garage and you wait again.
You pay in dollars. Many.'

'And if the *ribiata* fix it *na lyeva*?'

'Maybe three days. One bottle of Scotch, maybe two, and
one carton of cigarettes.'

I kept my expression neutral. 'How soon can the *ribiata*
pick up the car?'

'I ask and then I tell you.' I pretended not to see his
knowing smile. 'Don't worry, Claire. You are being happy
when all is good.'

'I'll bet.'

I thought I would drive to the Ukraine after work and leave
the car there, but Yuri vetoed that idea and said the car stayed
right where it was. 'At the Ukraine, your car is kaput. At
night. Gone. Like that.' He snapped his fingers sharply under
my nose and I flinched. He added, 'Here the *militsia* look at
this car because foreign peoples live here. Then you are not
having a big nervous.'

I didn't want a big nervous. So instead of driving Ian's car,
I cleaned it. My dear, darling Ian had left it full of trash,
ankle-deep on the floor and littered across the back seat. A
rubbish can on wheels. Old newspapers, candy bar wrappers,
empty plastic tobacco pouches, the mouldy remains of an
ancient, half-eaten cheese and meat sandwich, among God
knows what else. Like I said, tidiness wasn't one of his
virtues.

Yuri helped me clean it out. We carried the revolting sandwich and all the other trash to a large, rat-infested dumpster
near one of the other entrances to the building. Getting rid of
the sandwich didn't get rid of the disgusting, lingering smell.
Yuri gave me a blank look when I asked him if there was any
such thing as air freshener, so finally I took a small bottle of
perfume from my purse and doused the interior with it. The
result was a peculiar odour of perfumed garbage that hopefully, in time, would dissipate.

After that we took the filthy floor mats and beat them
against the side of the building. Then Yuri left to get a bucket
and fill it with water so he could wash the car and I could find
out what colour it really was. It was when I was replacing the
mat on the front passenger side that I saw the large brown

envelope wedged under the seat. I pulled it out. Nothing written on it. Inside were papers, Ian's of course, and a stack of letters that had never been mailed. I took one look and groaned. Pre-printed envelopes addressed to banks and credit card companies. Lots of credit card companies. Ian's bills. How long had they been here? There was also a letter to his sister Susan. I ran my thumb over the address, written in his bold, boxy scrawl. All the letters, including this one, had stamps on them. Finnish stamps, not Russian. And on all of them the return address was 'Mr I. Kendall, c/o American Embassy, Helsinki, Finland'.

I shoved everything back in the larger envelope. I'd take it back to the hotel and have another look at it. As for the letters, I'd have to ask Annabel or Manning how to go about mailing them. Clearly Ian hadn't planned on dumping them in a local mailbox and letting them go through the Russian postal system.

After Yuri and I finished cleaning the car, I left for the Ukraine. I hadn't done anything about getting more food, so I ate breakfast for dinner – more brown bread with blackcurrant jam and juice from the box with dancing oranges – and then I spread the contents of Ian's envelope on the table. In addition to the bills and letters, there were old wire stories dating back a couple of months and what looked like notes from various press conferences or briefings or events he had covered. I read all the notes and looked at the wire-service stories. Nothing out of the ordinary. I could throw it all out. There was nothing worth keeping. Except the mail, of course.

I picked up the papers and took them over to the wastebasket by the desk. I dropped them in, one by one. One piece of wire copy landed on the floor. I bent to pick it up and saw something I'd missed. On the back of the story Ian had been doodling. In the middle of a starburst he'd written 'Call H about getting cash to M'. I turned the paper over. It was an AP story with a Moscow dateline, just like the other stories. It was written by Hugh Davis.

MOSCOW, August 10 (AP) Historians will be intrigued by the re-release of the autobiography of Marshal Georgy Zhukov scheduled for early next year. Zhukov served as chief commander of Soviet Occupation Forces in

Germany during World War II and defence minister under Premier Nikita Khruschev. It has now been revealed that the Communist Party's Central Committee heavily censored the previous edition of Zhukov's auto-biography, published fifteen years ago. The new version contains the full text of the original memoirs with the expurgated sections denoted in italics.

Marshal Zhukov's distinguished military career during World War II was abruptly terminated by Joseph Stalin in 1948 after a raid on Zhukov's dacha turned up hundreds of crates of valuable art, silver, and furniture reportedly looted from Nazi Germany. He was subsequently exiled to the Urals until he was reinstated as defence minister under Nikita Khruschev. Khruschev later dismissed Zhukov for displaying too much independence.

The three volume unabridged memoirs are a revealing insight into what information the secrecy-obsessed Communist Party hierarchy once deemed too sensitive to be made public.

Zhukov again. Ian probably wanted to get hold of the memoirs to use for researching his own book. But what was he talking about: 'Call H about getting cash to M'?

Was 'H' Harold, as in Harold Miller? Or was he 'M'? Who else, among Ian's friends, could be 'H' or 'M'? Hugh? Manning? Manning . . . now wouldn't that be interesting?

And the cash. Was it the fifty thousand or something completely different?

In those first days in Moscow, when I was still in freefall, before I got my bearings, I persisted in clinging to the easiest, most obvious explanation: Ian's crummy bookkeeping habits had finally tripped him up, leaving fifty thousand dollars of IPS money temporarily unaccounted for. And the cryptic notes pertained to the book he was writing.

Ian hadn't embezzled office funds for his own private use. He wouldn't. But if he had taken the money, then he had a valid, honest reason. Once it was retrieved or rediscovered, his motive would be revealed and he would be exonerated. Hopefully before Manning tarnished his name with the brass in New York.

When you sleep with a man, live with him day in and day out, love him so intensely you would die for him, you know him to the core. Even when the white-hot passion has cooled between you and you are no longer lovers, your handprints are still there on each other's hearts and that lasts forever.

I threw the paper in the wastebasket with all the others and went to bed.

Chapter Five

David Manning was alone in the office when I arrived the next morning. He looked like he'd been up all night, gutted and hollow-eyed. I said I would make a pot of coffee and he nodded without speaking.

He came into the kitchen while I was measuring coffee into the filter and threw himself into a chair. He rubbed his face with his hands and leaned back against the wall so his chair balanced on two legs.

'They did the autopsy in New York.'

I turned around.

'Ian died of liver and kidney failure.' His tone was matter-of-fact and without emotion.

I slammed the filter into the coffeepot. 'That's not possible. He was perfectly healthy.'

'The coroner thinks ...' Manning paused and stared at his fingernails. 'He says there was evidence from the extensive organ damage that Ian ingested mushrooms that were highly toxic. A poisonous variety called "cortinarius".'

Mushrooms? Ian died from eating mushrooms? He didn't even like them that much.

'How would he happen to eat mushrooms that were poisonous?'

'Mushroom picking is a great pastime here.'

'Ian wasn't the nature-boy type, David. He thought sticking something in the microwave was gourmet cooking.'

'Maybe someone fixed them for him.'

'Well, if whoever fixed them didn't know what they were doing, at least one other person in Moscow ought to be in the hospital or dead, right? Ian was dating Victoria Nobary. They apparently ate dinner together, the night before he got sick. I met her yesterday. She looks perfectly healthy.'

'The symptoms don't show up immediately,' he said. 'It can take anywhere from two days to three weeks before you realize something is wrong.'

'Oh.'

'Sit down,' he said.

I sat.

'New York's worried, what with the missing money and all, that Ian was in some kind of trouble.'

'You *told* them?'

He thumped his chair down on all four legs. 'Oh, for God's sake! Give me a break, Claire. How could I *not* tell them?' He stood up and flipped the switch to turn on the coffee pot. He got two mugs out of the cabinet above his head. 'What did you expect me to do? Lie?'

'Why did you have to tell them before you checked the books? Ian was an appalling bookkeeper.'

'No fooling.'

The coffee pot started to burble.

'So what are you saying? Ian stole the money and his death had something to do with it? Maybe someone fed him the mushrooms on purpose, intending to poison him?' Even for a place as out of synch with the rest of the world as this was, it sounded a bit far-fetched. 'You are out of your mind.'

'Am I.' It was a statement, not a question. That superior tone again. He knew something. He said coldly, 'New York wants this whole thing, the cause of Ian's death, that is, kept quiet until they get a handle on that money.'

'Then why tell me?' I shouldn't have asked that. I just set myself up to get kicked in the teeth.

He didn't say anything. He took the pot and poured coffee into the two mugs. 'How do you take it?'

'Milk and sugar.' I walked over and got the milk out of the refrigerator.

He took too long fixing my coffee. He handed me a mug. He picked up the other mug and wrapped his hands around it.

'Look . . .'

I hate it when someone says 'look' like that. I never like what comes next.

'Everyone knows how close you and Ian were.' He paused and let it sink in.

I have to say I was stunned. 'You think I know something about the money, don't you? And that's what you told New York. Maybe Ian called me before he got sick and told me where he'd stashed it. Well, sure, that's just what he did, but I don't plan to tell any of you. You'll just have to wait until I send you a coded message on a post card from my hideaway in Jamaica.'

I banged my mug down on the table. Coffee splashed everywhere.

Manning ignored it. 'Grow up, Claire. Of course they're going to ask you questions. You're the logical person to ask.'

'Me? Why me? He was sleeping with someone else the night he got sick. I didn't even get here until after he'd died. Or are you accusing me of having something to do with that, too?'

I picked up my mug and dumped what was left of the coffee in the sink. Then I took the sponge and started cleaning the mess I'd made, ignoring Manning totally.

He said nothing so I threw the sponge in the sink and left the room.

He found me, a few minutes later, at my desk, with my head in my hands. 'You seem to be under the very mistaken impression that I'm getting some kind of perverse pleasure or satisfaction out of doing this.'

I looked up at him. 'What difference does it make what I think?'

'I have no choice. I'm sorry you don't like it.'

I sat up. 'You probably didn't know that Ian was the sole support of his sister and her daughter. Jade, his niece, has cerebral palsy, by the way. Her father walked out on Susan before Jade was born so Ian was paying all of her medical bills. Everything. He had an insurance policy through the company. And a pension. No doubt if this works out right and Ian gets hung out to dry as a crook, Susan won't get a dime.' Dammit, why was he doing this? Couldn't he even give Ian a *chance?* I steamrollered on. 'Won't the guys in accounting be thrilled with you? What a prince you'll be. All that money saved. Especially since they're in such a budget-slashing mood these days.'

Okay, that was low. I admit it. I shouldn't have said it. Manning looked like someone had just slapped him.

But how could he turn against Ian like this? How *could* he? Ian had told me they were friends.

Some friend.

He left the room without a word, face like a volcano. I heard the reverberating slam of the office front door, like he'd pulled it off its hinges. I jumped a mile. What if I'd gone too far this time? What if I'd really provoked him?

He came back about half an hour later and I waited for the other shoe to drop. But it never did. He ignored me so completely that I got frostbite. He left again, just before lunch. Annabel told me he'd gone to an interview and wouldn't be back for the rest of the day. She shoved a stick of gum in her mouth and lit up a cigarette. 'What's going on? You two lovebirds have a *spat*?'

'It's nothing.'

'I see. *Excuse* me while I scrape the layer of *permafrost* off the furniture.' She took the cigarette out of her mouth and blew a large bubble.

Obviously Manning hadn't said anything to her. I guess she didn't even know about the missing money. To change the subject I said, 'Do you know where I can mail a letter around here?'

She looked at me curiously but all she said was, 'Yeah, sure. The American Embassy. They take our stuff in a diplomatic pouch as far as *Helsinki* and then dump it in the regular Finnish mail. Otherwise the Sovs would read our bank statements, you know, *snoop* through everything if we sent it from here. It's only once a week, on Friday, but at least it's *something*. But you've got to get your letters to the Embassy by Wednesday afternoon or they don't get sent for another week.' She blew another pink bubble. 'Wait until you start getting the "Dear Deadbeat" letters from your credit card companies because your bills are so *late*.'

Wednesday. That was today. I left for the Embassy with Ian's stack of overdue bills. He probably got a truckload of

'Dear Deadbeat' letters. When we were together I paid all the bills. Left on his own, Ian could be a bit ... cavalier ... about these things. So it was only natural that I should make sure his bills got mailed, although knowing Ian, the cheques in these letters were minimum payments on maximum debt.

The Embassy wasn't far away so I walked. It was down the street and across the Kalininsky Bridge, so close I could see part of the red-brick walls of the compound from my window at the Ukraine. When I got back Annabel and I did not discuss David Manning again for the rest of the day.

Manning didn't show up at the office either Thursday or Friday. I didn't miss him.

On Friday morning I asked Larisa where I could find the Moscow telephone book. It was not on the bookshelves with the other reference books.

'We have none,' she said. She was sitting at her desk, her long, graceful neck bent as she studied a page of numbers, her bejewelled fingers rapidly tracing across the columns as she made notes on another piece of paper.

She obviously hadn't heard me correctly. 'I meant the Moscow telephone book.'

This time she looked up. 'Yes, I know. We have none.'

'Well, maybe we should get one.' How could she be so nonchalant? What news organization functioned without a telephone book? 'Maybe we could borrow one. Or one of the Yuris could get one from the telephone company.'

'We ... have ... none.' She spoke with the exaggerated patience reserved for a child who does not understand, stressing each word. 'There is no telephone book for Moscow. It does not exist.'

'That's impossible.'

'Why?' She raised her eyebrows and smiled with benevolent, but fraying, tolerance.

'Because this is a city with nearly nine million people, that's why. No city with that many people can function without a telephone book. How do you find the telephone number of someone you want to call?' I was getting a bit exasperated myself.

'You already know the numbers of people you want to call.'

She was still acting as if I was asking something completely unreasonable.

'But if you don't?'

'Then you find out.' She opened a drawer of her desk and reached inside, pulling out a battered black ledger held together with a rubber band. She opened the ledger and showed me pages and pages of names and phone numbers on paper now nearly transparent after years of use. There were numerous crossing-outs and several colours of ink. 'This is my private telephone book,' she explained. 'If there is someone you wish to telephone whose number you do not know, perhaps I can help you.'

I knew for certain Larisa's book did not contain the telephone number I needed. It belonged to a friend of my mother's, a woman named Nina Revchenka. I'd found her letters to my mother in a trunk in Kathleen's attic two weeks ago, when her lawyer had gently urged me to get on with the task of sorting through my grandmother's estate. The letters had been a shock. In fact, everything I'd found in that trunk had been a shock.

Particularly the theatre programme. It was for a performance by the Bolshoi Ballet over thirty years ago. My mother's black and white picture was on the cover. She'd danced the lead in *Gisele*. At first I didn't believe it was my mother, except there was her name, 'Natasha Orlova', right there in the programme.

I hadn't known she was ever a dancer, much less a prima ballerina with the Bolshoi Ballet. A little oversight on her part, never to mention it to her daughter? Or maybe some other reason not to tell.

You don't just forget something like that.

Kathleen had never breathed anything about my mother's illustrious past, either. Of course the fact that she'd hated my mother probably had something to do with it. Kathleen blamed her for my father's death, for killing her golden-haired son, even though he'd been driving when the car went over the embankment and they'd both been drinking. But the way Kathleen remembered it, my mother had baited my father, goaded him into taking the car out, so it was all her fault.

When I found Nina Revchenka's letters, it was like blowing the dust off Pandora's box. And it was screaming: 'Open me'.

Who wouldn't want to know?

The answer to all the unanswered questions. All the years of guilt and shame because of the scandal-driven account of my parents' accident. Afterwards, the whispered remarks I wasn't supposed to hear or understand. The looks the other kids gave me at school.

The painful things I suspected Kathleen wouldn't tell me because she didn't want me to be hurt further.

Nina's letters were ancient, postmarked from Moscow more than two decades ago, and fragile as dried leaves. They were also indecipherable. The faded, old-fashioned flowery Cyrillic script was impossible for me, with my fourth-grade Russian, to translate, except for a word here or there.

But now I was in Moscow. Now I could find Nina herself, if she were still alive and living here. She could tell me about my mother, a woman of whom my memories had become so insubstantial, so ephemeral, I sometimes wondered if I had dreamed or invented her.

Still, my search for Nina wasn't something I wanted to broadcast. That's why I didn't want everyone in the office looking over my shoulder while I tried to find Nina in the non-existent Moscow telephone book. But now I'd put my foot in it with Larisa, and she wasn't going to let me off the hook until I gave her an answer that sounded vaguely truthful.

She was staring at me, poised and regal, like a school-teacher waiting for a pupil's answer, dead certain it's going to be a bluff. 'Claire? Whose phone number do you wish?'

I said the first thing that came into my head. 'The phone number of the Sovremennik Theatre.' I'm a terrible liar. Thank God I'm not Pinocchio. I'd just seen the name on a poster stuck up on a bulletin board in the kitchen.

She smiled and managed to look like she believed me. 'Ah, but of course I have that number. Do you want to attend a play there? The director is a good friend of mine. I can get you tickets.'

We both knew I was lying. I could tell by her wide-eyed look of sincerity. 'No. No, thank you. I mean, that's not necessary. But ... yes. That is, I was thinking about it. Attending a play, I mean.'

'Then you must let me arrange the tickets for you. I insist.'

'I wouldn't want you to go to any trouble.'

'It is no trouble at all. How many tickets do you need?'

'Two. Two would be perfect.'

'How nice you want to improve your Russian.'

So I was going to the theatre.

As for Nina Revchenka, I was back where I'd started. The only way I was going to find out if she was still alive and living in Moscow was by going to the address on the letters and knocking on the door. I had Saturday off work. I would go then and meet her, if she still lived there.

But would she want to meet me?

I offered Annabel a lift to Victoria's dinner party on Friday night. I figured I might as well start learning my way around the city, and besides, the short Yuri had just filled the petrol tank so there was no danger of being stranded on some dark street without petrol.

Manning wasn't coming since he had the late shift at work. Frankly, it didn't bother me.

'Good God! What *died*?' Annabel said as she got in the car.

'Ian left a half-eaten sandwich that started to rot.'

'I'm gonna be carsick if I have to ride in this vehicle, Claire.'

'Roll down the window.'

She opened the window and the night air rushed inside, whipping our hair in to our faces. 'I guess it's all right if I don't breathe.' She cupped a hand around a cigarette and tried to light it. 'What's that other weird smell? It's probably something toxic. We could *die*, you know.'

'It's perfume. I was trying to get rid of the odour.'

'These matches won't light. There's something wrong with the air in this car.' She flung the matches out of the window and shoved her cigarettes back in her bag. She pulled out a dark brown bottle and shook some pills into her hands. 'Here, have a few. Chewable vitamin C. It's an antioxidant. God *knows* what we're breathing. And you'd better slow *down*. There's a GAI up ahead. You know, those traffic cops who ambush you from behind bushes or parked cars and say you've been speeding or you're drunk. You can't avoid them, either. If you get pulled over, one whiff of this car and they're going to think you've stashed a *corpse*.'

I took my foot off the accelerator. 'I'm not speeding.'

'Speeding, schmeeding. The limit is *sixty* in the city. *Kilometres*, that is. You're going at least a hundred.'

'Sixty kilometres? That's only thirty-six miles an hour.'

'No fooling. And wait 'til you get pulled over. Foreigners are sitting *ducks*. You'd think we were wearing "kick me" signs on our tushes. The GAI *love* us. Although you can get out of being written up if you slip a twenty-dollar bill between your driver's licence and your press accreditation. Just don't look too obvious or smug about it and let them give you their spiel.'

'You mean, bribe them?'

'Claire, you *sweet* child. They *expect* it. Why do you think they pull you over in the first place?'

Victoria lived in one of Moscow's oldest foreigners' compounds, a place called Sad Sam. It was just off the Sadovoye Koltso, the inner ring road known as the Garden Ring, which changed names sixteen times as it circled Moscow's sprawl. Victoria's part of the ring was called Sadovoye Samotechnaya or 'Sloping Garden Road', a whimsical description, since there wasn't a garden in sight, sloping or otherwise.

She opened the door for us, waving a half-full glass of red wine like a semaphore, radiant and lovely in a lilac silk blouse and fitted black velvet trousers. 'Come in, come in. Make yourselves at home. We've started drinking already.'

Her apartment smelled of the drifting aromas of dinner. It was a home, with surprisingly airy rooms, carved woodwork, and high ceilings with sparkling chandeliers that hung from elaborate plaster medallions of cherubs and twining vines painted in pink, celadon and dusty blue. The contrast between my stark hotel room with its dowdy shades of sepia and brown and this cosy place, with its book-lined walls, photographs, plants and comfortable furniture, made me suddenly, desperately homesick for Kathleen's house. My house.

The living room was full of people. Ella Fitzgerald sang Gershwin from somewhere in the candlelit shadows. Annabel knew everyone, of course. Victoria introduced me and the men stood up. Hugh nodded from across the room. He was wearing an expensive blazer, cashmere by the look of it, and well-cut trousers. This was obviously a man who ironed his pyjamas. I nodded back. The golden light from half a dozen fat red candles on the coffee table glinted off his glasses, turning them to mirrors, obscuring his eyes so I couldn't read them.

'You know Hugh,' Victoria was saying,' and that's Paula Engel with Radio Canada, Simon Westacott with BBC television, and Nick Ivory with Reuters.'

I shook hands with everyone. Simon Westacott winked at me.

'Someone get them a drink,' Victoria ordered. 'I've got to get back to the kitchen.'

Simon handed me a glass of red wine big enough to drown in and Hugh made space for me next to him on a chintz-covered sofa. Annabel poured her own wine and sat on the arm of another sofa, next to Simon. She bent down and lit a cigarette off his, their faces nearly touching. She kept her hand on his shoulder.

'Bloody shame about Ian,' Simon said to me. 'Annabel says you're taking his place.' He had the wholesome good looks and sex appeal of someone who was probably a television heart-throb. Straight blond hair, dark eyes, tanned and outdoorsy. A combination James Bond-Boy Scout. Except for his eyes. They were calculating.

'I'll be here for a while. At least until they find a replacement for him.'

'Is this your first time in Moscow?'

'Yes. First trip.'

We got through all the polite chit-chat you make when someone's new in a group. These were Ian's friends, all right. They had the same edgy restlessness as he did. I could tell when the talk drifted to work. Their stories were sort of a 'can you top this' banter about who'd been caught in the bloodiest gun battle in some ancient nationalist feud or who had the worst story about being stranded in some hellhole when all the flights were cancelled for lack of fuel and there was no food except beer and black bread.

Maybe it wasn't so improbable that Ian had gone foraging for something to eat. Everyone in the room had stories about

70

living on nothing but booze, or something equally unimaginable and bizarre, while they were travelling away from Moscow. They all talked lightly of appalling food shortages and poverty.

Maybe Ian had picked those mushrooms after all. Maybe he'd been out in the woods while he was in Smolensk and ... got hungry.

Or maybe someone had fed them to him. Someone in this room.

It could have been an accident.

Except then whoever it was would be sick, too.

Simon was pouring wine as freely as if Victoria had a vineyard outside her kitchen window. I held out my empty glass for a refill.

This was a dinner party, not a police line-up.

I must be nuts to be sitting here speculating about which of Ian's friends might have poisoned him, even accidentally. Or that he might have stolen fifty thousand dollars from the office.

I would have known if something were wrong. Ian would have said something. And surely Victoria would have known, too?

She came into the room just then, holding half a dozen photographs in one hand and an empty wineglass in the other. 'These were all I could find,' she said, passing them around. Her voice was shaky.

The photos were of Ian, of course, and I caught my breath when Hugh passed the first one to me. There were dates and places written on the backs of the photos in Ian's broad scrawl. Ian when he had been with Victoria, on a trip to Georgia and another to Azerbaijan, exotic and remote places I did not know, with magnificent backdrops of mountains or snow or water. There was one picture that stood out from the others, of the two of them in front of a small house, their arms intertwined, heads thrown back laughing, caught in a moment of unmistakable intimacy. I held it longer than the others did before I passed it to Nick Ivory.

He hadn't spoken much all evening. Instead, he'd been fiddling with his wedding ring like he wasn't used to it yet. He looked like an eighteen-year-old school boy but was probably

71

twenty-one or -two which still made him the youngest of all of us by seven or eight years. Handsome in a baby-faced way, ruddy cheeks, athletic build, earnest, youthful innocence. The air of someone who'd been the captain of the rugby team at an elite boarding school and won the debating prize as well. He was wearing jeans and a white dress shirt with no collar under a tweed blazer.

Ian had told me about meeting Nick when he arrived in Moscow, an extremely bright kid who'd just graduated from Cambridge and got sent to Russia hours after he married some gorgeous creature whose father was Lord Somebody-or-Other. I think Ian planned to take Nick under his wing. Ian was always doing things like that. Once I'd been the new kid. Then we got physically involved and I was a lot more than under his wing.

But in Nick, I suspect Ian saw a younger version of himself. He told me Nick had real compassion and a good intuitive feel for his stories. As long as he didn't get too cocky or jaded.

That was Ian, all right.

Nick looked up just then and caught me staring at him. He immediately looked down, but before he did, I saw his eyes, which were troubled and maybe a bit ... scared. He'd been the last person to see Ian before he died. He was the one the hospital sent home.

He passed the photo I'd given him to Paula like it was too hot to touch. He did the same with all the others.

Victoria filled her glass unsteadily. 'We're almost ready to eat,' she said, as some of the wine splashed on the coffee table. She swiped at it with her hand. 'I guess I'd better see about everything. Hugh ... be a darling and carve the meat for me.'

'I'll come.' Nick got up so quickly his wine glass rocked crazily on the table. Paula Engel reached out and caught it just before it tipped over. 'So sorry,' he said. 'Terribly clumsy of me.'

He left and no one spoke, except for Ella crooning dreamily above the roar of traffic outside the curtained windows, below us on the Sadovoye Koltso.

Dinner had come from Paris. Filet mignon spirited into Russia in a carry-on suitcase the last time Victoria was there.

72

'I was saving it for a special occasion,' she said, 'although I never thought . . .'

There were no mushrooms on the menu.

We talked about Ian during dinner. We even told jokes about him and laughed a little. Ian would have enjoyed it, actually, if he could have been there. He wasn't much on church or God or anything spiritual, so a dinner party would have suited him fine. No mourning, no hanging crepe, nothing sad or weepy.

Anyway, funerals aren't for the person who's died, are they? They're for the rest of us who get left behind, so to speak, with a big hole in our lives, wondering how we're going to fill it. And, of course, we drank. Hugh placed bottle after bottle on the sideboard like he was setting up bowling pins. We were finishing dinner when the doorbell rang. Victoria turned scarlet. 'I'll get it,' she said, and started for the door.

'Who are we expecting?' Simon called after her.

'Another friend of Ian's,' she called back. 'I don't think you know him. He said he couldn't come. I guess he changed his mind.'

'I'll get another place setting,' Paula said. She stood up. She was a large-boned woman, every bit of six feet tall. A physique that might have been better suited to a man, except for her face. Classic, arresting features that made me think of pictures of Egyptian princesses in books on ancient civilizations and dark shoulder-length hair that shimmered like liquid silk when the light caught it. She'd been quiet for most of the evening. Watchful as a cat, regal in an almost feline way. She turned to Annabel and me. 'Is David coming?'

'He has to work,' Annabel said.

I could hear Victoria's voice, greeting the latecomer. Paula came back from the kitchen with the place setting. There was quiet laughter down the hall, then a moment later Victoria walked into the dining room with Philip Robinson.

I think I stopped breathing.

He glanced around the room, taking us all in, pleasantly, cordially, in complete control. Philip never entered a room. He owned it. His gaze passed over me, as cursorily as it passed over the others. Then he looked back at me again. I bet he recognized me but forgot my name.

'This is Philip Robinson,' Victoria was saying breathlessly. 'He's teaching at Moscow State for a year while he's on sabbatical from Harvard. Ian and I met him in Smolensk last summer.' I couldn't help noticing that she had laced her arm through Philip's. 'Why doesn't everyone introduce themselves?'

We went around the table. When it came to me, he said, 'I know you. I'm sorry but I've forgotten your name.'

'Claire Brennan. I was one of your students at Harvard.' I left out the research assistant part. No point dragging that up. He'd probably had dozens of nubile young women working for him since my day.

'Yes,' he said. 'Of course. Now I remember you.' Which obviously translated into 'I still haven't got a clue'.

Victoria fussed over getting Philip something to eat. I thought she seemed flustered. Philip could do that to people. Especially women. I ought to know. He'd done it to me. And probably a million others, give or take a few hundred thousand.

If I were a betting person, which I sometimes am, I would have put money on Philip and Victoria being an item in, say, a week. There was something about the way they were connecting, Victoria's self-conscious distractedness, Philip's deft grace and self-assured charm. She was captivated. As for him, he still had that way about him of a man who's never, ever, ever been turned down by a woman.

Besides, I knew his technique. I'd seen it often enough. Sure, he was a little older and greyer. But he'd aged well, as they say. I think it only made him sexier.

He apologized profusely for disrupting the dinner, and of course we all said he hadn't. But his presence did change the chemistry of the evening and suddenly we were spectators to the budding relationship between Philip and Victoria and we were all playing to that. No one spoke about Ian any more.

I would like to say that I watched this little tableau in a calmly dispassionate way, but I didn't. Frankly it was with anger, more than jealousy or even sour grapes. I was angry with both of them. Here we were at what was more or less Ian's wake. And Victoria, who one minute could hardly contain her grief, was suddenly looking like she was about a heartbeat away from having sex with Philip on the dining room table. And Philip ... what friend of Ian's was he? He came for Victoria, not Ian. An intruder who stole Ian's evening and made it a setting for another conquest, another notch in his bedpost. I couldn't even remotely imagine him and Ian getting along. Two brainy men with monumental egos who never shared the limelight. No, they'd have clashed together, that's for sure.

The person I felt sorriest for was Hugh. He had a bottle of wine next to him on the table and had been refilling his glass as soon as it was empty ever since Philip arrived.

Victoria brought dessert while Philip finished his dinner. A really spectacular chocolate mousse. Conversation had dwindled, although it was probably due more to the amount of alcohol we'd consumed than to the effect of Philip's presence.

Hugh opened another bottle of wine. Like we really needed it.

Paula said, into the silence, 'So what are you doing at Moscow State, Philip?'

'I'm researching a book on Napoleon's Russian campaign of 1812,' he said. 'I've been following the route of the French army from where they crossed the Niemen River all the way to Moscow and back again ... it's been fascinating.'

Quite honestly no one was ready for a discourse on Russian history, given the general state of weary inebriation. Simon put an arm around Annabel's shoulder. He murmured something in her ear and she nodded.

Hugh was murderously silent, Victoria too smitten to talk, Annabel and Simon were completely taken with each other all of a sudden, and I was keeping my mouth shut, so it fell to Paula and Nick to make a few polite inquiries about Philip's work. We made it through dessert. Then, mercifully, the party broke up.

Annabel pulled me into a corner. 'I'm going home with Simon,' she said. 'Do you think you'll be all right, driving on your own?'

'Sure. No problem.' What choice did I have?

Paula leaned over and drawled in my ear, 'Do you suppose he's asking if he can help with the dishes?' We were both watching Philip, who was bent over Victoria, saying something she clearly found mesmerizing.

'I used to work for him. Philip's the kind of guy who thinks the dishwashing fairy floats down from a star and cleans up while you're in bed.'

'Why am I not surprised.' She rolled her eyes. 'Come on,' she said, 'help me get him and Hugh out of here. I'll stay and do the dishes. She's had way too much to drink and she's missing Ian. This isn't a good night for her to be having a slumber party ... they both want to spend the night. Hugh looks like he's ready to do battle.'

She marched over to Victoria and put a hand on her shoulder. 'I'll go in the kitchen and start the dishes, honey. They're too much for you to do by yourself ... then, if you don't mind, maybe I could just sleep on your couch tonight? I really don't think I ought to drive.'

Well, Philip got it. He left, looking unhappy I'd say, but with a meaningful look at Victoria. Paula disappeared into the kitchen. Annabel and Simon had gone already. That just left Hugh and me. He asked me to wait for him while he said goodnight to Victoria alone.

He found me in the parking lot. 'You okay to drive?' he asked.

'Perfectly fine.' The road was wide and straight, probably not too many cars at this hour, either, with any luck. There was only one turnoff I had to make at Kalinina Prospekt.

I could do this.

Hugh was watching me. 'Just take it easy and if you're lucky the GAI won't pull you over. If they do, don't let them breathalyse you with that paper cup crap, either.'

'What?'

'Sometimes they give you a paper cup and tell you to breathe into it. Then they light a match to see if your breath is flammable.'

'You're joking?'

'Not exactly. Look, do you want me to follow you?'

'Thanks, I know where I'm going.' Unsteadily I started to unlock the door of Ian's car. 'Hugh?'

'Yeah?'

'Are you all right?'

He knew what I meant. 'I'm fine.' He took the key from me and unlocked the door with quick, deft motions. Obviously impervious to the two gallons of wine floating his kidneys. After I got in he handed me Ian's key and bent down and kissed my forehead. 'Thanks for asking. Look, why don't I drive you back to the Ukraine? We'll come back tomorrow and get your car.'

I shook my head. He knew I would. He kissed me again, a sweet, brotherly kiss. 'Take care of yourself.'

I left the parking lot before he did and figured out almost immediately that I was going the wrong way on the Sadovoye Koltso. Or maybe it was the right way. I wasn't in the best condition to judge.

I should have waited and followed him.

A few street lights gave off a pale, ghostly glow and there were no lights at all in any of the buildings I passed. I couldn't see landmarks well enough to tell if they looked familiar. I pulled the car over to the shoulder and turned on the interior car light. Damn. Something else to be fixed.

There was a flashlight and a map in the glove compartment. I'd seen them when I cleaned the car. I snapped open the glove compartment and fumbled around until my hand closed around the smooth metal barrel of the flashlight. I pulled it out and switched it on. It didn't work, either. I banged the steering wheel with my fist and sat in the dark.

Since I was on a ring road, I could just keep going and eventually I'd end up where I wanted to be. But it might be the long way around, possibly miles out of my way.

I'd just do a U-turn and go back the other way. The short Yuri had already explained to me about making a U-turn in Moscow. It was called a '*razvorot*' and was only permitted in specified lanes with special arrows painted on them. He also said sometimes you could drive for ages before you found a place where you were allowed to make a *raz*.

Well, not tonight. It was late. I was tired. There was no one around. I pulled out on to the road.

He vaporized like a genie out of a bottle the moment I swung my car in the other direction. I saw his lighted white night stick wave up and down in the darkness ahead of me like a fluorescent drum majorette, gesturing for me to pull over. For a moment I thought I would just accelerate and pretend I didn't see him, but Annabel already told me that was pointless. He would just radio his buddy up ahead and the next and the next.

They would catch me. I wouldn't escape.

The road was deserted.

I was at his mercy. I would have to do anything he said or wanted. I tried not to think of the cab drivers Manning had warned me about who stripped and robbed their clients after taking them to some remote, isolated place. Surely the GAI, who were, after all, ersatz police, had to behave honourably when they stopped a solitary woman in a foreign car at two o'clock in the morning.

In a moment I'd know, wouldn't I?

I held my breath and listened as the sound of heavy footsteps on the gravel shoulder came closer and closer to where I waited, alone, in the middle of nowhere in the ink-black night.

Chapter Six

He strolled up to the car window. '*Dobre vecher. Documenti, pozhalusta.*'

I pulled out my press pass, my US driver's licence, and my passport and handed them over. My hand shook but maybe it was too dark for him to notice. My GAI officer looked everything over in silence. Then he said I had made made an illegal U-turn. Did I know that?

Yes, I said in Russian. I was sorry, but I was new in Moscow and I was lost.

He was sorry, too, because he would have to write up a citation and fine me. He pulled out a formbook from his back pocket.

'And where are you coming from just now?'

'Dinner at a friend's house.'

'And you had something to drink.'

Here it was. 'Yes.'

'How much?'

'Two glasses of wine.'

'I see.' He rocked on his heels and waited.

We both knew I was lying. I sat waiting for him to write up the citation. But he did nothing. I didn't dare to look at him.

Instead I picked up my bag from the passenger seat as though I expected a snake to slither out and bite me. I felt my wallet and pulled it out. He didn't stop me. The first bill I pulled out was a ten. I took out another bill. Another ten. I laid them on top of my documents. 'Perhaps I can just pay the fine right now,' I said. I still didn't look him in the eye.

He didn't answer. An eternity passed. Did he want more

money or was he really going to throw the book at me, now that I'd added bribery to my other sins?

'See that I don't catch you again.' He handed me my documents, minus the money.

I slumped against the seat and listened to the sound of his boots crunching on the gravel as he walked back to his hiding place. My mouth tasted of sawdust. I started the engine and drove excessively carefully back to the office parking lot. Then I ran, as fast as I could, all the way to the Ukraine.

There was a note from Nigel, which he'd slipped under my door, inviting me to stop by for a drink if it wasn't too late when I got in. Another drink. Just what I needed. I crumpled the note into a ball and threw it in the wastebasket.

Then I went to bed.

I passed out at once, but it was a heavy, alcoholic sleep and soon the dreams came, terrifyingly vivid and real. For the first time in years, I dreamed about my parents. My mother was shouting at my father. They were arguing. They always argued. I couldn't hear the words, but I knew they would be brutal and venomous. Then my parents faded, first my father, then my mother, vaporous as ghosts, and I was running for my life through the dirty, littered corridors of Ian's hospital. Someone was chasing me, breath hot on my neck, fingertips brushing my clothes, closing in on me. I ran through one of the locked metal doors, and another and another like they were holograms, and spurted ahead of him. I lost him in the twists and turns of the corridor, which was now a funfair maze. Then I tripped. I lost my balance and pitched into darkness. A light beam shone like a spotlight, showing me the way, and caught on something in its swath. I hurtled down, towards it. It was Ian. He leered at me from inside a block of ice, eyes wide, mouth open. A frozen scream.

I hit something hard, like concrete, and woke up.

I think I cried out. Next thing I knew, I was sitting bolt upright in bed, my heart slamming against my chest. I could feel it through my nightgown. I reached for the bedside table lamp in the darkness. I knocked something over and it clunked on the floor. My alarm clock. I found the switch for the lamp and sat there in the dirty light of a forty-watt bulb, panting, ecstatically relieved to be in my dingy, familiar hotel room.

When I was little I used to look under the bed each night, checking for monsters that would pounce as soon as the lights went out. I looked under the bed and saw the alarm clock. I pulled it out. Four-thirty.

My throat was as parched as if I'd swallowed a desert and my nightgown was drenched with sweat, sticking to me like a second skin. I needed a shower, but there would be no hot water at this early hour. It was something to do with the hotel's prehistoric plumbing system which couldn't handle the water needs of guests in more than a thousand rooms. Nigel had told me about it, warning me never to count on a hot shower before six or seven in the morning. He said sometimes they even turned off the water in the middle of the day with no warning. Russian roulette. Ha, ha.

I stripped off my soaked nightgown and pulled on an old sweatshirt that came down to my knees. Then I went and stood in front of the refrigerator with the door open and drank juice, straight from the box.

Even if I could have slept, I didn't plan to go back to bed. I seem to have the talent, if you can call it that, for slipping back into a dream where I left off, the way you pick up a book and start reading again. It doesn't always happen, but it's happened often enough when I've had a nightmare like the one I'd just had.

I had no intention of replaying the horror show of Ian's death mask or my parents' bitter matrimonial *jihad*.

There would be nothing on television because they turned it off at night. And I'd already read everything I'd brought with me from the States.

I got the saucepan from behind the television. I set it on the hot plate and poured mineral water into it. A cup of coffee, then.

Ian's flashlight and my bag were still sitting in the middle of the table where I'd left them when I came in a few hours ago. I had brought the flashlight with me so I could replace the batteries. No more episodes of attempted map reading in total darkness. Manning had left some batteries in the desk drawer while he was living here, probably spares for his tape recorder and radio. I took a package of batteries out of the drawer.

81

Size C. The tape recorder took Cs. So did the radio. Flashlights took Ds.

I picked up the flashlight. I don't know why it didn't occur to me earlier that the reason it felt so light was because there were no batteries in it. It was probably broken. It would be just like Ian to keep a broken flashlight in his car. He couldn't be bothered to fix or replace it. It wasn't a cerebral enough matter to make a claim on his time. I unscrewed the top and then I knew why he'd kept it.

There was a wad of money inside it, rolled up tightly inside the barrel.

He'd really stuffed it in.

They were dollars, not roubles. Hundred dollar bills coiled tightly in two rolls. I broke a fingernail trying to fish them out. Wrapped around one of the wads was a page torn from a diary. The date was July 25 and the handwriting was Ian's. '*Luminous, like the dust of crushed pearls. Sensual face, wearing blue hat. Black background. Approx. 20x15. So-so condition, some mildew, bottom left. Dutch, probably – 17th cent. Vermeer??? Also, Madonna and child??? No details. Can get it 2-3 wks, maybe less.*'

The water spat at me from the saucepan. I turned off the burner, sat down, and started counting. Exactly five thousand dollars.

Cash had a way of slipping through Ian's fingers like water, so it was pretty stunning – no, more like unbelievable – to find a wad like this that he'd actually managed not to spend. And given the way things were going, it didn't take a genius to figure out where he'd got it.

So maybe Manning was right.

Maybe Ian did take the fifty thousand.

But why park it here? Some of it, that is. And where was the rest?

Maybe he didn't have enough time to get it back to the strongbox. Maybe he figured it was a safe place to keep it temporarily. Ian would do something quirky like that and think it was perfectly logical.

As for the note . . . what? He'd actually found a painting by Jan Vermeer? Or thought he had? A painting like that was worth millions. You didn't just stumble on them. And you

82

couldn't buy it for fifty thousand dollars, much less five thousand.

So what was he doing?

Oh, Ian.

Tell me you weren't fencing stolen art?

Ian had a passion for art but surely it didn't run to stealing it? In New York he was always haunting the museums. I think most of the staff at the Guggenheim knew him on a first name basis. He loved modern art; he even collected it. Our tastes were diametrically opposed, though, and I remember one rather heated discussion, all right, argument, about whether a tiny red dot on the corner of a white canvas was really worth eight hundred dollars. Particularly as we were broke when he bought that little number.

I turned on the burner to re-heat the water. It boiled almost at once and I fixed a cup of sludgy coffee. I drank it and looked at the pile of money on the table.

Damn it, Ian, what were you doing?

I got dressed while the inky sky faded to the colour of pewter. I didn't feel like waiting until the gnomes in the basement got around to turning on the water so I splashed mineral water on my face from my dwindling supply of bottles and called it a bath.

I'd go back to the office and make one more stab at trying to find something in Ian's files or on his desk. At least now I had an idea what I was looking for.

Sort of.

Fortunately it was Saturday so no one would be there this early except whichever intern had overnight babysitting duty. None of those kids would ask questions about what I was doing.

I was practically out the door when I remembered the money. It was still in the middle of the table. Not too smart. It wouldn't be there when I got back.

Either Zoya would figure it was an extra-generous tip or one of the Ukraine's ubiquitous staff, like the exterminator, who was getting to be a pal, or the plumber, another habitué, might be tempted to liberate it from my room.

Anyway, it was a stupid slip-up, forgetting to put it away.

Which left me with the question . . . where?

Return it to the safe? Or stuff it back in the flashlight?

If I returned it to the safe, Manning would be all over me like a bad rash, wanting to know where I'd found it and what had happened to the rest of it. I have to say, under the circumstances, it wouldn't look too good for Ian. So I stuffed it in the flashlight and then put the flashlight underneath my underwear, in the dresser.

I'd give the money back. But not now.

When I was ready.

Manning wasn't going to ruin Ian's good name and trash him to the bosses in New York if I could stop him.

When I got to the elevator, Nadya was at the *dejournaya's* desk by the elevator, patiently knitting something long and pink, the Madame Defarge of the eleventh floor. She was small and fragile as a bird. She could have known Moses personally.

Of all the *dejournayas*, the hotel's posse of vigilantes who informed on its guests' comings and goings, I liked her the best. Unlike the others with their heavy-handed questions, Nadya never seemed fussed about what I did. In a movie she'd be the sweet-faced grandmother who'd slip the inmates the keys to the prison and no one would ever guess. When the hotel's senior snoops asked for her reports she probably had the nerve to say whatever she wanted and didn't lose sleep over it.

I gave her my key and smiled.

'You are off so early today,' she said.

'*Rabota.* I have to work.'

She clicked her tongue and watched me, bright-eyed and alert, assessing my face, my clothes. '*Rabota, rabota.* You work too much, *dorogaya moya.*'

My darling, my dear. My mother had called me names like that, though less and less frequently after her drinking got really bad.

'*Do svidanya*, Nadya.' I stepped into the elevator.

'*S'bogom.* Go with God.' I heard her knitting needles clattering again.

I was in the pedestrian tunnel under Kutuzovsky Prospekt when I finally figured out what was bothering me. Ian's note was written on a page from a diary. The day-a-page kind of diary.

84

Ian didn't even wear a watch, much less carry around that kind of diary.

So, whose diary had a page missing from it?

When I got to the office Justin, our intern from Princeton, was there. He was in the kitchen, hell-bent on devouring the entire contents of Tanya's refrigerator.

'What do they feed you at Moscow State?' I asked.

He looked up. 'Air.'

I grinned.

'Hey, no joke, I've dropped ten pounds in six weeks. I told my parents not to waste money on my return airfare next June. I'll mail myself home in an envelope.' He was slabbing mayonnaise on a thick piece of bread, ready to set it on a mountain of meat, cheese, and other things hidden under yesterday's borscht that he'd already heaped on another piece of bread. 'Want one of these? I'll make you one.'

'What's in it?'

'You don't want to know. It's kind of a Russian club sandwich.'

'You eat that for breakfast?'

'I eat *anything* for breakfast. Especially if you saw what they feed us at school.'

'Like the Ukraine, I guess.' I'd ventured into the hotel's dining room one night but left after I saw one of the serving ladies scrape the plate of a departed guest and put the uneaten food on a platter she then slapped down on the buffet table. 'All right, fix me one, but leave out the borscht, please.'

'You want the borscht.'

'Okay, I want the borscht.'

I went back to the main room to Ian's desk. My desk. It was still cluttered with his things. I'd been too busy to do anything about seriously cleaning it since that first morning, so I just heaped things on the sides and on the floor next to me and cleared a space to work in the middle.

I sat down in his chair and checked under piles of things the way you do when you expect to find bugs until I unearthed the desk calendar IPS issued to everyone. It was kind where you tear off the page at the end of each day. This year IPS, in a moment of uncharacteristic extravagance, went all out and splurged on calendars with little quotes on each page. I'd already seen Ian's; the date hadn't been changed since August 15. He had doodled all over it, probably while talking on the phone, turning the two 'u's in August into smiley faces. The quote of the day was an English proverb: 'A stumble may prevent a fall'. I flipped through the pages from the twenty-sixth until . . . .

Until he died.

On three pages he'd scribbled the word 'Tretyakov'.

The art gallery.

Well, that figured. The Tretyakov Art Gallery contained the finest collection of Soviet and Russian art in the world. I could imagine Ian hanging out there like he'd done in New York. Except for one thing.

The Tretyakov had been closed for renovation for months.

So what was Ian doing lurking around a closed museum? Maybe he'd befriended one of the security guards, like he did at the Guggenheim, and they let him in anyway.

It looked like he'd been there three times in the last few weeks. The final entry was Wednesday, September 20, but this time he'd written '4 p.m.' as though he had an appointment.

I looked through the calendar, all the way to December 31, but the last time he'd written anything was that appointment on September 20.

Of course. The next day he'd been rushed to the hospital.

I looked at the quote of the day.

'When it's a choice between two evils, I always pick the one I never tried before' – Mae West.

Then Justin yelled, 'Come and get it.'

I wolfed down his mystery sandwich in about two minutes and paid for it. It sat in my stomach like a cannonball while I continued to go through the filing cabinet. I found nothing about the Tretyakov, though Ian did have an art file. He'd covered Wolverhampton's hugely successful art auction last year in Moscow. Ian could write about the telephone directory and make it sound sexy. This story was pure Hollywood. Famous auction house sells sought-after avant-garde paintings of the 1920s, conceived in the dark and stony heart of one of the darkest realms of twentieth-century Europe. For the Soviet government it was the equivalent of selling off national treasures, but the quid pro quo was a deal to showcase works produced by their current crop of artists, whose market value in the West was presently nil. The auction hit the international art market like a high explosive bomb and made overnight celebrities of the previous *inconnus*. Ian had written profiles of several of them, which I skimmed. But there was nothing in the file that made mention of any paintings prior to the twentieth century. Nothing by Jan Vermeer, or any Old Master painting for that matter.

The front door to the office opened and closed. I slammed the drawer to the cabinet and whirled around to sit at Ian's desk. I was busy tidying papers when Annabel came in, singing 'Oh, What a Beautiful Morning' like she meant it.

That would be Simon's doing.

She stopped when she saw me and looked puzzled. 'Aren't you . . .you're *off*, today.'

'I know.' I waved vaguely at the disarray around me. 'I've got to get some of this stuff cleaned up. Plus I need to read in on a lot of the files since I don't know the story as well as I ought to.'

She lit a cigarette and studied me. 'If you ask me, you look *beat*, Claire. You're not even here a week and you've already got the kind of black hollows under your eyes that usually take a *month* to get. Why don't you give yourself a break and get some sleep?'

'Uh . . . sure.' I couldn't really go through Ian's files any more. 'Don't you need some help?'

'Nah. That's okay. I can cope. It's usually really quiet on the weekend. The whole Politburo hangs out at their *dachas*.' She looked at the end of her cigarette and studiously watched the ash grow. 'You run along.'

Ah, a little tryst in the office. I said innocently, 'Everything work out last night?'

She grinned and turned red. 'He, uh, might stop by in a while.'

I picked up my raincoat. 'Maybe you're right. I am tired. I guess I'll take off.'

She looked grateful, but her voice was gentle. 'Get some rest, kiddo. I mean it. This place'll eat you *alive*, if you don't watch it.'

I stopped in the doorway and said, 'Do you mind if I ask you something?'

She looked wary but said steadily, 'Shoot.'

'Where did you learn to sing like that? Your voice is ... fabulous.'

'What?' She started to laugh. 'Oh, *that. Jeez*, Claire, I could sing before I could *talk*. When I was a kid I used to think about going to Julliard.'

'Why didn't you?'

She lit another cigarette. 'Ah, you know how it is. Who makes a living singing? I wasn't sure I had what it takes to make it, you know? At least now I can pay the rent.'

She'd probably been saying that for so long she finally believed it. 'You're good,' I said, 'I'll see you later.'

I was waiting for the elevator when I heard her again. Opera, this time. Verdi. Whoever talked her out of singing professionally hadn't done her any favours. She was dynamite.

I didn't go back to the Ukraine for a nap. Instead I headed for Ian's car, and found it where I'd left it last night, badly parked too near the militiaman's booth. This time it was broad daylight when I looked in the glove compartment for the map, so at least I could figure out how to get to the Tretyakov.

It was the most logical place to go. Ian had been there, apparently, the day before he got sick, and met somebody. Someone who worked there? Or was it just a meeting place?

I found the map and pulled it out before I lost any more of my nerve. It was the CIA map which, Nigel had told me during another nocturnal vodka session, was the only reliable map of Moscow. He said Russian maps were deliberately misleading, to confuse the enemy in case of an invasion. I said okay but it seemed a bit weird to think of some general of a potentially hostile nation using a street map to figure out his lefts and rights for the quickest route to the Kremlin, only to find himself ending up on the highway to Berlin.

Not to mention how confusing it must be for the locals.

I found a listing for the Tretyakov in the index and flipped through the map. An envelope fell out and hit my lap. No writing on it, nor was it sealed. I lifted the flap and pulled out two postcards. Actually, two black and white photographs, sepia-coloured with age and quite fragile. Both were of the same elderly gentleman. In one, he was leaning against an ornately carved desk in a room that was probably a study or a library, the kind you see in coffee table magazines on interior decoration. He was frowning at the camera, the kind of arrogantly dismissive look that said the photographer was an insignificant cockroach taking up valuable space and wasting oxygen. In the second picture, he was seated in a striped wing chair next to a fireplace with a blazing fire in it. His hands were folded in his lap and he had the same unobliging, mordant expression on his face like he'd eaten a lemon. I turned over the photograph. Someone had written 'Baron Caspar von Müller, 6/12/47' in faded, flowery ink on the back. The same thing was written on the other picture.

I squinted at the photo of Baron von Müller leaning against his desk. Behind him, there were several paintings on the panelled wall. Impossible to tell what they were without a magnifying glass. It would be too good to be true if one of them was Ian's Vermeer. Of course if it was, I couldn't ask von Müller about it anyway. If he were alive, he'd be about one hundred and twenty years old.

The chances of that were probably slim to none.

I slid the pictures back in the envelope and put it in the glove compartment.

Then I started the engine and looked at the useless petrol gauge. Hopefully there was enough to get me to the Tretyakov and home again.

The Tretyakov was something out of Old Russia, all red and white gingerbread with ornately decorated portals and elaborate windows that made me think of the enchanted castles in my childhood books of Russian fairy tales. Above the main door was an ogee-shaped gable with a bas-relief of St George slaying the dragon, the emblem of ancient Muscovy long before the double-headed eagle of the Tsars and the hammer and sickle of the Communists. To either side of the door was a thick stripe of words written in floral Cyrillic script.

The place looked deserted. Not a soul anywhere.

I walked up to what appeared to be the main entrance and knocked on one of heavy wooden doors, bruising my knuckles. The sound was flat and shallow. No one could possibly hear me. So I rapped on one of the panes of the lattice windows instead.

I kept it up for a while, then I finally stopped. There was a stillness about the place that was unsettling. I stepped back and looked up at the bank of windows below St. George, half-expecting to see a kabuki face peering down. But there was no one.

The gallery was built so that part of the façade, to the right of the main doors, was recessed like an inverted horseshoe, creating a small courtyard that adjoined another wing of the gallery. I walked around to the courtyard and knocked half-heartedly on another set of doors. On the opposite wall was a large bank of windows. I stood on tiptoe, cupped my hands around my face to keep out the daylight, and peered inside. A huge, empty room.

Well, so much for this wild-goose chase. What had I expected? Some benevolent docent, standing on the doorstep, with the answers to all my questions?

Ian's contact at the Tretyakov probably met him only by prearrangement. I walked back around the corner to the main entrance and was on my way to check out the statue in the dusty, bedraggled garden in front of the gallery when I saw a man standing by my car. He looked like he might be trying to open the door. Certainly he was peering in the window on the driver's side.

'Hey! Leave my car alone!' I shouted in English, instinctively. He probably didn't understand, but in Moscow even a two year old recognized the standout black and yellow licence plates with the big 'K' followed by the country code '004', which meant it was the car of an American correspondent. Already a few Russians had pulled up next to me at stoplights and badgered me for cigarettes. They knew who I was and where I came from.

Nigel and the Yuris had warned me to be careful where I parked the car. I should have known better than to leave it some place where there was no one around and walk away.

I ran toward the Volvo. If he was going to steal it, at least I wasn't going to stand by and watch while he did it.

He looked up from whatever he was doing and came toward

90

me. I slowed down. He had one hand in the pocket of a battered leather jacket. What if he had a gun in that pocket? A gun would definitely change the dynamics of the situation. He was about ten yards away. 'You want my car?' I called. This time I spoke in Russian.

He stopped dead in his tracks. 'What? What do you mean, do I want your car?' His English was heavily accented but I could tell he was fluent.

I pointed to the Volvo. 'You were ... examining ... my car.'

He took his hand out of his pocket and walked over until he was standing in front of me. He folded his arms across his chest. No gun. Possibly in his mid-to-late-thirties, tall and thin, with straight brown hair. The slant of his pale blue eyes and the high Tatar cheekbones were unmistakably Slavic, giving him a languid look of sleepy astonishment. Or else it was a look of calculated assessment which, I'd say, was probably more accurate just now. He knew I'd just taken him for some low-life carjacker.

'That is *your* car?'

'Yes.'

'And who are you?'

Besides the beat-up jacket, he was wearing jeans so faded they were practically white, except where they were covered with splotches of paint, and a dirty black sweatshirt, also paint-stained. Maybe he was the Tretyakov's janitor. Or one of the construction workers. But somebody like that wouldn't be so fluent in English and besides, there was something ... noble, I guess you'd say, about him.

So I said, 'I'm Claire Brennan. I'm a journalist with International Press Service. I ... stopped by to see if it might be possible to get a tour of the gallery.' I gestured behind me. 'I'd like to write a story about the work you're doing here.'

'Really?' His eyes became slits and then he looked positively Oriental and remote as the Himalayas. 'Perhaps I can arrange something for you, but today is not possible.' His voice was flat and hard, as though he were angry.

'Maybe I could call you, Mr ...'

He didn't finish the sentence, like I expected. 'As you wish.'

91

I opened my bag and fished in it for my reporter's notebook and something to write with. But his cold demeanour rattled me and my bag slipped out of my hands and fell to the ground, scattering the contents. I bent to retrieve things and so did he.

'This is yours?' He was holding the keyring I'd given Ian, the silver horseshoe, between his thumb and forefinger, like it was contaminated.

I snatched the keyring. 'Yes. Look, I'm sorry to be taking up your time. If you'd like to give me your name and a phone number where I can reach you, I'll be on my way.'

'If you want to contact me, you can call the main number at the Tretyakov.'

'And you'll answer?' I didn't mean to sound sarcastic, but he wasn't being any too friendly.

'They'll find me.'

Oh, brother. 'And who would I be asking for?'

'Nazarov. Alexander Nazarov.'

'Oh!' We both straightened up at the same time. 'You're Alexander Nazarov?'

'Yes.' He spoke warily. 'I don't know you.'

'I don't know you, either,' I said, 'but I've read about you. You sold a painting at the Wolverhampton's auction last year ... to one of the Beatles or Rolling Stones, wasn't it?'

'It was purchased by a former manager of the Bittles,' he said, 'I am not as famous as you think.' He paused. 'And how is it that you read about me?'

I looked at the keyring in my hand. 'My ... colleague ... wrote about you.'

'Who is your colleague?'

He knew the answer. He was just testing to see if I was legit. He was looking at the keyring, too. How many silver horseshoe keyrings could there be in Moscow?

Maybe he recognized it.

Maybe he was the one I was looking for.

'Ian Kendall.'

He nodded, cool as a cucumber. 'Ah, yes. Mr Kendall. I met him several times. He interviewed me after the auction.'

'Yes. He was very passionate about modern art. He liked your work.'

'What do you mean "was"?' His voice was quietly ominous.

He didn't know Ian was dead.

I said carefully, 'Mr Kendall . . . became ill suddenly and was rushed to the hospital last week. He . . . didn't make it.'

'Didn't make it', he repeated. He paused, then said, 'You mean, he is dead?' He seemed genuinely shocked.

I nodded and bit my lip.

He muttered something in Russian that could have been a prayer or a curse, and looked at the ground.

'You knew him well?' I asked.

His head jerked up. 'Did I?' His eyes, now the opaque colour of slate, were challenging.

I said casually, 'You had a four o'clock appointment with him here on September the twentieth. The next day he collapsed and was taken to the hospital. You saw him right before he got sick.'

It was a bluff, and I'm not a great liar, but this time I got lucky.

He looked startled, so I knew I'd hit a bull's-eye. Then he squinted at me with those assessing eyes, like he was deciding whether to trust me or not. 'Your friend was buying one of my paintings,' he said finally. 'You are right, he was not well that day. You must be talking about the day he came to the gallery to pay me.'

Unless he meant Ian was going to pay with Monopoly money that wasn't too likely. Alexander Nazarov probably didn't take plastic or a cheque either. He would be talking about cash. The green stuff.

Oh, Ian. Don't tell me you took the fifty thousand from the safe to buy a couple of blue dots and a yellow squiggle on a canvas? The ex-manager of the Bittles coughed up five figures for the painting he'd bought.

'Excuse me, but I can't imagine that Ian could afford one of your paintings.'

He didn't seem surprised that I knew about Ian's financial status, but after getting the friendly but nosy third degree about intimate details of my life from Tanya and the two Yuris, I guess Russians figured everybody knew everything about everybody else. 'He paid me part of the money.' 'He was going to pay the rest when he picked it up.'

Then he cleared his throat and looked around as though he

expected someone to leap out from behind a bush and say 'boo'. 'He was paying me in *valuta* . . . hard currency. Obviously that is illegal as Russians are not allowed to own hard currency, only roubles. You understand what I'm saying?'

You bet. *Na lyeva.*

'I understand,' I said, 'but Ian still didn't have the kind of cash it takes to buy one of your paintings.'

He shrugged. 'I gave him a . . . how do you say? . . . a good price. It was to thank him for the story he wrote about my work. Am I understanding that you will be completing the purchase for him?'

'You must be joking!' It slipped out, an American idiom, without thinking.

He took me literally. 'I do not joke about my work.'

He sounded mortally offended and I cringed. 'I beg your pardon, that came out wrong. I'm afraid I can't. Pay for your painting, that is. But I would like to ask a favour.'

Another slitty-eyed look of cold assessment. 'You want me to return the money?' He didn't say, 'Forget it, honey,' but I heard it, anyway.

'Please,' I said. 'Ian has a niece who is very ill. He was helping his sister pay this child's medical expenses, but now he's gone. They have nothing.'

That was, of course, only part of the truth. Before Susan and Jade got anything, there was still the little matter of the missing fifty thousand. I already had five back in my hotel room. If Nazarov had the rest of it, Ian's troubles were over.

I could kill Ian, so to speak, for using the office safe as a personal bank, but at least I could get the money back before things really got out of hand. I could conveniently discover it in his car or some other innocuous place like that.

Careless old Ian. Always leaving things around. Here's the money. End of story. It would clear his name and Susan could get whatever life insurance policy and pension Ian had coming.

If, that is, I could persuade Alexander Nazarov to return the money Ian had paid him for the painting.

Snowballs probably had a better chance of freezing in hell, judging by the expression on his face.

'I cannot give Ian's money back,' he said at last. His eyes met mine.

Oh, no.
Dammit, dammit.
'You spent it?'
He nodded slowly. 'All of it. There is nothing left.'

Chapter Seven

We stood looking at each other. I don't know what he was thinking but I was wondering what, exactly, did he buy for forty-five thousand dollars? You couldn't spend that kind of money here.

There was nothing to buy.

No food in the shops, no clothes or household items in the stores.

I mean, really nothing.

'I'm very sorry,' he said, and sounded like he meant it. 'I spent it, also for medical expenses. My mother has a problem with her heart. With *valuta*, I could pay for the surgery now, you understand. Otherwise she would have had to wait many months. She is so fragile ... I used the money to bribe the doctors. And, of course, there was medicine. Anaesthesia. I wanted her to have the best. Things from the West.' He held out his hands, palms upward. 'What would you have done?'

The first time I answered no words came out. The second time, I croaked, 'The same.' And my heart hit the ground.

'I would like to give you the painting,' he was saying. 'Perhaps you can send it to the child. The mother can sell it if she wishes. I have some ... reputation. It will bring some money.'

I nodded. Susan and Jade could use the money, all right. But the cash in the safe was gone, up in smoke. It had been too good to be true to hope that he had it and would just hand it back over. 'Thank you, Mr Nazarov. That's very kind.'

'Sasha,' he said.

'Sasha.' What in the hell was I going to tell Manning? New York would go nuclear when they found out about this.

'So I will telephone you,' he was saying, 'and arrange a time for you to come to my studio.'

'Thank you,' I said again.

'Come,' he said, 'I will take you to your car.' He took my elbow and we walked over to the Volvo. 'This news has surprised you. You are having a big nervous.'

Well, actually a king-sized nervous. But what could I say? He thought the money was legitimately his. He'd spent it, on something very worthwhile, too.

He held the car door while I got in. I rolled down the window. 'I'll wait to hear from you.'

He said gently, 'If I had another five thousand dollars, I would give it to you. You look . . . destroyed.'

'*Five* thousand?'

He nodded. 'Yes. That is what Ian paid me. Five thousand dollars.'

Wait a minute. 'He only paid you *five thousand dollars*?'

He looked puzzled. 'I told you it was a good price. I am sure his sister will get at least that much money for it. More, even. So you see, it all works out well.'

He was smiling broadly, happy to have solved my problem.

'I see what you mean,' I said. 'It's very generous of you to do this.'

I could see him waving in my rearview mirror as I drove off. I stuck my hand out of the window and waved back, trying to think how and where Ian had spent the other forty thousand dollars. Sasha had five, which was gone. I had five, tucked away under my bras and panties back at the hotel.

So where was the rest? Was Ian subsidizing some of the other artists he'd written about, painters who'd made names for themselves at the Wolverhampton auction, buying their work speculatively, more or less, hoping his prescience would make him the incredibly rich owner of a future Picasso? And then there was this business with a painting he thought was an original Vermeer.

Ian, Ian, why did you dig such a deep hole?

And why was I such a fool that I'd fallen right into it, with my eyes wide open?

97

*

I was so worked up about the meeting with Sasha that I missed the turnoff for Kalinina Prospekt. But here I was, flying down Prospekt Marksa, the National Hotel to my left, the dull red Historical Museum at the edge of Red Square to my right.

I turned left on Gorky Street, another main street, but there was no chance of stopping to get my bearings in the middle of all this traffic. If I did, I'd surely be out another twenty bucks when one of my good friends in the GAI appeared with that trusty citation book. So I turned right on the first possible side street and pulled over.

I hate to admit it but I'm one of those hopeless people who has to turn the map upside down and sideways to figure out which way I'm going, so it took a minute or two while I flipped around the CIA map and squinted at the street sign on the side of the building next to me before I understood where I was.

A left at the Ring Road, which I'd intersect in a few blocks, would put me on the road home to the Ukraine, but a right would put me on Karetny Ryad, the street where my mother's friend Nina Revchenka lived. After everything that had just happened at the Tretyakov, I probably didn't need another nail in the coffin of an already catastrophic day.

I turned right.

I'd already read about Karetny Ryad in one of the guidebooks. The name meant 'Coach Row' because it had been the nineteenth-century neighbourhood of carriage- and coachmakers. It still seemed like a place more suited to horses and carriages than Ladas and Zhigulis or my Volvo. Nina's building was grand and shambling, prominently occupying most of the block and asserting its past elegance like an old dowager still convinced of her beauty. I probably had nothing to lose after that session at the Tretyakov, so I took the creaky, carriage-like elevator to the eighth floor and knocked on the door of Flat B. A gimlet-eyed crone wearing a black turban peered through a crack in the doorway and shouted at me that no one named Revchenka lived there. Then she slammed the door in my face so hard I felt like I'd been slapped.

So I left.

If Nina Revchenka were still in Moscow, I'd have to figure

out some other way to find her before I returned to New York. Or maybe I should just write off the day as a total loss. I was going to have to finger Ian, a man I'd loved and adored, as an embezzler and a crook, assuring that his sister and niece would probably end up on welfare. And I might have just come to the end of the faint trail of information that could lead me to any knowledge about my mother's hidden past.

Well, big deal. The part about my hidden mother, I mean. It wasn't going to be good news anyway. What difference did it make now? What really mattered was what was going to happen to Susan and Jade. Jade worshipped Ian. It would destroy her if she thought people believed her uncle was a crook. No child, especially one who already had enough battles to wage, needed a burden like that.

I had to find out what Ian did with the money, why he took it.

When I got back to my room, I found a note from Nigel under my door asking if I would have a nightcap with him later. He was out for the evening, back by eleven. It was getting to be a little habit with him to tap lightly on my door between ten and eleven each night and wave a bottle of vodka or wine under my nose. At first I'd suspected ulterior motives, but it was obvious almost immediately that the Casanova act and the silly tabloid stories about women in Uzbekistan giving birth to multi-headed babies were a façade. What I couldn't figure out was why. He said it was for the money, the tabloid work that is, but I had difficulty buying that completely.

I'd probably be miserable company, the way I felt, but I didn't want to be alone tonight, either. I didn't want to think about how or what I was going to tell Manning about the money.

Not yet, at least.

The phone rang as Nigel knocked on the door. I let him in and strolled over to answer it. I wasn't too worried about whoever it was hanging up before I did. It would ring until I picked it up, however long that took. Manning was right. There were calls at all hours of the day and night. At first the voices, Russian voices, asked for David Manning. When I said he was no longer at this number, the line went dead in the space of a heartbeat. But within a matter of days the voices asked for Clara Brennan. The journalist, Clara Brennan. They had stories to tell, all of them, and if I would just write their stories, some compassionate soul would surely help them get a visa to America, that great shining land where the streets were paved with gold. The first few times I was caught off guard, stammering in my best Russian that I couldn't help, that I had no influence in the matter of visas to the United States. They didn't want to believe me. I stayed on the phone for hours, listening, consoling, murmuring that unfortunately I could do nothing, while they ignored everything I said and continued pleading.

Finally I began cutting the conversations off almost immediately. It was less agonizing to sever the calls quickly with a terse, 'I'm so sorry. I cannot help,' than to prolong the heartache, only to have to say the same thing forty-five minutes later when everyone was emotionally wrung out. Either way I still felt like a heel for turning my back, closing my eyes as I let go of a lifeline.

Nigel poured our drinks silently while he listened to me disentangle myself from another soul-destroying story. 'No, I'm so sorry ... I have no authority in these matters ... no, so sorry ... no, I cannot. No. It's completely impossible ... I'm sorry ...so, so sorry.' Then I hung up, numb with guilt like I always was.

He walked over to where I sat at the desk and handed me a glass of red wine. 'You all right, love?'

'No.'

He stroked my hair. 'You can't save everyone, darling. No one can. And you can't blame yourself for these things, either. It's not your responsibility. It's just the way things are.'

'That's easy for you to say.'

'You think so, do you? You're the only one with a conscience around here? Come to do the right thing while the rest of us sit back and watch, have you? How nice.'

I turned red. 'I'm sorry.'

'You mustn't let it consume you, Claire. It's no good. Besides, what are you going to do? What can you do? Realistically ... nothing.'

I got up and walked over to the window and stared at the thin ribbon of white and red lights as cars criss-crossed the

Kalininsky Bridge below. The clock tower of the Russian Parliament, the large white building across the river, was still illuminated, pristine and elegant against the night sky. I took a big gulp of wine. It was Georgian wine, syrupy and sweet. His favourite.

I guess, after all that had gone wrong during the day, I was spoiling for an argument. Nigel didn't deserve to be my punching bag, but I was mad at the world and here he was. 'So just write the whole country off as a loss. Let it all go straight to hell? Is that what you mean?'

He looked at me sharply over the top of his glasses, then took them off and began polishing them on the sleeve of his threadbare jacket. He let the silence lengthen between us. When he spoke, his voice was mild, as though he were continuing a pleasant tête-à-tête. 'My dear, you've got it all wrong. You're trying to live like a Westerner in a country that is completely Byzantine, completely Eastern. You're applying your own ethics, your own morality, your own values to a system that doesn't embrace any of those things. Look at their religion. A thousand years ago when Prince Vladimir of Kiev decided his pagan subjects should worship God, he chose the Eastern Christianity of Constantinople, not the Western Christianity of Rome.'

He tipped his wine glass and drained it. 'Let me tell you something. In the West, we obey our laws. We pay our taxes when they're due, our parking tickets when we get them, and a handshake means we give our word on a promise we intend to keep. You know what happens here? None of those things. In the Soviet Union everything not expressly permitted is forbidden. Do you know what that means?' He shook a finger under my nose with the orgiastic excitement of a Bible-belt preacher revving up in front of a captive audience. 'I'll tell you what it means. *Everyone* bends the law. They ignore the unreasonable ones entirely. Or else they bribe to get around them. Whatever it takes. It's a national pastime, for God's sake. The whole country lives in a bloody amoral vacuum. It runs on *blat, na lyevo,* scheming, bribing. Everyone's on the take and no one respects you for following the rules. There's no honour in doing it. Instead they think you're a bloody fool, a poor naïve bugger to be taken advantage of.'

'It sounds pretty bleak, Nigel.'

'It does, doesn't it?' He put on his glasses again and blinked like an owl. 'You mustn't let your anger and frustration overwhelm you, my love. Life is different here. The boundaries between reality and imagination aren't so sharply drawn. Things can get blurred and confusing. You don't know what or who to believe. So you'd better keep your wits about you.' He swept his hand around to encompass my faded hotel room and the rest of the city outside the window. The lights on the clock tower blinked off as though he had orchestrated it and a gibbous moon slid eerily from behind a bank of clouds. 'Russia intrigues you, Claire. It's in your blood because you're half-Russian. Don't forget that.'

He grabbed my shoulders and turned me so I faced him. He leaned his face close to mine and shook me. 'Listen to me. You don't realize how this place can possess you, but I can tell you are starting to understand it and it bothers you. I know it because I am part-Russian, too.'

I tried to wriggle out of his grasp, but he was strong and held on. 'Nigel, please, you're hurting me!' Actually, he was scaring me.

He loosened his grip on my shoulders but still pinned me in his arms. 'So many journalists who come here merely watch and record as though they are looking at animals in a zoo. But you must not. You must understand the *dusha*, the soul, of this place. It is worth knowing, Claire.'

He dropped his arms from my shoulders abruptly and walked over to the table to get the wine bottle. He held it out to me and I went to him obediently, like a sleepwalker. He filled my glass and I sat down. 'Is that why you've stayed here so long? To know the soul, the *dusha*, of Russia?'

He moved his glass around on the ring-stained table in slow, small circles. 'Don't be angry with me, love. I am only looking out for you.' He pulled out a chair and sat opposite me.

'Then tell me.'

He drained his glass and slapped it on the table. 'I curse this place and at times it tears me apart. But there is also something utterly . . . gripping. I love it here as much as I hate it. A macabre fascination? A desire to live in a place where life is stripped to its essentials? Sometimes I don't know myself.' He tilted his wine glass theatrically and stared through the red-stained bottom like he was looking through a telescope.

He began spinning it around. 'A kaleidoscope,' he said. 'Hundreds of brightly coloured pieces of glass that make pretty patterns until you shake them and everything changes. Then there's another pattern and another and another, all different, from the same pieces of glass.' He set the wine glass on the table and reached for the nearly empty bottle. 'They do it with mirrors, you know.' He poured a refill for himself and topped off my glass. '"A riddle wrapped in a mystery inside an enigma". You know who said that?'

'Winston Churchill. About Russia.'

'Good girl. By the way, Kisya is back.'

I somehow missed the free association that got us to that part of the conversation. I was still working out the relationship between kaleidoscopes and Winston Churchill. 'One of the *dejournayas*?'

He laughed and slapped his knee at my hilarity. 'No, love. The cat. She went missing for a few weeks, but now she's back. She lives here, you know. On the eleventh floor. She looks like she hasn't had much to eat while she was gone, though. She's looking a bit thin.'

'A cat? Who does she belong to?'

He shrugged. 'Everyone and no one. David used to feed her quite regularly. Don't be surprised to find her at your door. She used to make herself at home here.' He stood up and walked around the room, stretching like he was trying to straighten out the creaks and kinks of age. He stopped in front of my desk and stared down.

He was looking at the photographs of Baron von Müller.

I'd brought them back to the room with me, along with the CIA map, figuring I'd hone my navigational knowledge of the city, to minimize becoming hopelessly lost again.

He turned to me, holding the pictures. 'Where did you get these?'

'I found them with some of Ian's papers. Why? Do you know who he is?'

'It says who he is on the back.'

'I *know* that. Baron Caspar von Müller. But who is he?'

Nigel came over to the dining room table and set the photos in front of me like he was about to let me in on a huge secret. His voice was conspiratorial, practically a whisper. 'He was the only person in the world who really knew what happened to the Amber Room.'

'The Amber Room?'

Nigel's fuzzy eyebrows telegraphed surprise and shock over the top of his glasses. 'My dear, what *planet* have you been on? I wrote about this only last week!'

'I thought you wrote about the alien community that plans to colonize the world and make Novosibirsk their capital.'

He said severely, 'There's a *market* for that sort of thing. There are plenty of good, decent folk who love the stories I write.'

'I wasn't criticizing,' I said. 'Are you going to tell me about the Amber Room or not?'

He picked up the bottle of wine and stared into it. Empty, of course. Our second. He looked up and said brightly, 'Any vodka in the freezer?'

'Nigel . . . '

'Get the vodka, love, while I tell you a bedtime story.'

I made a face at him and walked over to the refrigerator.

'I take it you don't know who von Müller is, then?'

I said, from the depths of the freezer, 'No!'

'All right, then, I'll start at the beginning. Caspar von Müller was a wealthy industrialist who worked directly for Hitler. He was an urbane and cultured man.' I set a shot of vodka in front of him. 'The nectar of the gods! You'll join me? No?' He knocked back the vodka in one swift motion and held out his glass for another.

'All in good time,' I said. 'After I get my bedtime story.' I set the bottle on the floor next to me.

'Bloody hell, you're not my mother.'

'Lucky for both of us. Now talk.'

'I've forgotten . . . '

'You were saying that von Müller worked for Hitler.'

'Yes. I was, indeed. You know, of course, how Hitler plundered the national treasures of the countries he conquered? Art, sculpture, books . . . anything. Looted whatever he wanted and had it brought back to Germany. I'm not sure whose idea it was to take the Amber Room ... do you know its history, my love?'

'Only that it was a room, made completely of amber, in one of the Russian palaces.'

'A firm grasp of the obvious,' he said, disgusted. Then added, 'I'll tell you everything. After I've had another little drinkie.'

I poured his vodka. He still looked perky as anything. He might have been guzzling water.

'The Amber Room,' he continued as he set his empty glass on the table, 'was a room in the Catherine Palace in Tsarskoe Selo, just outside Leningrad. As you said, it was made completely of amber. The walls, the furniture, everything. Supposedly dazzling. The Prussian king Frederick William I gave it to Peter the Great who'd admired the panels when he first saw them on the walls of a palace in Berlin called Mon Bijou.

'When World War II started, the Russians decided to dismantle their precious room and store it safely out of the way of German bombs. But they botched the job and the first panel they tried to remove crumbled in their hands. So they left the Amber Room intact and covered it with cloths and paper. Later the Germans took Tsarskoe Selo, including the Catherine Palace and of course the Amber Room as well, succeeding where the Russians had failed. They removed all the panels from the room and installed them in Königsberg Castle in Germany.'

He grinned evilly and slid the glass toward me.

I ignored it. 'So the Amber Room is in Germany?'

'I'm just getting to the good part, but it's hard to talk when your throat is parched.'

'You're rotten.'

'I'm thirsty.'

So I poured him another shot, which he drank and then continued. 'The Allies bombed Königsberg in August 1944, but apparently the Amber Room survived the fire caused by the bombs. After that, it starts to get confusing. The last document connected with the Amber Room is dated January the twelfth, 1945. The Germans packed up the panels once again, intending to send them to Saxony. No one knows what happened to them then. The Amber Room seems to have disappeared. The Russians looked for it for thirty years. Some people say it was destroyed. Others say it's somewhere here in Russia. Or that it sank on a boat bound for Hamburg and is now at the bottom of the Baltic Sea. There are even those who say ...' he paused to add a bit of melodrama '... that it's somewhere in America.'

'The person in charge of the German operation to safeguard the Amber Room was Caspar von Müller. He died shortly after the war and there are those who believe the secret of the Amber Room's whereabouts died with him.'

'Do you know where it is?' I asked.

'Don't be daft. If I did, I'd have the world at my doorstep. It's one of the great twentieth-century mysteries.'

I shivered. 'I guess Ian was going to write about it, too,' I said. 'That's why he had the pictures.'

Nigel picked up the photograph of von Müller leaning against his desk, and looked at it. 'Mmm. Perhaps.'

'Where do you suppose they were taken?' I asked.

'Germany, I should think. After the war. The date is 1947.'

'But I mean *where* were they taken?'

Nigel looked at me curiously. 'Is it important?'

'No ... just wondering, that's all. The art on the walls looks like the real thing. And it's just that ... Ian was interested in art, too.'

Nigel's eyebrows went up again but he said, 'Yes, he did rather frequent the Pushkin, didn't he?' Then added, 'You seem to be looking for a deeper meaning where the truth is obvious. Any particular reason?'

I blushed. 'You're the one who said something was bothering him before he died. I guess I'm just questioning everything, that's all.'

'Really? And what have you discovered?'

I was never going to get away with lying to him. So I said, 'I found a lot of old bills – Ian was always in debt – and some notes he was making about a book on the Russian front during World War II. Nothing very ... connected.'

If Nigel thought I wasn't coming clean with him, he decided to ignore it. Instead he said, 'Maybe the photos had something to do with his book since von Müller was linked to

106

the war and to the Amber Room.' Then he added shrewdly, 'What's so important about the art on the walls, Claire?'

'Nothing. Just covering all the bases.' My voice was flat. 'You can't even see what the paintings are, anyway.'

'Let me look at those photographs again.' He peered over my shoulder. 'Of course you can. The one more or less behind his head is some bloke standing next to a dog.'

'What? How can you tell? I don't see any dog.'

He pushed his glasses higher on his nose and took the photographs, examining them more closely. 'Well, maybe he's sitting on a horse, then. But it's some chap with an animal. Large as life.'

'Where did you get eyesight like that?' I said. 'I can't make out anything.'

'Drinking,' he said, and held up his shot glass. 'Gives you great vision. Give us another, love.'

I poured the last of the vodka.

Nigel squinted at the photograph. 'And that one's a ... woman, I think. The other ... I can't make it out ... it's too dark.' He knocked back the vodka and looked at me. 'You're looking exhausted all of a sudden, my love. I think it's time for me to leave.'

'That wouldn't have anything to do with the fact that the vodka's all gone, would it?' I said.

He laughed. 'You are charming, my dear, absolutely charming.' Together we walked toward the door. I reached out to open it. 'You know, if you need anything ... anything at all... you only have to ask. I'd do anything for you.' The levity was gone from his voice. He wasn't teasing any more.

I took my hand off the doorknob.

'What is it?' he asked shrewdly.

'Nothing, really.'

He waited.

'It's a bit silly, actually ...'

'I'm sure it's not.'

'All right. It's about what happened earlier tonight. And every night.'

He looked worried. 'Go on.'

I bit my lip and said, 'How is it that my telephone number ... a private number in a hotel in Moscow ... is known by absolute strangers in Alma Ata? And Kishinev? Those places are hundreds of miles away. And you know what else? When I answer the phone, someone just starts speaking. They don't even have to ask who I am. They already know. How do they do it? This city doesn't even have a telephone book.'

Nigel smiled a Mona Lisa smile. 'Everything is known here, Claire. That's how it is. There are no secrets. Officially that information isn't available but unofficially ... anyone who wants to find you, will find you.'

He spoke as casually as if he were talking about the weather or some other innocuous topic of conversation but he was giving me the creeps. 'Well, what if I wanted to find someone?' I kept my voice as light and casual as the better part of a bottle of wine would allow.

His eyes were like lasers. 'Oh, word gets out ... osmosis, telepathy, whatever. They'll know you're looking for them. You just have to wait.' He didn't ask the obvious question but by now I knew he wouldn't.

'Wait for what?' I said.

'Wait and see what happens.'

After he left I leaned against the door and held my breath until his footsteps faded away down the corridor and his door clicked faintly as he closed it. Then nothing, except the empty, aching stillness of the night and my own confused, uneasy thoughts. That man knew too much. Either I'd just spent the evening with my guardian angel or else I'd been with the devil in disguise.

Chapter Eight

I had Sunday duty at the office, so I went directly to work after going to the early-morning Catholic mass at the US Embassy. When I was a kid, Kathleen had marched me to church every Sunday and then, of course, there were the six years of school at St Teresa's. At graduation some of my friends rocketed through the arched doors down the road of libertinism, but not me. Through all the horrible months of Kathleen's illness, I'd leaned into my faith.

Ian never understood that, but what could I expect? He was your basic pagan who absolutely could not comprehend how an educated person like me could believe, as he put it, 'that three-in-one thing, especially the dove'. And don't even get him started on the Immaculate Conception. But to my everlasting gratitude, he was by my side at Kathleen's funeral mass, even though he spent most of the time hyperventilating and looking around when he thought I didn't notice like he was waiting for someone with a tonsure, sandals and a brown robe to throw a net over him and haul him off to a life of serene celibacy. He was pretty negative on celibacy, too.

So this morning, after I'd said my prayers for Kathleen, I said them for Ian too even though I knew he thought lowering your casket into the ground and saying 'rest in peace' was the cue that you were about to become worm food or fertilizer, and that was all she wrote. Of course, by now he knew for sure just what exactly did happen.

The Russian soldier who guarded the entrance to the utilitarian office building that metamorphosed into a church for an hour stopped me and demanded to see my passport, which he then scrutinized. Why did he care? He stonily watched every-one leave too, like he was mentally taking photographs of a subversive group plotting mayhem under the guise of religion.

When I got to the office, Justin was still there, asleep on the tattered sofa in the back room where we kept files and the photocopier, his mouth open, a pillow clutched to his stomach, finishing up overnight duty. I let him sleep, made a pot of coffee, and checked the overnight file and the wires. It was quiet, only one story to write.

I finished it and sent it to New York. The dulcet sounds of Justin's snoring serenaded me. I went into the kitchen to refill my coffee mug. It was just as well that Justin was sleeping. I could go through Ian's files one more time, in private, this time to see if there was anything on Baron Caspar von Müller. He hadn't been part of the equation when I'd trawled through Ian's mountain of papers yesterday. Maybe I'd missed some-thing.

An hour later I was ready to call it quits. Nothing on von Müller and nothing that yielded any more clues as to where Ian spent the rest of the money. I reread the profiles of Sasha and the other new artists who'd sold their work at the Wolverhampton's auction. I could always track the others down and ask if Ian had danced through their studios with a fistful of dollars, collecting paintings bartered at a steep discount, his little *na lyeva* deals. The Pied Piper of the avant-garde Moscow art world, preparing a future nest egg so he could buy some island and retire in style.

Forget it.

Ian would *never* do something like that.

He'd mentioned something about money twice that I knew about. In his note about the phone call he was expected to make or get from Harold Miller, written on the back of the file containing the Zhukov biography and the reminder he'd scribbled on the back of Hugh's wire story. Which was also about Zhukov.

Too bad I'd thrown it out, though I remembered what it said.

'*Call H about getting cash to M.*'

What if 'H' was Hugh? And was it so implausible that Manning could be 'M'? Maybe Manning, Mr Squeaky Clean,

110

had been involved in this all along, just like I'd accused him on that first day in the parking lot at the Ukraine. And Hugh, too, the rat.

Letting Ian take the blame for everything, now that he was dead. How convenient.

Maybe that's why Manning had moved into Ian's apartment, as soon as he was hospitalized. Maybe he knew Ian wasn't going to make it.

I'd seen the spare set of keys to the apartment in the top drawer of his desk. Annabel told me one of the bedrooms was used as storage for overflow files and supplies. Everyone went down there from time to time to get something.

Manning was in Lithuania for the weekend. He'd be back tomorrow.

I walked over to his desk and opened the drawer. There they were, on a key ring with a tag that said 'Kv. 134'. Apartment 134. I was just reaching for it when a quiet voice behind me said, 'Have you been here long?'

I slammed the drawer on my thumb and spun around. 'Damn! What did you do that for?'

'Gee, Claire, I'm sorry,' Justin said, 'I didn't mean to scare you.'

I sucked on my throbbing thumb. 'Mmm.'

'Can I get you anything for that?'

'A new thumb. Next time cough or something. I thought you were still passed out in the other room.'

Not to mention I'd left the keys in the drawer. Well, big deal. I hadn't been doing anything illegal. I needed a file that was probably downstairs. I opened the drawer and calmly took out the key. Then I said, 'I need something in the other apartment.'

'Sure thing. Look ... sorry about crashing back there on the sofa. I think it was only for a few minutes.' He sounded so nervous I felt sorry for him.

'It was two hours,' I said, 'but your secret is safe with me.'

'Oh.'

'There's coffee in the kitchen. Why don't you get yourself a cup and finish up whatever you're supposed to be doing?'

'Okay.' He sounded cheerfully surprised, relieved at getting off the hook so easily. 'I'll refill yours, too.' He sauntered over to my desk then went off to the kitchen, whistling.

'Leave it 'til I get back,' I called.

'Hey, Claire?' He met me on my way out of the door.

'Hey, what?'

'I'm not sure what I'm supposed to do with these.'

'With what?'

He held out a stack of letters to me. 'It's Mr Kendall's mail. It came in on Friday. I don't know who . . . can I give it to you?'

'Of course, Justin. Thanks.'

I took the letters and headed straight for the sofa in the back room. The indentation of where Justin had been sleeping was still there. I kicked off my shoes and sat down.

Then I started to go through Ian's mail.

Bills. More bills. The man got nothing but bills. An offer from a history book club in America. A letter from Susan. I started opening letters. As expected, his credit cards were more or less maxed out. The total balances, as I mentally added them up, were pretty steep. He hadn't exactly been living a life of deprivation, either. He'd been to London again at the beginning of August, his second home after New York. He'd been the bureau chief there ten years ago, before he and I were an item. I think he would have stayed forever if it hadn't been mostly a desk job.

So he went back to visit whenever he could. And spent a bundle.

I shoved the bills back in their envelopes. Who was going to pay back all this money? Not Susan and Jade. And not me, either. I was as broke as he was. In my case, it was college loans. And Kathleen's house, which I desperately wanted to hold on to. We'd drained every penny of equity from it to pay the hospital bills after her stroke. I picked up Susan's letter. The postmark was dated before Ian got sick. She wouldn't have known anything when she wrote this. I slid my finger under the flap of the envelope and opened it.

A picture of Jade fluttered out, her school picture. Dark hair, dark-skinned, enormous velvet brown eyes, a sweet, crooked smile. Obviously the portrait of her father, who'd snowed Susan with a line of bull about being a Spanish nobleman, reduced to living in genteel poverty on his family's thousand-acre hacienda in the remote mountains of Venezuela.

He just happened to be passing through Queens on his way home. What fabulous good fortune that here he should meet the woman who would conquer his heart forever. Yuk. Susan fell for it, of course. At seventeen that kind of romantic mush would melt any girl's heart. The life of a barefoot countess and all that, worshipped by the simple people of the local village. She 'loaned' Jaime all the money from her savings so he could book passage on a ship for their trip to Caracas. Of course Don Juan, as Ian called him, didn't even bother to say 'adíos' the minute he got Susan pregnant, never to be heard from again.

I ran my thumb over Jade's picture. I hadn't seen her for about eight months. Not since before Kathleen's stroke. It was her smile that unhinged me, the Madonna smile on a million Christmas cards and church statues. Pained understanding and forgiveness for an unforgiving world that valued physical perfection and shunned aberrations like hers. Looked away at the sight of a deformed child in a wheelchair. Susan's letter was short and it twisted my heart in a knot. She thanked Ian for the gifts he'd sent from London and scolded him gently for spoiling them. She also thanked him for the money for the new wheelchair and the special swimming lessons. In the water, when you couldn't see, Jade almost seemed like a normal child . . .

I folded the letter and put it back in the envelope. Justin came into the filing room and found me with tears sliding down my face. He looked absolutely panic-stricken. 'Oh, God. Excuse me . . . I'm sorry . . . I didn't mean . . .' He turned and fled.

I sat up and wiped my eyes with my fists. Justin returned a few moments later with a large glass of water. 'Here. Drink this.'

I took the glass and swallowed a mouthful. I choked as it burned my throat. Vodka. I started coughing violently, trying to catch my breath, and Justin was thumping me on the back. 'You all right? You all right?'

I nodded and held out my arm to stop him from whacking me again. More tears streaming down my cheeks but these were from the lethal dose of vodka I'd accidentally inhaled. 'Why . . . didn't you tell me it was vodka?' I was still sputtering. 'You nearly killed me.'

'Gee, Claire, I'm sorry. I thought it would help.'

I leaned back and closed my eyes. After a moment I said, 'Next time, try a shot glass. Vodka's supposed to be served in shot glasses, not an eight-ounce water tumblers.'

'Okay.' He sounded humble.

I opened my eyes. 'I'll live. You can go back to whatever you were doing.'

'It was the letters, wasn't it?' he asked quietly.

'Yes.'

'I shouldn't have given them to you.' He put his arm around my shoulder, like a kid brother comforting an older sister. 'I'm really sorry.'

'Don't be.'

He gave my shoulder a squeeze and got up from the sofa. Some of Ian's mail fell to the floor. He picked it up and handed it to me. 'Sorry about that. I'll be in the other room if you need me. I was in the middle of fixing something to eat. You hungry?'

I guess I didn't hear him because I was looking at one of the letters I must have missed seeing earlier. It had my name on it. My name and Ian's, sent to both of us at his address in Moscow, care of the American Embassy.

'Claire?'

'Yes?'

'I said, do you want anything to eat?'

'No, thanks anyway, Justin.'

He left and I ripped open the envelope.

It was a bank statement from the New York bank where we'd had our joint account when we were living together. A truly disastrous experience. One of us put money in and the other took it out. Of course the one who took money out never bothered to inform the one who put it in. So if you have two people gleefully writing cheques all over Manhattan against the same pitifully small balance, it doesn't take a genius to figure out what happens.

I thought Ian had closed that account ages ago.

Obviously not. I stared at the statement. He'd been a busy boy.

Opening balance was ten dollars and twelve cents. Enough to keep the account open these last few years, even without any activity. The statement probably kept going to our old apartment where Ian had still lived after I moved out. I never knew he hadn't closed it.

Then, boom, all of a sudden on August 22 there's a wire deposit of forty thousand dollars. And three days later, on August 25, a cash withdrawal.

What a surprise. Forty thousand dollars. Final balance: ten dollars and twelve cents.

Of course Ian himself had withdrawn the money. That was the week he'd been in New York with me. And August 25, the day he took the cash, was the day of Kathleen's funeral. Not a date I'm likely to forget. Somehow, in the middle of everything, he'd found a minute to slip away from my side and take a little stroll over to 92nd and Broadway where he did the dirty deed.

I could call the bank in New York and find out where the wire transfer had originated. As for the withdrawal, well, it was cash. They probably didn't give Ian the third degree about 'what are you planning to do with it' and 'don't spend it all at once', though he would have had to give advance warning that he planned to make a serious dent in some teller's cash drawer. Still, this was New York. The second most blasé people in the world, after Californians, live there.

So why did he do it? Go to all the trouble, I mean.

The money missing from the office safe was cash. That would mean Ian had deposited it somewhere, then wire transferred it to New York, only to take it out as cash again?

That sounded ... dumb.

Why leave an audit trail?

Especially when our accountants in New York could find out about this account in a heartbeat, once they started poking around, looking for the money. A little credit check and *voilà*. If Manning had any idea about this, he'd be up one side of me and down the other before you could say 'jack rabbit'.

Wouldn't that be something? He'd be accusing me of taking the money and I'd be accusing him. Of course, he'd have more than a little ammunition to make his accusation stick.

And what about the five thousand I had stashed in my underwear drawer? If I handed it over now, how could I possibly keep my mouth shut about everything else? Sooner or later

I'd end up pointing the guilty finger at myself which, as Manning said, was already twitching in my direction, anyway. How could I expect them all to believe I had nothing to do with this now?

I sat back again on the sofa and closed my eyes.

In retrospect, maybe I should have finished off Justin's tumbler of vodka. My head was throbbing wickedly.

I don't know how long I stayed on that sofa, trying to rationalize what Ian had done and why. He took fifty thousand from the office safe. He spent five as a down payment on a painting and stashed another five in his car. Then he took forty, put it in our account in New York and took it right back out again. Possibly chasing a painting by Jan Vermeer.

It made no sense.

I unkinked myself from the sofa and went into the kitchen to tell Justin I was going downstairs to the other apartment.

Not that I thought Ian might have conveniently left the Vermeer hanging in his living room or shoved it under his bed along with the dust bunnies or that Manning hadn't already had the identical brain wave of looking through Ian's stuff when he moved into the place. But no one knew Ian like I did. Maybe Manning just didn't know where to look.

There was also the other possibility. Maybe Manning still had the painting. Or the money. Maybe he hadn't gotten rid of them yet.

'Sure thing, Claire,' Justin said when I told him I was leaving. He sounded excessively cheerful, probably because my absence gave him the opportunity to indulge in a late-morning snack, like his favourite tunafish and ketchup sandwich or spaghetti with *smetana* and soy sauce.

The hallway was quiet as a tomb, except for the echoing sound of my footfalls on the spiralling marble staircase. I jiggled Manning's doorknob. Locked, of course. I sucked in my breath and inserted the first key in the top lock. Wrong lock. Being from New York you'd think I could open a Fort Knox system of locks and deadbolts blindfolded, but maybe it was nerves. I finally got it right. Then a door slammed, several floors above me, and I nearly jumped out of my skin. It was nerves, all right.

I opened the door and slipped into the apartment. I was expecting it to look like Ian still lived here, the kind of place where you step on dirty underpants at the front door, marking the beginning of a trail of unwashed plates, half-full glasses, discarded clothing, and heaps of unopened mail piled on stacks of yellowed newspapers. And that was when he'd cleaned up a bit.

You could walk through this place with white gloves and never smudge them. It was as antiseptic as a hospital.

Manning had moved in, all right. The place was immaculate.

I found the spillover filing room which had a row of cabinets along one wall, stacked boxes with the logo of a German moving company on another, and a small put-u-up pushed against a third. I opened the top drawer of the first cabinet and smelled the fustiness of old papers. I pulled out the drawers, one by one, but they all held what looked like old files and records, jammed in crazily over the years, probably not in any logical order any more. If Ian had stuffed anything in here, it would take me a year and a day to find it. But if intuition counts for anything, I could swear that what was in these cabinets was exactly what it appeared to be. Old, yellowing, dusty files.

The moving company's boxes were full of junk. Used cassettes, broken tape recorders, discarded, leftover items that probably belonged in the trash.

I took a file from one of the filing cabinets anyway, to justify my little visit, and closed the door to the room.

The next room down the hallway was Manning's bedroom. The door was ajar. I opened it and walked in. I expected something spartan and impersonal to go with the rest of the hospital décor, but I was wrong. This room was someone's. A handmade log cabin patchwork quilt on the bed, primitive gaily coloured scatter rugs on the floor that looked like they came from one of the Soviet republics, plants rioting in the window, a bedside table overflowing with books and a photograph in a large silver frame. It looked like he was in the middle of reading *War and Peace* since it was lying open face down on the edge of the table nearest the bed, but there were also books on Russian history, two books of

117

poetry, and a biography of Lenin. I couldn't help looking at the photograph.

She could have been my twin sister.

I mean it, we were identical. I stared at a darker version of myself, someone who was nearly me.

A sister? His mother?

A girlfriend, left behind somewhere?

And then, just as I set the picture back on his bedside table, I heard the metallic sound of a key turning in one of the locks and the front door squeaking as it opened.

Only one person would have another key to this place.

In something like two milliseconds, Manning was going to find me in his bedroom and, sure as hell, was going to wonder quite justifiably what I was doing there.

He wasn't supposed to be back until tomorrow.

Isn't life just full of little surprises? He was here now.

I expected him to head straight for the bedroom and then it would be all over when he found me, but instead, by some miracle, he went into the kitchen, which was on the other side of the apartment. Weak-kneed, I walked into the hallway and called out: 'Who's there?' I admit, it was a dumb thing to say, but I couldn't think of anything else.

He walked out of the kitchen and leaned against the doorjamb. He looked dead tired. Maybe he forgot to take a razor with him on his trip because he looked like he hadn't shaved the whole time he'd been away. Or maybe he was trying to cover up how hollow-faced he was becoming.

'Want a cup of tea?' He said it laconically, like finding people lurking in his apartment when he got home was something that happened all the time.

'Uh . . . sure.' I couldn't match his nonchalance.

His eyes strayed to the file I'd taken from the cabinet, which I was clutching to my chest like a shield.

'Find what you were looking for?' he asked, in that same lazy drawl.

'Hope so,' I said, and prayed we were talking about the file and not something else. I walked into the kitchen to avoid his probing gaze. 'I'll fix the tea. You look exhausted.'

Manning followed me. 'I decided to come back early,' he said. 'I found a stringer in Vilnius who'll keep on the story for us.'

'Oh. Great.' I filled the kettle with bottled water and almost dropped it when I tried to set it on the stove. 'Where do you keep your tea?'

'Cabinet above your head. So what's been going on while I was away?'

'Nothing, really. It's been quiet.'

'The money's not here, Claire.'

This time I dropped the tin of tea, which thudded dully on the tile floor. Tea bags spilled out.

I bent over to pick them up, stalling for time. Finally I straightened up. 'I wasn't looking for the money.' I sounded huffy as I stuffed tea bags back into the dented canister.

'You weren't looking for Brezhnev's speech to the Twenty-sixth Communist Party Congress in 1981, either.'

I looked down at the file, where I'd left it on the counter.

I turned around and faced him. 'How do you know?'

'I've been through the place. I'm telling you, it's not here.'

'I'll bet you have,' I said bitterly.

'You want to look? Be my guest. See if you can turn up anything. Ian's things are in the boxes in the living room, next to the sofa. The shippers are coming for them next week. Or have you already been through them?'

I slammed the canister on the counter. 'No!'

'You're lying. Are you going to tell me what you're really doing here? What are you looking for?' He sounded more angry than irritated at the invasion of his privacy.

Maybe he *was* hiding something. And nevertheless had managed to turn the tables so I ended up as the guilty party, having illegally broken into his apartment and rifled through his things. Well, okay, he'd caught me. I'd made it dead easy for him. Not that he needed another reason to exact revenge.

He'd had it in for me ever since our public verbal punch up in the newsroom five years ago, right after I started working for IPS. I'd been right, he'd been wrong. I'd made him look like a fool and I'm sure he'd nursed a grudge ever since. I bet he'd dance with glee if he could tie me in with the missing cash. If he ever found out about that bank statement he'd have all the evidence he needed to do it.

He'd hang Ian out to dry without blinking an eye, if it

119

meant he could take me down, too.

'All right, I am looking for the money, same as you are,' I admitted.

'He took it, didn't he?' The kettle whistled and Manning turned off the burner.

'If that's what you think, why don't you tell New York Ian stole it and it's not just unaccounted for?' I asked. 'What are you waiting for, if you've got it all figured out?'

'I don't,' he said. 'All New York knows is that some cash went missing while Ian was bureau chief. Considering his untimely death, there are a few eyebrows raised. So they want to know what's up. What am I supposed to say? It's a hell of an accusation, if I say he stole it, particularly without any tangible proof. Besides, I can't figure out why Ian would do something like that.'

'Me neither.'

'Oh, come on. You must know something or you wouldn't be here.'

That got me. 'Look,' I said. 'Ian stealing the money makes as much sense as you stealing it. You had access to that safe, just like he did. Who's to say you didn't take it?'

'*What*?' He slammed his fist on the kitchen counter. 'Dammit, Claire. What is it with you? *Ian* took the money. We know that. It's not missing or lost in some accounting ledger. It is *gone*. You came down here snooping around because you have some idea what he might have done with it, don't you?' He moved toward me. I backed away from him until the edge of the counter dug into my back.

'Don't be an idiot! Of course I don't know!'

He grabbed my arm. 'You know why, too.'

It was pointless playing games at this point, pretending I didn't know something when I did. 'Let go.' He dropped his hands instantly and I wriggled out from under him, escaping to the other side of the kitchen. 'Okay. I think he might have taken it,' I admitted. 'But I don't know where it is or why he did it, except that he didn't steal it. Most likely he borrowed it because he needed it for something and then got sick before he could replace it.' Then I said, without looking at him, 'I don't think he ever managed to . . . deliver it.'

120

'Nice theory,' he said, sarcastically. 'What if he needed it because someone was blackmailing him? Or he owed somebody the money and had to pay up? What if it's gone for good?'

That came out of nowhere. 'Where did you get such a ridiculous idea?'

'What makes you think it's so ridiculous?' he said. 'Ian died under suspicious circumstances, didn't he? Maybe his death had something to do with the money.'

'Well then, why don't you enlighten me on your theory, since you know so much?'

'I don't have a theory. Just like you.' Manning pulled the rubber band out of his ponytail and ran his hands through his dishevelled hair so it was practically standing straight up. 'Look, I haven't slept in a bed for three days. I'm beat. Why don't we talk about this some other time? I can't even think straight. I'm going to bed.'

Then he stumbled out of the room and a moment later, I heard the sound of his bedroom door closing.

I stood there, numbly, for what seemed like the longest time. Finally I turned and pushed a tea bag into one of the mugs with shaking hands. I gripped the edge of the counter until the shaking stopped. Then I picked up the kettle and poured boiling water into the mug, managing not to slosh anything on the counter.

Underneath that don't-come-near-me exterior was a don't-come-near-me interior hiding a heart of stone. What if Manning knew something about the money, as I'd suggested, and this little scene we'd played out was a giant bluff? God knows he was cold and emotionless enough to be capable of acting that ruthlessly.

How would I ever know? The way things were going he could slap this charge on Ian and make it stick for good. Ian certainly wasn't going to speak up for himself and contradict him.

I began opening cabinets until I found the sugar. Then I opened the refrigerator to get the milk.

Which is how I happened to see the bowl of mushrooms, in a see-through plastic bag, on the shelf below the milk. I'd bet a million bucks these hadn't come from one of the hard currency stores. There was still a lot of dirt on the stems, like maybe he'd picked them himself, possibly in Vilnius.

I closed the refrigerator door, dumped my tea down the sink, and fled his apartment.

Chapter Nine

It occurred to me later that night back in my room at the Ukraine that what I was doing might be dangerous. Blundering around the edges of Ian's life with my bull-in-the-china-shop tactics like a well-intentioned Girl Scout or a Nancy Drew wannabe probably wasn't too smart. But as the days passed in Moscow, my life – as Nigel had predicted, or did he warn me – seemed increasingly surreal and dreamlike. I felt oddly invincible, the way you do in dreams, when you can walk through walls, run faster than bullets, survive underwater by holding your breath for hours. The consequences of my actions no longer seemed the same as they would in New York.

Anyway, my time in Moscow was running out. I'd heard Manning on the phone Monday morning talking to one of the overnight editors in New York about Ian's replacement. They were almost finished interviewing candidates. It was only a matter of days before they announced the new Moscow correspondent and then I'd be on a plane back home.

Manning and I had the rest of our talk about the money in the office one evening after everyone had gone. He talked and I listened. He said he'd been thinking about everything and had decided not to say anything to New York for another week or two.

In case something turned up.

What could I say? That's what I was hoping for, too.

And if I thought he was using the time to cover his tracks, I was surely no less to blame. For one thing, Ian had sewn me right into whatever this was. Running the money through our joint account ... and then there was the matter of the five thousand in my lingerie drawer. I'd cast in my lot with Ian when I'd kept that bit of news from Manning.

Now I didn't want to be found out, either.

Sooner or later, though, the suits in New York would have to be told. Something. I could just imagine the scene around the conference table with everyone discussing 'damage control'. They'd write off the loss and make the problem disappear, but not before hauling Manning over the carpet, and possibly me, too. If Manning gave them his cockamamie theory about Ian being blackmailed by the Russian mafia because he'd gotten in with the wrong crowd, it would really hit the fan.

Under those circumstances, I couldn't imagine Stan, or our big boss Mark Weinstein, making a scene about Ian's death with the Soviet Foreign Ministry. They wouldn't demand an explanation, much less justice for a wrongful death. Already the Russians were becoming increasingly sticky about granting additional visas for new IPS staff and Mark was pretty firm on just how much bribing he would do to get something that should have been a normal part of business, so we weren't exactly the favoured children at the moment. If Mark went to the Russians with information that one of our correspondents had been buddy-buddy with guys who didn't exactly bake cookies for a living, they'd be furious. An IPS correspondent engaged in criminal dealings? A charge like that would sink us.

By that time, everyone – Mark, Stan, Manning, me – would be on the same page.

Make the money disappear. Whatever it took to keep the IPS shield untarnished.

Whether or not the bosses would exact a quiet revenge for Ian's illegal dealings and withhold his pension or the money from his life insurance policy was another matter. If they did, they would put an innocent woman and her sick child out on the street.

Could they be that crass and inhumane?

I guess we'd find out.

And then there was me.

If they found out about the joint account, it was over. At

best, I'd get a reprimand and be put on probation. If they believed I was innocent.

At worst, they'd fire me.

At least, I hoped that was the worst they could do.

As for Manning, he'd probably skate away clean. Who'd believe me if I pointed the finger at him? There was too much evidence stacked against me. Nope. He'd get away with it, damn him.

Unless I could find out what happened to that money while I was here.

There was still one place I hadn't checked. One person who might know something. Hugh.

He'd told me to call him that day we met at the Kremlin. And Victoria, if you could believe the rumours, was really steaming things up with Philip. I guess she'd managed to contain her grief about Ian, all right.

So Hugh wouldn't be spending his nights consoling her.

I called him Monday afternoon, after Manning had sloped off to a press conference. It was just Annabel and me and Larisa in the office.

He answered his own phone with brusque efficiency. 'APDavis.' It sounded like one word.

He startled me. 'Hugh?'

'Yeah?'

'It's Claire Brennan.'

'Hi, Claire.' He sounded weary.

'I was wondering if you were free tomorrow night for dinner.'

'Can't,' he said. 'I'm playing poker.'

I said without thinking, 'Draw or stud?'

'Stud. You play?' He sounded doubtful.

'Don't tell me it's guys only?'

'I didn't say that. But we play for real money.'

'Money? Oh, yeah. That green stuff. I'll bring some.'

He laughed. 'Okay, you're in. My place. Leninsky, 45. Fifth floor, apartment eighteen. Eight o'clock.'

'Uh . . .'

'What's the matter?' he teased. 'Cold feet?'

I hesitated. 'Did Ian . . .?'

'Yes. You're taking his place.'

I should have guessed.

125

I hung up the phone. If Ian played poker with Hugh, then maybe they were close enough friends that Ian had included him in whatever little scheme he had going. Maybe Hugh was 'H' after all. Maybe he knew something.

Tomorrow I'd get there early while it was just the two of us.

Then I'd ask him. One way or another.

The minute I put the phone down Annabel came over to my desk. 'I couldn't help overhearing your conversation.'

Unless you wore earplugs, you could hear everyone draw breath in this shoebox office. I was surprised she didn't say she'd overheard Hugh's end of the conversation, too.

'Are you *serious* about playing poker with those *barracudas*?' she demanded. 'It's not bingo at the *Y*, Claire. If Simon loses any more money, he's gonna be walking around Moscow in his *underwear*.'

I smiled. 'Thanks. I'll remember that. So who else plays beside Hugh and Simon?'

'Nick. And Ian ... did. Then there's a couple of others who show up from time to time. A woman from Canadian Press who can drink *anyone* under the table. If she's there you've really had it. I mean, she takes no prisoners. She's the reason Simon's practically a *pauper*.' She lit up a cigarette and settled herself on the edge of my desk. 'So. Where'd you learn to play poker, anyway?'

'From a man called Fast Eddie Graziano. He used to let me watch him.'

She squinted. 'Graziano ...that wouldn't be the New York Grazianos, would it? You don't mean them, do you?'

'Fast Eddie was a distant cousin. I don't think he got too involved in the family business. He lost both legs in Korea, so he was in a wheelchair, if you're asking whether he went around wasting people in between teaching me the difference between a straight and a flush.'

'*Jeez*, Claire! You learned poker from the *mob*? What were you doing hanging around with *those* guys?' Annabel's eyes were huge. She sucked hard on her cigarette.

'I worked summers during college at his wife's beauty parlour.' The Nail and Lash. A cute, kitschy place on Main Street painted bubblegum pink inside and out, the same colour as Lola Graziano's hair. Lola and Eddie became like an aunt and uncle to me, much to Kathleen's dismay. It was that Old World thing the Irish have about the Italians. 'Fast Eddie and his buddies played in the back room.' The nerve centre of his little bookie's operation. I knew a lot about horses, too, but this wasn't the time to say so.

Annabel ran a hand self-consciously through her frizzy, overbleached curls. 'So, um, does that mean you know how to cut hair, by any chance?'

'Well . . . more or less. I mean, yes.'

She hesitated then said, 'Would you consider . . .?'

'I didn't exactly train under Vidal Sassoon, Annabel.'

'Who cares?' she said happily. 'Getting a haircut in this city means some nebbish asks what size *bowl* to use . . . do you have any idea how *rich* this could make you? This is a highly marketable *skill*. The nearest hairdresser who knows the difference between the sharp end of the scissors and the little holes for your fingers is in *Helsinki*. I think you should *exploit* this, Claire. You could have every foreigner in *town* coming to you for a haircut.'

'Annabel . . .'

'I mean it.'

'The average age of the clients who came to the Nail and Lash was a hundred and two. Blue rinses and concrete hairdos designed to withstand gale-force winds. I don't do anything trendy. I think you've got the wrong idea.'

She stubbed out her cigarette and grinned. 'Well, okay. But you should still think about it. You'll cut mine, won't you?'

I said I would as long as she didn't hold me responsible for the final outcome.

'Yeah, yeah. I know. Hair *grows*.' She ran her hands through her dishevelled puff of fluffy straw again and said airily, 'This'll be great.'

She wandered back to her desk and I knew she had fallen under that mythmaking spell of being transformed by a hairdresser's scissors, that she thought I could turn her into Marilyn Monroe or Madonna. Little did she realize she could just as easily look like Bozo the Clown when I was done.

The phone rang again and Larisa answered it. 'Claire,' she called, 'a man for you. He didn't say who. An American.'

127

I figured it was Hugh, calling back, with some new instructions about the poker game.

'What's up?' I said.

'Hopefully you are, for dinner.'

I'd know that voice in my sleep.

Philip Robinson.

'Dr Robinson . . . I'm sorry, this is Claire Brennan.' Surely he'd got his numbers wrong and thought he was calling CBS? Philip Robinson wanted to take *me* to dinner? No way.

He laughed, like I'd just said something incredibly witty. 'Philip, please. You make me feel like an old man, otherwise.'

'Philip . . .'

'Claire, darling,' he said with easy familiarity, 'I do like to keep up with my former research assistants. I didn't get a chance to talk to you the other night at that dinner. I thought I ought to do something about it.'

Of course you didn't talk to me, you chump. You were too busy slobbering all over Victoria Nobary.

For a horrified millisecond, I thought maybe I'd actually said it out loud.

'So,' he was continuing, 'I'd love to take you somewhere and catch up on what you've been doing these past ten years. I'm proud of you, Claire. Ever since I saw your by-line, I've been following your work. You're a good journalist.'

It was about as unlikely a speech as I ever would have imagined him making to me. The luminary star of Harvard's history department telling *me* he'd read my work? And that it was good? That was like Michelangelo telling a house painter 'nice paint job'.

There was silence at his end, lengthening, and I realized he was waiting for me to say something. 'Thank you,' I said. And that was it.

'Does that mean 'thank you' for the dinner invitation and you'll come?' he asked. He sounded amused.

This man could get any woman in the world to have dinner with him. To cook dinner for him. Why was he trying so hard with me?

'I'd love to,' I said, and found my heart beating like a little rabbit's.

128

'Great,' he said, and sounded like he meant it. 'I'll make reservations some place for this Friday and call you back.'

'Fine,' I said, and listened to him hang up the phone.

After a moment Annabel drawled, 'You're giving off your own *light* just now, Claire. Who called? Gorbachev?'

'Very funny,' I said. 'As a matter of fact, it *was* Gorbachev.' Then I picked up my cup and escaped into the kitchen for a cup of coffee I did not need. I was already wired enough after Philip's phone call.

He called back at the end of the day, with directions to the restaurant.

He hadn't wasted any time.

I'd told myself earlier that I'd be cool ... oh, so cool ... when he called me. Actually, I'd said 'if'. I wasn't sure if he really would go through with this. But he did and I took down his dictated directions to the restaurant with a research assistant's efficiency and said I'd find it, no problem.

Afterwards I told myself I'd accepted his offer because I was hungry for a decent meal, something other than the meagre vegetables and rice or soup I'd been fixing myself each night on my little hotplate, hungry for companionship, hungry for the breathtaking, intellectually stimulating conversation I knew I'd have with Philip. And yeah, sure, I saw the rest of it, too.

Ian was gone, Kathleen was gone. I was probably going to lose my job and I was on the verge of losing my home. Escape. Lovely, obliterating escape. Just one night. I could live on one night with Philip Robinson for a long, long time.

There was one thing, a tiny thing, that jarred about his phone call. A catch, a hesitation so slight that it was almost not worth mentioning. Except it did bother me. It was the precision, no, the calculation perhaps in his voice when he gave me those directions to the restaurant. Silly to think he would actually drive all the way over from the university to the Ukraine to pick me up, like it was some kind of date. Wait in the lobby with the thug-like Mafioso guards who stood by the door while I wafted through the atrium, past the hookers with their makeup and short, tight dresses, and the hotel eccentrics who wheeled and dealed favours, past the defunct fountain surrounded by a stained, beaten up sofa where a shifty-looking crowd of men in cheap suits and wraparound mirrored sunglasses held court at all hours of the night or day. I couldn't expect him to wait there, could I?

Of course not.

So I dismissed Philip's clinical efficiency as part of his professorial nature, the way all university types, especially the real heavyweight academicians, think they're demigods and the rest of us are only there to serve and obey. But when I'd heard the smooth expectation in his voice, I'd wanted, foolishly, there to be something like eagerness, or anticipation, or even . . . delight. Did he have to sound so detached?

Nah. He'd done this too many times before. Take a number, honey. You're on a conveyor belt.

In retrospect, it was the *sang-froid* in his voice that kept me on my guard, kept me from making a fool of myself. Because Annabel told me later that Victoria had confided things were pretty torrid between Philip and her. So what was he doing, taking a Friday night off from the affair of the century, asking a drippy former research assistant to dinner?

Maybe he was just being polite.

Maybe it was like writing a thank-you note for something you didn't want or like. You did it as a courtesy, even if your heart wasn't in it.

Maybe that's all it was.

I was early for the poker game. Hugh met me at the door holding a beer, a cigar clamped between his teeth. He was wearing faded jeans and an expensive-looking shirt made out of fine, soft cotton. It was butter-coloured and there was a designer logo on it.

'Hi, sweetheart.' When some men call you 'sweetheart' it's patronizing. With Hugh, it was tender and he sounded like he meant it. He took the cigar out of his mouth and bent down to give me a kiss. I wasn't sure where he was aiming so I moved and the kiss landed on my eyebrow. He set the cigar on a brass ashtray on a table by the door and helped me off with my coat. 'I like your perfume. The others aren't here yet, you're early. How about a drink?'

'Thanks. I know. Water or juice, please.'

He led me down a long, narrow corridor lined from floor to

ceiling with leather bound books and prints of old maps. I heard him chuckle and then he muttered something about Fast Eddie Graziano, so I knew Annabel had told Simon who had obviously told Hugh that they would be playing with a ringer tonight.

At the end of the corridor was his kitchen. It was as well ordered as the rest of the apartment. I peeked into other rooms en route. Cooking utensils in an earthenware crock by the stove. Copper-bottomed pots, polished even, hanging from hooks nearby. A plant in the window and starched, striped curtains. A stack of magazines in a woven basket on the floor by a table where it looked like he ate his meals. *GQ*, *The Economist*, *Ogonyok* and *Nash Sovremmenik* in Russian, *The New Yorker*, *Playboy*. A masculine apartment. Tidy, almost meticulously so, in the way of someone who'd organized his life so there were few surprises. I notice things like that after living with Ian, a man who'd never met a pot he wanted to wash or a bed he wanted to make.

'Orange juice all right?'

'Great.'

He opened the door to his refrigerator on which there was a nearly life-size poster of a nubile young thing wearing nothing but a G-string. Implants. No woman could possibly look like that without surgery unless they'd changed the laws of gravity recently. The poster had been strategically sliced in two so her body was on the refrigerator door and her head was on the door to the freezer. At the moment, all I could see was her head. Moist lips, pouty smile, let's-have-fun eyes. Then Hugh decapitated her again when he swapped over doors to get me some ice, so I was left fixating on her other ... assets.

He closed the door and grinned. 'That's Natasha. She's my girl. We talk about everything. She understands me.'

'Barefoot and in the kitchen. I always knew you were a down-home guy, Hugh.'

He roared with laughter and stuck his cigar in his mouth and puffed. 'So how good *are* you?'

'I assume you're asking about poker?'

He laughed again. 'Something like that.'

'I haven't played for years.'

He waved a hand. 'Don't give me that.'

131

'Okay, I won't. How good are you?'

'Ah ... I'm all right. It passes the time, you know?'

'Did Ian play regularly?'

'Up until a month or two ago. Then he was on the road all the time.'

I drank some juice. 'Did you know him well?'

Hugh held his cigar between his index and middle fingers and rubbed his chin with his thumb. I watched the ash curl slowly at the end of the cigar. He said slowly, 'Oh, I don't know. As well as you get to know anybody in a place like this, I guess. When there's such an obvious foreigners' enclave the way there is here, the way the Sovs have segregated us, you get thrown together with the same people a lot. Ian and I went out for drinks a number of times. He really liked the bar at the National Hotel. A wonderfully atmospheric dump where every second chick is a honeypot and every second guy has documents revealing some country's nuclear codes sewn into a secret lining inside his fedora ... he missed you like hell, Claire.'

A comment like that still turned me inside out. 'I know.'

He held up his beer glass and stared through the amber-coloured liquid at Natasha's overt voluptuousness.

'Was he in trouble, Hugh?'

He looked from Natasha to me. 'I wondered that myself.'

My heart started thudding like a drum. 'Do you know what it was?'

He shook his head. 'I didn't pry. I figured if he wanted me to know, he'd tell me.' He looked at me shrewdly. 'Suppose you tell me what it was?'

He'd turned the tables nicely, asking questions without having given anything away and I'd set it up for him, like a dolt. He was probably a hell of a poker player. I shrugged. 'I don't know. Right now I'm trying to make sense of his affairs. You know he's got a sister in New York who has a handicapped child with massive medical expenses, don't you? Ian was supporting them. And he, er, left some bills that didn't get paid.' There was no point telling Hugh the figure could be mistaken for the national debt of a small country. 'I'd like to straighten out his finances so Susan knows where she stands.'

His cigar had gone out. He reached for a box of matches

next to the stove and lit it again. He shook out the match and said, 'Ian was always cadging money from people. I think he was into me for something like two hundred bucks ... I don't want it back, of course.' The doorbell rang. He walked by me towards the door and laid a hand gently on my shoulder. 'I didn't know about his sister's kid until you told me just now. Figures, though. If Ian had to borrow a lot of money to help her and it got him in trouble, he never mentioned it to me. I know he was preoccupied these last few weeks ... I didn't know why.' The doorbell sounded again. Someone was growing impatient.

'If you find out and it's something I can help with, let me know.' Then he left the room and I heard him say, 'Hold your horses, I'm coming,' and then the sound of the door opening and more voices.

Somehow I believed him.

He didn't know what Ian was involved in.

He wasn't 'H'.

The poker game was played with ruthless efficiency. Simon, Nick, Hugh, me, and Fiona, the woman from Canadian Press, who showed up in combat fatigues and sported a tiny dragon tattoo just above her right wristbone. She took a cigar from Hugh and looked me up and down with the clear conviction she would wipe the floor with me before the night was over. I lost the first two hands on account of nerves and saw Fiona's smirk. After that I won, fairly steadily, and Fiona looked like she might be capable of murder.

Simon loved it, clearly overjoyed to see her being taken to the cleaners for a change. He kept winking at me which got on my nerves, not to mention getting Fiona so torqued I wanted to check if Hugh's kitchen knives were tucked away safely. It wasn't fun like this. When I used to play with Fast Eddie and his buddies in the back room at the Nail and Lash they were fairly serious about their poker, but at least we had some laughs. The way Fiona played you would have thought the winner got to decide The Future of Civilization As We Know It.

I lost the next hand on purpose and saw Hugh frown into his cards. Then Nick, who had been betting wildly all evening and losing a lot of money, threw down his cards and said, 'I'm out,' in a disgusted voice. He scraped back his chair and headed for the kitchen.

A moment later he came back with a handful of beers, enough for all of us and three for himself. Then he let himself out on to a microscopic balcony where he leaned against the concrete parapet and stared at the dark brooding hulks of the bunker-like apartment blocks that surrounded the dark brooding hulk of Hugh's bunker-like apartment block. I could see the glow of cigarette after cigarette as he chain-smoked and the light glinting off the bottles of beer as he drank, steadily.

'What's with young Nicko tonight?' Fiona asked. It was her deal. 'Bet, Simon,' she commanded, 'if you're playing.'

Simon's card was high. The jack of hearts. 'I'm in,' he said, and threw a chip into the centre of the table. 'I don't know. Maybe he had an argument with his wife.'

Hugh threw in a chip. 'Me, too ... Lady Rebecca's not in Moscow. I think she's taking photographs in Italy.'

I threw in my chip. 'Same. His wife's a photographer?'

'Photojournalist,' Hugh said. 'A good photojournalist. She works for all the top magazines ... I think she's shooting something for *Vanity Fair* at the moment.'

Fiona threw in a chip and dealt another round of cards. 'So what is it, then ... Ian's death still got him all bitter and twisted? I hear he's been drinking a lot. I saw them drag him out of the National twice last week.' I froze. I could feel Hugh's eyes on me, but Fiona was oblivious. She continued her monologue, without looking at any of us, fiddling with her cards. 'I mean, of course, he should be upset. We all are. Makes you think about your own mortality when you get sick in a bloody stinkhole like this ... no one gives a damn if you bleed to death right in front of them. The Sovs are capable of utterly subhuman behaviour. Do you know what I saw last night?'

I didn't feel like guessing. Besides she was going to tell us anyway.

'I saw a Lada plough into a drunk in the middle of Ulitsa Mosfilmskaya. I mean, the guy was weaving down the middle of the street, completely smashed. He went down when the Lada hit him but the jerk who was driving didn't even stop the car. The drunk just crumpled in a heap and then a couple of people hauled him to the side of the road like he was roadkill and left him.' She shook her head. 'What a bunch of heartless bastards.'

'Are we playing poker here or what?' Hugh asked sharply.

I lost that hand, too, but it wasn't intentional.

'Deal me out of the next round,' I said to Simon. 'Hugh, the bathroom?'

'Down the hall where you came in. By the coat rack. Door on the right.' He had a cigar clenched between his teeth, captivated by whatever hand Simon had dealt him. He didn't look up.

My bag was underneath everyone else's backpacks and holdalls, since I'd been the first to arrive. Fiona, the dragon lady, certainly belonged to the ratty-looking satchel with the Harley-Davidson logo on it. Simon had the leather-trimmed Billingham bag. Nick's was the beaten up backpack he'd probably used at Oxford or Cambridge or wherever it was. It was half-open and over full. It was also on top of my things. I picked it up and the thin cord that had been wound around some button to keep things inside gave way. Everything spilled out. I groaned and crouched down. I was on my knees, stuffing things back inside, when I found his diary.

It wasn't that I meant to go through it. But the shape of it, rounded corners, oddly-sized, reminded me of the diary page I'd found with Ian's money.

So I peeked. Who wouldn't?

And, big surprise, July 25th was missing.

I was kneeling there, holding the diary, trying to work it out, when a shadow blocked the light. Nick's voice was thick. He was very drunk. 'What are you doing with that?'

He grabbed the diary out of my hand. 'You always go through other people's things?'

I said evenly, 'Your backpack was on top of my bag. When I picked it up, everything fell out. I'm sorry, Nick. I was trying to put it back.'

I don't know whether he believed me or not because Hugh was on the scene microseconds later. 'Everything all right here?' I had a feeling he'd heard our little exchange.

'No,' Nick said in that same thick voice, and bolted for the

135

bathroom. Hugh went in with him and held his head while he threw up.

I was in the kitchen, drinking a beer with Natasha, when Hugh came in. 'Simon and Fiona are playing black-jack,' he said, 'and the kid's in bed.'

'I ought to go,' I said.

'Sure. I'll walk you to the door.'

Nick's things were still scattered on the floor where we'd left them. Hugh bent over and picked up my bag. 'You all right?' he said.

I smiled a brittle, broken-glass smile. 'Never better.'

'Look, don't worry about Nick,' he said. 'He's been biting everyone's head off lately. As for Fiona, she's always that way.' He bent down and kissed me goodnight on the top of my head. 'Good night, sweet Claire.'

'Good night, Hugh.' I kissed him on the cheek.

The sky was wild and disordered with stars and the night air was cold and sharp. It cut through my raincoat and the thin, summery clothes I wore underneath. I ran to Ian's car.

Then I drove back to the Ukraine.

First thing tomorrow, when that kid was sober, I'd get hold of him and get him to talk. He knew something.

I just needed to catch him in between drinking binges. Hopefully tonight's little show of hostility was just the booze.

Hopefully he'd tell me what I wanted to know.

Hopefully he was still on Ian's side.

Chapter Ten

I called Reuters the next morning but Nick wasn't in so I left a message. When he hadn't returned my call by the middle of the afternoon, I called again.

'He's not in today,' a clipped female British voice said. 'Can someone else help you?'

'No, thanks, I'm really trying to get hold of Nick.'

'Well, in that case, you need to call back in about ten days' time. He's on leave.'

'On leave?'

'Is this urgent?' She pronounced it 'ah-gent'.

'Yes. No. I mean, sort of.'

'Well, then, you could try ringing him in London. Would you like the number of our office there? They can get a message to him.'

'He's in London?'

'I'm not at liberty to give out details, but yes, I do believe he'll at least pass through London,' she said, and now she sounded bothered. 'But he's on holiday until the beginning of November.'

'When did he leave?' I asked. With the hangover he'd probably had, I'd bet someone had to pour him on the airplane. 'Was this trip planned?'

'He left this morning. As to whether it was scheduled, why don't you ask him?' she said firmly. 'I've got another call.' And she hung up.

Great. Just great.

I called back later and got the number for Reuters in London from another voice, fortunately. Then I called

London and left a message for Nick.

He might get it, but I'd bet he wasn't going to call me.

And when he did get back to Moscow, I'd be long gone. I'd be back in New York.

I was edgy and restless over the next few days. I almost called Philip and cancelled our dinner. I was feeling increasingly foolish about it, dreading it even, now that his raging affair with Victoria was the talk of Moscow. I didn't need any patronizing or avuncular favours from him.

Then out of the blue the weather turned warm and the air, for once, was sweet. The two Yuris called it 'grandmother's summer', Moscow's Indian summer, although this year it was unusually late. Two days later the fragile warmth evaporated as though it had never happened and we were back to the cold again. Overnight the trees in the small park in front of the hotel changed from vivid green to clear yellow. I stood at the window of my room, sipping burned-tasting coffee, and watching it rain yellow leaves on the statue of Taras Schevchenko, the Ukrainian national poet. Then two peasant women, shapeless in padded workers' jackets and stooped over besoms, methodically swept them off the sidewalk below in a losing battle to keep the paths clean.

My thin clothes were now hopelessly inadequate against the sharp winds and cold, slanting rain. Two weeks ago we had a freak hot spell in New York. My air conditioning gave out and I packed my suitcase for Moscow in my bra and panties. I hadn't wanted even to look at a sweater and, of course, I counted on being here two weeks maximum. Well, twenty-twenty hindsight and all that.

Soon enough I'd be back there and none of this would matter. In the meantime, I was living the life of a schizophrenic, going through the motions at work like everything was normal, trying to focus on what I was supposed to be doing. But I felt rudderless and uncertain, constantly waiting for the other shoe to drop. And then all of a sudden Manning decided that the official time of mourning for Ian was over and adopted a 'let's move on' policy.

Talk about crass.

I said something about it to Annabel who told me what he'd said. 'David thinks we should, you know, bring this whole Ian

138

thing to *closure*. He says it's the best thing.'

'That's his opinion,' I said.

She shrugged. '*Jeez*, Claire. We all miss Ian. But nothing's gonna bring him *back*.'

After that I swear Manning made a point of assigning me every complex, arcane story that came up on the Tass wire, knowing that most of the time I didn't know the first thing about the subject. I think he enjoyed it too, pushing to see how much I could take before I said 'uncle'.

So I said nothing, never reacted, just did my work. But underneath the surface was a simmering mutual anger. I'm sure everyone else in the office felt it too.

He started spending less and less time there during these cold war days. In fact, some days I didn't see him at all.

'I guess David really *hates* it that Stan made him bureau chief,' Annabel said one day, when we were alone. 'I think he still wants to be a correspondent, not a pencil pusher, if you ask me. He was working on a series of feature stories on Moscow children before Ian died. He told me he wants to finish it. That's why he's gone so much.'

'He's gone so much because he and I loathe each other and you know it,' I said.

'Here.' She tossed me a sheaf of papers. 'Read this.' I did. It was his story about Moscow's orphanages. It was a heart-breaking piece, poignantly written without a trace of mawkish sentimentality. He was as good as Ian had said he was. If I were speaking to him other than when strictly necessary, I might even have told him so.

But instead I was testy and impatient and tired. And hungry.

Oh, yes, hungry.

In fact there were days when I went to bed hungry, too bone-weary to bother with the time-consuming chore of hunting down dinner. A couple of glasses of wine, two aspirin from my shrinking supply, and straight into my lumpy bed at the Ukraine.

It's not like there wasn't food. You could find things if you didn't mind paying outrageous prices for crummy quality. Annabel took me to a *rynok*, one of the indoor farmers' markets near the office, where we paid a usurious sum for some bruised fruit and vegetables. And near the hotel I found a bakery that usually had bread, if I got there early enough in the day. We'd also gone to one of the hard currency grocery stores, reserved only for foreigners, on the other side of town. You paid in dollars or deutschmarks or francs. Anything but roubles, a currency so worthless even the Russians didn't want to use it. When we got to the store, a large shade had been pulled over what was supposed to be the dairy section.

I stared at it, hoping it wasn't what it looked like. 'Why did they do that?'

'Why do you think? No milk, no eggs, no butter, no yogurt, no cheese. *Zilch.*' Annabel shrugged. We bought several bottles of red wine and some packaged soups, paid a fortune and left.

'Does that happen often?' I asked as we put our bags in the back of her car.

'You get used to it.'

Then there was the matter of fixing Ian's car. The tall Yuri informed me one morning that the *ribiata* were 'ready' for me. I didn't ask for details and he didn't give any. The next morning the car was sitting in the parking lot at Kutuzovsky, exactly where I'd left it. I found Yuri, standing next to one of our two blue Volvos, lighting up a cigarette.

'Didn't they fix it?'

There was a bucket of dirty water near the Volvo. The windshield wipers stuck out like a giant wet bug with its antennae extended, the signal that the car had been washed, practically a daily necessity since Moscow was such a dust-bucket.

Yuri blew a puff of smoke. I think I'd hurt his feelings. 'Of course they fixing it,' he said. 'You didn't look? Your *machina* is beautiful. Like new.'

'But I thought you said it would take two or three days?'

'The *ribiata,* they can many do. They can be quickly when they want.'

They were quickly, all right. Especially the bill. Two bottles of Scotch, a bottle of Blue Curaçao, and two cartons of cigarettes, all brand-specific, all top drawer stuff. But Yuri was right. Everything was fixed. The petrol gauge and the odometer worked, although the *ribiata* had reset the odometer

140

to zero like it was a new car instead of the clunker it was. The next day Yuri told me he and his buddies liquidated their winnings, so to speak, practically as soon as I paid up. I would have guessed anyway, especially as none of us had missed Larisa's octave-spanning lecture threatening the consequences to befall the next dimwit who showed up for work still drunk the morning after, expecting to get behind the wheel of a car.

He slunk around the office with his tail between his legs for a few hours, but then I heard his laughter, booming and slightly raucous, while he sat with the other Yuri and some of the other drivers who came to the little waiting room by the front door to smoke and drink tea. He was a real practical joker as well as a shameless flirt and a tease. Once or twice I'd heard him bragging about his sexual prowess with women, which drove Tanya crazy.

'All Russian men is like that. Women is nothing. Wife is nobody,' she told me one afternoon when he left the kitchen as I walked in to pour myself a cup of coffee. She scrubbed hard at imaginary spots on the table. 'Me, I don't need men, every men. They many drink, but they nothing do.' She snapped her forefinger against the side of her neck, the Russian gesture for drunkenness.

But for all his swaggering machismo and boyish pranks, the tall Yuri could also recite poetry, beautifully, from memory, which he did with unselfconscious naturalness and passion. So, on the occasions when he would drive me to the Press Centre or the Kremlin or wherever, he would quote long passages from Pushkin, Akhmatova, Tsvetayeva or Pasternak, leaving me completely humbled that I only remembered fragments of Whitman or Frost or Longfellow, which I recited for him as best I could. I was teaching him part of Longfellow's 'The Midnight Ride of Paul Revere'.

Then there was his music. He owned only one tape. A bootleg copy of Frank Sinatra singing 'Songs for Swingin' Lovers.'

He'd turn it up as loudly as possible and sing to me, in a rumbly off-key baritone, all tender sincerity, one hand usually over his heart instead of on the steering wheel where it belonged. He drove, like every Russian it seemed, like a madman, as quickly and perilously as possible, slaloming through traffic, belting out the lyrics to a song he didn't quite understand, la-lahing when the words were utterly beyond his comprehension or he was intent on overtaking a car which wouldn't give way. His favourite was 'Old Devil Moon' which he sang as 'That Whole Double Moo,' generally while roaring along the Sadovoye Koltso at breakneck speed.

'Yuri,' I would say, with one hand on the dashboard, the other clutching my seat, 'maybe you should slow down.'

Slowing down was obviously for wimps.

The short Yuri didn't drive as fast as the tall Yuri, but he had a nerve-racking habit of looking at me intently when I was talking to him or he was talking to me, which meant he wasn't looking at the road. We had a few really close calls, which didn't do much for my blood pressure, but he was as cool as a cucumber. I don't know how he did it. Personally, I was considering valium.

He confessed to me, once, that he was taking English lessons. I think he must have been trying out on me what he learned in class because every so often he would slip a rather startling *non-sequitur* into the conversation like, 'My grandmother is clean' or 'Your lips are like a bowl full of cherries'. He read, avidly, anything he could get his hands on. He had read all the Russian classics and the complete works of Shakespeare.

'I like Gamlet best of all the plays,' he said, 'it is a true Russian tragedy. At the end, everyone dies, Gamlet, the king, the queen ... everyone. Russians understand this. Gamlet should have been a Russian.'

He liked American authors, but books were almost impossible to get. I gave him the paperback copy of Harper Lee's *To Kill a Mockingbird* which I'd picked up at Kennedy when I realized I'd forgotten to bring something with me to read, and you'd have thought I had given him the crown jewels. The next time he drove me somewhere he plied me with questions about Jim and Scoot and racism in America and said Mr Garper Lee was a fine writer.

From him and the tall Yuri and Tanya, I heard the latest rumours in Moscow, recounted with grave solemnity and assurances that this information was obtained from unimpeachable sources and therefore absolutely reliable. The stories always started the same way. Someone's cousin knew someone who had a friend who'd heard from his brother who'd had it on good authority that a space ship had abducted two people in Tashkent. Or Mikhail Gorbachev had come down with some mysterious illness and was being treated by a faith healer who could bend spoons with his thoughts. Or whatever.

I was starting to think I would miss them all when I left, except Manning of course, which was bizarre because most of the time I couldn't wait to get on a plane headed West. But New York didn't have Annabel's lilting voice singing Gershwin or Cole Porter or even Verdi as she moved through the office, or the pungent aromas of Tanya's cooking and the no-nonsense way she bossed us around, or the laughter and pranks of the Yuris, or even Larisa's schoolmarm efficiency administered with a cool, graceful charm and a lovely sense of irony.

Maybe Nigel was right and the place did get under your skin. New York was great and exciting, but there wouldn't be the adrenalin rush of Moscow, the stabbing, energizing feeling of living on the edge in a city that was either the most lawless place I had ever lived or the most oppressively despotic.

Well, as they say, when the gods want to punish you, they grant you your wish.

I found out on Thursday, the day before my dinner with Philip Robinson. Tanya made *kulebiaka* for lunch and all morning the fragrant smells of cabbage and onions and spices had been drifting through the office. Everyone was there, including Manning in a rare guest appearance. No one missed Tanya's *kulebiaka* if they could help it. We crowded into the kitchen as soon as she called us. While she was serving, Manning leaned over and said in my ear, 'I need to talk to you about something. Afterwards.'

The expression on his face was unfathomable, but I knew. They had found a replacement for Ian. I bit into pastry and dilled rice. 'Sure.'

After that I picked at my *kulebiaka*. Tanya saw me dawdling and jumped all over me. 'You are theen, too theen.

You must eat many! I eat many and look!' She slapped a well-padded thigh. 'You must not be half-past!'

In a few days I'd be back in Manhattan eating hot pastrami on rye with coleslaw, a kosher pickle, and a double cappuccino to go. Or a bagel with cream cheese and lox. Or dim sum. Or anything else my heart desired at a million restaurants and delis. I smiled and obediently dug into my *kulebiaka* and tried not to think about my little tête-à-tête with Manning or how many hours Tanya must have waited in line to buy the simple food on my plate.

After lunch, Annabel left for a press conference. She gave me a knowing look and told the short Yuri she'd meet him at the car as soon as she got her equipment together. The tall Yuri was going to look for petrol. While we were eating he'd told Manning he'd been to two petrol stations that morning and found the hoses coiled on the ground next to the tanks, which meant there was none. It was more serious than it sounded since there were only a few places in Moscow that had the high-octane fuel foreign cars used. The watered-down spit the Russians put in their tanks would destroy the engine of a Volvo or a Mercedes and was the reason Russian cars rocketed along the Sadovoye Koltso with the velocity of a golf cart motoring up a mountainside. 'Maybe a problem, boss,' Yuri told Manning. 'Maybe petrol is *defisitni* for a while.'

'Have we got anything left in the jerry cans?'

'*Nyet.*'

Manning looked exasperated. 'Do what you can. Take them with you and fill up where ever you can find anything. Don't come back until you try every station.'

'You bet, boss. I sound the alarm in every Middlesex village and town.' He grinned at me and winked, before he vanished.

'What's that supposed to mean?' Manning snapped.

I said in a cool voice, 'He thinks he's Paul Revere. Coffee, David?' No answer. 'David?'

'What?'

'I said, would you like some coffee?'

'Oh. Sure. Thanks.' He glanced over at Tanya who was washing dishes. 'Tanya, could Claire and I have a moment here, please? Alone?'

She looked up and wiped her soapy hands on her apron. 'Yes, of course.' She fished a battered pack of cigarettes from under several plastic-wrapped packages of dried pasta. 'I go smoking.' She smiled serenely and left and I suddenly had the feeling that everyone else was already in the picture about what Manning was about to tell me.

While I poured the coffee he said, ''They've made a decision in New York about Ian's replacement.'

I set the pot back on the warming plate. 'When do I leave?'

He stirred his steaming coffee until I thought his spoon would melt. Then he looked up. 'You don't.'

'What do you mean, I don't?'

'You're staying.'

'You mean, staying because they want to keep looking for someone?'

'I mean, you got the job.'

'You can't be serious?' I said. 'I didn't apply for it.'

'Stan and I discussed it last night. I'm completely serious.' He sounded like we were chatting about some news story instead of deciding my future.

Ask me to do something, I'll go to the moon for you. Tell me to do it, I won't walk around the block. 'Well, you can discuss it again. And this time you can tell Stan I said it's no-go. I heard you two on the phone talking about all the people he interviewed for the job. Why didn't he pick one of them? Why didn't he pick someone who actually wanted to come here instead of pressganging me?'

He shifted in his seat, but still looked unfazed. 'We agreed you were the best candidate.'

'We?' I set my coffee cup back in the saucer and pushed it to one side. 'Who's "*we*"?'

He set his spoon on the table and looked at me. 'Stan and me, that's who. And I'm the one who pushed for you to stay. Stan said Mark Weinstein was ready to yank you home but he gave in when I wouldn't back down. I told them what your Russian's really like but you'll get it up to speed in a few months. The real reason, though, is that you have a good feel for the story.' He hesitated then said testily, 'Look, I know you don't like me because of this business with Ian, but that's all over with. They're dealing with it in New York.'

145

My heart constricted when he said that last part. 'What do you mean, "dealing" with it?'

'I told them the money's missing for good and no one knows what happened to it or where it is. I said it's highly unlikely we'll find it. I . . . didn't say anything about Ian taking it.' He looked at me meaningfully. 'Or your involvement.'

'*My* involvement?' This was blackmail. 'So what did Stan say when you told him?'

Manning got up and poured us more coffee. 'Well, he had to tell Mark and Mark went ballistic, of course. My conversation with Stan wasn't much better. It was ugly, to say the least. But the bottom line . . .' He paused and set the coffee pot back on the warmer, probably enjoying making me squirm. 'The bottom line is that I told Stan the smartest thing to do is not to stir up trouble with the Sovs. Let sleeping dogs lie. Write off the loss and move on.'

Sure, why not? Make it all go away. That had been his plan all along.

'What about Ian's pension?' I asked.

'Ian's pension?' He sounded irked that I'd brought it up. 'I got him off embezzlement charges, for God's sake, Claire. How can you be talking about a pension?'

'Susan and Jade will have *nothing*,' I said. 'He was their sole support.'

Manning blew out a long, exasperated breath. 'Look, I did tell them about his sister and her little girl but I have no idea how much ice that will cut with Mark. You forget, he's firing people left, right and centre. Those people have families to support, too.'

'Susan has no one! She has to take care of Jade.' I slammed my fist on the table. 'They can't do this to her!'

'Why don't you call Mark?' he said sharply. 'See if you can do any better.'

He banged his coffee cup on the table. Then he said, 'Congratulations on your promotion,' and stomped out of the kitchen.

He was sitting at his desk, head buried in the *International Herald Tribune*, when I walked back into the office. I went over and stood in front of him. 'I can't live like this,' I said. 'And what promotion?'

He lowered the newspaper. 'Live like what?'

'I've got a suitcase full of summer clothes and I'm living in the cockroach hotel, cooking on a hotplate.'

'New York will get your things here,' he said. 'Whatever you want. Call Stan and give him a list. They'll hire a moving company and someone from IPS will supervise. As for your living situation at the Ukraine, we're getting another apartment in a new building that's been designated for foreigners. You'll live there.'

So I'd actually have a place of my own. 'When?'

'A few months, give or take. And it will probably need to be fixed up. You know, a *remont*. We've been bribing some vixen at UPDK, the organization that takes care of foreigners, to speed things along. But you know Mark and bribes.'

'Mark and bribes? Oh, brother. I could spend another year at the Ukraine, especially if the apartment needs this ... *remont*.'

'Get over it. We all did.' His voice was curt and it was the old hostility again. 'You're getting per diem, you know. For as long as you live there. It stops when you move into the apartment but first, let me tell you, you'll make a bundle. Plus the hardship pay. And the pay raise that comes with this job ... like I said, it's a promotion.' He raised his newspaper. From behind it he said, 'No need to thank me.'

The man could take my breath away. 'I need to clear my head,' I snapped. 'I'm going for a walk.'

I ran into Tanya, red-cheeked and smelling heavily of smoke, climbing up the stairs as I was going down. 'Everything is okay?' she asked.

I patted her arm. 'Just dandy.'

When I got outside, it took about thirty seconds before I regretted flouncing out of the office in that high-handed way because the wind was cold and stinging and it was starting to spit rain. But I walked anyway, toward the river, because I can be incredibly bull-headed when I've a mind to, and I was damned if I was going back to the office too soon.

Well, give Manning credit for that slick move. I should have seen it coming. Putting me right under his thumb, where he could keep an eye on me. Now he wouldn't have to worry about a loose cannon in New York. The money, the manner of

147

Ian's death, all of it ... dispensed with, swept neatly under the rug. Now Manning could make sure, at close range, that I didn't do something stupid and open my mouth, asking a lot of questions he didn't want answered. If he'd taken the money. Which I still didn't know for sure.

But if he *was* guilty, he'd set it up so no one would ask anything any more.

Maybe New York wasn't even going to check into Ian's personal finances. Maybe they were too scared of what they'd find ... considering the circumstances surrounding his death. No point rocking the boat with the Soviet Foreign Ministry, just as Manning advised them. Now they might never find out about the joint account. Ian was off the hook, Manning was off the hook ... I was off the hook.

Five thousand dollars richer, too. How could I give it back now? All I had to do was take my raise and my promotion and keep my mouth shut.

Sign my own private pact with the devil in Ian's blood.

I was no better than Manning, stumbling on the money like maybe he'd done, then rationalizing why I should keep it. Even if I gave it to Susan, it didn't change anything.

How had Manning managed to justify it?

Finder's keepers?

By the time I got back to the office, I was soaking wet and sneezing. Manning was gone but Tanya met me at the door, scolded me like a truant child, and dried me off like a wet dog. Then she force-fed me a cup of scalding tea laced with a shot of vodka.

After that I called Stan when everyone else had gone home for the day.

He told me to get him a list of the clothes and things I wanted them to send from home. He said they'd ship it as soon as possible. In the meantime, if there was anything I needed to tide myself over until my warmer clothes came, I should just toddle off to the Moscow equivalent of Bloomingdales and get myself a little something. The company would cover any reasonable expenses, Manning would okay it.

I thanked him and thought of the pathetic queue of mothers who waited in front of the children's shoe store across the

148

street from the office every single day. The whole city was like that, full of sad, twining queues, until I finally wondered why they didn't all join together, circling Moscow in one enormous ribbon of melancholy men and women, waiting for something they might never get. There was hardly anything in the stores, anyway. 'We have shops so you can remember what you cannot buy,' the tall Yuri said to me once, when we were out driving together, passing yet another queue, this one in front of a store that sold light bulbs. I think he meant it as a joke, but neither of us laughed.

I said nothing to Stan about how shockingly empty the stores in Moscow were and how I had just seen a father and son scrounging in the rat-infested dumpster outside our building, picking through our stinking garbage.

Then we talked about Ian, which was rough. Stan made a couple of barbed comments about him and the money, asking me what I knew. I told him quite truthfully that I had known absolutely nothing before I got to Moscow. Ian and I had talked regularly up until he was hospitalized but he'd never mentioned any problems or worries. I said nothing about what Ian had done or what I'd done to cover it up.

Finally, thank God, I hung up the phone and ended my charade.

Nothing made sense. Ian taking the money, the circumstances surrounding his death, Manning's effort to keep New York out of it.

But it didn't matter any more, anyway. There would be no more questions, no public humiliation for Susan and Jade, no one punished for wrongdoing.

It was over.

Unless . . . Ian died before he finished whatever business he was involved in. Left a few loose ends. Which, frankly, was something I'd wondered about.

In other words, what if the game was still afoot?

If it was, someone, somewhere, would be making their move.

Any time now.

Chapter Eleven

Despite the directions, I got lost on the way to Philip's restaurant on Friday night so I was late. There was no place to park as usual, but I had already fallen into the Western habit of parking on the sidewalk. Everyone at the Press Centre did it. I left the car a block from the restaurant, smack in the middle of the first available patch of sidewalk I saw, and ran.

Hugh told me not to worry about parking tickets. For some reason the GAI seemed to give foreign correspondents a special dispensation so far as parking was concerned. Maybe it was to make up for pulling us over for all those bogus citations they threatened us with, then withdrew if you bribed them. Russians would get their cars towed, but Hugh said we could probably park in front of Lenin's tomb.

Philip was waiting for me inside the main door. I nearly collided with him, breathless from my little sprint.

He caught my elbow. 'You found it.'

'Either that or we're both in the wrong place.' Why did I say that? I had just finished driving here, listening to Elton John on the tape deck moodily crooning in the silky Moscow twilight, telling myself I'd keep cool.

But Philip actually laughed, like I'd said something incredibly witty, and then, thank God, the maître d' appeared and led us to a table in the corner, next to a grand piano. The room was small, but pretty and cheerful, with modern paintings of flowers and soulful-looking women on exotic beaches scattered about on whitewashed walls. It looked distinctly un-Russian.

As though he read my thoughts Philip said, 'It's a cooperative restaurant, the first one to open in Moscow. The menu's not the standard *zakuski* and cardboard *bifstek*, either. I thought you might like it.'

A waiter hovered near the table.

'What do you drink these days?' Philip asked.

'White wine, please.'

'A glass of white wine and a Scotch.'

We discussed the menu. Philip asked whether I preferred dry or sweet wine. He ordered for us both, suggesting the salmon. We would start, of course, with caviare and *blini*, he said, if I liked caviare. Then he ordered a bottle of Chablis, horribly overpriced but the only French wine on the wine list. His Russian was flawless.

After God made Philip, I bet He rested.

Since I'd split up with Ian there hadn't been anyone steady in my life, and since Kathleen's stroke eight months ago and her death, there hadn't been anyone at all. I had forgotten how much I liked being with a man who took charge of things like ordering in restaurants in that caressing, commanding way of those who know what they're doing, who know exactly the right thing to say.

Lucky Victoria.

I asked Philip where he'd learned his Russian while a waiter brought our drinks.

'I needed it for my research,' he said, 'I spend a lot of time here.'

'You speak with almost no accent.'

He smiled the way people do when you compliment them on something they already know and I blushed. He lifted a *blini* off the pile of pancakes on the plate between us and put it on his own plate. 'Shall I fix this for you?' he asked. I nodded but he was already heaping caviare in the middle of the *blini*. He rolled it up with his fork like he did this every day of his life. '*Smetana*?' he asked. 'It's Russian sour cream.'

I could have said, 'I know.' Instead I said, 'Oh, really? Please.'

He cut a piece of the pancake and held it to my mouth. I opened it, like an obedient bird. 'Do you like it?' he asked.

It's hard to talk with food in your mouth and caviare is notorious for sticking between your teeth. So I just smiled

151

with closed lips and nodded and felt like the wet-behind-the-ears kid who used to work for him ten years ago. I took a sip of wine and cleared my throat. 'Delicious.'

'Good.' He looked pleased and I remembered, of all the quirky things, the day he'd taught me how to use a corkscrew, practically the first day I'd started working for him. I'd come into his office with some papers as he was opening a bottle of wine. Within five minutes I was opening the bottle of wine under his directions and then we spent a sweet, tender afternoon drinking and chatting like old friends. Later we walked the crisscrossed paths of Harvard Yard and I'm sure there has never been another autumn day as perfect as that one, when the leaves were as fire-coloured and brilliant and the magical light that danced through them was spun gold. So began our romance.

Unfortunately, it was a one-sided event.

After a week, when I'd seen the parade of long-limbed, doe-eyed beauties who sashayed into the den of ecstasy, otherwise known as his office, I figured he'd had a freak cancellation in his full schedule the afternoon he'd spent with me. It's a wonder he didn't have one of those 'take-a-number' dispensers, like they do at the post office.

That's when I knew he was capable of breaking my heart in a million pieces, so I'd tried to keep my distance as much as I could, which was a chore considering I was working for him. And never, ever tried to speculate whether he might, just maybe, perhaps ... have actually enjoyed that incandescent, sun-spattered autumn afternoon we spent together.

He was watching me now, in between more bites of *blini*, with a scrutiny that made it impossible to eat and nonchalantly return his gaze. On top of all his other attributes, God help me if he was a mind reader, too. I lifted my napkin to my mouth and ran my tongue furtively over my teeth, on the off chance he was fixating on black specks I didn't know about.

'Are you going to tell me about your book?' It came out abruptly but I knew it was a safe subject. He could talk for hours when you got him started on his work.

'My book?' He grinned charmingly and we both laughed, me self-consciously and too loudly, he in complete control. 'You are very lovely,' he said.

152

I know I turned scarlet. He picked up one of my hands and held it. 'You really want to hear about my work?'

'Absolutely.' I slithered my hand out of his and reached for my wineglass, which I picked up with both hands, to eliminate all possibilities.

I'd thought this was to be a no touching, I'm-just-being-polite dinner.

'You know all about Napoleon's Russian campaign, of course,' he said in a matter-of-fact voice, and I panicked. I'd forgotten that Philip always assumed everybody had a PhD. in history.

I have to admit that if I'd thought things out in a clear-headed way, I would have looked over one of the Russian history books in the office, just to avoid a situation like this. I wasn't exactly knowledgeable about Napoleon and all his comings and goings.

'Ah ... as I recall, Napoleon was angry because the Russians wouldn't cooperate with the French blockade of Britain. He thought the Tsar, Alexander II, was trying to undermine him. So he marched on Russia but was so poorly prepared he lost most of his army because of the brutal weather and lack of supplies. Then he went back to France, but with his army so diminished, he barely made it.'

'It was Alexander I,' Philip said mildly. 'You're about fifty years ahead of yourself.' He ordered another Scotch and asked if I wanted another glass of wine. I could feel him start to relax.

'No more wine just now, thanks,' I said. Better to keep my head. I leaned my elbows on the table. 'So tell me.'

He smiled and our eyes met. I could have sworn his were full of promise, except that he was currently unavailable for that sort of thing. Surely he didn't think I was unaware of his affair with Victoria? 'Napoleon was obsessed with the idea of sitting on the throne of the Russian Tsars, of sleeping in their beds, taking over their palaces and making them his own. He had the romantically exotic vision of Moscow as the glittering city where Europe and Asia met. He had vastly more troops than the Russians and the supreme confidence that he could overwhelm them and force Alexander I to surrender.' He was tracing a map of Russia with the tip of his knife on the damask

153

tablecloth, making swift indentations in the cloth. 'Of course he completely underestimated Kutuzov, the one-eyed Russian commander-in-chief, remembering only that he had defeated him in 1805 at Austerlitz. But by this time Napoleon was so corrupted by his own power he thought he was invincible.'

I sat with my chin propped on my hand and forgot about eating. Philip moved his knife across the tablecloth map. 'Kutuzov lured Napoleon deeper into Russia during the autumn of 1812. The first big battle was here.' He stabbed the damask cloth. 'Smolensk. Then Borodino.' He dragged the knife further. 'Then Moscow. The prize.' He made the salt shaker Moscow. 'Kutuzov retreated and let Napoleon chase him. All the way to Moscow, where he was completely stranded, cut off from his supplies. But Napoleon was triumphant. He had reached Moscow. He thought he'd beaten Kutuzov.'

The waiter was not amused by Philip nearly carving up the tablecloth. 'Let me take that for you, sir.' He removed our *blini* plates as a second waiter laid the silverware for the salmon. I thought he hesitated before giving Philip another knife.

'Where was I?'

'Moscow.'

'Kutuzov set fire to the city, as you well know,' he said, 'with Napoleon and his men inside the Kremlin.'

I shuddered. 'How gruesome.'

'But so magnificently Russian ... the ultimate patriotic gesture. Kutuzov wouldn't let Napoleon take Moscow so instead he destroyed what Napoleon wanted more than anything, what he had risked everything to win. Kutuzov made him watch Moscow self-destruct, knowing it would also destroy Napoleon. He had it all planned. The city had been evacuated by Rostopchin, the governor of Moscow, before the French ever set foot in it. Everyone was gone, except the prisoners in the jails ... it was a ghost town.'

The waiter appeared just then to open the Chablis. He poured a small amount in Philip's glass, spilling some on the tablecloth. I saw a muscle twitch in Philip's jaw and remembered his one teeny-weeny flaw: how viciously caustic and impatient he could be when someone screwed up in his presence. I'd been on the receiving end of his rage just once, but it had been unforgettable. I'd fled his office in tears and quit the next day. He'd sent flowers and an abjectly apologetic note, saying he'd torn up my letter of resignation. So I came back. But after that, any time he seemed just a wee bit annoyed, I'd go out of my way to placate him or distract him or whatever it took to derail him and forestall another firestorm.

'What was I saying?' It was still there. The knife-edge of irritation in his voice.

But some spilled wine was a little thing, wasn't it, even if the bottle did cost thirty dollars? The waiter obviously knew he'd committed a blunder. 'You were talking about Moscow being a ghost town,' I said in a rush. The waiter caught my eye and fled.

Even after all these years, there is something vaguely frightening about trying to defuse the dark anger of another person when it's ticking like a bomb without a timing device. But the explosion never happened. Nothing. Zero. Instead Philip said mildly, 'Oh, that's right. Sorry. I got distracted.'

Then he leaned over and clinked his glass against mine. 'To us.'

'To us?' I drank uneasily.

What 'us'?

And what had happened to that legendary temper?

Maybe he'd learned to control it.

He could have changed.

People do.

Our salmon arrived and was served without incident. Philip even joked with the waiter before he began his story once more. 'So ... as I was saying ... three hundred thousand people vanished. Gone. And Napoleon never suspected a thing. Can you imagine what it must have been like to be one of those French soldiers? Walking through dark silent streets until you realized the only inhabitants were a group of half-crazed prisoners, released from the jails for the purpose of burning the city to the ground?' He was at it with his knife again, stabbing the air as he spoke. 'Napoleon's shining city of a hundred gilded domes, that he had seen from the hills the day before, reduced to ashes and rubble. He couldn't believe Kutuzov would do it.'

'What happened after they set the city on fire?' I'd abandoned any pretence of acting like I remembered the details of these events, but I don't think he noticed. He was too caught up in his story. He was mesmerizing, as always. Philip could hold a packed classroom completely in his thrall for hours.

'The French sacked the place,' he said, 'pillaging everything they found, helping themselves to whatever they could find to eat and drink. Their rations had nearly given out and they were cold, their uniforms in rags. It was the middle of September, just a few weeks earlier than it is now, but it was cold and raw. In a few days it would snow.'

Snow. I shivered involuntarily.

'By the time the fire began to spread through the city,' he continued, 'the French soldiers were drunk out of their minds, incapable of any action. Then the winds started and the fire spread to the Kremlin.' He'd finished his glass of wine already so he reached for the bottle in the silver wine bucket next to our table. I'd only taken a few sips of mine, so he splashed some in my glass, then refilled his own. He drank and said, 'When that happened Napoleon knew he had to abandon Moscow. But by then they were trapped in the Kremlin, inside a wall of flames.'

'But they did find a way to leave, didn't they?'

'You know they did.' This time he frowned at me as though I'd forgotten something as elementary as the order of the letters in the alphabet. 'Napoleon didn't die in Moscow. He and his officers escaped through a gate among the rocks in one of the back walls. It brought them out to a narrow, winding street that led out of the city but it, too, was completely engulfed in flames from one end to the other. The Count de Ségur, one of Napoleon's aides, wrote in his journal that it was like passing through the entrance to hell.'

I shuddered, imagining the Kremlin in flames and sooty, wild-eyed prisoners, slightly mad with unexpected freedom, running through dark, empty streets, igniting the beautiful homes and palaces with their blazing torches. What part of the Russian psyche could endure such self-immolation in order to destroy an enemy? Had Kutuzov flinched when he gave the order to burn Moscow to the ground?

'The Russians wanted revenge on the French for what they

did to Moscow,' Philip said as though he'd read my mind. 'Napoleon had horses stabled in Uspensky Cathedral in the Kremlin. He planned to destroy Novodeivichy Convent . . . he was defiling holy places, places sacred to the Russians. He authorized the churches to be stripped of whatever the army could carry away, claiming that as the victors they were entitled to the trophies of war. He wanted to fill the Louvre. . . he wanted these things for France. So his soldiers took everything they could . . . tons of silver, hundreds of pounds of gold from Uspensky Cathedral alone. They took the gilded silver cross, more than thirty feet long, from the bell tower of Ivan the Great, knowing the Russians believed it had mystical powers to protect them as long as it remained in Moscow. Napoleon said he would have the cross for the dome of Les Invalides in Paris. Later, as the French retreated, on the way back to Smolensk, they were forced to dump the cross in Lake Semlevo, along with the art they had looted from the Kremlin. It had become too much to carry and by then all they cared about was survival . . . they were diseased, exhausted . . . there had been incidents of cannibalism. Of the four hundred thousand men who started the Russian campaign with Napoleon, only a few thousand crossed the Niemen River when they finally left Russia five months later . . . Napoleon never recovered from the loss.'

Our waiter showed up to take our dinner plates.

'Would you like dessert?' Philip asked.

'Just coffee, please.'

He ordered two coffees and a brandy for himself.

'Are you here for the whole academic year?' I asked.

'Depends,' he said. 'I may leave sooner than that.'

'Oh. So you're almost done with your research?'

He didn't answer the question. Two men in tuxedos had just walked into the room. 'Listen,' Philip commanded. 'You'll enjoy this.'

The musicians. One held a violin. The other sat at the piano.

They played Mozart.

'How lovely.'

'Better than the usual Moscow after-dinner entertainment, isn't it?'

'I beg your pardon?'

He looked at me curiously. 'Depending on the restaurant and level of raunchiness, it's usually a striptease and maybe simulated sex. It's pretty desperate. I always feel sorry for the girls.' Then he said, 'You haven't been out much, have you?'

'Usually I cook on a hotplate in my hotel room or I eat at work. I've only been here two weeks.'

'When do you leave?'

'I don't. I was told yesterday that I'm staying permanently.'

'Really?' He seemed genuinely surprised. 'So you're taking Ian's place?'

'I'm trying,' I said and my voice wavered. 'No one can take Ian's place.'

He began turning his empty brandy glass around, making neat quarter turns, which seemed to fascinate him. 'I'd heard you two were close,' he said. 'Is it true, then?' He was staring at the brandy glass.

Surely he wasn't jealous? 'Yes.' I looked over at the musicians who had just finished playing. 'Did you know him well?'

'No.' He moved the glass to one side and looked up. I couldn't read his expression. 'Unfortunately. Drinks a few times. We had a shared interest in history. But life here gets so . . .' He shrugged. 'Complicated.'

There was scattered applause. The music had finished. I looked up and clapped, too. The violinist caught my eye. He moved toward our table and I saw Philip grimace.

The musician's smile was pure silver and directed at Philip. 'I play for your beautiful lady,' he said. Philip nodded. I was expecting more Mozart but instead it was 'Lara's Theme' from *Dr Zhivago* played with the quivering passion of a man serenading two people deeply in love. I stared at the tablecloth. I'm sure my cheeks were scarlet.

After he'd finished, we applauded and, mercifully, he slid over to the next table. 'Now that he's finished playing our song, maybe we should go,' Philip said.

I laughed, then, completely mortified, and he signalled to the waiter to bring our bill. Behind us, the violinist launched into a peppy rendition of 'Moscow Nights'. It was the song they played every night on the main news show.

'If we're going to have a song, it should at least be

Russian,' I said. 'I prefer "Moscow Nights".'

'Have it your way.' He grinned. 'Come on. I want to show you something.' Then he looked at my thin cotton dress and my blazer. 'Don't you have something warmer than that?'

'My raincoat ... unfortunately I packed for New York weather when I came here. I didn't expect to be here long. My office is sending the rest of my things, my warm clothes, in the next few weeks.'

'Darling, it will be snowing by then ... you'll freeze.'

The unexpected term of endearment caught me off guard. 'I ... I'll be all right.'

He put his arm around me as we left the restaurant and I could feel, rather than see, that every female pair of eyes in the place was watching us. Ogling him. Envying me.

Philip helped me on with the raincoat and kissed my neck. He smelled of brandy and a lingering trace of cologne, something cool and masculine. 'I've got some sweaters I'll loan you until your things get here. They'll be too big, but at least you'll be warmer.'

'Thanks, but you really don't need to.' My skin burned where he'd kissed me.

'I insist.'

We stepped outside into the chilly night air. I shivered and his arm tightened around my waist.

'Come on,' he said, 'I'm taking you to the outdoor swimming pool.'

'*Where*?'

He laughed. 'You really haven't been around much,' he said.

'Some of us have to work for a living.' I could hardly concentrate on what I was saying. All I could think of was the pressure of his arm around me and how good it felt to be this close to him.

'You need someone to take care of you,' said Philip, brushing a strand of hair off my face, 'so you don't work yourself to death.'

I couldn't believe he was coming on to me like this. Victoria...? Maybe he was into serial affairs these days because he was most definitely making a pass at me.

We walked for a few minutes down dark, empty streets

without speaking. He started to whistle under his breath. 'Moscow Nights'. Then he stopped. 'Look over there.'

I did. Suspended in the black silhouettes of the bare trees was an enormous cloud of grey-white mist. We walked toward it and suddenly we were engulfed in the fog. The city had vaporized behind us. 'What is it?'

'It's the outdoor swimming pool. Haven't you heard about it? It's huge, bigger than a football field. The largest outdoor swimming pool in Europe,' he said. 'The heat from the water that causes this mist . . . at night it makes this part of the city look like something out of a Hallowe'en horror film, don't you think?' He moved his hands slowly so they encircled my neck and said, in a choked Boris Karlov whisper, 'Dark shapes emerging from the shadows . . . returning from the dead to stalk their prey . . . terrifying innocent people. Like you, my darling, the next victim.' He grinned. 'Scared you, didn't I?'

He had. I'd never thought of Philip as the kind of guy to clown around. The way he spoke, in this deserted place, was a bit too realistic. I pulled his hands away from my neck and threaded my fingers through his. 'Yes, you did.'

I spoke sharply and he pulled back to look at me. 'I did, didn't I?' He sounded surprised.

'Forget it.' I tried to look away but he put a finger under my chin and tilted my face so that I had to look directly at him.

'No,' he said, 'I won't. I really scared you . . . you're afraid of water, aren't you?'

'I don't want to talk about it.'

'Honey . . .' He pulled me into his arms. 'Now I remember. That pool party I gave the year you worked for me. You wouldn't swim . . .'

'Do we have to discuss this?' My voice was still sharp, muffled from his shoulder. I'd made a complete fool of myself at that party. All my life I'd been terrified of water. I wouldn't even change into my bathing suit then. I'd been teased mercilessly.

Later that summer I tried to take swimming lessons to avoid future humiliation in case I was ever forced at gunpoint to attend another pool party, but the terror was firmly embedded

160

in my brain. I quit after the doggy paddle and floating on my back.

'It was something about being thrown in the water when you didn't know how to swim, wasn't it?' Philip asked gently. 'No wonder you were terrified, poor darling.'

I nodded and buried my head on his shoulder.

'We can leave here if you want,' he said. 'I don't want to upset you.'

'No,' I said, 'it's okay. Just promise me we're not going swimming?'

He chuckled and stepped back to look at me. 'Okay,' he said. 'No swimming. But I did want to tell you a ghost story. That's why I brought you here.'

I shivered, this time not from the cold but because I'd remembered his story of Napoleon's men entering a ghostly, deserted city, just before it went up in flames. Moscow was still a city of shadows and secrets, a place where reality was made fantastical in the mist or obscured by darkness. 'Oh, a ghost story. Much better.'

He laughed again and his eyes, I swear, danced as he looked into mine. I stopped breathing. He pulled me to him again. And then the handsome prince kisses Cinderella . . .

'Do you know the history of this place?' he asked brightly.

And then the handsome prince gives Cinderella a history lesson.

'No, but I'm about to hear it.'

I felt him shake with laughter. 'It's fascinating, I promise.' He moved back from me and stared down into my eyes. 'Like I said, it's a ghost story. But it's a historical ghost story.'

'You really are trying to scare me.'

He chuckled. 'Maybe a little. But it does have something to do with what I was telling you about at dinner. I could have finished the story at the restaurant, but it's much more atmospheric to tell you here.'

'*Philip*!'

'Okay, okay.' He kissed my forehead. 'No one's going to jump out of the fog, I promise.' His arms tightened around me. 'This place wasn't always a swimming pool. There was a cathedral here, the Church of Christ the Saviour. In 1812, Alexander I decreed that a church should be built to commem-

161

orate Russia's victory over Napoleon. His successor, Nicholas I, took up the idea years later. He chose the architect, a man who was known for building railway stations. So, of course, he designed the cathedral on a big scale. It was huge ... soaring. An enormous basilica with five domes and a giant cupola. The interior was gilded with nearly a thousand pounds of pure gold. It took forty-five years to build. Right ... here.'

His words echoed in the night stillness and I buried myself deeper in his arms. Philip stroked my hair absently. 'Then Stalin, that great humanitarian, a former theology student who destroyed ninety percent of his country's churches, decided he wanted to build a monstrosity called the "Palace of Soviets" in this same place. It would be a "museum of world art" where he could display the treasures the Russians had confiscated from the Axis powers during the war. You see, they had learned well from Napoleon about looting art ... to the victor go the spoils. Stalin believed it was justly deserved compensation for what the Germans did to them.

'So he ordered the Church of Christ the Saviour to be blown up. They dynamited it. Demolished a magnificent church into a pile of rubble.' A siren wailed somewhere in the distance and I jumped. 'It's all right,' Philip murmured, 'it's nothing.' Then he said, 'Stalin's vulgar "Palace of Soviets", was to be six times larger than the Empire State building. There would be a statue of Lenin on top, his hand outstretched, three times bigger than the Statue of Liberty. Just the index finger alone would be twelve feet long and the eyes were to glow with red lights, like some kind of ideological beacon of Communism, trapping people the way animals freeze when they're caught in the headlights of a car.' He stopped and looked down at me.

For a moment I couldn't speak. Then I said, 'It sounds ... ghoulish! How could they *do* something like that? Blow up such a beautiful church?'

He shrugged. 'They never managed to build the museum. The ground became completely waterlogged. No one could explain it. So the building began to sink and it became impossible to build anything on the site. Finally they took the marble and used it to build the Metro when they realized it was a lost cause. Thirty years later Khrushchev decreed that the hole in the ground should be turned into an open-air, year-round swimming pool.'

There were more sirens in the distance. His voice came back to me, remote and detached in the darkness. 'The Russian people, being intensely superstitious and naïve, say it was God Himself who made the ground so unstable. It was His revenge against Stalin for destroying the church.'

'Russians are also intensely religious, Philip. You make them sound primitive and childlike. They're not pagans. Maybe it *was* God taking revenge.'

His voice was cool. 'Oh, come on, Claire. Don't be absurd. You sound like a Russian.'

I pulled away from him. 'Quite possibly because I am Russian.'

He was stunned. 'You're ... Russian? Brennan? Are you *serious*?'

'My mother was born in Moscow.'

'I didn't know that.'

He didn't know anything about me. We'd never spoken of my personal life. 'She died when I was eight.'

'I'm so sorry ... I had no idea.'

'It was a long time ago.'

'Look.' He laid his hands on my shoulders. 'All I meant was that many Russians are simple, dumb peasants. I don't mean the educated ones like your mother. After all, she left the country. But the *narod,* the common people, are totally dependent on the state, unable to think for or take care of themselves. They *are* like children, with little understanding of money or the real value of things.'

I'd forgotten how Philip always had to win.

For some reason, it irked me now. Maybe it was the wine. Maybe it was the cavalier way he wrote off the Russian population as a bunch of no-brains. Either way, I guess I took it personally. So I snapped at him: 'They understand well enough the real value of things. The real economy here is the black market, the shadow economy. Everything else is a joke. Their poverty and dependence aren't their fault ... they have no choice in the matter.'

I'd annoyed him, tripped that hair-trigger switch. He spoke with professorial brusqueness. 'No one said anything about fault, Claire, except you. I stated facts that obviously offended you. I didn't know you were Russian. I apologize for the slight. Accept the facts or don't. It doesn't change them.'

Then he leaned forward and kissed me, so bruisingly, so insistently, shoving his tongue inside my mouth with such brutal force that it ached and I was breathless. After an eternity he stopped and took my face in his hands. 'You get too overwrought over trivialities, darling. Let's not talk about it any more. It doesn't matter.'

'Philip!'

He put his finger over my lips to hush me. 'I want to be with you tonight,' he said, sounding almost business-like. Matter-of-fact. 'Unfortunately we can't go to that cell of mine at the university ... there's no privacy. But we could use your hotel room. I've a meeting in the morning so I'll have to leave early, but that shouldn't be a problem, should it? I can grab a shower before I go.'

I had waited ten years for him to say those words to me. Why had I thought they would sweep me off my feet, make me swoon with ecstasy? It felt like we were discussing an airline reservation.

'I'm sorry,' I whispered. 'I can't tonight.'

Give him credit, he didn't miss a beat. 'Of course. Forgive me if I misunderstood things between us. Why don't I walk you to your car, then?'

A perfect gentleman.

'Yes. Thank you.'

I have no idea what he made of my blunt rejection, but you would have thought we'd just been talking about the weather instead of sex. He took my elbow rather formally and we walked, in complete silence, back to the restaurant where my car sat, like a beached white whale, in the middle of the sidewalk.

He held the door for me as I got in and brushed his lips against my cheek.

'Thanks for dinner,' I said, 'I enjoyed it.'

'Pleasure. I'll call you,' he said, and I knew I'd blown it and he wouldn't.

I was shaking as I backed the car off the sidewalk and on to the road. He didn't wait for me to leave. He left, making for his own car, I suppose, and disappeared into the shadows.

Why had I said no? Why did I do it?

Loyalty to Victoria?

Wasn't it 'every woman for herself'?

I was an idiot. I wanted him. I hadn't rebuffed his advances all evening. He was right about that.

And I'd just told him to get lost.

Was it because I didn't want him to consume me, possess me ... be my obsession? Or because I didn't want to get involved with a man who two-times another woman?

It was neither.

It was that Jekyll-Hyde thing. That character change he could do, from tenderness to ice in a heartbeat. It still scared me.

Even though the explosion hadn't occurred earlier at the restaurant, I still felt the undercurrents. That kind of unpredictable volatility ... I'd be holding my breath again, like I did ten years ago. Although brilliant people – and Philip was brilliant – could be like that.

Ten years ago I had worshipped him. I still thought he was an incredibly sexy man. A night with him would be magic. The earth would move.

I was probably the only woman who'd ever turned him down. I'll bet he'd been floored, though he hadn't shown it.

So now it was finished between us. A man with an ego like his and the bedroom credentials to back it up doesn't take rejection too well from an insipid little nobody.

I drove slowly back to the hotel, while Elton John sang about sweet temptation in a voice that curled around my thoughts, which were all over the place, insubstantial and disquieting, like the mist above Stalin's doomed swimming pool.

Chapter Twelve

As soon as I got back to the hotel, I went straight to bed. For the first time since I'd arrived in Moscow I slept deeply and dreamlessly until the early hours of the morning when I was jarred awake by the unnamed dread that comes, sometimes, when you know something is wrong but can't remember what it is.

So I got out of bed and padded, restlessly, through my dingy hotel suite and drank cup after cup of bad-tasting coffee until I heard the sound of creaking pipes that meant the hot water had been turned on.

What would it be like if I'd said yes to Philip last night, if I were waking up in his arms this morning, instead of alone and bone-weary and bad-tempered?

And sick.

Last night's little jaunt by the haunted swimming pool and that stroll in the rain the other day in thin cotton clothes had finally done me in. My head ached, my throat hurt, and I was sneezing and coughing.

If I didn't get some warm clothes soon, God knows what I'd do when the snow came. Philip had said last night that it could happen any day now and this was only the third week of October. What would this dreary city be like in December or January? Annabel had told me winter could leech into April.

Stan's suggestion that I should pick up a few warm things in one of the Moscow department stores was a nice gesture, but I know he didn't have a clue about life in the city he called 'The Big Cabbage'. This was a man whose idea of foreign travel was an annual Christmas holiday on St Croix and to whom roughing it meant no *New York Times* on the doorstep each morning to go with his cappuccino and croissant. He couldn't possibly fathom the wretchedness of what passed for Moscow's shops and grocery stores or he would have bitten out his tongue. I couldn't explain it to him, either. How can you expect someone to believe a major foreign capital, the other superpower no less, has streets lined with dreary little shops that are nearly devoid of merchandise?

He couldn't even imagine it.

The one time I'd cruised through GUM, after attending a hearing at the Kremlin, the barren, threadbare poverty had shocked me the way blood on a child's face is shocking. I'd left, my throat closing against tears, almost immediately.

How the Russians survived, I did not know. The searing poverty and crushing hardship of their lives was everywhere. Even the irony of their struggle was sickening. Two days ago I'd written a story about the annual harvest. Manning had given it to me to write, saying only, 'Here. You do this one,' but I'd seen something flash in his eyes. I went back to my desk and read what he'd handed me.

This year there would be a bumper harvest; there should have been more than enough food to feed the population of a country that sprawled across two continents. But the reality was a nightmarish prediction of food shortages and ugly threats of starvation. The reason could make you weep. Crops were rotting in the fields because of a chronic lack of people and equipment to get them out of the ground in time.

How could there be even more empty shelves where there was already so little? How on earth did Larisa, Tanya, and the two Yuris cope? They were well paid, by Russian standards. At least that's what the tall Yuri told me one day when he drove me to one of the hard currency food stores on the way back from a press conference. We were listening to Ol' Blue Eyes singing 'You're Getting to be a Habit with Me', or, as Yuri liked to call it, 'You're Going to See a Rabbit with Me'. As always, he had turned the volume up full blast.

'I am rich man, Claire,' he shouted above the music. 'I have many roubles, very many roubles. But there is nothing to buy in our shops. What good is money when you can nothing buy?' He laughed uproariously as usual, but this time I could tell he didn't mean it.

We didn't talk for the rest of the trip.

He was watching me when I came out of the food store with its painted-over windows, a pathetic attempt to hide the fact that it was full of things Russians could not buy. Of course, nobody was fooling anybody about what was inside. He was leaning against the car, chewing on his toothpick. As I shifted my overstuffed shopping bags, I saw the look on his face and faltered.

Instantly he was at my side, brushing aside my embarrassed protests. 'I have forgotten what cheese tastes like,' he said, looking at the contents spilling out of my bags as he took them from me and placed them in the back of the car. 'And we have no eggs in our shops.'

Like a fool, I tried to give him my groceries.

He helped me into the car, a perfect gentleman. In flawless English he said, 'Thank you for offering, Claire. But it is not necessary.'

He closed the car door. But when he got in on his side, before he started the engine, he pulled the Sinatra tape out of the tape deck and slipped it into his jacket pocket. I said nothing when he carried my two shopping bags into the office for me.

The next time I needed groceries I would get them myself. I couldn't face that look in his eyes again.

The phone rang as I was getting out of the shower and I ran for it, leaving a wet footprint trail through my suite. Philip? Maybe he didn't hold a grudge. Maybe he wanted . . .

'*Jeez*, Claire, for a moment I thought it was some *guy* answering,' Annabel said. 'You sound like the living *dead*.'

'Thanks bery much.'

'Honest to *God*, hon, why don't you come over *here* tonight for dinner? I'll fix a little something for us.'

Annabel and I had eaten together a few times, usually when Simon was busy at work or out of town. The first time we'd made plans for dinner she'd admitted she couldn't boil water and that her idea of a three-course dinner was two bags of crisps and a bottle of wine.

'Do you eat like that every night?' I'd asked.

'Doesn't everybody?'

So I generally did the cooking. 'I'll cumb but I'll cook.'

'Okay,' she said breezily. 'Twist my arm.'

'Annabel, I deed some clothes. I'm freezing. I bean it.'

'Well, *hey*.' I could hear her sucking on a cigarette. 'I can loan you a few things. We'll just roll up the sleeves and put cuffs in the trousers. You'll look cute!'

I would look like a child dressing up in her mother's old bag of theatre costumes. 'Tanks. Dat'll be great.'

The phone rang about half an hour later and I lunged for it again. This time it was Victoria.

'Claire.' Her voice was low and musical. I knew who it was immediately. 'I'm sorry I didn't think to offer before this, but Annabel just told me you're about dead with pneumonia. You and I are practically the same size. Why don't you come on over and we'll pick out some clothes for you? The closet and dresser in my extra bedroom are completely stuffed with things. I don't wear half of them. I could probably open a boutique.'

She spoke without a hint of jealousy or apprehension. Maybe she didn't know I'd had dinner with Philip last night. Or else she knew and wasn't worried. Maybe she thought she had a lock around his heart. Little did she know she'd padlocked the wrong body part.

I still didn't understand it myself.

How many women did Philip Robinson need to sleep with at one time?

The third time the phone rang I was on my way out of the door to Victoria's place.

It was a man this time, but not the one I'd hoped for.

Sasha Nazarov.

Over the phone his voice was abrupt and toneless, the way all Russians sound when they don't know you well, lacking warmth or enthusiasm. He shouted, too, in the Russian way, as though he was calling from Siberia rather than the other side of town.

I held the receiver slightly away from my ear. 'I am calling to invite you to my studio,' he said. 'This evening, perhaps, would be fine.'

I couldn't tell if that was a question or a statement so I said, hesitantly, 'I'm sorry, I can't tonight. I'm ... having dinner with one of my colleagues.'

'Ah. You cannot come tonight.'

'No . . . but some other time?'

'Tomorrow, then.'

'Sunday. Yes. What time? And where?'

He gave me directions to the studio, which turned out to be on Arbatskiy Pereulok, a little hook of a street off the Arbat, Moscow's pedestrian artsy outdoor market, the one place in the city where capitalism was mostly above ground and flourishing rampantly. Then he said goodbye and hung up. Once they were done talking, Russians acted like telephones were snakes that were going to bite them.

I got to Victoria's just after noon.

She looked, as always, heartcatchingly lovely. She greeted me serenely and said she had a million things for me to try on. Then she pulled me into one of her bedrooms and I realized she meant it literally, not figuratively. I'll bet she could have outfitted half the women of Moscow.

Most of her clothes were French, with labels that said haute couture and you-don't-want-to-know-the-price. There were a couple of little shops in Paris she just adored, and I'll bet the owners just adored it when she walked in the door, too.

'Clothes are my weakness. I can't resist them.' She smiled and gave one of those casual Gallic shrugs that said 'And I don't care, either'.

With the body of the Venus de Milo, sackcloth would look stunning on her.

I have to say, everything I tried on was, well, gorgeous. I was hoping for a sweater or two and maybe a pair of wool trousers, but she acted like it was her missionary duty to make sure I had clothes for every occasion, imaginable and unimaginable.

'I'm probably not going to go riding,' I said, when she threw a buttery-soft pair of dove-coloured jodhpurs on to the bed. 'I'm only taking a couple of things, anyway. There's no way I'm letting you loan me all this fabulous stuff. It's too beautiful.'

'Don't be ridiculous. You're taking it all. I know it sounds horrible, but I get tired of my clothes so quickly. This room,' she waved her hand at the bulging armoire and the overstuffed dresser, 'is full of all the things I don't wear anymore. I'm

170

probably going to give it away, donate it somewhere. You're doing me a favour, making space in that jammed wardrobe.'

After the fashion show, she said, 'How about a bite to eat?'

The 'bite to eat' was another literal statement. She got out a box of crackers and then opened a bottle of wine. 'A little drink?'

'I might have to work later on so I'll pass,' I lied. I had drunk more alcohol since I'd arrived in Moscow than I had during my entire life, but I had not yet resorted to drinking with lunch.

'Busy at work?' she asked.

'I guess it's always this way.'

'You know,' she said with the subtlety of a ton of bricks, 'that I'm involved with Philip Robinson? It's pretty serious. We haven't talked about making any permanent arrangements yet but he does keep some clothes here.'

I had no idea what to say. Was she warning me off him? Was this the right moment to tell her 'Philip' and 'fidelity' were mutually exclusive terms, even when your girlfriend is Helen-of-Troy beautiful? Or that he'd asked me to share his bed last night?

'That's great,' I said. 'I heard you were seeing him.' I shoved a handful of crackers in my mouth.

'I hope you don't think it's disloyal to Ian,' she said, and I almost choked.

She splashed wine into a glass and handed it to me. 'Drink this.'

I did, but it took a few minutes before my coughing spell subsided. Finally I croaked, 'Victoria, Ian's dead.'

'You don't understand,' she said.

'Understand what?'

She ran a finger around the rim of her wineglass and stared at the floor before looking up at me. 'I've been wanting to tell you this for a while,' she said, and my heart started to pound. 'I began seeing Philip before Ian . . .it's not true what I told you about spending the last night with him. I mean, I did go over that last night. But it was to tell Ian I wanted to end things between us.'

She knocked back her entire glass of wine and reached for the bottle. I covered the top of my glass with my hand. 'No,' I said.

171

Victoria looked miserable. 'We had a huge fight. He guessed there was someone else and when he found out it was Philip ... well, Claire, he really lost it. Told me Philip was trouble, said I'd regret getting involved with him ... he said horrible, hateful things. I've never seen anyone in such a jealous rage. We were screaming at each other. I stormed out of there. That was the last time I talked to Ian. And I screamed at him.'

Of all the adjectives I'd ever heard anyone use to describe Ian, 'jealous' was not one of them. He was too much of a free spirit to be jealous. Hurt, yes. Angry, sure. Resentful, maybe. But not jealous.

'Why are you telling me this?' I asked.

'Because he was still in love with you, that's why. He never said so, but you can sense these things, you know? And now I feel so *guilty* about everything, it's just been torturing me. If only I'd stayed with him that night, maybe I would have been there when he collapsed. He might still be alive ...'

She was crying now, huge gulping sobs. She even looked beautiful when she cried. I went over and held her. 'I don't think it would have changed a thing, Victoria,' I said. 'You couldn't have done anything anyway. He was already very sick.'

'I don't know,' she said in a hiccupy voice from my shoulder. 'Maybe.'

Manning said Ian could have ingested the mushrooms anywhere from two days to three weeks before the symptoms showed up. Victoria wasn't sick, nor were any of Ian's friends. And now, after what she'd just said, it didn't even sound like she and Ian had been spending that much time together.

Either Ian ate the mushrooms by accident or someone deliberately tried to poison him. Even though Victoria had a motive now, it was a pretty feeble one. How likely was it that she decided to bump Ian off so she could take up with Philip Robinson?

Their big split-up argument had occurred days, possibly weeks, after Ian had been poisoned. The timing was wrong.

I left shortly after that, my arms full of the clothes she insisted I take. She was still pretty weepy, brandishing the corkscrew. I think she was going to head straight for the liquor cabinet as soon as I left.

Under the circumstances, I dropped the subject of Ian's death. Nor did it seem like a good moment to mention my date last night with Philip.

So I bit my tongue and said nothing about him being a liar and a cheat because it probably would have provoked a rerun of that last screaming argument she'd had with Ian.

And that hadn't ended so well, had it?

Especially for Ian.

I showed up for dinner at Annabel's wearing a pair of charcoal grey wool slacks and a cream-coloured angora turtleneck.

'*Jeez*, Claire,' she said when I slipped out of a stunning camel cashmere coat, 'You look fabulous. Is this what you borrowed from Victoria? I didn't know you could look so good.' She stopped and clamped her hand over her mouth. 'Excuse me while I chew on a piece of foot.'

'It's okay,' I said. 'You happen to be right.'

We walked into her postage stamp-sized kitchen. 'I didn't get *any* of the things you asked me to get at the *rynok*,' she complained, 'they were out of *everything*.' She held up a bouquet of pale green leaves tied together with purple sewing thread, the fine mesh of roots covered with dirt. 'No basil. So I bought this stuff. *Khinsa*. I think that's coriander. Straight out of the ground, obviously. Can you make anything with it?'

I took the leaves from her and smelled them. 'It is coriander. We'll figure something out.'

She splashed wine into two glasses. 'And I bought walnuts instead of pine nuts.'

'Okay.' I unravelled the thread from the coriander and started to wash it.

'I'll do that. I'm not a total klutz, despite what it looks like.' She leaned over and took the coriander. 'So where did you learn to cook like this?'

'Like what?'

'You know. Making up things when you don't have what you need.'

'My grandmother taught me. People were always dropping by our house when I was growing up and she'd always invite them to stay for something to eat. You learn to improvise when you think you're going to be two for dinner and instead it's seven.'

'So you actually *cooked* for all those people?'

She made it sound like I'd just admitted to boiling them in oil.

'Yep.'

She helped me chop and cut and then she disappeared and I heard her playing the piano while I put everything together for our dinner. It was the first time I'd heard her play. It was Chopin's *Sonata Pathétique* and there was something haunting and melancholy in her rendition that made me put down my knife and lean back against the wall and close my eyes.

We ate by candlelight in her living room, at a small table next to the window.

Annabel told me she'd heard something funny about the autopsy results on Ian. I set down my fork. 'What do you mean? Where did you hear that?'

'*Jeez*, Claire, the New York office is one big sieve. You know *that*.'

'So, what are they saying?' I dug my fork into coriander pesto and stared at my plate.

'I thought you'd know.' Her voice was coolly appraising, very un-Annabel.

There was no graceful way to avoid answering her. 'He died of liver failure,' I said flatly.

'Ian wasn't a boozer, Claire.'

I shrugged. 'I don't know. But that's what I was told. What does the rumour mill say?'

'It's pretty weird. That Ian was a spy and someone bumped him off.'

'That's ludicrous.'

'David said the same thing. He said it was just paranoid New York gossip.'

'Did he?'

'You really don't like him, do you? Come on, Claire, ease up a little. I know he can be a bit touchy. But when you get to know him, he's a real *mensch*.'

'We had a huge fight in New York about five years ago. I know him as well as I'd like to.'

174

'I heard about that fight,' she said, 'who didn't? But you know, he *likes* you. He asked for you to be kept on here. If he thought you were an idiot, he'd never have done it. David doesn't suffer fools gladly.'

'How very flattering. Can we change the subject? How about dessert?'

'Will you stop being so uptight about this?' She lit a cigarette. 'How about another bottle of wine? You need to loosen up a bit. You know,' she added, 'this Cold War you're waging doesn't exactly make the office much fun any more. Not that it was a barrel of *laughs* to begin with. But how about cutting the rest of us a break? Give the man a *chance*.'

The phone rang then and she got up to answer it.

I could hear her voice from the other room, agitated and angry. Simon. She was obviously talking to Simon. I heard the phone being slammed into the receiver and then she returned to the table, tight-lipped, and poured wine hastily into our glasses.

'You all right?'

'Nope.' She drained her glass and refilled it. 'He says he's tied up all weekend, doing God knows what. Something to do with work.' She did not meet my eyes.

I had seen Simon a few days earlier at the Press Centre, flirting with some blonde I didn't know. Annabel was head over heels about him and he had already moved on.

'I have an idea,' I said. Why don't we clean up and then I'll cut your hair? Remember you asked me a few days ago?'

She smiled tiredly. 'Yeah, sure, that'd be great. Something different. Maybe I can knock him dead with the new me.' But I knew she had figured out that maybe it was already too late.

Her haircut turned out to be one of the big successes of my career. I had to cut it quite short to get rid of all the frizz and split ends and the result more or less accidentally turned out to be a lopsided hairdo that was chic and immensely flattering. Annabel loved it.

She hugged me at the door when I left and I knew she was thinking that now she might actually win back Simon's affections, hoped that something as superficial as a new hairstyle would make him see her in a different light, make him want her again.

I walked back to the Ukraine in the raw cold of a starless night and thought of Annabel and Simon. And Philip and Victoria. Two women in love with two men who were cheating on them.

Annabel knew; Victoria didn't.

Ian, I am sure, had always been faithful to me when we were together. There was none of the tortured jealousy between us that destroys a relationship from the inside out. Makes you wonder where he is if the phone doesn't ring. If he really was . . . at the office. With the guys.

What a couple of cads, Simon and Philip.

Annabel was hurt to the bone.

And Victoria? What would happen when she found out?

What would happen when she found out . . . it was me?

I ran up the steps to the front door of the Ukraine. Tomorrow . . . I'd tell her. Or I wouldn't. It wasn't my place. Philip was never going to call me again, anyway.

No, better to say nothing.

I walked through the second set of double doors into the lobby and stopped.

The place was deserted.

Empty. Nobody. Not even the security guards. It was eerie.

My footsteps echoed so loudly as I walked across the marble floor that twice I was sure someone was walking behind me. I looked over my shoulder, but I was alone in the lobby of a hotel with a thousand rooms. Maybe the security guards were making their rounds, maybe they were sleeping somewhere, maybe they were in some bolt hole with a bottle of vodka and didn't care if the Great Unwashed made it through the golden arches tonight and got a taste of Shangri-La.

One of the elevators was waiting, the door open. I stepped in, pressed the button for eleven, and watched the numbers change above the door as the carriage hummed quietly. Silence on the eleventh floor, too. The *dejournaya*'s desk was closed down for the night.

I put the key in the lock of my door and turned it.

The door was already unlocked. My heart started to pound.

Nigel? Perhaps Nigel had come by for the vodka. Maybe Zoya, my cleaning lady.

I pushed the door open and felt for the light switch by the door. I flicked it on and flooded the little anteroom with sallow yellow light. Something moved in the darkness beyond, somewhere in the main room, quiet as a whisper. Before I could cry out a black cat padded toward me, blinking in the dingy light. She stopped and did one of those lazy stretches all cats do when they wake up after a long nap.

I scooped her into my arms and buried my face in her fur. 'Who let you in, sweet thing?' I murmured. Kisya, the cat Nigel had told me about. She purred and rubbed her head against my cheek. My heart slowed to a more normal rhythm.

It had to be either Nigel or Zoya and one of them had forgotten to lock the door. I closed the outside door and walked through the suite, turning on lights as I did. By the time I got to my bedroom, I knew for sure. Nothing seemed to be out of place, but someone had been here and gone through my things. Not Nigel. Not Zoya. Someone else. I ran to the dresser and pulled open the top drawer with hands that shook like I was palsied.

It was still there. The flashlight was still under my lingerie. I unscrewed the top. The money was there, too.

So what was it?

What did I have that anyone would want? What did they *think* I had that they wanted?

After all the wine I'd drunk at Annabel's, I didn't need more alcohol but I went straight to the freezer for the vodka bottle anyway. It was still there, too, untouched since the last nightcap. I poured a shot that would have made Nigel proud and downed it in one gulp. Then I walked over to the desk and opened the drawers.

The one with all my bills and letters was empty. My bills, Ian's mail, the joint bank statement, Susan's letter, my mother's letters from Nina Revchenka, – the theatre programme with her picture from the Bolshoi, and the two pictures of Caspar von Müller were gone. All of them.

I've never been robbed before, not in New York, not anywhere, but it's true what they say. You feel violated, scraped raw. And terribly, terribly vulnerable. After that, you're ready to kill whoever *dared* ... I would never, *never* have anything of my mother's again. What could her letters possibly mean to some two-bit thief? What did any of those papers mean to anybody, besides Ian or me?

Was some good fairy going to pay off his debts?

I would not report this.

How could I?

What, exactly, would I say? Excuse me, someone took my mail. No, no money. The five thousand dollars is still right there in my underwear drawer. No, nothing missing except personal letters and some bills. Sure, that would go over really big. They'd think I was nuts.

What bizarre things to steal. No one except Justin knew I had Ian's mail.

Whoever had been in here was probably looking for the money and didn't think to check the flashlight barrel. Or else they thought they'd find some clue to the whereabouts of the supposed Vermeer.

Meaning I was right. Whatever Ian had been involved in hadn't ended with his death.

Someone was still looking. For something.

And here I was, Ian's ex-girlfriend, come to town.

They knew that, too, or they wouldn't have pawed through my things.

Maybe I needed to start looking over my shoulder from now on.

Or maybe it was someone I saw every day.

Before I went to bed I shoved the two armchairs in the living room over to the little foyer and stacked them on top of each other so they barricaded the door to the hall. Not that I thought I would have another visitor tonight. The room had been well and thoroughly searched by someone who had taken his or her time. It's just that it made me feel better to have some kind of alarm system, just in case.

Then I stripped off my clothes and slid under the bed covers, careful not to disturb Kisya who had come to sleep at the bottom of my bed. I stroked her and she began to purr like a Rolls-Royce engine.

I couldn't sleep at all for what was left of the night. Whether my restless tossings and turnings disturbed Kisya or whether she heard noises of her own, each time she raised her head and pricked her ears, I sat bolt upright in bed.

But it was always nothing.

The loudest noise was the slamming of my heart and my own breathing, hard and shallow, like I'd been running a marathon. Then I'd lie back down and the fear would trickle through my veins again like slow paralysis while I waited for this endless night to fade to daylight.

Chapter Thirteen

I fell asleep after all, dozing off in the safe pale grey hours of the morning. When I woke up, it was just after ten o'clock. Kisya was still at the foot of my bed, blinking at me, slant-eyed and haughty as a sphinx. I leaned over to stroke her.

'Morning, sweet thing.' Her head swivelled around at the sound of my voice, which resembled, frankly, a bullfrog with adenoid problems. Tanya and the Yuris had already told me I needed to take a steamy hot bath, as hot as I could stand, while drinking numerous shots of vodka. It was a great way to get rid of a chest cold, apparently. It wouldn't hurt, either, the tall Yuri said, if I poured half the vodka bottle in my bath water as well. The vapours would clear my sinuses.

A vodka bath seemed a bit extreme first thing in the morning, but a hot shower was a definite necessity. I swung my legs out of bed and headed for the bathroom. Kisya followed me, threading herself between my bare feet.

Nothing. No water. No hot, no cold.

Great, just great.

I pulled on a sweatshirt and a pair of jeans. I walked into the living room preparing to storm the *dejournaya*'s desk and stopped. The armchairs were stacked in front of the door, as I'd left them last night. I moved them back into the living room with the false bravado and general feeling of foolishness that daylight brings after you've been spooked by night terrors. Maybe I should have a cup of coffee first and calm down. Then if there still wasn't any water, I could throw my tantrum. For all the good it would do.

I poured bottled water into the saucepan and set it on the

180

hotplate on top of the desk. Then I poked around the refrigerator until I found a slice of ham for Kisya's breakfast. I filled one chipped bowl with water, another with cut up ham, and set them down next to the desk. The poor little thing was ravenous. Maybe they sold catfood in one of the hard currency stores.

I opened the empty drawer where Ian's bills and my mother's things had been. Why was I so sure that those papers had been taken last night? I hadn't actually opened that drawer since I'd stuck Ian's mail in there and that was a whole week ago. What if my room had been searched earlier? My papers and Ian's things could have been missing for a few days and I wouldn't have realized it.

Why was I sure the intruder had been in my room while I was at Annabel's? Maybe it had been Zoya or the refrigerator repairman. I'd been complaining about the leaking water. I'd told both Lydia and Nadya it was getting worse. Maybe the Ukraine staff had decided to fix it. Or at least look at it. Kisya could have slipped in then.

There was another possibility, ridiculous as it might seem. Maybe the hotel staff had taken my papers. In the West, of course, that would be preposterous. But here there was no privacy. The Ukraine and every other hotel in this city behaved like it was their God-given right to snoop on their guests, invading the most intimate parts of their lives. Microphones in the walls, telephones that were tapped. So why not read the mail, too?

But would they leave such obvious tracks? I thought they were supposed to pretend this spy stuff was clandestine, even though everyone knew they were doing it.

Maybe the papers would reappear, once they'd been scrutinized for evidence of subversive behaviour.

Maybe.

The water boiled and I made my coffee. I carried the mug over to the window and stood in front of it. Another dull day. Sky the same leaden colour as the brackish water of the Moscow River. These past few days it had felt like snow was in the air. Everyone said we were way overdue for the first snowfall.

I finished my coffee and went back to the bathroom. The

gnomes in the basement still hadn't turned on the water. Dammit. It was half past ten.

I marched out to the *dejournaya*'s desk. Kisya slipped out behind me and disappeared into the shadows of the hallway. Lydia was on duty, painting her nails. She was always painting her nails. I asked her about the water and I guess I probably sounded a bit sharp about it. She gave me one of those elaborate Russian shrugs that means everything and nothing and said she was desperately sorry. No, there was no water, all right. No, she didn't have a clue when it would be turned on. No, it wouldn't even be possible to find out. She was really, really sorry. Another theatrical shrug and a look of wide-eyed innocence that was a sure sign of complicity with the chief gnome who controlled the hotel's sluice gates somewhere in the bowels of the building. She held out her hands and blew gently on blood-coloured nails. The signal for 'this conversation is over'.

I marched back to my room, slamming the door so the china in the armoire rattled. Now there wasn't even enough time to shower at Annabel's before I was supposed to meet Sasha. Someone pounded at my door. Probably Lydia telling me I'd broken the Ukraine's sacred no-door-slamming rule. She'd already told me off a couple of times for cooking in my room.

It wasn't Lydia, it was Zoya. I shook my head. '*Nyet*. I don't want my room cleaned now.' That was a dumb move on my part because she'd probably have an attack of amnesia and forget to clean it at all. That's what had happened the last time. Zoya didn't like anybody telling her what to do.

But this wasn't about cleaning my room. 'Come,' she said in Russian. 'You must follow me.'

I stared at her. She and I didn't exactly have what you'd call a cordial relationship, ever since that first morning when she'd made it clear I had to bribe her in return for such basic elements of hotel life as soap or fresh towels or toilet paper. I knew she thought I went through far too many rolls of toilet paper and used up my quota of wafer thin bars of soap much too quickly. Imagine my surprise therefore when I came across her one afternoon, counting supplies in a surprisingly well-stocked linen closet, like a miser with gold bricks. When she realized she'd been caught, she'd looked guilty. Then she'd become defiant and let me know my newfound knowledge didn't change the rules. I still had to bribe her.

And she never, ever thanked me for anything I gave her.

'Come,' she said again, 'you must do as I say.'

I shrugged and followed her out to the lobby and the large defunct bar directly opposite the elevators along the entire length of the back wall. It was an old fashioned affair of polished mahogany and worn, patinaed brass rails. Above it, a dull mirror dimmed and distorted reflections. It was the type of place where assignations were made, secrets were traded, and the bartender already knew what everybody drank. Probably a relic of the hotel's grander days. No one had poured tea or served drinks since I'd been here, and for a lot longer than that, too, by the looks of things. Behind the counter were tarnished shelves of bottles, glasses and silverware. The worn leather barstools stacked on top of each other were thick with dust.

Except that wasn't what Zoya had brought me to see. It was the sink. She turned on the taps. Water. Hot and cold. She smiled triumphantly like she'd just found buried treasure. 'You can wash here.'

I don't know if I was more astonished by her uncharacteristic generosity in sharing this fabulous secret or the realization that, clearly, someone was lying through their teeth with impunity about the availability of water. All I could say was, 'You mean here? In the lobby?'

She shrugged. 'Who comes? Most of the guests are gone for the morning.'

I had not lost so much of my Western sense of propriety that I was willing to strip naked or nearly naked in the lobby of a large hotel and bathe. But at least I could wash my hair.

'Okay,' I said. 'Thanks.' The payoff for this was probably going to involve something major, but so what? I saw her hands when she turned on the taps. They were bright pink and raw, like someone had scraped a layer or two of skin off them. Her face, which I'm ashamed to say I'd never really noticed before, was a mass of fine veins and deep lines. She could have been in her mid-forties except I knew she would be younger, much younger, maybe even my age. Russian women aged so brutally they looked like most of the life had been sucked out of them once they got past their twenties. What was left was dry and withered.

So I washed my hair in the hotel lobby while the elevator door opened and closed and tried to imagine this happening in New York. But already, in the time I'd been here, New York was becoming increasingly remote, replaced by the surreal, debilitating atmosphere of Moscow. I could feel it slowly soaking into my skin and infiltrating my mind. I no longer even noticed the smells which had seemed so repulsive when I'd first arrived. Lately I'd caught myself wondering, as I waited in line at the bakery or stopped by the local *Produkti* where the only food was a few rancid-looking jars of puréed vegetables and some rotting meat, if maybe this situation of appalling shortages and poverty had transmitted itself to New York, too, and no one had told me about it yet. Was there still food in Gristedes? Did Zabar's still have their fabulous epicurean delicatessen? And Bloomingdales? Could you still buy clothes that fit there? Or had they, too, reverted to selling shapeless, one-size-fits-all-large-people garments begrudgingly surrendered by sales clerks who threw your purchase at you, wrapped in a scrap of brown paper rolled up like a sausage?

So I finished washing my hair and went back to my room to dry it with my hair dryer. Then I changed my clothes, quickly, because it was late and Sasha would be waiting.

I must have written down the address he'd given me incorrectly because the once-beautiful Neo-Classical mansion I was standing in front of had obviously been incinerated by a fire, probably a couple of years ago by the looks of things. The windows were boarded up, the façade was soot-black, and officials of Mossoviet, the city hall, would probably be coming any day to condemn the place, if they hadn't done so already. Inside there'd be the treasured possessions of the vagrants who no doubt slept there, and the clutter of used needles, cigarette butts, empty vodka bottles, and various rotting substances.

I was thinking that I should at least find the nearest alley and check out the back of the building when the door, which hung on one hinge, creaked open and Sasha came out. He was in the same paint-stained faded jeans and black sweatshirt he'd been wearing the day we met. 'Beautiful, isn't it?' he said. He wasn't smiling.

I honestly didn't know if he was serious or pulling my leg, so I said, 'It's ... really ... something.'

'Don't tell me you don't have a sense of humour,' he said, 'or did you think you would hurt my feelings?' His voice was lightly mocking.

His defiance reminded me of the tall Yuri, the little litmus tests he loved to try on me, checking to see if I'd be honest and tell the truth about something, or wimp out and say something innocuous and inoffensive. Where I walked the line between pity and honesty.

So I said tartly, 'I thought I had the wrong address. You didn't tell me about the *remont*.'

He roared with laughter and said, 'Good. Come on. I'll take you to my studio. You don't mind a little creosote, I hope. Be careful not to touch the walls or you'll get it all over you. And try not to breathe until we get upstairs.'

Oh, brother.

The building was as derelict on the inside as it was on the outside, at least on the main floor. The stairs were marble, though they were chipped and stained and worn. There was the familiar stench of urine. 'Don't touch the railing,' he said. 'It's completely rotten.'

He reached for my hand and I gave it to him. 'Some stairs are uneven,' he murmured. 'You wouldn't know.'

When we got to the second floor, he led me down a long hallway. Most of the doors were padlocked but one was open and I could tell by the canvases lining the paint-spattered floor inside that it was an artist's studio. The heavy chemical smells of turpentine and varnish hung in the air. Sasha gestured to the open door. 'Valery Yekimov,' he said. 'His work is really popular right now. He is probably going to emigrate to the West soon, if he can. He wants to go to Paris.'

'You know, for a building full of artists,' I said, 'I'd have thought you might have done a bit of redecorating around here.'

'No way,' he said. 'It's too dangerous.'

Then we walked into his studio. It was small and cramped but he was lucky enough to have a window, so the room was floodlit with dull daylight, even though the view was of the cracked and flaking salmon-coloured wall of the building next door. There were canvases stacked along two walls for the length of the room and in the middle was his easel and a rickety paint-stained table with a piece of old wood that he obviously used as a palette. Next to it were jars and tin cans full of brushes of different thicknesses and sizes as well as several trowels, like small gardening tools. Then there were his colours, squeezed out like used-up toothpaste tubes. He painted in oils.

Modern art, as I've said, really isn't my thing and I wasn't sure what I was going to say when I saw some of his work, especially since he'd already shown he could spot insincerity a mile away. But as it turned out, I didn't have to fake any reaction.

Sasha's work took my breath away. 'These are wonderful,' I said.

'Thank you.' He sounded pleased.

No squiggles or single lines or boxes on empty canvases. His paintings exploded with colour and energy, reminding me a little of the later shimmering works of Gustav Klimt. In a city where life existed in such a monochrome palette, he favoured colours that were sundrenched and passionate. I walked around to the front of his easel to see his current project. The canvas was completely blank, although it looked like he'd painted it with white paint.

'Do you like it?' he asked. 'I think it's my best work ever.'

I looked up at him and saw the flicker of amusement again in those exotic ice blue eyes. I said neutrally, 'You've outdone yourself,' and he laughed.

'Actually,' he said, 'I'm preparing the canvas for painting. You know, of course, that you cannot paint directly on a new canvas.'

'What will you paint?'

'That is a long story.' He walked around to my side of the easel and stood in front of me. His eyes had changed from pale ice to cobalt.

I didn't have a good feeling about this. 'Tell me.'

186

'I don't have Ian's painting any more.'

'You mean, you sold it to someone else?'

He smiled ruefully. 'I didn't sell it. I gave it away.'

'You *gave* it away?'

He pulled over a paint-spattered wooden stool. 'Sit down,' he said. 'I will make us some tea. Then I'll tell you a story.' He walked over to an ancient electric kettle that was on the floor. He knelt down and poured water into it from a plastic bottle. Then he plugged the kettle into the wall.

The tea wasn't real tea; it was yellowish in colour and tasted like stewed grass. He had no sugar or honey. I drank it black. Rather, yellow.

Sasha leaned against the rickety table, crossed his legs, and sipped his tea. For someone whose profession wasn't very physically demanding, he had the powerful, graceful build of an athlete nonetheless. Just now he reminded me of a panther or a jaguar caged in a zoo. He had the same alert restlessness, like he was waiting for someone or for something to happen. He kept glancing at the door.

'Are you expecting someone else?' I asked.

'I hope not.' He looked startled. 'Do you remember what you said earlier? You asked why a group of artists wouldn't paint their own studios or even this building?'

'Yes.'

'Do you know what the best and the worst things are that have happened to me in the last year?'

'No.'

'The best thing that happened to me is selling a painting at the Wolverhampton's auction. It is also the worst thing that happened to me.'

'Really?' When was he going to stop speaking in parables? What happened to Ian's painting?

'I'll tell you a joke,' he said.

When I'd first met him, I'd immediately taken him for the same kind of hustler as so many other Russians I'd encountered, motivated by a lifetime of privation, playing all the angles, whatever it took to make a crummy substandard life marginally less crummy. Of course, when I first met him, I thought he was trying to steal my car.

He was poor, all right, like everyone else here was poor.

You could tell by the clothes, the worry lines around his mouth that seemed carved in stone, and the silver hair at his temples, years before it should have been there. Whatever weed we were drinking that was supposed to resemble tea. But Sasha seemed to bear his poverty lightly, almost dismissively. It hadn't ground him down to bitterness and lack of compassion, the way it had so many people in this city, at least when you dealt with them in shops and on the street.

His art was too passionate, too sensuous, too . . . exuberant, I guess. Somehow, he'd figured out how to circumvent a system hell-bent on draining the joy out of life.

He was looking at me steadily and I happened to meet his eyes. He must have read all my silly thoughts as though I'd transmitted them directly to him because there was one of those unmistakable lightning connections of searing intimacy that pass between two people and irrevocably change the chemistry of a relationship.

I said, self-consciously, 'Okay, tell me a joke.'

He acted as though he didn't notice my embarrassment. 'Do you know the story about the Frenchman, the American, and the Russian who were asked what their dearest wish would be?'

'Er . . . no.'

'The Frenchman wanted to spend the night with the most beautiful woman in the world. The American wanted to be the richest man in the world. And the Russian . . . his wish was to see his wealthy neighbour's house burn to the ground.'

'That isn't very funny,' I said.

'No, it isn't. But it's true. What the Russian wished for, that is. Russians despise wealth in others. Anyone who has any money or any appearance of wealth in my country is hated. If we seem more fortunate than others we should be punished.'

'We?'

'Yes,' he said. 'We. I. Me. My mother.'

'I don't understand.'

'I know,' he said. 'You wouldn't.'

He stood up and began pacing the room with that catlike prowling restlessness again. He was counting the steps from one wall to the other, I could tell. Something a prisoner would do in a cell.

'Will you explain it to me?' I asked.

He stopped pacing and stood in front of me. 'Do you know much Russian history?'

'Some.'

'Then you should know that what I've told you is nothing new. Russian society has always been ... extreme. We have the very wealthy and then the peasants, who have nothing. We do not really have what you Americans call a 'middle class', only about fifteen percent of our population, compared with sixty or seventy percent in the West. In my country, eighty percent of the people are hopelessly poor. So poor that anyone who has more, who has a little something his neighbour does not, is thought to have gained it unfairly. It is insulting to the others.'

'That's ... crazy.'

'Try living here,' he said. 'I mean, *really* living here. Not inside the cocoon of your Western cars and shops and your special hard currency hotels and restaurants. Then tell me it's crazy.'

He said it simply, without a trace of resentment or reproach, but it made me cringe, anyway. I squirmed every time Tanya or Larisa or the Yuris made some offhand remark that slammed into my brain the reality of the punishing harshness and struggles they went home to every night. The guilt was starting to eat at me. 'I didn't make those rules,' I protested. 'I hate them.'

'You don't mean that you would like to live here as a Russian,' he said. 'Like I do. And despite your elite status, the riches of a king to the average Russian, Westerners still consider their life here to be a hardship.' He added quietly, 'Don't you?'

I made myself look him straight in the eye. 'Yes.'

He walked over to one of the canvases stacked on the floor and picked it up. It was a surrealistic painting of what looked like a little Orthodox chapel, in the middle of a birch forest.

'Our religion glorifies poverty,' he said, staring at the painting. 'Our fairy tales portray the poor as heroes while the rich are cruel and stupid. For centuries the wealthy have ruled the poor with a ruthlessness that is savagely inhumane. Do not forget, we did not abolish serfdom until 1861.' He put the painting back where he'd found it. 'And as for Communism . . .' He practically spat the word. It was the first time I'd seen him angry. 'It glorifies the worst ideals of the past. First Stalin obliterated the super-rich class and burned into our brains the idea that getting rich was morally unacceptable. While all the while our new class of leaders, the *nomen-klatura*, the Communist bureaucracy, was busy spinning itself a web of privileges and favour.'

He drained his teacup and stared into it.

Finally I said, 'Is the reason you're telling me all this because someone destroyed the painting Ian bought?'

'No,' he said, 'not that.'

'Then . . . what?'

He sighed wearily. 'My fame, my supposed wealth, has been a nightmare. Suddenly I am the enemy. There are people who want to destroy my work, my home, my life. I think they would even go so far as to physically harm me. Or. . .' he swallowed '. . . my mother.' He paused then said, 'I do not dare possess anything that shows I have any kind of material wealth. Of course my name has been in the newspapers, in the media. Everybody knows about the auction. It's no secret what I was paid. And so . . . I need protection. Not that I asked for it, you understand.'

'You mean, the KGB?' As in the guys in trenchcoats and black fedoras turning into the white-hatted good guys? Taking care of him?

He shook his head. 'No.'

'Then . . . who?' He waited to see if a light dawned. It did. '*Mafia* protection?'

He said, with quiet sarcasm, 'Is there another kind?'

So that's why he'd been watching the door. I hadn't actually thought about it until just now, but he had never turned his back to it during our entire conversation. And his easel. Placed in such a way that he could see clearly if anybody . . . dropped by. 'Who is it? How do they . . . protect you?'

'He is called the "Gypsy",' Sasha said, and the way he spoke made me, glance uneasily at the door, too. 'I have no idea what his real name is. Not that it matters. He arrives in a large black car with mirrored windows. No licence plates. His

190

own private bodyguards. We call them "the goon squad". Then he tells you that you must make a "donation" in return for protection. He came to my studio after I called you. He chose Ian's painting as my donation. This time.'

'The police ...?' As soon as I said it, I realized it was dumb.

'The police! I would have to bribe them, too, so they would protect me from my protectors!' There was no mirth in his laugh. He waved his arm at the collection of paintings. 'Do you think this studio is officially registered? That I am painting here with permission? And the police ... they are as corrupt as the rest. They hate us as much as the others. How can a painting they believe looks like a child's mistakes be worth more money than they'll earn during a whole lifetime?' He laughed again. 'Why should they help?'

Sasha walked over to the window and leaned on the sill, with his back to me, like he was memorizing the tracery of the cracks in the paint on the salmon-coloured wall of the building across from us.

'What will you do?' I said finally.

He turned around. 'I wanted to emigrate,' he said, 'with my mother. Most of the money I've earned has already gone for bribes. I'm trying to keep what is left, but my mother's health is not good. I have to pay the doctors, bribe to get good medicine. It never ends. The friend who was helping me get to America is ... no longer able to do so.' A muscle twitched in his jaw and he looked down at the floor.

'Ian.'

'Yes.'

It wasn't as though he'd asked. And this time, it was no stranger calling my hotel room in the middle of the night. 'I only just arrived here,' I said, stammering. 'I don't know what I can do.'

'I am not asking you for anything,' he said. 'Ian offered as a friend.' It was a statement, not an indictment. Not a shred of disappointment or self-pity in it. 'Ian was a good man,' he continued. 'That is why I want to paint again the painting he liked so much. It was of a woman, standing on a beach. He said he liked how wild and free it was. He said the woman reminded him of someone he knew.'

191

Then he paused and said, 'The moment I saw you, I knew it was you.'

'Me?'

'Yes,' he said. 'If you will stay for a while, I would like to sketch you.'

'But the other painting . . . you did it from your head.'

He nodded. 'Yes, I did. But now I have the model in front of me.'

There was something he wasn't telling me.

'So . . . if I were to pose for you, would this be standing or seated?'

'The woman is nude,' he said matter-of-factly, 'she's on the beach. You would be standing. I promise I would not let you get too tired.'

'Oh.'

'It's professional, Claire,' he said gently. 'I use models all the time. Most of them are friends. I couldn't afford to pay anyone for many years. I could ask someone else, if you'd rather not. But there is a . . . light . . . about you that I want to capture. I really need you to pose. Please say yes?'

'Look.' I ran my hands through my hair. 'How about giving me a little time to think about this? I don't know . . . I mean, I've never . . . it's pretty cold in here . . .'

He grinned. 'I have a heater. Or we could work at my flat, if you'd rather.'

He saw the wariness in my eyes. 'Although the room is much smaller and the light is not as good as here,' he said blandly. 'You would meet my mother. She would probably feed you and talk to you the whole time. She does that with all my models. She is quite distracting. It always takes longer.' He said it affectionately. I don't think he minded either the distraction or the delay in his work.

I smiled. 'I'll think about it.' I gestured to the stacks of paintings around the room. 'Do you have some of the . . . er . . . other models among these paintings?'

'Of course. Why don't you look? I'm going to Valery's studio for a minute. He has something I need.'

Later I wondered if things would have been different if he'd been in the room with me when I found the painting.

I don't know.

If his current style was anything to judge by, I'd say this was from an earlier period, accidentally mixed in with some of his more recent works. This painting was quite realistic. And I'd seen it before, though not as a canvas.

I'd seen it as a photograph.

It was my mother, exactly as she was on the cover of the Bolshoi programme that I'd found in the trunk in Kathleen's attic. The programme that had been stolen from my room, along with all the other papers and bills.

Of course there had to be more than one programme with my mother's picture on it. The Bolshoi didn't just print one single copy and I had the only one. But how bizarre . . .

I'd buy it. Offer him any sum he wanted. Help him emigrate. Pose nude for twenty paintings. Anything.

I heard footsteps behind me and jumped practically out of my skin.

I spun around, half-expecting to see a man in mirrored sunglasses surrounded by a group of gorillas. 'Oh, it's you . . .'

'I'm sorry,' Sasha apologized. 'I should have called your name . . .' His voice trailed off. 'Where did you find that?' He was looking at the painting of my mother.

I said breathlessly, 'I want to buy this. Name your price. I must have this painting.'

His eyes narrowed to slits. 'No,' he said. 'I'm sorry but that painting is not for sale.'

'Please, I have to have it,' I said. 'I mean it. Any price.'

He said curiously, 'Why do you want it so much?'

I knew, then, that our conversation was about to take a wrong turn.

'It's a painting of my mother,' I said.

'That's not possible,' he said.

'What do you mean?'

I already knew what he was going to say.

Sasha said it. 'She's my mother, too.'

Chapter Fourteen

'That's impossible,' I protested. 'My mother died when I was eight years old. Your mother still feeds tea and cookies to your models.'

'My adoptive mother,' he said. 'My real mother died when I was a baby. I never knew her.' He added gently, 'Perhaps this painting reminds you of your mother. A case of mistaken identity.'

'No,' I said. 'I'm not wrong. I have that same picture of her. The one you used for this painting.'

Well, had.

Until it had been stolen from my room.

Sasha looked at me strangely. 'Her name was Natasha Orlova ...she danced for the Bolshoi.' He stopped as the colour drained from my face. 'Oh, come on,' he said. 'This has to be some kind of joke.'

'I don't believe it either,' I said and ran a finger discreetly over the edge of the painting. Of course the paint was dry. But how long ago had it been painted? In the last week, maybe? Or years ago? There were all kinds of tricks to age paintings. Maybe he knew a few.

Maybe he was conning me. Maybe he did know Ian, but not in the way he'd explained it. Maybe they weren't ... friends.

Otherwise, I was his American half-sister, if this were true. And he'd be ... my half-brother.

'Maybe they were ... cousins.' He sounded puzzled. 'I cannot believe my mother ... I mean, my adoptive mother ... would lie to me.'

'Your adoptive mother ... her name is Nazarova?'

'No,' he said, 'Nazarov is my father's name. My real father. I decided to use it when I began painting. Before that I used my adoptive mother's name – Revchenka.'

'Oh, God. Don't tell me . . . she's Nina Revchenka?'

He looked stunned. 'How do you know her first name?'

'She wrote to my mother in America.'

'Can you prove that?' he demanded.

As family reunions go, if that's what this was, it wasn't such a good one. Neither of us believed or trusted the other.

Could he be telling the truth . . . had he really just discovered that his mother had abandoned him, left him for a new life in America and another family, when all these years he'd thought he'd lost her because she died?

'No,' I said, 'not any more. Her letters were stolen from my hotel room. Along with a programme from the Bolshoi Ballet with her picture on it.' I pointed to the painting. 'This picture.'

It was true, what Nigel had told me. Sometimes you didn't know where reality stopped and fantasy began in this place. How did I know this little drama wasn't some elaborate hoax? What if he'd engineered the theft of the papers and documents from my hotel room and made up this cock-and-bull story about being a relative, knowing I was looking for Nina, knowing who my mother was?

Maybe he was more desperate to get a visa than he let on.

Or there was the other possibility. What if he had something to do with Ian's death and had lured me here so he could find out just how much I knew?

And I'd come. Alone in an abandoned building with a total stranger.

He took a step toward me then and I panicked. I stepped back to the door, but before I could turn and bolt, he reached out and grabbed my wrist. 'Please don't go.' His grip was firm, but I could have broken away easily. I looked up at him. His face was troubled, concerned, but there was no malice in it.

'Okay,' I said. 'I won't. But this whole thing is so . . . bizarre.'

'Yes.' He let go of my wrist and rubbed his chin.

'Why don't you ask your mother?' I asked. 'She's the only one left who really knows the truth.'

'It's not that easy,' he said. 'If what you say is true, then she has been lying to me all my life. I can't believe she would do that, but if she did . . . *if* she did . . . she must have had her reasons.'

Maybe this wasn't an act, maybe I'd been wrong thinking this was a big charade. If Sasha forged that painting in order to dupe me and persuade me we were blood relatives, he was starting to carry the performance a bit far.

What if it *were* true? Maybe my mother, or our mother, if that's who she was, had actually walked out on a life in Moscow where she had a husband and child, and never looked back.

She was, I have to say, the type. My mother never thought of anyone but herself.

'What about your father? Mr. . . er . . . Nazarov. Could you ask him?'

'My mother – Nina, I mean – told me he left after my birth mother died. He was also a dancer in the Bolshoi. He was always away, on tour. How could he take care of a baby? I think he helped with money for a while. I've never seen him. I have no idea where he is now.' Sasha shrugged. 'Maybe it's all lies.'

He bit his lip and stared at me for the longest time as though he could see right through my flesh into my bones. Then he stared at the painting.

'My God.' His voice shook. 'It could be.'

And so Pandora's box was open.

I left soon after that. I think we were both in shock. Sasha said he'd call me as soon as he'd figured out how exactly to ask Nina about his mother. Our mother.

'Her heart is so weak,' he said. 'This could kill her. Give me time. It might take a week, two even, before I find the right moment. I'll call you.'

Then I drove back to the Ukraine and wondered what I'd stumbled into. Once, just before my parents' accident, I'd overheard an argument between Kathleen and my father. I remember it particularly because I was scared to death of the harshness in my grandmother's voice. 'I warned you!' she'd shouted. 'I told you she was trouble!'

Twenty years later she was still trouble.

As much trouble dead as she'd been alive.

I wasn't sure I could face going to the Sovremmenik Theatre with Annabel that evening after that episode in Sasha's studio, but I really didn't have much choice. The tickets were mine, the ones I'd accidentally wangled from Larisa during our long-ago conversation about the Moscow telephone book when I was first trying to find Nina. Larisa had presented them to me at work on Friday afternoon with a little flourish, saying they were practically front row seats to the hottest play in Moscow. Her connections were gold-plated but this was apparently quite a coup, even for her. The play had been sold out for months.

I'd asked Annabel to go with me and she'd said, no, thanks, she was busy.

'Doing what?' I'd said. 'Waiting for the phone to ring? Annabel, you need a life.'

She'd finally admitted that 'busy' meant washing her hair.

'Wash it some other time,' I told her. 'You're coming to the theatre.'

She bit her lip and nodded and said she'd come. But she looked so forlorn I knew her heart wasn't in it and that she was pretty cut up about the way Simon was treating her these days.

Neither of us knew anything about the play we were seeing. Living in New York, I have to admit I'm spoiled when it comes to theatre. Other than London's West End, no other city in the world holds a candle to Broadway. So I wasn't expecting much, though I'd thanked Larisa profusely.

But I'd never been to a play where I sat on the edge of my seat for the entire performance with my heart pounding so hard I could feel it thudding against my chest. It was a real low-budget production, a nothing of a set, the cast in street clothes. Except the acting was brilliant and the story, set in Stalinist times, taut and well-written, but so depressingly bleak you knew from the start the heroine wouldn't make it. It was the agony of waiting until she finally ended it all that was unbearable. The actors turned up the tension like the slow tightening of a screw. I don't think anyone in the audience breathed for the entire second act. When it was finally over, there was tumultuous applause and cheering and the cast took

197

endless curtain calls on a stage that slowly became carpeted with pink and red geraniums, the most popular flower in the Moscow flower markets.

Annabel was really low as we left the theatre. It wasn't hard to figure out why. The boyfriend of the play's heroine was a sadistic misogynist who had beaten and raped her, then left her for another woman. The audience hated him. While it wasn't precisely a case of art imitating life, it was close enough. Simon's name hadn't come up all evening.

'I don't feel like going home right away,' she said. 'Why don't we go to the hard currency bar at the Savoy?'

There was the usual beefy guard at the front door to the hotel, just like at every foreigners' hotel in Moscow. They were bouncers more than security guards, their real purpose being to make sure no Russian made it past the front door. I always thought it was ironic that the guards themselves were Russians. The ones at the Ukraine were particularly merciless. On several occasions I had seen them humiliate their own countrymen who had actually been bold enough to try to slip through the front door. There was always a lot of shouting and then everyone was herded back outside like cattle. I usually tried to look away, vaguely ashamed that I could witness such inhumanity without doing anything to stop it.

But if you were dressed like a Westerner, no one hassled you and you sailed through the front door with no questions asked. That's why when Annabel and I started to walk into the Savoy's opulent marble and gilt lobby, we were stunned when the guard grabbed me by the arm and told me in curt Russian that the hotel was for foreigners only. I must have looked completely nonplussed until Annabel hissed in my ear, 'Oh, *jeez*, he thinks you're a *prostitute*.'

Then she drawled loudly in her broadest American accent, 'I believe there's been a mistake here. Please allow us to pass or I'll speak to the manager.'

He let go of my arm like he just touched hot coals. '*Izviniti pazhalsta*. Excuse me, please.'

Annabel grabbed my elbow and dragged me with her. 'The entrance to the bar is next to the reception desk. Let's *go*.'

The bar was more ornate gilt and elegance, an anomalous reminder of the West and places that tonight seemed impossibly remote. The wasn't a seat anywhere in the main bar so the waiter took us up to the balcony and gave us a table with a view of everyone below. The noisiest group was a party of German businessmen who took up several tables and were already pretty drunk. With them were three stunning Russian girls, heavily made up and more undressed than dressed.

'He obviously lets some Russians in here,' I said to Annabel, after we'd ordered champagne.

'The three graces? They bribed Bubba at the front door, of course. He'd have let you in if you'd bribed him too. If you were really Russian, that is.'

We drank our champagne, gloomily silent.

Then Annabel said, 'I know about that blonde.'

'I'm really sorry,' I said.

She shrugged. 'Yeah. Well.' She tipped her head back and gulped her champagne. She set down the flute and said, 'Simon's a *schmuck*, anyway.'

We both laughed like it was funny, then the waiter reappeared and we asked for two more glasses of champagne. Our bill would be outrageous, but I don't think either of us cared at the moment.

'I was talking about it with David,' she said, pulling her cigarettes out of her purse. 'He says Simon's one of those guys who get their buzz from the chase. As soon as they catch you, they get *bored*. So they move on.'

'David said that?' I must have sounded startled.

She lit a cigarette and blew out a cloud of smoke. '*Jeez*, Claire. I mean, he used different words. By the look on your face, you'd think I went to Jack the Ripper for advice for the lovelorn. I don't get why you don't think he's human.'

'Because I find him very cold, that's why. Obviously he's different with you.'

The waiter arrived with our champagne. 'You don't know anything about him,' Annabel said. She flicked the ash off her cigarette and I could tell she was annoyed.

'You don't have to be so defensive. I didn't realize you were so fond of him.'

She picked up her glass. 'Bottoms up.'

'Mud in your eye.'

After we drank she said, 'If you knew what I know, you'd

change you mind about him toot sweet, honey. I mean it, the guy's an absolute *prince*.' She sucked hard on her cigarette.

I didn't say anything.

'I'm not supposed to tell you this, you know,' she said finally.

'I didn't ask.' I picked up my champagne glass and drank.

'Claire,' she said, 'you gotta swear . . .'

'Okay. I swear.'

She sat up a little straighter and leaned toward me. 'David met a little girl named Yulia, one of the kids he talked to while he was doing that series of articles on Moscow kids. She's *adorable,* except she needs an eye operation and I'm talking *major* which, like I need to tell you, is about as likely to happen as Mikhail Gorbachev giving the kid an all-expenses paid round trip ticket to Disney World.' She expelled a cloud of smoke and said on the same breath, 'So whaddaya think? He's paying for Yulia's operation. Isn't that fabulous?'

'Gorbachev?'

'No, you idiot, *David*! There's some super-duper eye doctor here in Moscow, if you can believe it, who works miracles with lasers. The surgery's gonna be next week, I think.'

I nearly choked on a mouthful of champagne.

She looked smug. 'I knew that'd floor you. Isn't that just the neatest thing?'

'Terrific.' A guy who looks like he buys his clothes at the thrift shop once every decade somehow comes up with the big bucks for a child's highly specialized eye surgery?

'You can't breathe a word about this,' she said. 'He doesn't want anyone to know he's doing it.'

Of course he didn't. Me, particularly. That way he didn't have to deal with those pesky questions I might have about how or where he managed to come up with such a hefty chunk of change.

We didn't talk after that, just sat and drank our champagne in silence. Then Annabel started looking drifty and a bit melancholy and I'm sure she was thinking about Simon again. Manning's agony-aunt advice, notwithstanding.

The laughter from the German table below was becoming more boisterous. So were their advances to the Russian girls.

'Let's get out of here,' Annabel said abruptly. 'I don't want to spend the rest of the evening watching those guys grope a couple of hookers.'

So we left.

Manning was already at his desk Monday morning when I got in, reading a sheaf of telexes from New York. He was wearing another plaid shirt worn white at the elbows and a dark grey tee shirt underneath. He had his hair pulled back with one of those coated wire twist-things they have in the vegetable section of the hard currency stores next to the roll of plastic bags so you can tie up your bag of tomatoes or zucchini or whatever.

For better or worse, we were stuck working with each other. Annabel's point the other night about our feud making life miserable for everyone else in the office hit home. I had no idea any more whether Manning took the money or didn't. It seemed doubtful he was involved in Ian's scheme from the beginning and had been lying to me ever since he'd picked me up at the airport. But maybe somewhere along the line he'd come across all or some of Ian's stash and decided that since it was lost anyway, he could put it to better use than to further the crass monetary interests of The Almighty Ones in New York.

A little girl's surgery.

Maybe he'd been sucked into that 'amoral vacuum' Nigel spoke about where the boundaries between right and wrong grew blurry the longer you stayed in Moscow and you started thinking of Machiavelli as a good guy who knew how to get things done, even if his technique was a bit rough.

Even after a few weeks, I already understood how the frustration and absurdity of life could push you to do desperate or reckless things. Ian had done it. Maybe Manning did, too, but he was lucky enough not to get caught.

He looked up when I came in and said there was news of the shipment containing my personal effects. He said it was sort of a good news-bad news message.

'Tell me the good news first,' I said neutrally and sneezed. It was the first time I'd spoken all morning. I sounded like an exhilarated foghorn. My cold was getting worse.

'God bless you. They found your shipment,' he said. 'You sound rotten.'

'I feel worse than rotten. That's the good news? I didn't even know it was lost,' I said and sneezed again. I reached for the box of tissues on my desk and blew my nose. 'I don't want to know the bad news. '

He handed me the paper. It must be really bad if he couldn't even tell me.

A flowery little message from the shipping company. They were pleased to inform me that they had located my clothes and personal effects. Unfortunately the shipment was in Morocco. Even more regrettably, that country was in the midst of a transportation strike that apparently was going to drag on for a while so it was uncertain when my things would be forwarded to Moscow, given the backlog of freight that was piling up in their warehouses. They apologized profusely for any inconvenience, which was spelled 'inconvienients'.

'Boscow. Borocco. Why don't they hire someone who can spell?' I slammed the paper down on my desk. 'What if they screw up again and my things end up in Bonaco? Or Banila?'

'You're forgetting Bexico.'

'You're a regular barrel of laughs today, aren't you?'

I stomped out of the room to get coffee in the kitchen. He followed me.

'I'm sorry I teased you,' he said. 'You look pretty wretched.' I glared at him and he held up his hand, to ward off whatever I was going to say. 'I've got some other news for you. It's good news, I promise.'

'What?'

'You've been assigned an apartment. Things finally broke loose at UPDK, thanks to Larisa who's been rattling their cages pretty regularly.'

The apartment was in a relatively new foreigners' compound on the outskirts of the city, on a street called Rublevskoye Shosse. It sounded like the place Paula moved into a few weeks ago. If it was, then it was where Nick Ivory lived, too.

'It's probably a twenty- to thirty minute drive in rush hour,' Manning was saying. 'You go straight out Kutuzovsky Prospekt, away from the city until it turns into the Minsk

Highway. Then you take a right out near some birch woods and it's only a few miles after that. It shouldn't be too bad a commute.'

Spoken by someone who merely had to trot up two flights of stairs to get to work. I'd heard from the interns that he had been known to show up in the middle of the night in a bathrobe when there was an urgent on the Tass wire and he was on duty.

He told me that the apartment, not surprisingly, needed a *remont*. The plumbing was modern, if you were living during Peter the Great's reign, and my hotplate was state-of-the-art compared to what they'd installed in the kitchen. I couldn't move in until after the *remont*.

'I'm still trying to line up a contractor to fix the place up,' he said. 'So don't pack your bags yet. Whoever we hire will have to ship in everything from the West, right down to the nails and screws. In the meantime maybe you should take a drive out there during the week and see the place for yourself.'

But I never got anywhere near my apartment.

On Tuesday, Annabel asked me to go shopping with her after work at the Dorogomilovskaya *rynok,* the farmers' market around the corner from the office. Annabel enjoyed food shopping about as much as anyone likes getting a root canal, so I knew something was up.

The building housing the *rynok* always made me think of a child's crude drawing of a wooden circus tent. Inside were noise and people and the overpowering earthy smell of over-ripe vegetables and dusky unfamiliar spices. The first time I came here had been a shock, particularly the meat section where severed sheep's, cow's and pig's heads were propped up against the wall to show you what type of meat was for sale. An American health inspector would have had a coronary. Huge slabs of meat lay on bloodied marble counters, along with large, scaly tongues, pools of intestines, hooves, and puddles of brains. It's funny how you get used to things, though, and after a few times I no longer turned my head away when I passed the butchers in their blood-soaked aprons, but looked and even asked a few questions about what was for sale.

We walked past the flower sellers with their sparsely filled vases of carnations and a few roses and started going up and down the rows and rows of plain wooden tables where men with gold and silver teeth and women with ancient faces like shrivelled nuts sold things I'd never heard of, weighing them on quaint, antique scales. Then they calculated their prices on abacuses, zinging black and white beads back and forth across the small wires quick as a blur. We passed stands heaped with lingonberries, gooseberries, whortleberries, quinces and pomegranates, and then the tables lined with canning jars of marinated whole garlic cloves. The tall Yuri had told me once that eating a garlic clove soaked in pomegranate juice was a sure-fire cure for a hangover, but after I took one whiff of the sharp, pulverizing scent I figured it was probably also a sure-fire way to make sure no one came near you for a week, either.

Along the back wall tables were heaped with dirt-covered potatoes and mountains of cabbages and beets, like someone had dumped them there. It was the antithesis of the shrink-wrapped hygiene, pretty displays and abundance of every grocery store I'd ever been to in America, but it was starting to grow on me and I was beginning to like the vulgar hustle and bustle. Usually I lingered at the stalls where dark-coloured spices with musical-sounding names like *khmeli-suneli*, *adzhika* and *sumakh* spilled out of small burlap bags, but today we went directly to the tables that were selling what we needed, ignoring the old women calling to us, cackling as we passed them, urging us to buy.

I bought dill, parsley, eggplant, zucchini, tomatoes, and several bunches of carrots tied together with sewing thread. I stuffed the packages into my *avoshko*, the string bag Russians called a 'perhaps bag', their equivalent of 'be prepared'. Everyone carried an *avoshko* because 'perhaps' you might find something to buy in this used-up city. Tanya had given it to me a few weeks ago.

'I need some pomegranates and apples and then I'm done,' I said to Annabel. 'What about you?'

She'd bought three tomatoes and six potatoes.

'Claire, I've decided to quit.' She said it so quietly I wondered if I'd really heard correctly through the noise around us.

'Quit shopping?'

'No.'

I set down a pomegranate and stared at her. Across the table the little *babushka* who thought I was no longer going to buy her fruit vibrated with anger in some unknown dialect.

'*Da, da. Ya khatela bi kupit.* I want to buy.' I paid for the pomegranates and didn't even bother to collect my change. My diminutive *babushka* chortled happily at the oversight but I was watching Annabel who looked like she was a heartbeat away from tears.

'Let's get out of here,' I said, 'I think we should have this conversation somewhere else.'

Annabel nodded, zombie-like, and now I could see there really were tears glittering in her eyes. I grabbed her elbow and steered her through the congested aisles of end-of-the-day shoppers arguing with the farmers that their goods would be too old or too bruised to sell tomorrow but they would gladly liberate them today if the price was right.

It was dark when we walked outside, although the parking lot was bright as day, floodlit by two enormous lights shining down from the top of the *rynok*. We loaded the packages into my car in silence. I slammed the door shut and turned to her.

'You want to leave Moscow?'

'I want to leave journalism.'

I said, slowly, 'Are you sure you don't want to think about this for a couple of days?'

'There's nothing for me to think about. Nothing.' I had never heard her sound this bitter or vehement, so I knew she'd made up her mind before today and she wasn't changing it. She added tiredly, 'Let's get in the car before we freeze to death and I'll tell you the whole sordid story.'

It was Simon, of course. I should have guessed.

'I thought I was pregnant. It wasn't impossible ... I got careless one night and forgot my diaphragm. Afterwards, like a big *jerk*, I went to him. He just laughed and told me to go to Helsinki for an *abortion*, if it was really true. Then he told me he was seeing somebody else. It's that Swedish blonde, Inga or whatever her name is.' She swiped at the tears sliding down her cheeks and said, 'That's it. Get lost and have a nice life ... what a *fool* I was.'

I said, 'Annabel, he's not worth giving up your career for
. . . don't do it. He's the jerk.'

She was laughing and crying at the same time. 'Oh,
Claire, come on. It's not *my* career. It never was. It's my
mother's. The whole time I was a kid she had this *thing*
about every woman journalist she ever saw on television. I
mean, she lived and breathed it. For crying out loud, I know
every detail of Barbara Walter's life! Want to know what
Barbara eats for breakfast? What her living room looks like?
Does she have her own teeth?' She laughed again and this
time it was really bitter. 'So here's my mother. Make something of yourself, she says. You can be somebody. You can
be as good as Barbara Walters. Your father'd be so proud.
I'd be so proud . . . my daughter, the foreign correspondent.
Think what I could tell your Aunt Sybil. All these years
I've had to listen to her talk about her daughter Rosie, the
D.A.'s assistant . . . putting the scumbags of Brooklyn behind
bars. *Jeez,* Claire, she rammed it down my throat. Your
cousin Rosie, the greatest little thing since sliced bread . . .
you have no idea . . .' She stopped talking and stared at her
hands in her lap.

The warmth of our breath and our body heat had completely
fogged the car windows and the windshield. We could have
been inside a cocoon. 'Simon?' I asked.

She looked up and practically spat the words. 'I . . . have
. . . spent . . . my . . . life . . . being who other people wanted
me to be. Trying to be someone I'm *not*. Nearly throwing
myself away on someone who's such a *putz* . . . such a
schmuck.' She stopped again and I waited. Then she said
softly, 'All I ever wanted was to do something with my music.
I'm good, Claire . . . I'm *really* good at it.' Then she was lost
in her thoughts until finally she said with unexpected compo-
sure, 'Come on, let's get out of here. I know we just bought
all this food, but I'm taking you out to dinner. Have you been
to that Georgian place over by Novodeivichy Convent?'

I shook my head.

'Good. We'll go there.'

'Annabel, you don't need to . . .'

'I *want* to,' she said fiercely. 'Don't turn me down.'

I started the car engine and we both rubbed at the opaque

206

windows until we made little spyholes and I could see well enough to drive.

'What are you going to do?' I asked as we pulled out onto the street.

'Go back to New York,' she said. 'I can *make* it there. I know a lot of people in the business ... it'll work out.' She started humming to herself and it hit me that I had missed her singing these last few weeks.

The Georgian restaurant was crowded; in fact, it was packed. The large room we ate in smelled of the dusky smoke of the braziers on which meat was grilled. I liked the place: the exotically pungent smells, the atmosphere, the food. For once, it wasn't an enclave exclusively reserved for foreigners since you could also pay in roubles, except for the bar bill, which was in hard currency.

We were drinking tea after dinner, served from a nearby samovar. It tasted vaguely of cardamom. Annabel lit up a cigarette. 'In a way I'll miss this dump,' she said. 'The place kinda grows on you, you know?'

'Changing our mind, are we?'

She smiled. 'Nah.'

'When are you going to tell David?'

She blew out a puff of smoke. 'The sooner the better. I mean, what's the point of hanging around?'

'Well,' I said, 'there is the little matter of filling your job.'

'You and David can cope. You're a great team.'

'Annabel, who else lives inside that mind of yours besides Tinkerbell and the tooth fairy?'

'Lighten up!' She looked indignant. 'You know, if you weren't so dense, you'd see that he actually *likes* you.'

'Don't be ridiculous. The guy has a heart of stone.'

'Is that so? Then how do you explain him paying for Yulia's eye surgery?'

'I don't,' I snapped. 'Unless it's all the money he's saved because he buys his clothes at the Salvation Army thrift shop.' I stopped and held up my hand before she could say anything. 'I didn't mean that. I know it was nasty. But honestly, Annabel, on our salaries who can afford to finance that kind of operation?'

It was as good a time as any to spill everything to her about

207

Ian, the missing money, and where I figured Manning had got the funds for his philanthropic gift.

She blew out another puff of smoke and looked at me. 'You can if your father's got enough bucks to buy Peru. Or some other cute little country,' she said flatly.

'Uh . . .'

'You don't know who David is, do you?'

There were several answers to that question. I shook my head, which seemed like a better idea than making another wisecrack.

'His father owns AmericaBank, dummy. David grew up with a piggybank as big as the state of California. The bill for Yulia's surgery is *pocket* money, hon.'

'You don't mean Cameron Manning? David's father is Cameron Manning? Are you serious?'

'*Jeez*, don't talk to *me* about the tooth fairy and Tinkerbell. Yulia's not the only one David's helped, for your information. He's been doing stuff like this ever since he lost his wife and daughter two years ago. Four years old, that's all his little girl was. She'd be about Yulia's age now. They were killed in a car accident when a truck ploughed into them. The driver was drunk as a *skunk*. He was killed, too, the schmuck. David used their insurance money to set up a foundation for sick kids. No doubt Daddy Warbucks kicks in, but *hey*, a good deed is a *good* deed.' She sucked on her cigarette and looked at me appraisingly. 'You had no idea, did you?'

'No.' How come I'd never heard about it?

Unless it happened during the time I'd gone back to Harvard for a six-week summer seminar. Maybe the accident had happened then . . . and somehow I'd never heard.

'I didn't think so,' Annabel said calmly. She picked up her teacup and drained it. 'Let's get the bill and get out of here.'

We didn't speak until I pulled into the parking lot at Kutvzovksy. 'I feel like a jerk,' I said.

'You are,' she said. 'But you're a nice jerk which is why I'll miss you. *Hasta mañana*, hon. Get some sleep.'

So I set off for the Ukraine and knew I'd miss her, too, probably a lot more than she'd miss me.

For some reason, it took Annabel until Thursday to tell

Manning and the rest of the staff she was leaving. To say everyone was surprised was putting it mildly. Especially when she announced she was quitting journalism completely to pursue a career as a professional singer. Manning looked like he was having a big nervous, what with another position to fill, Tanya and the Yuris thought it was incredibly romantic, and Larisa, I think, believed Annabel had temporarily lost her mind. In the middle of the uproar, the phone rang.

Annabel answered it. 'Claire. For you.'

'Who is it?'

She said in Russian, 'I don't know.'

I picked up the phone. 'Claire Brennan.'

'This is Sasha.'

One thing about my office, everyone had hypersensitive radar when it came to everyone else's business. I could feel the collective surge of interest crackling around me, shifting temporarily from Annabel's news to whatever was happening in my life.

'Hello!' I swivelled my chair so I was facing the back wall.

'Hello!' He sounded momentarily perplexed by the television commercial jollity in my voice. Then he said, 'Ah. You cannot talk.'

'It's a bit hectic today.'

'My mother wishes to meet you. Nina, that is.'

So he'd finally told her. 'Oh. Really?' I tried to make it sound like we were chatting about the weather. I said noncommittally, 'What did she say?'

'Do you know a place, "116 Reechlinstrit"?'

Fortunately I did not drop the phone. I'd lived at 116 Richland Street with my parents until their deaths. 'Yes.'

'My mother ... Nina, I mean ... she kept letters, too.'

I really, desperately wanted to believe that he was telling the truth, that Nina really kept letters from my mother. Because there was only one other way he could have known that address: it was also on the letters Nina sent my mother, the letters someone stole from my room, along with the Bolshoi programme.

Was he the thief? He knew I was out the evening I suspected the robbery occurred. Could he have bribed someone to let him into the Ukraine, into my room?

209

'I'll come,' I said.

'Good. Tomorrow night at seven. I will be home from work then.' He rattled off the address to me and I guess, in my shock, it didn't register until after I hung up that it was the same address on Karetny Ryad I'd visited a few weeks ago.

And when I'd asked the woman who'd opened the door if she knew Nina Revchenka, she'd hollered 'no' at me and slammed the door in my face.

So what was going on?

Tomorrow I'd get answers.

To everything.

Chapter Fifteen

I stopped at the *beriozka* at Hotel Mezhdunarodnaya on my
way to Sasha's place to pick up a gift for him and Nina. The
Mezhdunarodnaya was a starkly modern hotel as its Russian
name implied, across the river from the Gothic Ukraine, and
its hard currency store was probably the swankiest in
Moscow. Compared to the scruffy, dilapidated Ukraine, the
Mezh was sleek and Space Age, with glassed-in elevators, real
escalators, and a cavernous airy atrium dominated by a clock
tower with a whimsical-looking rooster who emerged from a
cage to cock-a-doodle-do every hour.

Despite its pseudo-Western ambience and the rooster, the
place had all the brittle charm of a high-tech corporate head-
quarters. The lovely shops were empty and museum-like.
Places to look, not touch. Occasionally an exquisitely dressed
Russian woman would drift by with glittering eyes and beautifully manicured hands. No Russian woman ever looked like
that unless she was a hard currency hooker. They always met
my eyes, all of them, and the look was always the same.
Something between hard-won triumph and calculating territor-
ial scrutiny.

My heels clicked on the marble floor, echoing in the stillness as I crossed the main lobby to the escalator. I walked
through the double glass doors into the store. Pallets with
boxes heaped on them littered the aisles, which meant there'd
been a delivery. I'd been to this *beriozka* and others in
Moscow when the shelves had been practically barren. There
was booze, of course, the one thing you could almost always
find unless there had been a recent holiday when everything

211

remotely flammable was cleaned out. I took a bottle of Scotch and a bottle of Bordeaux. Then I debated whether I should buy something else, something sweet or some fruit. In the end I bought nothing more since I hadn't figured out yet the Byzantine code of behaviour that defined where Russian pride and dignity began and the wheeler-dealer culture of need and greed bred by appalling poverty ended. The same people who wouldn't lift a finger to help you unless bribed to do so, unless there was something in it for them, would turn around and spread a feast fit for a king if you dined in their home. Give you the shirt off their back if you said you liked it.

I set down the Scotch and the wine in front of the Russian woman sitting at the cash register. Her cheeks were two bright circles of rouge and her lips a cherry bow, exactly like the *matrushkas* lining one of the shelves of the store. My bill came to thirty-six dollars and change. I gave her a fifty.

'I do not have change for this,' she said in a high-pitched school mistress voice, 'you must pay with exact change.'

'I don't have exact change,' I said. I opened my wallet. Another fifty and a twenty. 'Look. That's it.'

She shrugged. 'Then you cannot buy.' She sat, staring at the cash register, willing me to disappear. Behind me, a queue started to form.

'That's ridiculous.' I pointed to the cash register drawer. 'You have change in there.'

'Not enough. Please. Next person.'

'Wait a minute.' But she was already gesturing for the man behind me to step around me and set his basket on the counter. I turned around and glared at him. He stepped back and I swung around again to the cashier. 'Look, I want to buy these things. Keep the change.'

'I cannot.'

'What do you mean, you cannot?'

'I cannot keep the change.'

'Give her a credit card,' muttered the man behind me. 'She has to take it.'

I opened my wallet again and pulled out a credit card. I slapped it on the counter and heard the man behind me mutter something indistinct. We all watched as the Russian girl rummaged around until she found a credit card slip. She wrote out the bill with what seemed like exaggerated slowness and finally took an imprint of my card on an antique machine. Sullenly she pushed the slip over for me to sign.

Then she shoved my purchases to the end of the counter and began to ring up the items of the man behind me.

'I could use a shopping bag,' I said, 'but don't put yourself out too much.'

She threw it in my general direction without bothering to look at me.

Linda Rondstadt, wailing about lost love in a break-your-heart torchy voice that blasted through the car's speakers, had calmed me down by the time I got to Sasha's apartment building. I shoved Linda in my purse and grabbed the hard-won *beriozka* bag. I left the car in my customary parking place, in the middle of the sidewalk.

The lobby smelled, as did all the other Russian buildings I'd been in, of urine and garbage. I took the rickety elevator to the eighth floor. Two apartments to a floor. Theirs was on the left. Flat B. The place I'd been to before. I hesitated, then rang the doorbell.

After a moment Sasha opened the door. He was elegantly dressed in a starched white shirt and new blue jeans. 'Please. Come in.' He held the door for me and I slipped past him into a poorly lit narrow corridor.

He was standing in such a way that the light at the end of the hall silhouetted his profile, the sharp cheekbones and slant of his eyes, so that he seemed more remotely exotic, more Oriental, than he had the day I'd met him. That he was my brother seemed quite incredible at that moment. We didn't resemble each other at all.

He took in Victoria's expensive cashmere coat and the fur *chapka* I'd bought recently. 'You look very lovely,' he said formally. He sounded as stiff and self-conscious as I felt.

'Thank you.' Sasha helped me off with the coat and took my hat. I handed him the *beriozka* bag. 'These are for you.'

He looked inside and I saw his eyes flash. 'You are too kind,' he said firmly and I was afraid I'd overdone it with the gifts. 'Please. Now you must meet Nina.'

He started down the corridor and I followed him. Photographs and paintings lined the walls from floor to

213

ceiling. The photographs were black and white, probably at least thirty or forty years old, and all of dancers. Ballerinas. In costume, on stage, in classes, applying makeup. The paintings were his, in the unmistakable style that had dazzled me in his studio the other day.

He led me into the large room at the end of the corridor. It was modestly furnished in the same browns, sepias and rusts as my hotel room, the lifeless tones that were the indoor colours of Moscow. But on one wall was a single enormous painting, magnificent and utterly Russian, a glowing, jewel-plumed Firebird, the enchanted fairy-tale bird whose magical rainbow feathers fell from the sky across the meadows and fields of Russia when the evil sorcerer Kaschei the Immortal tried to carry it off to his distant kingdom. I'd read the story as a child, imagining Russia as a fantastical land that existed at the back of the North Wind, where the magic feathers of the Firebird probably still glowed, visible to those who loved truth and beauty.

When I asked my mother about this, she lost her temper, worse than any of her usual screaming tirades, and forbade me to read anything about Russia ever again. Then she turned on me, I think I was about six when this happened, and shrieked at me until my ears hurt, telling me 'the truth' about the real Soviet Union and the inhumanity of Communism. How people who'd done absolutely nothing were carried off in the middle of the night, during Stalin's purges, to camps where they were tortured, which she'd described so graphically I'd had nightmares for weeks.

I do believe this was the first time I'd ever thought about that fairy tale since the day my mother delivered her Götterdämmerung lecture.

I must have been so riveted by Sasha's painting and the memories it brought back that I didn't realize Nina was in the room. Sasha took my arm.

'Please.'

I looked up.

She was sitting in the far corner, a little bit of a thing, so small she could have been a doll. Nina Revchenka sat propped up against embroidered cushions on a daybed, a crocheted afghan draped across her legs. She was white-haired and fair and fragile as fine porcelain. She stretched out her hand and said my name.

I turned my back on the painting and went over to kneel by her bed. She was wearing a dress the colour of dark amethysts. I kissed her hand, which was gnarled and arthritic, like the root of an old tree. I said in Russian, 'Nina Alexandrovna, how do you do?'

She tipped my chin so I looked up at her. Her eyes were bright and alert but there was something in the intensity of her gaze that reminded me of Kathleen in the last weeks at the hospital. As though she were trying to memorize me, every minute detail, before her time ran out.

She stroked my hair. 'It is as though Natasha has come back,' she said in a whispery voice that made me think of dry leaves, 'except your hair is russet and hers was black as the night. Only that difference. Otherwise you could be your mother, child.'

She rubbed her thumb across the back of my hand. Her touch was light as a butterfly's wing. Then she put her hand over her heart and I saw her chest rise and fall ever so slightly. Sasha was at her side in a flash and I leaned toward her, but she brushed us both away and said, 'No, no, children. It's nothing, I promise. But I would like to drink a cup of tea. Sasha, darling, take me to the table. Clara must have something to eat as well.'

I had seen the table by the window on the other side of the room. It was heaped with platters of meat and salads and hard-boiled eggs. There was a bottle of red wine and vodka. I knew they didn't eat like this every night.

This was for me.

Sasha began fiddling with a chair that stood next to the daybed. I hadn't realized it was a wheelchair, probably because I'd never seen a wooden one before. This was ancient, something you'd find in a museum of antique medical equipment. I stood up and whispered in English in Sasha's ear, 'Don't you think she should have her tea in bed?'

He whispered back, 'Her body may be fragile but her mind is stubborn as a mule. If she wants to sit at the table, she'll sit at the table. No one tells her what to do.'

Then he picked her up in his arms like a child and set her

gently in the rickety old chair. Nina patted his hand as he wheeled her to the table.

'I'll get the tea,' he said and left the room.

When he came back, he had my bottle of Bordeaux. 'You would prefer to drink this,' he said. He was treating me like a privileged Westerner all of a sudden. He thought I brought the wine for myself. He poured Nina's tea and set it in front of her.

'I like Georgian wine,' I said mildly, 'particularly *Khvanchkara*. Please keep the Bordeaux for another time.'

Khvanchkara happened to be Nigel's favourite wine – Stalin's too, he'd told me once. It was the tipple *du jour* when we drank together, unless it was vodka. It was also the only Soviet wine I knew.

Sasha looked startled at the comment, then he smiled, an incandescent smile that said I'd crossed the chasm from the Aladdin's cave of Western treasure that separated my world from his. His smile must have been his father's. Natasha, as near as I could remember, rarely smiled. And when she did, I always thought, in my little girl way, that her constricted grimace reminded me of someone who was being pinched.

Sasha poured the *Khvanchkara*, and then he and Nina insisted I put enormous amounts of food on my plate. I had known it would be like this, that they would insist I eat for three people as though I were about to cross the desert on foot, so I'd skipped lunch at work and had to spend the entire afternoon listening to Tanya lecture me about starvation.

So now I was genuinely hungry and I could tell they were pleased. We had a toast first, of course, to my presence. To friendship. To families.

To ... Natasha.

Each time, Nina drank little more than a thimbleful of wine, but Sasha was pretty heavy-handed about filling my glass as well as his own and I knew I needed to slow down. Then again, maybe I needed those drinks, to fortify me for what was coming. Nina clearly was waiting for some predetermined moment before she started her story which only ratcheted up my anxiety level.

She wanted another cup of tea. Then she said, 'Tell me, Clara, what do you know about her?' She didn't say 'Natasha' or 'your mother'. I heard, ever so faintly, the reproach in her voice.

If all Nina felt was mild annoyance at my mother's behaviour, she surely was an angel. I'd be more than a bit irritated with someone who dumped a baby on me then split for America, never to return again. It's not exactly in the same ballpark as asking if you'd mind looking after the cat for a week or two.

I wondered if Natasha ever sent her any money, to help out. I'd bet she didn't.

'I know very little,' I said to Nina. 'She died when I was eight and then I went to live with my father's mother, Kathleen Brennan. Kathleen . . . did not like my mother. After her death, we rarely spoke of her.' I had no idea what stirring up all these memories would do to her or Sasha so I didn't bother to elaborate. I would do that if they asked me outright.

Nina stared into her teacup. I couldn't tell if she'd heard me or just tuned out. I glanced at Sasha, whose expression was politely impassive.

Nina raised her head. 'But you did know, of course, about her career with the Bolshoi?'

'No,' I said. 'Not until a few weeks ago when I found a theatre programme in a trunk in Kathleen's attic. Along with your letters.'

'You knew nothing about her until then?' Sasha asked. He spoke with that same polite detachment. The bombshell revelations triggered by my appearance in their lives clearly hadn't stirred any feelings of filial attachment, judging by the way he was acting.

'Kathleen passed away in August,' I said. 'I was going through her things. That's how I found out.'

'How sad for you.' Nina's voice was gentle. 'About your grandmother.'

I shrugged and said in a voice that wavered only slightly, 'She had been ill for a long time. It was a blessing, finally. She was in a lot of pain.'

Sasha looked up at me, then at Nina, who nodded as if at some pre-rehearsed cue. He said to me, 'My mother . . . Nina . . . has told me everything. We agreed she should tell you, too. I'm sorry but it's not a pleasant story.'

217

'I lived with her for eight years,' I said. 'Do you think she was any different when she was in America? She never, ever said a thing about leaving a child behind in Russia. I'm sure my father ...' I closed my eyes and squeezed them tight. My father was a good man, with a conscience and a sense of decency and honour. His one flaw was his blind adoration of my spoiled, wilful, beautiful mother. 'I'm sure my father never knew what she'd done. If he had, he would have wanted to do something. To help ... I don't know ... he wouldn't have done nothing. He wouldn't have abandoned you.'

Perhaps I shouldn't have used the word 'abandoned' because a muscle twitched in Sasha's jaw and now he seemed provoked. 'What was she like?' he asked, his voice cool.

'She drank.' I said it acidly, automatically. It was my one, lingering memory of her. A drunk.

So much for pulling punches. The last thing I wanted to do was to upset Nina, with her fragile heart. But she was nodding, like it was no surprise.

'She was once a brilliant ballerina, destined for greatness. Another Pavlova.' I must have looked incredulous because she said, 'Yes, child, she was that good. And she was beautiful. Exquisite. A princess. When she danced with Grigorii Nazarov, it was truly perfection.'

I looked at Sasha, at the mention of his father's name, but he seemed as unmoved by the mention of it as he was by this conversation about his mother.

'She broke her leg,' Nina continued. 'Grigorii dropped her and she fell off the stage. Natasha was furious with him – I think she would have killed him if she could. She said he let her fall deliberately because they had been quarrelling. He had been Natasha's lover but then there was a new ballerina, there always is ... younger, more beautiful ... and he wanted to dance with her.' She paused then said, 'It was while she was convalescing that she learned she was already four months pregnant. I am not sure how she did not know she was going to have a baby before that. Perhaps it was complicated by the broken leg, but ...' She shrugged delicately. 'Natasha was a child, really. By that time, of course, it was too late to have an abortion. Not surprisingly she did not want the baby, especially Grigorii's child. I looked after

Sasha almost from birth.' She smiled at her son. 'He has been my reason for living.'

The look that passed between them went a long way toward explaining how Sasha could freeze out any memories of his biological parents. He leaned over and kissed his mother on the cheek.

Nina stroked his hand. 'By the time Sasha was born, Grigorii was dancing all the time with Katya, the new prima ballerina in the Bolshoi. Natasha was insanely jealous. She resumed dancing, but because of her injury it was painful and she was never the same. She went on the tour to America that spring. It was the last time she would dance. That's when she defected.' In the silence that gradually seeped into the room, I heard a clock tick quietly. Finally Nina said, 'I knew she would try something. I ... hoped ... she would never return for Sasha. You see, I could not have a child of my own.'

She stopped speaking and stared at her hands in her lap. Sasha spun a spoon around and around on the tablecloth and I contemplated the Firebird.

'She didn't love me, either,' I said to Sasha. 'The only difference is that I grew up knowing it.'

Between the two of us, he'd lucked out in the mother department. Life with Natasha had been like living with the Wicked Witch of the West.

'I'm sorry for you, Clara,' he said. 'But it's different for me. The heart can't grieve when the head doesn't know. I never knew any of this.'

I started to say something but there was the tiniest gasp and Nina's hand fluttered to her heart. Suddenly she was pale as death. Sasha was out of his chair so swiftly he knocked it over. 'You are going back to bed,' he said as he gently picked up his mother in his arms and carried her to the daybed.

I righted the chair and set it next to the table. 'What can I do?' I asked. My own heart was pounding.

'There's a bottle of valerian on the bookcase,' Sasha said urgently. 'It's her sedative. Get it, please.'

I found the dark brown bottle and handed it to him.

He gave her a spoonful, like coaxing a baby bird to drink, then Nina's eyes flew open. She looked straight at me, but I don't think she saw me. 'Natasha,' she said, and closed her eyes again.

I whispered, 'I think I should go.'

'Perhaps,' Sasha murmured.

He leaned forward and cocked his head, listening to her faint breathing. After a moment, he stood up. 'Come,' he whispered. 'She's sleeping. I can leave her for a few minutes.' He led me down the narrow hall of ballerinas to the tiny foyer, then disappeared into a nearby room. He came back with the cashmere coat and *chapka*.

'I shouldn't have come,' I said. 'It's upset her.'

'Did you think it would not?' He sounded gently reproachful. 'She's been carrying this burden for thirty-five years.'

'Maybe we should have left it . . .'

'No,' he interrupted. 'She's relieved that all the lies are finally out in the open. The truth is always better.'

'Will she be okay? What happens when you are not here?'

'Ah. My . . . aunt comes.'

His aunt. The friendly lady who'd thrown me out the first time I'd showed up at his doorstep. 'I met her,' I said. 'I came here because of the address on Nina's letters to my . . . Natasha. She told me you didn't live here.'

'Of course not,' he said laconically. 'Never tell a stranger anything.'

'Oh.'

He helped me on with my coat.

'Thank you for . . .' I didn't know what to say. '. . . dinner.'

'I'll call you in a few days. There are things we should talk about.' He put his hands on my shoulders and looked down into my eyes. His face was millimetres from mine. Ian told me once that Russians don't have the same sensibilities we have about the boundaries of personal space.

Sasha must have felt me go tense because he pulled back into a less intimate zone and brushed a strand of hair off my face. 'Are you all right?'

'Yes.'

'Then what . . .?'

How could I tell him I'd doubted him, wondered if he'd stolen the letters and theatre programme from my room so he could concoct some elaborate hoax about us being related?

After this evening, one thing was clear: he genuinely adored Nina and there was no way that sweet woman was part of some plot to dupe me, whatever the reason.

Which meant he really was my brother, as incredible as it seemed.

'I'm still trying to get used to the idea.'

'That we're related.'

I nodded.

'Well,' he said, 'it's not as if we have a life of shared memories, is it? Or spent years wonderng if we'd ever meet?'

'No.'

'I think we should go slowly,' he said. 'I think we should be friends.' He kissed my forehead. 'I must get back to her.'

I drove slowly back to the hotel, through dark, deserted streets, listening to Linda's smouldering voice singing about how lucky she was to find the man who'd been missing from her life.

Maybe I'd just done the same thing.

If Sasha was my brother – which, after today, I think I finally, truly believed – I'd do anything for him.

He was the only family I had left in the world.

Chapter Sixteen

On Friday evening I was in my room washing the dishes after another hotplate dinner when the elevator crisis in the Ukraine happened and all hell broke loose. I found out about it when Nigel showed up at my door after climbing up the eleven flights of stairs to our floor.

His face was bright pink and he was panting like he'd just run a marathon. He seemed on the verge of collapsing in a heap at my feet. I pulled him over to the sofa, worried about his heart and the spare tyre he wore around his middle. Nigel's idea of exercise was raising a glass of wine from the table to his lips.

'Are you okay?' I asked. 'Here ... put your feet up.'

His shoes were soaking wet and so were the cuffs of his trousers. I looked across the room to the door and saw a trail of wet footprints. 'What in the world ...?'

I had nothing, absolutely nothing to give him if there was something wrong with his heart. Maybe I should get him a doctor. Maybe we should go to the Kremlin clinic ...

He held up his hand. 'Some vodka. Do you have any vodka?'

Nigel believed, with the same childlike faith of Tanya and the Yuris, that vodka was the universal cure-all. Russian chicken soup.

'Of course.' I got the bottle from my freezer. I took a glass from the armoire and poured him a shot.

He knocked it back and said disgustedly, 'Bloody hell! No elevators for God knows how many days. The entire electrical system has been knocked out. Bloody cleaning staff decided to wash the roof of this place. Then they didn't know what to do

222

with the dirty water so they dumped it down the stairwells and the main elevator shaft. Twenty-nine floors. It was like a bloody waterfall.'

I started to giggle and he glared at me. 'It's not bloody funny. I practically got electrocuted when I was in the elevator and a huge wave of water came crashing through the ceiling. Then the lights went out and everyone started screaming and carrying on until we finally got to the lobby. Bloody hell!' He held out his glass for more vodka and I filled it.

Outside the door to my room, someone began shouting. I turned to Nigel. 'Now what?'

He stood up. 'I don't know.'

He padded over to the door, leaving another path of wet footprints. I followed him. Across the hall Lydia was shouting 'Nyet, nyet' at a closed door. On the other side of the door, angry voices shouted back at her.

The door was one of the fire exits. It should have been left open, in case of an emergency, but every time I tried to use it, it was always locked. Nigel told me later all the fire exits were locked. That way no one could leave or enter the hotel without passing the *dejournayas'* desks near the elevators. It was how they kept track of us.

'Lydia, *otkrivayte, otkrivayte,*' Nigel said. 'Let them in, for God's sake. The bloody elevator is broken.'

She turned around. She was wearing a pair of dirty pink high-heeled bedroom slippers and a tubular orange knit minidress with a deeply plunging neckline. She wore heavy eye makeup but no lipstick and had obviously been in the middle of painting her fingernails blood red. She looked like an escapee from a circus. 'I cannot. I cannot. They must go another way. Tell them. I think they speaking English.'

'It sounds like some of the Canadian hockey players who've been staying here,' I said. 'They played an exhibition match yesterday against the Russians. I saw a few of them in the lobby last night. They'd just lost the match and they weren't too happy ... I think they're saying they're going to break down the door.'

Lydia went pale. 'No – no, they must not. Please, Nigel. Please, you must send them another way. There is another door is open I'm thinking.'

223

Nigel shouted through the door, negotiating with the hostages on the other side. Finally, we heard what sounded like a herd of elephants clumping down the steps.

Lydia was grateful.

'You'd better unlock this door, Lydia, or you're going to have a riot on your hands,' Nigel said.

'*Da, da,*' she said. 'I know.'

But the door wasn't unlocked and for the rest of the evening I heard more banging on the fire door and voices shouting for someone to open up. Either Nigel or I would go to the door and tell some unfortunate out-of-breath soul they had to go back downstairs and find another fire exit.

At some point, Kisya slipped into my room. She was cold and wet and shivering. I dried her with one of the bathroom towels and fed her another slice of ham.

Nigel came by around eleven with a bottle of Georgian wine. 'I can't sleep with all that racket in the hall,' he said. 'And, by the way, I found out something about your Baron von Müller.'

I nearly sloshed red wine all over myself. I didn't need this right now. 'He's dead. I don't think he's anybody's Baron von Müller any more,' I said. My voice was probably a bit sharp. 'So, what did you find out?'

He peered over the top of his glasses. 'Interested, are we, love? All right, I'll tell you what I know. But first you tell me what you know.' His antennae were practically quivering.

'I don't know what you're talking about.' I wasn't about to hand him the front page of that rag he worked for. Suitably hyped and sensationalized, once he'd finished with it.

He spoke softly. 'Don't be daft, darling. Of course you do. I checked into those paintings. The ones in the photographs, the ones you were so interested in. I'll tell you what I learned, but first, tell me why you thought there was something so special about them?' He bored holes in me with his eyes until I felt the heat. 'It's something to do with Ian's death, isn't it? Ah ... I'm right. Although you don't know the whole story. Oh, my. Right again.' He looked, I would say, like a cat that had just polished off a large bowl of cream. He beamed. 'Between what I found out about the paintings ... and what you know about Ian ... we'd have a sensational story, love, wouldn't we? Come on, darling. I'll show you mine, if you'll show me yours.'

I banged my glass down on the table. 'Is everything in your life for sale, Nigel? I thought you were supposed to be Ian's friend.'

'That,' he said testily, 'was low, Claire. Ian's dead, for God's sake. And everybody's saying it was his bloody liver. You and I know better. Don't you want to *know?* The truth, I mean?' His eyes glittered.

I said cautiously, 'Then if it's not for a story, why are you so curious?'

He got up and walked over to my desk. He picked up my little Sony portable radio and brought it back over to the table. He turned it on and fiddled with the dial until there was music. Accordion music, something folkloric. He turned up the volume.

He leaned over and hissed in my ear, 'Because I'm worried about what you're getting yourself into, that's why. And I don't think you know just how dangerous it could be. Is that a good enough answer?'

The chill that went through me was so real I shivered. Whatever this was all about, it was the first time Nigel had thought we needed to muffle our conversation from the listening walls. These past weeks he'd been acting like a kindly but rumpled guardian angel who'd answered every silly question I had about life in Moscow. All of a sudden he no longer seemed like the harmless, bumbling garden gnome who wrote kooky stories about weird things.

'You're bluffing, Nigel,' I said, but my voice wavered and gave me away.

'Let me help you, love,' he said, softly, and I could tell he meant it. 'I'm not trying to scare you, just make sure you stay on your guard. I've got a nose for these kinds of things.' He patted his bulbous nose self-importantly with his index finger. 'Ian got himself into trouble and it got him killed. I've heard that from more than one person. But you're the only one who knows why. Or at least something about it.' He squeezed my hand and his eyes grew narrow under the caterpillar eyebrows. 'You need help, darling.'

I chewed my lip. Why shouldn't I trust him? He said he was

worried about my well-being, and I was making lousy progress on my own. Whatever he knew, I needed to know it, too.

'I really don't know much,' I whispered. 'Only that Ian was involved in some deal involving a painting. A valuable painting. I don't know if it was stolen or if he was fencing it for someone or what he was doing. But he took fifty thousand dollars from the IPS safe in the office and no one knows why or where it is. I think his death was related to the painting or the money. Or both.'

Nigel whistled softly. 'Fifty thousand dollars. That's a bit of dosh. Ian, my boy, what were you up to?'

'It's ancient history,' I said. 'They're going to write it off as a loss in New York. There won't be any more discussion about it or any investigation into his death, either. Whatever he was involved in was obviously reckless and my bosses don't want to mess around with the Foreign Ministry.' I finished off my glass of wine.

Nigel poured me another drink immediately. 'Well, it's not over,' he said, quietly, 'because that painting is missing. Ian never delivered it.'

I was listening to the song on the radio. It was 'Moscow Nights'. The song they'd played at the restaurant. The one Philip and I had agreed would be our song.

Philip ... had our dinner been only two nights ago? It seemed more like two years. Right now I would give anything to be talking to him instead of Nigel who, at the moment, seemed to be speaking in riddles. I needed someone with Philip's precise, incisive mind to set me right in all this.

'You think I know where it is?' I said.

'Claire.' Nigel laid a hand gently on my arm. 'I don't think you understand what I'm telling you. I'm worried there is someone *else* who thinks you know where it is.'

That registered. 'Someone broke in here and took some things of Ian's,' I blurted out.

'What?' He looked startled. 'What did they take?'

'His mail. Bills, mostly. The photographs of Baron von Müller. Some mail of mine, too.' I didn't say what it was. Nothing about my mother's letters, nor anything about Sasha. My mother's callous behaviour and her ignoble past were a private family matter.

'The photographs? Bloody hell! We need them.'

'Need them? Why?'

'They're proof,' he said. 'Proof the paintings really exist.'

All this furtive whispering under cover of the music, like something out of a bad spy movie, was making me jittery. I was drinking more wine than I ought to, if I wanted to keep my wits about me, but I knew I wasn't going to slow down. I knocked back another glass of wine, slightly giddy by now. 'I don't understand?'

'Do you remember the date on those photographs?' he asked.

I closed my eyes and tried to recall the spidery writing on the back of both photos. 'I think it was six-twelve-forty-seven. June the twelfth, 1947.'

'Wrong,' he said. 'It's December the sixth, not June the twelfth. You're doing your dates American style. Europeans write the day first, then the month.'

'Sue me. What difference does it make, six months?'

'Everything,' he said. 'I found an article written about ten years ago concerning the art collection of a certain Baron Caspar von Müller. It seems he had the largest private collection of Old Master paintings outside a museum in all Nazi Germany.'

'Do you mean Ian found a painting belonging to von Müller?'

Nigel looked exasperated, as though I'd just stolen his thunder by telling the punch line of his joke. 'Don't rush me,' he hissed. 'Or you're not going to understand.'

'Sorry.'

'On June the eighteenth, 1947 there was a fire in von Müller's castle. The place was gutted. Burned to the ground. Von Müller claimed he lost everything, including his entire art collection. It was a national tragedy.'

The radio slid into some hauntingly weepy music and things clicked into place. 'One of Ian's photos shows von Müller in a room full of paintings,' I said slowly, 'a photo that was taken *after* the fire. He found a painting the whole world thinks was destroyed forty-five years ago. '

Nigel nodded. 'And Bob's your uncle.'

'Why are you so sure those paintings are from the Baron's

own collection? Maybe that photo was taken somewhere else. You said yourself the pictures on the wall were nearly impossible to identify.'

'You're right, I'm not absolutely positive. That's why I wanted to borrow the photographs from you. I thought I could send them to a chap I know in London who could enhance them for us.'

'We don't even know what we're looking for,' I protested.

Nigel raised his eyebrows. 'You do,' he said. He paused and added, 'Don't you?'

I couldn't evade him, not after all this. 'You won't believe it if I tell you.'

'You'd be surprised what I'd believe, my dear,' he said in a dry voice. 'Try me.'

It was going to sound preposterous. 'I think,' I said, 'that Ian found a painting by Jan Vermeer.'

'A *Vermeer*?' Nigel's voice rose above a whisper, verging into the screeching zone. 'Good God Almighty! Have you any idea how *priceless* ... I think there are only something like thirty-five Vermeers in the *world*!' He sat back in his chair and fanned himself with his hand. He reached for the bottle of wine and poured out glasses for both of us.

'I know,' I said, 'and you certainly can't buy a painting like that for fifty thousand dollars.'

He looked at me like I was born yesterday. 'You can in this country,' he said. 'Fifty thousand dollars here is like fifty million anywhere else. Or even five hundred million. And that's presuming the, ah, seller knows the value of what he's got, of course.'

What an idiot I was. A couple of hundred bucks in the land of the nonconvertible and utterly worthless rouble made you a king or queen.

'So someone stole the Vermeer from von Müller's castle?' I asked. 'And brought it here?'

He shrugged. 'I should think it's trophy art. You know, after the war and even during it, the victors plundered the museums and national treasures of everyone they conquered. They've been doing it since the Romans started it. Conquer a country then strip it of the works of art which are its glory. Except the Romans, instead of hiding it, used to bring their booty back to Rome and carry it through the streets of the city in a triumphal procession.'

'I guess Ian found the same article you did, about the von Müller collection,' I said.

Nigel smiled cryptically. 'Not exactly, my dear,' he said. 'He wrote it. The story has a London dateline.'

Now things were really slotting into place. 'Ian was our London bureau chief ten years ago. And he was quite an art connoisseur.'

"Then he probably knows a good number of galleries and art dealers in London.'

'He was there for a visit the month before he died,' I said. 'I found some credit card bills with charges made to London stores . . . maybe that's when he made his deal, or whatever it was.'

'I've got my sources in the art world looking into that.' He made it sound like he had a fleet of minions at his disposal combing the lanes and back streets of London, though I did get the feeling he might have rehearsed that line in front of the bathroom mirror for maximum impact.

What he said next, though, was dead serious and this time it did scare me. 'You need to mind your back, love. I'm worried for your safety until we find it.'

My safety? As in, I might end up . . . like Ian?

'Nigel,' I said, panicked, 'surely whoever broke into my room must know by now I don't know anything about the painting?'

'The photographs,' he said. 'You had the photographs.'

'I don't know anything,' I repeated. 'If I did, I'd have the painting by now, wouldn't I? And I *don't*!'

'Calm down, darling, calm down. Of course you don't.' He patted my hand. 'I didn't mean to get you all upset.'

'Do you think the painting is still in Moscow?'

'You mean, did it make it to its final destination?'

I nodded.

Nigel got up and went to the freezer for the vodka bottle. He really meant to tie one on. I'd hate myself in the morning for this. But tonight, I didn't care. He cracked the Stoli out of the freezer and brought it over to the table. Then he got two clean glasses out of the armoire.

I didn't say anything. He was thinking. I could practically hear the gears whirring in his head.

Finally he said, 'I would guess it's still here. Let me tell you why.' He seemed, suddenly, comfortingly paternal. 'If it made it to London, there'd be no reason for someone to rifle through your hotel room. The only other possibility . . .' He paused.

'What?'

'Is that it's still in transit and is neither here nor in Britain.'

Great.

'What in the world makes you think we can find it?'

'There are other people involved in this,' he said. 'Whoever had the painting, to begin with, and whoever was going to end up with it. And I'll bet Ian had help.'

'Ian was pretty much of a hog when it came to limelight,' I said. 'I bet he was trying to pull off the whole thing by himself. The rescue of a priceless painting by Jan Vermeer . . . that's exactly his kind of thing. But evidently he did get the painting from someone and he was clearly trying to get it to someone else.'

'Any ideas?'

I shrugged. 'Ian being Ian, it was probably a museum in London. He was very philanthropic like that. He thought art should be accessible to everybody. He'd go nuts when some rich company or investor would buy a fabulous painting at one of the big auctions, then stuff it in a vault or hang it in their bedroom so no one else would ever get to see it again.'

'Claire,' Nigel said seriously, pouring two hefty shots of vodka, 'you can forget about the Robin Hood thing. The painting was stolen from Caspar von Müller. The whole world thinks it's been destroyed. No museum would touch something that hot.'

We clinked glasses and drank. 'Then I give up,' I said. 'I don't have a clue where he got it or where he was delivering it.'

'You need to *think*!' he hissed. 'Tell me everything, absolutely every detail you remember about your last conversations with Ian. You must know something. Some clue, something you didn't think was significant . . .'

It occurred to me then, in one of those belated flashes of

sobered-up awareness we all have when seriously in our cups, that I'd never asked Nigel how he knew so much about the hushed-up details of Ian's death, or how, even, he'd divined so precisely that it had something to do with a missing painting. And his connections in London ... who were they? The good guys?

Why, exactly, *should* I tell him everything I knew?

What if he were dyed more darkly than I'd ever suspected and his reasons for wanting to find the painting had nothing to do with feelings of friendship for Ian or me?

What if I were sitting here, having a chummy tête-à-tête, with the wrong person?

Maybe the danger he had warned me about was right here in this room.

Maybe the killer was Nigel.

I started to stammer some kind of reply, but I guess he could read minds.

'Darling,' he said, 'I don't blame you for not trusting me. But please, you must believe that I have only your best interests at heart. I'd be absolutely destroyed if anything happened to you. Don't you worry, love, I'm going to find out who's behind this.' His chest actually puffed out a little as he said that, in a swashbuckling Errol Flynn way that was so ridiculous it was charming. 'And when I do, they'll have to deal with *me*.'

I know he meant it but I couldn't imagine anyone, unless it was some kid with a water pistol, feeling too threatened by Nigel, all five feet five inches of him, a man with the cushioned physique of the Pillsbury Dough Boy and the seeming gravitas of Elmer Fudd.

But here he was, my self-proclaimed knight in shining armour, for better or worse. My alcohol-induced terror of a moment ago now seemed overblown. To be rescued by Errol Flynn was the stuff of movies.

I had Nigel.

Still, my head was spinning, not only because I was spooked by what he'd told me but also because of four glasses of wine and three vodka chasers. 'Nigel,' I said, 'can we finish this in the morning? I can barely think.'

He left shortly after that, making me promise to erect my

little chair barricade again in front of my door. If anything happened, I was to scream as loudly as I could and he'd come running. He'd even offered, quite nobly, to sleep with me for my own protection. I declined and opted for having Kisya share my bed, which she did, sleeping on my feet on top of the covers.

My nightmares were bizarre, crazy, disconnected. I dreamed Sasha was chasing me through the streets of ... I think it was London, hunting me down, threatening me with ... a paintbrush? I think Caspar von Müller and even Jan Vermeer were there in the fog-shrouded background. But then everything became incoherent and the screen in my mind went blank.

I slept, finally, the dreadful, heavy sleep that comes with utter exhaustion and leaves you tired beyond words when you wake up. The day fitted my mood precisely. Blustery, grey, rainy, gloom-filled. My cold was worse than it had been yesterday. My head was stuffed with cotton and it felt like someone's foot was on my chest, pressing against it so hard I had to fight to breathe. I stared out of the rain-spattered window in my living room, nursing an extremely nasty hangover, chewing on a piece of black bread and some of Tanya's homemade whortleberry jam. A barge left a muddy wake as it passed under the Kalininsky Bridge in the dull first morning light. Moscow, on a rain-wrecked day, seemed suicidally depressing.

I finished breakfast, got dressed, and left to get my car at the guarded parking lot on Kutuzovsky after dismantling the chair wall in front of my door. I needed groceries at one of the hard currency grocery stores. My refrigerator was more empty than usual.

The elevator was still out of order. There was no one at the *dejournaya*'s desk, either. I had to search for the one unlocked stairwell on the eleventh floor and then grope my way down the semi-dark staircase, like I was exploring a cave. Above and below me were disembodied voices and echoing footsteps, but I met no one. The way Nigel had talked last night, I half-expected someone to leap out of the darkness and pounce on me, so my heart was hammering in my chest like a tom-tom. Then I heard someone a floor or two below me push the

232

creaky lobby door open and the comforting sound of early-morning bustle in the Ukraine's seedy lobby.

When I got back from the grocery store, I left the Volvo in the Ukraine's parking lot instead of driving back to the office like I usually did. Surely it couldn't be too risky to leave it here just this once? No one would steal it in broad daylight. Anyway, I'd move it to the Kutuzovsky compound later on.

So I left Ian's car facing the river near the statue of Taras Shevchenko, among the Ladas and Moskvichs and Zhigulis, and shrugged off the hard stares of the taxi drivers who leaned against their battered cars and watched me. I was crossing the parking lot when I saw him. It unnerved me so much that I tripped, over nothing I think, and then on cue he looked up and came toward me. He was carrying a plastic bag with a logo from one of the *beriozkas*.

'Hello, Philip.' My voice was supposed to sound cool and composed, except he'd seen that stumble. He must have been shopping in the Ukraine's crummy *beriozka*. Vastly more downmarket than the one at the Mezh, it didn't seem like a place he'd bother with. They sold mostly touristy stuff and a few items of food like Danish butter cookies and outrageously expensive caviare. And, of course, alcohol. But it was a long way from the university to come here to shop.

'Hi.' He leaned down and kissed me on the cheek. He smelled of musky cologne, something masculine. 'I was just up in your room.'

'*In* my room?' I said it too sharply.

For a middle-aged man who'd just climbed up and down twenty-two flights of stairs, he looked unaccountably perky.

'Well, no, not *in* your room. I knocked on the door but you weren't there.' He looked at me curiously. 'I wanted to leave you these.' He handed me the *beriozka* bag. I opened it. Sweaters. His sweaters. 'You said you didn't have any winter clothes. It's going to snow soon, you know. Today or tomorrow, for sure. You need something warm.'

It was just about the last thing I'd expected. Especially after what had happened the other night. I'd thought that had ended it and I'd never hear from him again. And Victoria? What about her? What was he doing here, anyway?

Maybe he was doing exactly what he said he was doing.

233

Bringing me his warm sweaters because he was worried about me. It was a sweet, thoughtful gesture.

So I took the *beriozka* bag and thanked him and said he shouldn't have done it.

'You looked so cold the other night,' he said, 'I've been worrying about you.' He took my arm and we started walking toward the entrance of the Ukraine. 'By the way,' he added, 'if you're not doing anything right now, I was wondering if you'd go with me down to the Arbat? I need to buy a wedding present for my niece . . . I could use some help choosing a gift.'

He was smiling at me, completely beguiling, and I think that's when the ground started to dissolve under my feet. 'I'd love to.'

What a pushover.

Then I said, 'But first I need to get these groceries upstairs.' I hoisted the bags I was carrying in each hand. 'You know, obviously, that our elevators don't work.'

'Your service elevators do,' he said brightly.

The service elevators.

'I'm glad you found them,' I said. 'Why don't I take all this stuff upstairs and I'll meet you in the lobby in about ten minutes?'

Somehow I thought he'd offer to help me with the bags but he just said, 'All right. I'll have a stroll around your little park and then I'll see you inside in ten minutes.'

So I lugged the bag with his sweaters and my two sacks of groceries up to my room, in the service elevator this time, while he played tourist in the park. Zoya had been in to clean and Kisya was gone. The tube of lipstick I'd left for Zoya on the big table in the living room was gone, too. I walked quickly through the suite, looking at everything, but it didn't feel, as it had last night, like anyone had been here combing through my things again. So I locked the door and ran back to the elevator, downstairs to where Philip was sitting on the low marble balustrade waiting for me.

We took his car, a Lada, to the Arbat. He parked near the Metro station across from the Praga Restaurant, half-on, half-off the sidewalk. There was a crowd around a Russian jazz band playing in front of the Praga. They were playing 'In the Mood' and they were good.

I had been to the Arbat before when I'd had a Saturday or Sunday off. I liked the quaint pedestrian street with its eighteenth-century sherbet-coloured gingerbread architecture and pink cobblestones, liked the life and vibrancy that was so un-Soviet, that bit of bolshie rebelliousness that gave you hope about this place. The Arbat tried hard to be as hip as Greenwich Village or Soho but this was Moscow so the poverty and shabbiness bled through the façade and you saw the desperation, even in the chat-up lines of the fast-talking pedlars who hawked everything from Red Army medals to individual tampons. It was packed, as usual, and we had to thread our way between the card tables where they did business. When I'd been here on my own I'd felt like a walking target, as though a 'Made in USA' sign were hung around my neck, a magnet for all the slick young men standing nervously at their stalls, calling to me in bad English, naming their prices in dollars, at first sweetly cajoling, then heckling when I didn't buy.

'Hey, what's wrong, sweetheart? You no finding this in America. This is good Russian stuff. Genuine, the real McCoy. How much you pay? I make you a deal. Come on, honey, let's talk.'

Hugh had warned me not to get caught paying for anything in dollars. 'It's illegal,' he said. 'Russians aren't allowed to own hard currency. If the police catch you, it's a currency violation.'

So I kept my hands in my pockets and continued my stroll, shaking my head, smiling regrets, which only earned me more catcalls.

Philip and I left the jazz band as they swung into 'Chattanooga Choo-Choo'.

'What do you want to get her?'

'Get who?' Philip seemed distracted, staring at a row of kitschy paintings of St. Basil's and the Kremlin painted in surrealistic neon splashes of colour, propped up along the outside ledge of a chemist's shop window.

'Your niece. The wedding present, remember?'

'Oh.' He put his arm around me and pulled me to him. 'I don't know, actually. Something Russian.' We walked by a sad-eyed woman selling an antique silver samovar. Philip whistled. 'That's magnificent.'

235

He asked her how much she wanted. Her price was stratospheric and she wouldn't budge when he tried to bargain with her. 'This belongs to my family. It is very old, very lovely. You will not see others like it,' she said in Russian. Then she added, quietly defiant, 'It is worth my price.'

'No, thanks,' Philip said. He turned to me. 'Let's go. It's too much.'

'She doesn't want to sell that samovar. She has to,' I said, turning to look back at her as we walked away. She was standing where we'd left her, like a statue, holding the samovar and staring at nothing. 'She looks like she really needs the money.'

'Claire.' He gently propelled me forward. 'They all need money. Look around you at the poverty.'

'Then why did you try to bargain with her?'

Philip looked surprised. 'Hey! Why shouldn't I? Supply and demand, the free market and all that. The one street in Moscow where capitalism is king. No one's forcing her to sell. Is she better off if she doesn't sell her samovar at all?'

'No. Yes. I don't know ... it's just so heartbreaking to see.'

'Look, we talked about this the other night,' he said, turning me so I faced him. 'The Communists did this to themselves, to their own people. No one forced them. It's a sad situation, pretty pathetic actually, but it exists. You're not going to change it. The sooner you accept this place for what it is, the easier it's going to be for you to live here, darling. There's nothing wrong with taking advantage of an opportunity that presents itself ... like that woman selling her samovar.' He kissed me on the forehead and then put his arm around me again. 'Come on.' We started walking. 'I really need your advice for this wedding gift. I'm hopeless at these things.'

We stopped at various stands, little card tables where anything you wanted or didn't want was for sale. Once or twice Philip kissed me absently on the cheek. He asked my opinion about everything in such a sweet, tender way that I was falling back under his spell again, the way I had on that late-autumn day we'd spent, light years ago, strolling across Harvard Yard.

The only thing that didn't add up in all this was Victoria. Wasn't he going to move in with her or something? The way she'd talked, they were practically engaged. But Victoria, stunning as she was, wasn't exactly ... how shall I put it? ... discreet.

'Who *cares* what kind of sexy underwear her new boyfriend wears?' Annabel had moaned to me one day. 'I don't care if it's a G-string or Doctor *Dentons*, I wish she'd keep it to *herself.*'

'You mean Philip? She told you about Philip's underwear?' I'd asked.

'*Jeez*! That was the *least* of it. She was yakking away in my ear about their latest gymnastic orgy while I was trying to listen to the briefing. You should see my notes. I kept writing down what she was saying, instead of what the translator was saying. He was talking about economic reform but you'd think I was taking notes at a *porno* film.'

Maybe Philip didn't like the whole world knowing how cute his underwear was. Personally, I'd always thought he was a pretty private person. Maybe he'd had enough of his bedroom tactics being broadcast all over Moscow.

So we kept walking and looking until finally we decided to get his niece a Palekh lacquered papier-mâché box whose cover was an exquisite painting of a scene from the fairy tale of Ruslan and Ludmilla. Philip didn't know the story so I told him about Ruslan, the knight, rescuing the beautiful princess Ludmilla after she was kidnapped from her father's castle by the evil dwarf Chernomor, and being rewarded with her as his bride.

'It's perfect for a wedding gift,' I told him. 'See, the painting shows the wedding feast when Ruslan and Ludmilla marry at her father's court in Kiev.' With my finger I traced the gold filigree work outlining the miniature scene with its glowing jewel colours of knights on horseback with billowing capes, richly dressed ladies-in-waiting, and a sumptuous banquet table surrounded by noble-looking guests.

Philip paid for the box and gave it to me to put in my bag. We were only halfway down the Arbat. 'Do you want to walk some more?' he asked. 'There's a Georgian tea house further down on the right. We can go there for tea.'

I nodded. We passed a photographer posing two people beside a four-foot tall Marlboro cigarette box. Opposite him, a long snake-like queue of people had materialized. I couldn't see where it began.

'Why are they queuing?' I asked.

'Ice cream,' Philip said. 'An American company opened an ice cream parlour here. Just like home.'

'You're kidding?'

'Nope. It's great stuff.'

I smiled.

'Look,' he said, 'wait over there by that guy with the cigarette box. I'll be right back.'

He disappeared into the crowd before I could stop him. I looked for him, but he had vanished completely. One guess where he'd gone. I stayed where I was told and watched for him, trying to stay out of range of the Marlboro photographer's camera after assuring him twice that I did not want my picture taken with either the cigarette box or with his assistant dressed in a bear costume he had stashed in a plastic bag.

I looked through the crowd again, shifting from one foot to the other. The queue was hours long. Philip wouldn't be back until dark. The photographer's assistant showed up, dressed as a clown. Then I saw David Manning.

He was with a woman and a little girl, both of them obviously Russian. Even from a distance I could see that the woman was a beauty. Dark-haired and slender with fair skin and fine, delicate features. The child, who looked about six or seven years old, was sitting on Manning's shoulders, her arms twined around his neck. He was holding on to her wrists. As I watched, the woman turned towards him and laid a hand on his arm, laughing up at him with unmistakable affection, sharing some joke. I saw him throw back his head and laugh too, as though she'd just said something incredibly funny. He never did that at work. Then he swung the little girl down from his shoulders and buried his face in her neck, kissing and hugging her. She held out her arms to be picked up again, so he did. She snuggled on his shoulder, clinging to him like a little monkey and I saw the black patch, like a pirate's, over one eye.

That would be Yulia, then, the little girl whose surgery he

was financing. And her mother would be ... his girlfriend? I looked away, embarrassed to have spied on them in a moment of intimacy. He looked like a man out for an afternoon with his beautiful wife and daughter. All this time I'd thought he hibernated in a cave when he wasn't working, and instead he had a knockout Russian girlfriend. Annabel had never mentioned he was romantically involved with Yulia's mother.

'Claire!' For a panicky moment I thought it was Manning calling my name. Then I saw Philip, holding two vanilla ice cream cones. He handed one of them to me. 'You moved.'

'I was violating the photographer's personal space. I had to. How did you get these so quickly?'

He smiled, a heartstopping forgive-me-anything smile. 'I paid in hard currency so they let me go to the front of the queue.'

'Philip!'

He leaned over and licked the side of my ice cream. 'I know, I know. But it's only an ice cream cone, not a samovar.'

I still didn't want to walk past that queue licking my ice cream.

He figured that out. 'I'm sorry, darling. Let's forget the tearoom. I'll take you there another time.'

In front of us, the photographer found a mother who wanted her child's picture taken with the bear. The assistant began to transform from clown to bear. Manning and his Russian family had disappeared.

'Okay.'

We walked slowly back to Philip's car. 'I'm going away,' he said. 'Probably for a week.'

'Where are you going?'

'I'm following Napoleon's route to Moscow. Except I'm doing it backwards, of course. I've already been to all these places but I want to go again now since it's the time of year when Napoleon and his army were actually there. By the time they retreated after Moscow burned to the ground, they were starving and without supplies, a disorderly mob dragging themselves through ice and snow, desperate to escape the brutal climate. I want to get a sense of what it must have been like.'

239

'But it's not even snowing.'

'It will. Mark my words. Today or tomorrow. That's why I wanted you to have those sweaters.'

He drove me home in soft, grey twilight. 'How about dinner this evening?' he said. The look in his eyes was unmistakable. He meant dessert, too.

'Uh . . .'

'So it's yes.' He grinned, cocky and absolutely sure of himself. 'I need to get back to the university just now, but what if I come by for you around eight?'

We pulled into the Ukraine's parking lot.

'Eight. Sure. Eight would be fine.' But something didn't seem right. Why was he doing this again? He knew I'd turned him down the last time we went out. Was he, after all, another 'in it for the chase' guy like Simon, and I'd never realized it? Was that what this was all about? 'I'll see you later then,' I said, and reached for the door handle.

'You're forgetting Jenna's gift.' He held out his hand politely and I had the oddest feeling he'd thought I actually planned to keep it.

I was completely flustered 'Sorry, I forgot I had it.'

'That's okay.'

I put the Palekh box in its cheap cardboard packaging in his hand and he slipped it into his coat pocket.

'You'd better wrap it up really well,' I said, 'otherwise it might get damaged in the mail. It's so fragile.'

'I have an old friend from my Air Force days who flies in here quite regularly with some of the official delegations that come to Moscow. He's flying the Vice-President into town for some meetings next week on Air Force 2. Those guys have diplomatic immunity and none of their luggage is ever searched. He'll take it for me, it won't even go through the postal system.' Philip sounded almost dismissive and I was embarrassed that I'd asked.

'Well, that's lucky,' I said inanely.

Then he leaned over without a word and kissed me so savagely that it hurt. I couldn't breathe, but I felt like I didn't want that punishing kiss to stop, either.

Finally I pulled away when he was nearly drawing blood on my lips. 'I have to go,' I gasped.

'No.' He bit my earlobe and began devouring my neck with his tongue and lips. His hands raked me everywhere.

'Philip . . .' In a minute we'd have the entire taxi rank of the Ukraine standing around the car watching our little X-rated display until the windows steamed up. I groped for the door handle. I managed to open it and we both practically fell out of the car.

He pulled back just in time and grabbed my arm. 'We'll finish this later,' he said. 'I'll see you at eight.'

I fled to the hotel.

By seven o'clock I was having, as Tanya and the Yuris would say, a big nervous over this dinner. I took a shower to see if it would calm me down.

It didn't.

Then I couldn't decide what to wear. The dressy clothes Victoria had loaned me were, shall we say, jail-bait provocative. They were also the only winter clothes I had that fitted me. If I wore anything of Annabel's or Paula's, who were either taller or larger than I was respectively, I'd look about as sexy as dirt. No offence to them, of course.

Well, call me vain.

I ended up choosing a stunning close-fitting teal sweater dress with a thick brown belt and a pair of heavy brown leather boots. One look in the mirror and I knew I was asking for it. I'd have to prise him off me with a crowbar.

Or maybe I didn't want to.

The phone rang as I was putting on my makeup. I ran to the living room to answer it.

'Claire, I really need to see you.'

I had no idea who it was, but he'd clearly had a drink or two. 'Philip?'

'It's Nick Ivory. Meet me at the entrance to the National Hotel. Half an hour. It's important.'

Then the line went dead.

Chapter Seventeen

I drove to the National Hotel with butterflies in my stomach.
Philip would be furious that I'd stood him up, but that couldn't
be helped. I'd called his room at the university and there was
no answer. He was probably on his way over to get me. I'd
apologize later.

Whatever Nick wanted to tell me, I bet he didn't want me to
bring a chaperone.

He was waiting outside the front door of the National as I
drove up. He walked around the car and tapped on the passenger window. I unlocked the door and he got in.

'How about a walk on Red Square?' he asked. 'Why don't
we park by the Historical Museum?'

It was only on the other side of the square, across Prospekt
Marksa. We could have walked from the National. 'Sure.'

I saw his profile silhouetted against the light from a street
lamp. He didn't look drunk at all. In fact, he looked quite
sober and grim. Like he was about to tell me something
unpleasant.

I parked the car and we both got out and started walking up
the cobblestoned hill toward Red Square. Softly swirling
snow, fine as dust, was beginning to fall. Philip had been
right.

We reached the edge of the square. The gaudy domes of St
Basil's and the Kremlin towers with their glowing ruby red
stars looked like children's cutouts pasted on the skyline, lit
against the backdrop of the blue-black sky and softened by the
confectionery snow. It seemed unearthly, a fantasy. Nick was
pulling me into this surreal place of dark passions and ancient,

bloody history to tell me some secret he didn't want the listening walls that surrounded us everywhere to hear.

'I got your message,' he said. 'Or should I say messages? I heard you called our London office, not to mention the Moscow bureau, at least half a dozen times.'

He tucked my arm through his and we began walking toward Lenin's mausoleum because that's where he wanted to go. 'Have you ever seen the changing of the guard at Lenin's tomb?' he asked. Tourist stuff. What was he trying to pull?

'No.'

'They're about to do it now. It's quite a little ceremony. Come. Let's watch.'

I don't know why he wanted to do this when clearly there were other matters we needed to discuss. But now we were among a small crowd of Russians and a few tourists who had gathered to watch precisely this event, so talking was impossible. I think he wanted it that way. He must have known there were a million questions I wanted to ask. Why was he making me wait? We could see the changing of the guard any time. They did it every hour.

I looked at the clock tower on Spasskaya Bashnya, the Saviour's Tower. Nearly eight o'clock. The only noise in this vast, lonely square was the soft hissing of falling snow and an occasional murmur from someone in the crowd. Then, eerily, there was the echoing sound of footfalls from somewhere in the darkness by the Saviour's Tower. The noise grew steadily louder, clicking sounds on the cobblestones, until two soldiers and an escort carrying rifles and dressed in long grey coats, white gloves and high black boots, swung into view. They goose-stepped toward us with military precision that made my skin crawl. Nick must have felt me shudder because he laid a hand on my arm and squeezed it. Exactly as the clock struck eight, the two new guards did some nifty trick of footwork that I didn't quite see, so all of a sudden they were standing where their predecessors had been, on either side of the door to the mausoleum. Then without missing a beat the escort and the two retiring guards began their vacant-eyed goose-step back into the darkness of the Saviour's Tower.

'Have you ever seen him?' Nick asked softly after the

243

haunting echo of the soldiers' boots on the cobblestones had faded. He was standing with his back to Lenin's tomb and the Kremlin wall so the floodlights were shining behind him, leaving his face partially shadowed. There was a fine dusting of snow in his hair and on his clothes, which the strong light turned to tiny diamonds. He glittered in front of me.

'Who?' I asked.

'Lenin.'

'No.'

'They change his tie.'

'They do *what*?'

'Change his tie. He's dressed in a business suit, preserved under glass for all eternity. But from time to time his keepers decide his tie is getting a bit tatty looking, so they change it. You know, jazz him up a little.'

'How absolutely fascinating.'

We stared at each other then he said, 'Walk away from this, Claire. You don't know what you're getting involved in. It's too dangerous.'

We were moving again, a little stroll around Red Square on a snowy night, taking in some fresh air. Two friends, maybe two lovers. Who would guess?

'Are you the one who searched my room?'

'Oh, God. Someone searched your room?'

'Yes.'

'You really *are* in trouble.'

We were in front of St Basil's now, standing next to the monument dedicated to Minin and Pozharsky, the two patriots responsible for leading an uprising in the early-1600s against the Poles who invaded Russia and captured the Kremlin. 'Do you know where the painting is?' I asked.

'Bloody hell, Claire. Of course I don't,' Nick said sharply. 'How did you find out about it, anyway?'

'It's a long story,' I said. 'So how about we skip that part and maybe you can tell me why Ian got involved. What's this all about, anyway?'

He grabbed my arm and said in my ear, 'Keep walking. And look like you're enjoying yourself.'

'I'm not.'

'Well, pretend.'

244

'Look, Nick,' I said, irritated. 'I didn't ask to get stuck in the middle of whatever this is.'

'You and me both,' he said. 'I got the deathbed confession. That's how I found out.'

'*What*?'

'Claire.' He took my hand and looked around, like he was enjoying the scenery. 'First tell me what you know.'

'Very little,' I said. 'Ian took fifty thousand dollars from the safe in our office and I think, illogical as it sounds, he was trying to buy a painting by Jan Vermeer. And now half of Moscow is trying to find it because no one knows what Ian did with it.'

Nick scanned the crowd around us again and groaned. 'God,' he said, 'that bloody Vermeer.'

Red Square, fascinating as it was, was occupying entirely too much of his attention. 'Are we being followed?' I asked.

'I don't know.'

'Nick,' I said, urgently, 'tell me what this is all about? Please.' My head swivelled around, too.

'Don't do that,' he said, 'just act natural.'

Oh, sure. Natural.

Then he said, 'Did you know Ian was working on a book before he died?'

I nodded.

'A couple of months ago, he and Victoria went to Smolensk on a research trip. I happened to be there at the same time. We were all staying in the Intourist hotel, of course. Their room was down the hall from mine. One night the power blew in our section of the hotel so Ian and I went to find the Commandant or whatever they call the guy in charge. The clerk at the front desk sent us to the bloke's office. When we walked in on him, he was, shall we say, sharing a biology lesson with one of the maids. He was pretty embarrassed at being caught with his pants down and insisted right there that we move to the next room for a friendly drink. So we left his girlfriend looking for her underwear and went into this other room.'

'Do I need to know all this?' I asked.

'Of course you do,' Nick snapped. 'Now listen. The bloke was ... well, a peasant, really, but he had this incredible

245

painting on the wall. You could tell it was from the Dutch School, but I wasn't quite sure who ... anyway, it was pretty dim in there, despite the fact that his part of the hotel had lights. So we're knocking back the vodka with this chap who probably needs to be told to come inside when it starts raining. I figured at first that the painting had to be a fake.'

'But it wasn't?'

'No.' Nick's hair was covered with snow by now. He looked like Father Frost in the Russian fairy tales. 'We talked about it back in my room and Ian said just for kicks he'd see what he could find out about it. I didn't give it another thought. But Ian went back to Smolensk specifically to have another pint with Igor and told him he knew the painting was stolen.'

'Stolen?'

'Stolen. And, of all the weird things, Ian knew the chap it belonged to.'

'That's impossible,' I said, 'Caspar von Müller is dead.'

If Nick was surprised I knew about von Müller, he didn't show it. 'His son isn't. He's a fifty-year-old art dealer in London.'

We were passing in front of GUM just now, but far enough away that we avoided the lights of the building, cruising the edges of the shadows. I stopped walking and turned to Nick. 'His son?'

He pulled on my arm. 'Keep moving,' he said. 'Does "Harold Miller" mean anything to you?'

'Yes,' I said slowly, 'it does. Are you saying he is Caspar von Müller's son?'

Nick nodded. 'A German name, especially considering who his father was, isn't a huge asset in Britain,' he said. 'We have a long memory when it comes to the war.'

'Ian wrote Miller's name on the back of the folder that held the notes for his book,' I said. 'It was next to Georgy Zhukov's name. You know, Marshal Zhukov, the war hero? Ian drew arrows between the two names. I figured Miller was probably a historian who was an expert on Zhukov. I never connected him with von Müller. Or the Vermeer.' I put my arms across my chest and hugged myself. The cold was starting to bite. 'So what does Harold Miller have to do with Zhukov?'

'Zhukov was in charge of Soviet Occupation Forces in Germany after the war and ran the Soviet Military Administration there,' Nick said. We had come full circle and were walking past Lenin's mausoleum again. The snow was falling faster and thicker. 'Zhukov, along with everyone else who showed up to carve up what was left of post-war Germany, helped himself to anything of value he could steal. The spoils of war.' Nick leaned over and brushed snow off my hair. 'The Sovs felt the Germans owed it to them. They sent in special "trophy brigades", art historians, to make sure they only took the best stuff. They had lists.

'Zhukov, being the big boss, was able to siphon off art that was supposed to go back to the Hermitage and the Pushkin and divert it to his *dacha*. He took hundreds of crates of stuff. Jewellery, paintings, furniture, silver, the lot. Supposedly his place looked like a small museum. At the same time, his popularity at home was growing, he was a real war hero and his troops loved him. When Stalin realized this, he became so jealous he decided to get rid of Zhukov. So he got Lavrenty Beria, the head of the secret police, to stage a raid on Zhukov's *dacha* and then had Zhukov denounced for stealing stolen art, if you can believe that. Beria ordered all of Zhukov's war booty to be confiscated, then Stalin exiled him to Odessa in disgrace.'

'And the things Beria took . . .?'

'Disappeared. Vanished into thin air. Nobody knew what happened to them.'

'Until Ian found them.'

'Ian found only two paintings,' Nick corrected. 'I told you, there were crates and crates of plunder. Still, he found the two most valuable works of art in the entire collection.'

'*Two*? You mean there was another painting beside the Vermeer?'

He seemed surprised. 'I thought you knew?'

I shook my head.

'Igor said his cousin had another painting, in his barn of all places,' he said. 'God, can you believe it? The other painting was a Bellini, Giovanni Bellini. A madonna and child . . . Ian just about cried when he heard the bloke left it where it was exposed to cold and heat.'

247

'Nick, I'm lost.'

'Look,' he said, 'it's taken me a while to put this thing together, too. Ian left out one or two details which would have helped considerably when I had the pleasure of meeting Harold Miller last week.'

'You met him?'

'Unfortunately.'

'What do you mean?'

'Harold Miller thinks Ian was having him on. When I showed up at his shop on Bond Street, he wasn't exactly cordial. You'd have thought he'd be grateful to the man who tried to help him recover his father's lost art collection. But he turned out to be quite a nasty piece of work.'

'I don't get it,' I said. 'Why?'

'Because the Vermeer Ian sent him ...' Nick paused and said softly ' ... was a fake.'

'A *fake*? You mean, Ian made a mistake?'

'Ian said he didn't. He took the painting to an art historian in Moscow, some Russian he trusted, and the chap said it was the real thing.'

Oh, God.

'What was his name? The art historian, I mean.'

Nick turned toward me but the shadows obscured his face so I couldn't read the expression. 'I don't know.' He paused and said, 'You want to tell me?'

What was I going to say? 'I think it might have been Alexander Nazarov. He works at the Tretyakov and knew Ian from the Wolverhampton auction.'

Nick shook his head. 'Nah. It's someone else, then. Ian didn't tell me his name but he said the chap worked for the Pushkin.'

We were starting on our third slow loop around Red Square. Another crowd had gathered to watch the changing of the guard at nine o'clock. My feet were blocks of ice and my fingers beyond feeling. In the distance I watched three new soldiers goose-stepping towards Lenin's tomb.

An hour. We'd been talking for a whole hour and I understood less than I had when we'd started. The soldiers arrived in front of the entrance to the mausoleum and the clock on Saviour's Tower began to chime.

It wasn't Sasha. Thank God it wasn't Sasha.

'So based on this art historian's say-so, Ian was sure the Vermeer was genuine?' I asked.

'Ian,' Nick said, as the crowd around us evaporated into the snow shadows, 'had taken the precaution of photographing Igor's painting. He told me to take the roll of film from his jacket pocket when I was with him in the hospital. The Vermeer wasn't in museum condition, for one thing. There was mildew in one corner. He was really upset about that. The painting Miller got didn't have the same wear and tear, so to speak.'

'Someone forged the Vermeer and switched it?' I said. 'That sounds almost impossible.'

'Well, you and Harold Miller agree on something,' Nick said gloomily. 'And guess what else he thinks?'

'Don't tell me. That Ian did it?'

Nick nodded.

'But that's stupid,' I said. 'Why would he offer Miller the painting in the first place, then deliver a fake?'

'According to Miller, Ian used the painting as bait to get him to provide cash, supposedly to pay off Igor. Miller figures Ian scammed him out of forty thousand dollars and gave him a phoney painting. Miller thinks Igor is some figment of Ian's imagination.'

'And the Bellini?'

'Miller said he wasn't dumb enough to fall for that ploy a second time. So Ian borrowed fifty thousand from your office to pay Igor's cousin . . . the price for the second painting went up . . .and was going to take the Bellini to London himself. He said if Miller didn't want it, he'd sell it for more like fifty million.'

'I don't get it,' I said. 'What was in this for Ian?'

'Originally Miller promised him a finder's fee. He'd already paid ten thousand dollars, I think it was. And he had something Ian really wanted . . . information he'd promised to reveal in return for his father's paintings.'

'The Amber Room,' I said flatly. 'Miller knows where the Amber Room is.'

'My, my, you *are* a clever girl.'

'Ian would have the story of the century then, wouldn't he?' Bingo.

'Until it all went wrong.'

'Who faked the painting? Who even knew about it?' I asked. I didn't really like the choices on that list. 'Igor? His cousin? The art historian? Victoria . . . you?'

'Or you.'

That threw me. 'Me? I was halfway around the world when this happened! How could I be involved?'

'The painting went to America first, then it was sent to London. In the regular post, if you can believe it. How do I know you weren't the recipient in the States?'

'Oh, come on, Nick! That's ludicrous! I loved Ian . . .'

'I cared about him, too,' he snapped, 'or I wouldn't be here with you right now, strolling around Red Square like a pair of sitting ducks. Come on.' He scanned the horizons of Red Square again. 'We've got to get out of here. We've been here entirely too long. Look, why don't you meet me at my place tomorrow morning, say around nine? Do you know how to cross-country ski? There are trails in the woods near where I live. We'll have to finish this conversation then. It'll be more private.'

I looked around us. Red Square was now practically deserted. Behind us, the lights on St Basil's went out and there was blackness where it had been bright, as though someone had suddenly snuffed a candle. 'I don't have any skis,' I said. 'Who's following us?'

'You can borrow my wife's.' He took my arm and steered me toward the Historical Museum where we'd left my car. 'No one, I hope.'

'Do you know who did it?' I asked. 'Swapped the painting and . . . murdered Ian?'

He shook his head. 'Ian said he was reasonably sure he still had the original Vermeer when he sent it to Miller. It was only out of his hands when he left it with that chap from the Pushkin. The courier, the person who got it out of the country for him, didn't even know what it was. Ian said someone with diplomatic privileges at your Embassy owed him a favour . . . crikey, Claire, you know what Ian was like. He figured he was getting the painting back to its rightful owner, so what he was doing wasn't really illegal. Ian had his own ideas about morality. He'd feel no twinge of conscience about this.'

'Yes, I know. The Robin Hood of Moscow. But who . . . how . . .?'

'He thought maybe someone at Miller's end did it . . . maybe Miller blabbed about the painting, that it was coming to London, and someone intercepted it.'

We were at my car, which had become a shapeless hulk under the snowfall of the last hour and a half. Nick started to clear the windshield with his gloved hand.

'I think Ian left a brush somewhere,' I said. I unlocked the door and groped around on the floor at the back until I found it. Nick took it from me and cleaned the snow off in slow, methodical strokes.

'What about the Bellini?' I asked. 'David Manning has been through Ian's apartment with a microscope, looking for the money. And this is Ian's car. There's no painting here or in his apartment. So where do you think he stashed it?'

I saw Nick's face clearly in the harsh light of the search-lights on the Historical Museum. He looked like he'd aged ten years since we'd started talking. 'I think he gave it to someone. I think he was trying to tell me who when his Gestapo doctor came in and threw me out. He said Ian was too ill for visitors. I never got another chance of a word with him.'

'What about Victoria?'

Nick snorted. 'Hardly! She may be a knockout, but she's not too bright. Ian would never have trusted her with something like that. Besides, the only way Victoria would have been interested was if it was something she could wear. She's a bit obsessed by her wardrobe, in case you hadn't noticed.'

I let that go by. 'Then who has it?'

'Beats me.' My car had a new sugar dusting of snow on it, just from the few minutes we'd been talking. 'You'd better go,' he said. 'We'll talk tomorrow.'

'Can I give you a lift home?'

Nick shook his head. 'No, thanks. My car's back at the National.'

'I'll drive you there.'

'Better not.'

'You do think someone's following us, don't you?'

'Not while we were in Red Square. But let's not take any

251

chances.' He leaned over and kissed me on the forehead. 'You know, when Ian asked me to take the film that day in the hospital, I don't think he realised he was going to die. I think he thought he would beat whatever he had and then finish this himself. He really thought he was invincible.'

'Yes,' I said. 'He would.'

Nick waited until I got in my car and slowly backed out on to Prospekt Marksa. Then he disappeared into the shadows of the snowy night. Walking back to the National, I suppose.

I drove back to the Ukraine in a kind of numbed state of panic, checking my rear-view mirror to see if the same head-lights made the turns I did and stayed with me.

No one tagged along.

It wasn't actually that late, just before ten o'clock, when I pulled into the Ukraine's parking lot. To hell with it, tonight the car was staying here. I was spooked enough not to want to make that solitary hike from the guarded lot at Kutuzovsky back to the Ukraine.

There were people in the brightly lit lobby, just like any other Friday night, and I had company in the elevator, a couple of Germans. The door to my room was locked, as I'd left it.

I could feel my heartbeat slow down to something not too far above normal.

I stepped on the piece of paper lying on the floor where it had been shoved under my door.

WHERE ARE YOU?

Underlined twice. Angry writing. Philip must have come and gone. I'd apologize tomorrow. Tell him it was an emergency and I'd had to work or something.

Kisya slipped in behind me and went straight for her dish under my desk. She finished the scraps in her bowl, then came back and rubbed against my ankle.

I didn't want to be alone tonight so I scooped up the cat and walked down the hall to Nigel's door. Even before I knocked, I knew he was out. There was no slash of light under his door. I went back to my room and wrote on a piece of paper that he should come for a drink when he got in. Then I slid it under his door, as Philip had done with his note, and went back to my room.

Tomorrow I'd see Nick again and we'd finish this discussion, then after that I was going straight to Sasha. Maybe he knew who Ian had talked to at the Pushkin. He was my brother, after all.

He'd help me.

At precisely midnight Nigel banged on the door. I flew to it before he woke up anyone else on the floor. Usually he was quieter.

I opened the door, ready to shush him, and Philip stumbled in.

'Where've you been?' he said. His voice sounded thick. It could have been dulled anger or maybe he was a bit drunk.

'Uh ... work. I'm sorry, I tried to call but I guess you'd already left. It was an emergency ... I'm really sorry.'

He was staring down into my eyes with an odd expression on his face as though he didn't see me at all and was looking right through me at the same time.

'Are you all right?' I tugged at his sleeve and tried to pull him over to the couch, but he didn't budge.

'Where were you?' he said again.

'I told you, I had to work.'

'We were supposed to have dinner,' he said. 'Did you eat?'

I'd been too hyper to eat, or actually remember to eat. 'No.'

'Good,' Philip said, 'because I've brought dinner for you.' Then he bent and kissed me as savagely as he'd done earlier in the car. He meant to finish tonight what we'd started then. I'd never realized, in all the years I'd known him, what a physically strong man he was. And a heartbeat later I knew he had no intention of letting me escape. He would do what he wanted.

When we finally stopped that marathon kiss, he murmured roughly, 'As for me, you're my dinner. I plan to devour you completely, the price you'll pay for standing me up.'

Then he lifted me in his arms and carried me into the bedroom like a rag doll. For most of the hours and hours we spent that night locked in each other's arms in my lumpy bed, I could have sworn he was oblivious to my presence. He seemed almost self-contained, primally programmed for a night of rough, bruising sex. He was a fierce and skilled lover, technically adept at manipulating me until I cried out from pain and pleasure. Touching, stroking, caressing, kissing me everywhere . . . exquisitely.

But he was overwhelming me and I kept feeling as though I were drowning in him, that he really was, as he'd said, devouring me until I was completely used up. Once, when I caught my breath, I imagined the end of this torrid session of hardcore sex and knew it would be cold. I also knew I could not stop this until he wanted it to end, which I found vaguely frightening.

It wasn't that he neglected me, or any of my desires or wants. No, he anticipated everything perfectly, read me like a book. But he was using me and I finally understood it. What he was doing to me was utterly devoid of passion – I mean the feeling of passion, of love, of caring, of . . . wanting.

There was a time when my mind went blank and I no longer thought about him, either. Just used his body to obliterate all my gnawing fears and apprehensions, let his driving intensity crowd out all rational thought about why I was letting him do this to me, leaving only my own wild need to escape the demons that chased me.

Unexpectedly he sat up and it was as though a switch had clicked off.

'I'm going to fix you something to eat,' he said, and touched the tip of my nose with his finger. 'Stay here.'

He got out of bed and padded naked into the living room. There was almost nothing in my refrigerator. At best, we were going to have bread and jam. I got up and followed him into the living room. He was getting something out of his coat pocket.

'I don't have much to eat,' I said.

He turned around. 'Hey! I thought I told you to stay in bed?'

I stopped in my tracks. He'd sounded angry. 'Oh. Sorry.'

He held up what was in his hand. 'I've brought you some caviare. The best,' he said. 'You have black bread, of course?'

'In the armoire.'

'I'll get it. Now back to bed.'

I did as I was told. I heard him rummaging around in the other room. 'Finding everything?' I called.

'I'm fine.'

254

He came back into the bedroom a minute later and sat on the edge of the bed. 'There's something I want to ask you,' he said, and bent to kiss my breasts. I pulled his head down and thought we were going to start all over again until we heard the crash in the other room.

Philip's head came up instantly. 'What was that?' he said sharply.

'I don't ... my cat!'

'Your *what*?' He shoved me back against the pillows and ran into the living room. He swore violently and then I knew he was going to unleash that volcanic temper of his that still terrified me.

I ran into the living room after him. The caviare, what little was left of it, was smeared all over the carpet. Kisya, fizzy-tailed with fury, was on the back of the sofa, hissing at Philip who'd picked up the empty jar and was aiming it in her direction.

'Don't!' I cried.

He didn't even turn around but hurled it at her, full force.

It hit her on the side of her head and she yelped. She fell off the back of the sofa and scrambled out of the room into the hallway, flattening herself until she was completely under the armoire. I think she was hurt, though I hadn't been able to tell if she was bleeding.

'You hit her!' I shouted. 'How *could* you? What did you do to my cat!'

'Your goddamn' cat ate my caviare,' Philip shouted back. 'How could you be so stupid as to keep a cat in a hotel room? Do you know how much that cost?'

'I don't care what it cost, you had no right to hurt her!'

'I had every right in the world! She's a goddamn' stupid animal!'

'Get out of here!' I screamed. 'Get out right now!'

Philip turned to me and raised a hand. 'Don't tell me what to do.' His mouth was contorted with fury. I'd never seen him in a rage like this.

I stumbled backward and shielded myself behind a chair. 'Philip, don't!'

The outer door burst open. Whoever it was hadn't even bothered to knock.

'Darling! Are you . . . oh my God!'

Nigel to the rescue.

'What,' said Philip venomously, 'is one of the Seven Dwarfs doing in your room?'

We were quite a little group, standing there. Philip and me, completely naked, and Nigel, in a ratty-looking striped bathrobe and scuffed bedroom slippers, carrying a lamp from his room which he held as if prepared to conk someone over the head with it.

'Nigel, don't throw that!' I shouted. 'Please, don't throw that! Everything's okay.'

Behind him, I saw Kisya scramble out from under the armoire and disappear down the hall. But she was moving in a peculiar way and I figured Philip had injured her more than I'd realized.

'Oh, I can tell that,' Nigel said. 'A regular little scene of bliss, this is.'

He was managing, quite manfully I thought, to keep his eyes riveted to my . . . face. Philip's, too.

'Is Jack the Ripper here your boyfriend, love?' Nigel asked neutrally.

'Philip Robinson,' I said, 'meet Nigel Bradford, my neighbour.'

Philip looked at me, a look to freeze over hell, and said, 'I'm leaving. I'll get my clothes and go.'

'That sounds like an excellent idea,' Nigel said. He took off his bathrobe and handed it to me. 'Put this on, love. You look like you could do with a cup of tea. I'll make it for you while we wait for Mr Robinson to depart.'

He walked over to the hotplate and I cried out, just in time, 'Watch it! There's caviare all over the rug.' Nigel stepped around the mess and I went over to the armoire to get some paper napkins.

Luckily the rug was already stained enough that one more wouldn't show. I was on my knees scrubbing at it when I heard Philip return.

'I'll see you, Claire.'

I stood up. 'Tonight was a mistake,' I said. 'I don't want to see you any more.'

He stroked my hair. 'I'm sorry I lost my temper,' he said

gently. 'You have to let me make this up to you.'

'Tea's ready,' Nigel snapped.

Philip looked over at him. 'I'll be going then.' He bent and gave me an absolutely soul-melting kiss. 'Tonight was magic,' he said, 'you're really something else. I'll call you.'

Then he turned and walked out of my room, closing the door behind him.

Chapter Eighteen

Nigel handed me my tea. 'How about a shot of vodka?' he asked.

'No, thanks.' I sat down and drank the steaming tea. I didn't look at him. Finally I said, 'I don't want to talk about this.'

'Your boyfriend has a hell of a temper, love.'

'I know. I used to work for him. He isn't always like that, Nigel.'

'I'm not going to tell you your business, Claire.'

'Okay.'

'Are you . . . hurt?' he asked.

I shook my head. 'He was furious with Kisya for eating his caviare. He didn't know I had a cat in the room and he left it on the table. He hit her with the glass jar. I think she's hurt.'

Nigel looked at me, mute as a sphinx.

'He wouldn't have harmed me.'

I know he didn't agree. But all he said was, 'It's nearly six in the morning, love. I'm going back to bed. First I'll have a look round for Kisya, though.'

'I'll come, too.'

'Not dressed like that you won't.'

'Wait, then. I'll put some clothes on.'

But though we looked in all her favourite hiding places, neither of us could find her.

'She's got a million bolt holes,' Nigel said. 'She'll turn up later, I expect.' Then he stood on tiptoe and kissed me gently on the cheek, like a sweet Dutch uncle, and said, 'You look like you could do with a bit of sleep, too, love. Get some rest and I'll pop in on you later on.'

I waited a few minutes after I'd heard his door close before I turned on the water for my shower. There was water, fortunately. Hot and cold.

I couldn't possibly go back to bed, tired or not.

I was meeting Nick in three hours.

Manning had told me how to get to my new apartment, which was in the same building as Nick's place. He'd said it was more or less a straight route out of the city, heading west away from the centre of Moscow. If I kept driving, I could be in Minsk ... Warsaw ... Berlin.

I drove down Kutuzovsky Prospekt, past the Triumphal Arch commemorating Kutuzov's victory over Napoleon and the circular museum with its panoramic murals of blood and carnage depicting the Battle of Borodino in the summer of 1812 when Napoleon still thought he could possess Moscow. The road changed names. It was now called simply Marshal Grechko. The scenery changed, too, from city to country. I drove past snow-covered forests of pines and birches.

I don't know what I was expecting the first time I saw my future home. I knew the building was new and modern. Why did I think it would be any different from all the other behemoth Soviet bunkers that dominated the outskirts of the city? Big, ugly, white. What did I expect? Something Tudor? Victorian? Colonial? A colonnaded entrance with a graceful fountain in front?

It was a dump. It was massive and hulking, with all the charm and character of a minimum security prison. It was huge, a giant rectangle of at least twenty storeys, set well back from the main road, accessible only off a slip road. It was picturesquely located in the middle of a construction area, ringed by unfinished buildings with giant cranes atop them like grotesque, prehistoric birds. The detritus of ongoing construction was heaped in a huge pile in front of the building, now softened by the snow. It looked suspiciously permanent, someone's twisted idea of post-modern sculpture.

I parked my car in between an overflowing rubbish dumpster and a small construction trailer and crunched through the snow to the first entrance which was on one of the short sides of the rectangle. The lobby was as cheerless as the exterior of the building, grey concrete with the usual bank of dilapidated mailboxes and two elevators. I pushed the button to call one of them and watched the lights until the door opened.

I almost collided with Paula. She was clutching a fistful of syringes. Annabel had told me that when Ian had been in the hospital she and Manning had taken him syringes, Western syringes they'd brought in their luggage. Otherwise he would have gotten reused Russian ones ... something like the way junkies shared needles.

'Who ...?' I couldn't finish. The look on Paula's face scared me.

'Nick.'

'What happened?' My mouth was sawdust.

'He was drinking at the National again last night. He wrapped his car around a lamp post near Mayakovsky Square. He never should have been driving. They said he was blind drunk. Thank God no one else was hurt. It's ... not so good.'

I said, without thinking, 'I don't believe you.'

She was stunned. 'Do you think I'm making this up? That's pretty rotten, Claire.'

I was about to open my mouth and tell her I'd been with Nick minutes before he got into his car last night and that he'd been sober as a judge, but then I thought maybe it might be better not to mention our little frost-bitten stroll around Red Square. So I said instead, 'No. I didn't mean that ... it's just that it's such a shock.'

Paula reached over and squeezed my arm. 'I know.'

'How bad is he?'

'Unconscious. He was haemorrhaging pretty badly when they brought him in. I don't know ...' She stopped and looked at the syringes in her hand. 'I'm taking him these. I'm on my way now.'

'I'll come with you,' I said, 'we can take my car.'

She shook her head. 'Actually ... it would be better ... I mean, there's something else.' She paused and I knew what was coming next. 'Rebecca. Nick's wife. We've been trying to find her. She's got to get here as soon as possible. And somebody needs to tell her what happened.'

She waited.

'You want me to do it.' Tell some kid who still counted her

260

marriage in days that her husband was bleeding to death in a Soviet hospital where they probably didn't have a clue what to do for him. I closed my eyes. When I opened them, Paula was watching me with that serene, clear-eyed look of hers and I knew she understood what I'd been through with Kathleen's death and Ian's and that I still wasn't over them.

I shrugged and said helplessly, 'Of course. I'll try to track her down.'

'Thanks.' Paula squeezed my arm again. 'I think she's on assignment somewhere. She was in Italy but I remember Nick saying something about Paris. You might call Gamma, the French photo agency. She freelances for them from time to time.'

Annabel took one look at my face when I walked through the door to the office and put a hand to her throat. 'Oh my God,' she said, 'what happened?'

Rebecca Ivory was in Paris. Someone at Gamma gave me the phone number of a friend of hers named Céline and it turned out she was staying in Céline's apartment somewhere in the Latin Quarter. When I finally got through to Paris again, Céline told me in heavily accented English that Rebecca was out having lunch *'avec des amis'* and one didn't know when she would return. *Quelle dommage*, she regretted she couldn't be more *'exacte'*. So I told Céline it was urgent, but I didn't say why and left my number in Moscow.

Then Annabel chain-smoked and I wore a path in the carpet in front of one of the windows that looked out on Kutuzovsky Prospekt and watched the snow sift past the window like it was never going to stop. Every time the phone rang we both jumped and I kept rerunning last night's conversation with Nick through my head in a continuous loop until I drove myself nuts. I never actually saw him get into his car. He'd just *said* that's where he was going. I'd offered to drive him there, hadn't I? But he'd turned me down because he'd said it wasn't a good idea for us to be seen together. So did he change his mind after he left me? Did he go back to the National and have another drink ... or ten or twelve, given the condition Paula said he was in, according to the hospital?

Rebecca called first. She had the cut-glass English accent of money and breeding and the breathy, whispery voice of a little girl. She took it better than I'd expected. She did not fall apart over the phone. Instead she said she'd book a flight immediately and call back with the details. Then she asked if, perhaps, someone could pick her up at Sheremetyevo because of all that business with rogue cab drivers. When she called back half an hour later I could tell she'd been crying. She said, tiredly, that the first flight to Moscow with a free seat didn't arrive until tomorrow at seven in the morning and it left from Zurich. She was leaving for Switzerland in an hour.

'Bring boots and a winter coat,' I told her, 'we're in the middle of a blizzard.' I heard her gasp. 'I'll have to borrow them,' she said, 'here it's sunny and cool. Perfect late autumn weather.' There was a pause, then she said in that soft, fragile voice, 'When I met Ian last summer he talked about you constantly, Claire. I know you don't know me but I feel as though I know you quite well. Thank you for telling me about Nick.'

It was a relief when the call ended. I don't know what I would have said if she'd asked me when I'd last seen him and if he'd seemed all right. Or anything wifely like that.

I think I would have lied.

I tried calling Sasha after that. No one answered at the apartment. Then I called the main number at the Tretyakov and a slurred voice said that he was *ne na rabote*.

Of course they didn't know where he was. Nor did they care, either.

That left his studio as the only other place I knew of and there was no telephone there.

'I'm going out for a while,' I said to Annabel.

'To do *what*? In this blizzard?'

'I need to see someone,' I said.

'Can't it wait?'

'No.'

I had to dig the car out of the snow, which took more time than I expected because first I had to remember roughly where I'd parked it and then I had to figure out which lump of snow it might be. I finally got it started and out of the parking lot without skidding into any other cars which, let me tell you, was a major accomplishment.

Then I ploughed slowly through the snowy streets of Moscow until I finally pulled up in front of the derelict building where Sasha had his studio. There were footprints by the front door, not terribly recent but several sets of them it seemed, so maybe he was here after all.

My boots clattered on the marble stairs, echoing loudly up the stairwell. The place seemed darker and more forbidding than I remembered. But that other time, I'd been with Sasha, not alone like I was now. Perhaps whoever had been here had come and gone because not a single door was open when I got to the second floor. The hallway was dark and silent.

I turned to leave, then stopped.

What if he were here, working in his studio with the door closed? I should at least rattle the doorknob. And say what?

Did you do it? Did Ian bring the painting to you? Did you tell him it was the real thing, then paint a fake and slip it to his courier?

How could I ask my own brother if he was a thief ... a forger ... a killer?

The door was locked.

I think I was relieved.

I started back down the hall and knew, with sickening fear, that someone had slipped out of the shadows behind me. He must have been there the whole time.

I didn't have a prayer.

I ran anyway, but he was on me in a flash. He clamped a hand over my mouth from behind me and threw his other arm around my waist like a vice.

'*Kto eta?*' His voice was harsh and he jerked the arm around my waist in a modified Heimlich manoeuvre, which hurt. He removed his hand, fractionally, so I could speak.

'Claire Brennan. Please let go of me. I haven't done anything,' I said in Russian.

'American,' he said. 'Who sent you?' His hand dropped away from my mouth, but he hung on to my waist.

'No one sent me.'

'Then what are you doing here?' Another little jerk around the waist.

'Looking ... ouch ... for Sasha Nazarov. Please let go. That hurt!'

He let go of me completely after I mentioned Sasha, and turned me around so I faced him. Hawk-like features, hooded eyes, narrow lips, stringy black hair. Thin as a walking stick. And obviously stronger than he looked.

'Why?'

I felt slightly bolder. This was just another artist with a studio here, not one of the Gypsy's goons. He probably just wanted to scare me. Which he'd done quite well. 'I want to talk to him.'

'He's not here.'

'I know. I was just leaving when you ... ran into me,' I said. 'You have a studio here, too, don't you?'

He nodded. 'Are you with the Englishman?'

'Am I *what*?'

'Are you with the Englishman?' he repeated. 'He was also looking for Sasha.'

'How do you know he was British and not American?'

'I know the difference between a British accent and an American one,' he said in a flawless British accent.

'Oh.'

He spoke again in English. 'So I'm asking, are you also with the Englishman?'

'Er ... no. What Englishman? I mean, who was he? What did he look like?'

'Short. Perhaps in his fifties. Some grey hair, not much. Glasses.'

Nigel.

'No, I'm not with him. Do you know what his name was?' Maybe this guy had prepared a little Welcome Wagon greeting for the Englishman and squeezed his name out of him the way he'd done with me.

No such luck. 'I don't know.'

'What did he want?'

'The Englishman,' he said caustically, 'accused Sasha of stealing a painting that belonged to him. They had a violent argument. Then finally he left.'

'Who? Sasha or the Englishman?'

'First the Englishman. He was shouting obscenities at Sasha, threatening him. I could hear him all the way down the stairs. Sasha waited until he was gone. Then he left as well.'

'Did he say where he was going?'

'Yes. To the Pushkin.'

'The Pushkin? Why?'

The man shrugged. 'He works there occasionally. Well, not exactly the Pushkin Museum itself. But he works for the museum at the Church of Saint Antipii, which is next door.

I asked, with slow dread, 'What does he do there?'

'Oh, once a week, people . . . you know . . .' he gestured in the air with a hand, like he was mixing something '. . . common people, the *narod*, may bring a painting or a sculpture or whatever they wish and for three roubles they can learn its worth and possibly something about its provenance.'

'And Sasha tells them about their paintings and sculptures?'

'Sasha and the other art historians.'

'Oh.'

He looked at me suspiciously. 'Sasha has something of yours, too?'

'No,' I said. 'Do you think he is at the Pushkin now? Or the church you mentioned?'

We were walking down the hall toward the stairs. He stopped outside one of the studio doors. The one that had been open the last time I was here.

'You must be Valery Yekimov,' I said. 'You were working here the other day when I was with Sasha.'

'Yes,' he said. He put his hand on the doorknob. 'If Sasha is smart, he didn't stay long at the Pushkin.'

'What do you mean?'

'I think you are a friend of Sasha's,' he said. 'But that Englishman . . .' He paused as though he were searching for the words. He shrugged. 'That Englishman is trouble.'

The snow had stopped falling by the time I got into my car. Valery Yekimov had nothing else to say about the Englishman, beyond the fact that Sasha hadn't seen the last of him.

How had Nigel managed to track Sasha down? Osmosis? Or maybe he'd been out for a little nocturnal stroll last night on Red Square and happened on Nick and me? Maybe he'd caught up with Nick afterwards and . . .

Nigel? My friend? My protector?

The one who'd stormed into my room, to rescue me when Philip was attacking my cat?

It didn't sound right. Or did it?

I drove back to the office with a heart of lead.

Manning was alone when I got there. Except for my luggage. All of it. I practically tripped over a suitcase when I came through the front door.

I walked into the main office. He was staring out of the window, his back to me. He must have heard me come in but he didn't turn around.

'What are my things doing here? Why aren't they at the Ukraine? What's going on?'

He still had his back to me. 'David!' I practically stamped my foot. 'Why are my suitcases . . .?'

He did turn around then, slowly, and I saw that there was something odd about his eyes. Like he'd been . . .

Funny, isn't it, how you can communicate devastating news by nothing other than the briefest glance?

'Oh, no,' I said, and the rest of my anger died inside me. 'When?'

It seemed like ages before he said, 'About two hours ago. Paula called from the hospital.'

I walked over to my desk and heaped my *chapka*, my gloves, my scarf and Victoria's coat in the middle of it in a big pile. Then I locked myself in the bathroom and cried as quietly as I could until I was completely cried out.

When I came out, Manning was in the kitchen. The phone rang and I answered it. My voice still sounded ragged. It was Hugh, but he sounded worse than I did, old and incredibly weary, asking for Rebecca's flight information. He said he'd talked to Paula and that they'd decided he should be the one to meet Rebecca at Sheremetyvo and take her to the hospital to sign all the paperwork. When he said that I grew cold because it was history repeating itself. I mean, *exactly* repeating itself. Last time it was Manning, Ian, and me. This time it was Hugh, Nick and Rebecca.

Manning walked out of the kitchen then and handed me a cup of tea. 'I put rum in it, along with the honey,' he said. 'I made it pretty strong.'

'Thanks.'

266

'I know this is lousy timing,' he said, 'but they kicked you out of the Ukraine.'

I was in the middle of sipping my tea and choked when he said that. He waited until I stopped coughing.

'Come on,' he said, 'let's go and sit on the couch in the filing room. We need to have a little chat.'

I didn't like the way he said that.

'Where did everybody go?' I said. We were completely alone.

'Annabel went to tell Simon about Nick.'

'Oh, God.'

'I know. As for the rest of the staff ...' He shrugged. 'They took off because of the holiday.'

'Holiday?'

'November the seventh. Revolution Day. Have you forgotten? They're getting tomorrow off, anyway, the sixth, but I sent them home early after ... all this.'

I nodded.

'And now,' he said, 'would you mind telling me what in the hell you were doing "brawling" at the Ukraine at four a.m. this morning?'

'*What*?'

'You heard me. That's the official explanation for your departure. The unofficial explanation, according to Larisa, is that they've got someone who'll pay them more *valuta* for their crappy suite. Wait 'til the Foreign Ministry hauls me in over this. We could really get our ticket punched, thanks to you.'

I said faintly, 'Oh.'

'They could yank your visa in a heartbeat, Claire. So what were you doing?'

What exactly was I going to tell him? The truth was somewhere between humiliating and embarrassing. God, he'd think I was an absolute idiot.

How much did I have to tell him? Our night of torrid sex? Philip hurling the caviare jar at Kisya and wounding her? Or Nigel bursting in on us, stark naked, carrying that lamp like it was a javelin, ready to hit Philip on the head?

'There wasn't any brawling,' I said. 'Just a loud argument.'

'Who were you arguing with at four in the morning?'

267

'Nigel Bradford.' I took a deep breath. 'And Philip Robinson. It was a misunderstanding.'

'Really?' He looked like he wanted to strangle me. 'You were spending the night with both of them?'

'It's not what you're thinking,' I said. What *was* he thinking? An orgy? 'Philip showed up at midnight. I think he was a little drunk. He got carried away.'

'I didn't know you were seeing him,' Manning said icily.

'I'm not,' I said. 'Victoria's ... seeing him, if you mean what I think you do.'

'Your affairs are none of my business,' he said, standing up. 'Unless they interfere with your work or somehow involve IPS. Which, at the moment, they do.'

'I'm sorry,' I said. What else was there to say?

'Save your apology for the Foreign Ministry. See if they believe you any more than I do,' he snapped and walked out of the room.

I sat on the couch for a long time, drinking my cold tea until it grew dark outside the window. Two deaths ... no, two murders. Nick's death wasn't an accident any more than Ian's had been. It had just been staged somehow to look like an accident.

It was a Russian superstition that deaths came in threes. If it were true, there would soon be another death.

Eeeny, meeny, murder ... me?

I was next. I was the only one left who knew about the paintings.

The killer would be looking for me.

Chapter Nineteen

I don't know how long I sat on the couch in the filing room, but it was dark outside when Manning came back and found me.

'Come on.'

I looked up. 'What?'

'Let's get out of here.'

'Where are we going?'

He looked exasperated. 'Are you planning to live here? Come on. You're coming to my place. You can sleep in the spare bedroom tonight. And I'm assuming you might be hungry.'

'Hungry?'

'You know, dinner. Food. You do eat, don't you?'

'Oh. Dinner.'

'Come on,' he said again. He held his hand out to me and without thinking I took it and let him pull me up. 'I've been thinking, you ought to move into Annabel's place after she leaves. Then the new correspondent, whoever that is, can take the apartment on Rublevskoye. For now, you can use my spare bedroom.'

'Oh.'

We were standing by the front door. 'Are you all right?' Manning asked. He picked up my suitcases and carried them into the hall by the elevator.

'It's been a long day ... what are you doing?'

'Bringing these downstairs,' he said. 'Isn't there stuff in them you might want tonight?'

'Oh. Sure.'

'Here.' He threw a key at me and I caught it. 'Why don't you take the stairs while I get these in the elevator? And do me a favour, will you? I've got something simmering on the stove. Can you give it a stir until I get there?'

A man who cooked? That was a surprise. Ian used to hyperventilate every time he got near the kitchen. If he opened a can of tuna you'd think a miracle had happened.

The 'something' Manning had on the stove smelled wonderful. He found me in the kitchen, stirring his pot. It was some kind of spicy tomato sauce.

'I didn't know you cooked,' I said, handing over the wooden spoon.

'My wife was a chef,' he said. 'She taught me everything I know.'

He'd never, ever mentioned his wife before.

He looked up and pushed a lock of hair out of his face with his forearm. 'Red or white?' he said, matter-of-factly. He walked across the kitchen and opened a drawer by the sink. He took out a piece of twine and pulled back his hair into a ponytail and tied it with the twine.

'White, please.'

He got a bottle of white wine out of the refrigerator and uncorked it. Pouilly-Fuissé. He knew his wines. He clinked his glass against mine but didn't say anything.

'Can I help you with dinner?'

'You want to do the salad?'

'Of course.'

It was, I have to say, a slightly bizarre scene of domestic tranquillity, given the state of relations between us, the horrible news about Nick, and my almost paranoid jumpiness when a door slammed, quite hard, somewhere close by.

'My neighbour across the hall just got home,' Manning said. 'Do I need to peel you off the ceiling?'

'Sorry. No.'

'You want to talk about anything?'

'Nick's death is bringing back a lot of memories about Ian,' I said. 'Is this enough salad or should I do more?'

Manning looked at me sharply. 'It looks fine,' he said. He pushed his hair off his face for what seemed like the hundredth time, where it had slipped out of the twine.

'Maybe I should sleep at Annabel's,' I said abruptly.

He set down a knife and turned to me. 'Suit yourself. I think she might be with Simon tonight.' He tried to fix his ponytail again.

'I know how to cut hair,' I said, 'if you're interested?'

He looked sheepishly relieved. 'I didn't have the nerve to ask you, but I'm about ready to take this knife and hack it off myself.'

'I've never cut a man's hair before,' I warned.

'So I'll look like Annabel,' he said. 'Worse things could happen.' Then he left to set the table.

He went to some trouble. A red tablecloth. Two fat white candles. And the dinner, chicken *cacciatore*, was excellent. I told him so, then covered my mouth with my hand to stifle a yawn.

'You didn't get much sleep last night,' he said, 'did you?'

I shook my head. 'No.'

'I know it's none of my business,' he said, 'but I think Philip Robinson is bad news.'

Jealousy. He was jealous of Philip's way with women, just like Victoria said Ian had been. I didn't think he'd be that petty.

'Thanks for your opinion,' I said.

'Why are you so defensive?'

'Why do you care?'

'You remind me of someone I cared about a lot,' he said. 'And I don't want to see you get hurt.'

It was the first time I'd ever heard him say anything remotely emotional and the second time this evening he'd mentioned his wife. At least that's who I think he meant. The woman in the photograph on his bedside table who looked like she could be my sister.

'Annabel told me about the little girl you're helping,' I said to change the subject. 'The one who needs surgery. I saw you with her and . . . your girlfriend on the Arbat the other day. I think it's very good of you to help.'

'You saw me with who?' He ignored the compliment and zeroed in on the girlfriend. He tipped his chair back against the wall and laced his fingers together behind his head. He stared at the dancing shadows the candles made on the ceiling.

In the soft golden light, his profile looked like it had been chiselled out of marble. 'Yulia's the same age my daughter would have been,' he said quietly. 'And I am not going out with her mother.' He set his chair back down on the floor and turned so he was facing me. 'I don't want you sleeping at Annabel's tonight,' he said. 'I want you here where I can keep an eye on you.'

I have to say, the way he said that, my blood ran a little cold. I licked my lips and said, 'Why?'

'I know about the painting,' he said, 'and I'm concerned about your safety.'

'Who told you?'

There were two possibilities. At least two I knew about. And one of them was dead.

He poured the last of the wine into our glasses. 'Nigel,' he said neutrally. 'He's worried about you, too.'

Nigel. Oh, God.

So were they in on this together?

Did he mean the Nigel who'd been skulking around Sasha's studio today? *That* Nigel, who was so concerned about me?

'Claire.' Manning reached over and took my hand. 'I'm not the enemy.' He rubbed a thumb across the back of my hand and his gentleness was unexpected. 'I think we need to get somebody from Embassy security involved in this. I'm going over there tomorrow. In the meantime, Nigel and I have agreed it's best for you to be with one of us.'

I pushed my chair back abruptly. 'Why don't I wash the dishes?' I said. I picked up our plates and went into the kitchen. I heard the clatter of dishes in the living room as he stacked the rest of the things, then finally he came into the kitchen. I couldn't look at him.

I was rinsing off the dinner plates when I felt his hand on my shoulder and it was one of those things that happened so fast I can't honestly remember how it began. But all of a sudden I was in his arms and we were kissing each other. I'm not sure who started the kissing, but I do know neither of us wanted to stop.

We broke apart after a few minutes and I felt like a sixteen-year-old on a first date. Something between terror, ecstasy and stunned disbelief. I turned back to the sink and started filling it

272

with water. He got a dishtowel and came over and stood next to me. I almost dropped a bowl when his arm brushed mine.

We talked about ridiculously mundane things, considering the events of the day and the conversation we'd just had in the living room. But honestly, I don't think I could have concentrated on anything except an almost carnal awareness that he was deliberately postponing the time until we would finish what we'd started with that kiss. So I let the tension in me grow like a slowly tightening coil, and we both knew he was purposely making me crazy with wanting and waiting. We finished the dishes and he took me in his arms again until I was utterly lost in him and I know he was just as lost in me. It was nothing like what had happened with Philip last night, no mindless, punishing, self-gratifying intensity. Finally I pulled away and brushed his hair from his face. 'Do you still want me to cut it?' I asked.

He bit my earlobe. 'Aren't you too tired?'

'No.'

'I'll get the scissors,' he said, but when he pulled away from me, he ran his hands over my body until I shivered.

'Bring me all the pairs you've got,' I said, 'and you need to get your hair wet.' And wondered how I'd ever manage to stay focused on his hair and not on everything else about him.

He brought me three pairs of scissors and then left to run his head under a tap. I heard him whistling 'Delilah' from the bathroom. He came back wearing only his jeans, with a towel slung around his shoulders.

'Is this wet enough?'

'Uh. Yes.' When you cut a woman's hair, she's usually got her clothes on. It is not an erotic experience. Manning was half-naked and he had a great body. I lie. He had a fabulous body. I'm a sucker for a guy with good muscle definition and his was perfect. I draped the towel so I couldn't see as much of him. At least he was sitting with his back to me.

'Can you use any of the scissors I gave you?'

'I think we'll skip the pinking shears. But the others are fine.' I ran my fingers through his hair. Okay, I'll say it. He had great hair, too. Thick. Lustrous. Gorgeous.

The only way this was going to work was if I could just pretend he was one of the little old ladies with blue hair who

273

used to come in to the Nail and Lash. 'What do you want me to do?' I asked.

He turned around and grinned.

'About your hair.'

'Oh. A regular haircut, I guess.'

'I remember your picture from the correspondents' wall in New York. How about if I cut it like that?'

He took one of my hands and kissed my fingertips. 'What a good memory you have,' he said gently. 'That would be great.'

We didn't talk while I cut his hair. I couldn't talk, actually, because I was biting my tongue the whole time. I'm not sure what his reason was. I was nervous as anything. What if I botched it and he looked like someone had run a lawnmower over his head?

But then I started to relax and it was, I have to say, an incredibly sensuous, intimate thing to cut his hair, touch his face, be close to him like this. I left it a little bit long. His hair, I mean. Sort of like James Dean. He looked terrific.

I was still cutting little stray hairs when he said, 'Can I ask you something?'

'Of course.'

'Are you involved with Philip Robinson?'

'No.' I was fiddling with the way his hair fell next to his left ear. 'Can I ask you something?'

'Of course.'

'Was that me you were kissing? Or was it whoever I reminded you of?'

He pulled me around and sat me on his lap. Now we were both covered with wet hair. 'It was you,' he said, 'it's always been you.'

Things got pretty steamy in the kitchen for a while and soon I was as undressed as he was, if not more so. Then little wisps of wet hair which had now dried started floating through the air and sticking to us like we were magnetized. I can genuinely say that there is nothing sexy about kissing someone under those circumstances. It's even worse than trying to look discreet when you're taking tiny fish bones out of your mouth. We were both trying not to look like we wanted to spit.

So we ended up in the shower since it was the only way to

get rid of all that hair and then in bed. I didn't sleep in the spare room, of course. As bruisingly hurtful as it had been with Philip, with Manning it was just the opposite. He poured himself into me, filling the hollow, empty places Philip had neither known nor cared about. He said my name again and again and once, I swear, I thought he whispered that he loved me.

Or did I imagine it, because I wanted to hear it?

He was curved around me and we were both lying on our sides, like a pair of spoons fitting neatly into each other. One of his arms was wrapped around me, his hand on my breasts. His breathing, steady and rhythmic, was soft in my ear. I thought he was asleep.

'Claire?'

'Mmm?'

'There's something else, isn't there?'

I know he could feel my muscles tighten since I was pressed up against him. 'What do you mean?' I said.

'I don't know. But I just have a feeling there's something else that's bothering you.' He reached up and stroked my hair. 'Do you want to talk about it?'

Sasha.

Maybe Nigel had told him something about Sasha and now Manning wanted to see if I'd finish the rest of the story for him. For both of them.

Not my brother.

Not even for him.

At least, not until I'd had a chance to see Sasha first, ask him about this face to face.

'There's nothing,' I said carefully. 'Really. Nothing. David, I'm so sleepy.' I took his hand off my breasts and kissed it.

He turned me over so we were facing each other. I couldn't see his face at all. The room was pitch black. In a way, I was glad. He couldn't see mine, either. His voice was rough. 'You still don't trust me, do you?'

'Of course I do.'

'Whatever you say.'

Then he turned over so he was facing away from me and his message was unmistakable. And even though we were still

275

practically on top of each other in that narrow bed, we spent the rest of the night the way we'd spent most of our relationship.

Miles apart.

The morning after the night before was, well, tense. I woke up early, but he was earlier. I could smell coffee in the kitchen. I found my clothes where we'd scattered them and pulled them on.

I walked into the kitchen. He was drinking coffee at the table. 'Morning.'

'Good morning.' I guess I wasn't going to go over and kiss him. He seemed just a bit forbidding.

'Did you sleep well?' he asked.

Oh, brother. Strained courtesy. 'Very well, thank you. And you?'

'Fine. Can I fix you some toast?'

'No, thanks. I'll do it.'

Over breakfast, we had an enthralling conversation about the weaponry that the Russians were expected to show off during the Revolution Day parade. Tanks. Rocket launchers. Nuclear missiles. Warheads. He did know his stuff, I'll hand it to him. Everything he said was strictly professional, cold, and impersonal as hell.

He didn't touch me or even act like there'd ever been any intimacy between us.

Well, fine. If he could be tough as nails, so could I.

'I'm going upstairs,' he said. 'Come along when you're ready.'

'I need a shower first,' I said. 'Give me half an hour.'

He left the kitchen and then I heard him rooting around in the bedroom. I stayed in the kitchen and drank another cup of coffee. He showed up in the doorway. 'Don't take too long.'

'Yep.'

He left.

I took my shower and, before I went upstairs, I called Annabel's place.

No answer. She must have spent the entire night at Simon's.

The phone was ringing when I walked into the office.

276

Manning was on another line, so I dashed over and picked it up.

It was Paula. She sounded exhausted. 'There's a wake tonight at Ni . . .Rebecca's apartment,' she said.

'A what? A *wake*?'

She knew what I meant. 'Rebecca . . . wouldn't let them keep him at the hospital. They found him on a stretcher on the floor. No blanket over him . . . nothing. It was . . . inhuman. Rebecca became hysterical when she saw him like that. Hugh said there was a big scene with everyone shouting at everyone else.'

It had been nearly that bad with Ian. Except at least he made it to the morgue. Then they froze him into a block of ice.

'So . . . how did they manage to . . .I mean, in what . . .?'

'Hugh took care of it. The AP is having some renovation work done on their offices so he went to one of the construction guys and paid him big bucks to build a makeshift coffin with some of the lumber they had.'

'Oh, God, Paula!'

'I know, I know.' There was a long silence. I heard her take a deep breath. 'Claire?'

'Yes?'

'You should know before you get here . . . they didn't have enough lumber to make a cover for the coffin. I think they're trying to find some more wood somewhere so they can finish it, maybe by tomorrow. But that means tonight it's . . . open . . . so Rebecca only wants his closest friends here.' She paused, then said evenly, 'His face isn't too disfigured from the accident, but I thought it would be easier if you knew before you saw him. Tell Annabel and David, will you?'

Manning had finished his phone conversation. 'I'm going over to the Embassy,' he said. 'I'll be back in a couple of hours. Was that Annabel?'

'Paula. There's a wake tonight at Nick's apartment. His wife is bringing his body back there until they get a flight to London. Paula says he doesn't look too good. She wanted us to be prepared.'

The expression on his face made me think me of the day I'd arrived and we'd gone to the morgue to sign the papers for

Ian. At least now I understood. He must have been through agony that was a hundred times worse when he'd had to identify the bodies of his wife and little girl, but still this would be like going through it all over again. 'You don't have to go,' I said, 'if you'd rather not.'

He misunderstood me completely. 'You can go with Annabel if you don't want to go with me,' he said coldly. Then he walked out of the office and a minute later, I heard the front door slam violently.

Annabel showed up about half an hour later looking, I have to say, completely wrecked. 'You look like hell,' I said.

'I feel like hell,' she said. 'I probably drank enough vodka to float a *boat* down the Moskva River. Ask me why I'm so stupid.'

'Why are you so stupid?'

'Beats me.'

'Are you all right?'

She lit a cigarette. 'I will be,' she said, 'as soon as I get out of this berg. *Jeez*, Claire, this city makes me do completely *meshuggeneh* things that I'd *never* do in New York. You know, it's like ... *voodoo* or something. Why did I ever go to him? I'm a *jerk*!'

The phone rang again and she picked it up. *'Kto eta?'* she said. She looked at me and frowned. She listened for a moment and said, 'Claire, I think it's for you. Do you know someone named Lydia?'

I picked up the phone. 'Claire Brennan.'

It was Lydia. The *dejournaya* from the Ukraine. But it took me a while to understand her because she was either drunk or she'd been crying. 'You must come,' she said. 'You must come. The little cat. Now.'

Then she hung up.

I put the phone back on the hook and Annabel said, 'What's going on?'

'I need to go over to the Ukraine,' I said. 'I'll be right back.'

'Uh, sure.'

Obviously Manning hadn't said anything to her about me being under house arrest. I'd be back before he would, anyway.

I counted on breezing through the Ukraine lobby the way I always had, figuring the guards probably weren't in the picture yet about my unexpected departure.

They weren't.

I took the elevator to the eleventh floor and felt, oddly, melancholy.

There was no one at the *dejournaya*'s desk, but I knew which guest room they all used as a hideaway to drink tea and watch television. Lydia wasn't there, either.

So I tried my old suite.

The door was unlocked. Whoever the new occupant was, they'd already moved in, which made me a trespasser. I took a quick look around the place and called Kisya's name, in case she'd come back to her old home. Then I stepped out into the hall and pulled the door shut.

Out of habit, I walked down the hall to see if there was a telltale slash of light under Nigel's door. There wasn't.

Then I checked all the hiding places where I'd seen Kisya in the past, but I found neither the cat nor Lydia.

Maybe Lydia had been drunk when she'd called.

Maybe she'd taken her lunch hour. It was the day before the Soviet Union's biggest national holiday, anyway. Maybe she'd taken the rest of the day off, and tomorrow, too.

I took the elevator back to the lobby and was heading toward the front door when a man who seemed to vaporize from behind one of the marble pillars came toward me. I moved sideways to avoid a collision, but so did he.

He walked up to me and took my arm. 'Claire Brennan, I presume,' he said. 'I've been looking for you. We need to talk.' His grasp on my arm tightened and he started to pull me toward the front door.

His physical description was familiar. Short, fiftyish, balding with frayed greying hair, horn-rimmed glasses, florid complexion. A dumpling.

English.

'Harold Miller, I presume,' I said, trying to match his coolness. 'You've been making the rounds, haven't you?'

The Englishman is trouble.

This guy looked about as dangerous as a bug you could squash under your shoe. I wouldn't have said he was trouble, more like ... weird, I think. Maybe Valery Yekimov judged him wrong, because he certainly was the one at Sasha's studio yesterday.

It wasn't Nigel after all.

I detached my arm from his grasp. 'Why should I talk to you? I haven't got the foggiest idea where your paintings are.'

'My dear,' he said, 'consider yourself extremely lucky that I ran into you as I did. This is for *your* benefit, not mine. I *know* where the paintings are. Now shall we go some place more ...' he looked around the lobby as though microphones were sticking out of every crevice, which they probably were '... accommodating?'

Trouble or not, he knew what I wanted to know. We walked over to the first of the two sets of doors that led to the outside, stumbling over the snow mats in the dark ante-room. Harold Miller pushed open one of the heavy wooden doors and we went outside together into snow-blinding brightness. 'Where are we going?' I asked.

'Why don't we take a little stroll down there by the river?' he said, as though he were talking about a pleasant amble by the Serpentine in Hyde Park, instead of slogging through the snow-clogged park in front of the hotel.

But the paths in the little park had already been shovelled so we could walk all the way to the Embankment. Snow etched the dark branches of the trees and coated Taras Schevchenko entirely in ermine. The sky was grey-white and heavy as though it had not disgorged all the snow it intended to send down on us. Below, the Moscow River was black and flowing thickly. Except for Harold Miller's vivid red ski cap which had a silly-looking pom-pom on top that bounced as he walked, we receded perfectly into the drab, faded colours of wintry Moscow. There was no one else in the park, no listening ears to eavesdrop on what he wanted to tell me.

'All right,' I said, turning to face him as soon as we reached the parapet overlooking the river. 'Where are the paintings?'

'Not so fast,' he said. 'You know as well as I do where they are.'

'Uh ...' I said, stammering. 'I don't.'

'Come, come.' He sounded playfully cajoling. 'Of course you do.'

'No, I don't. I mean it. I really don't.'

'You've been a step ahead of me the whole time,' he said, smiling. Though I have to say, it wasn't a pleasant smile.

'Beginner's luck,' I said. 'I don't know what you're talking about.'

'What were you doing at that artist's studio?' he asked, the rictus smile still on his face. 'And don't get clever and tell me you wanted to see his etchings.'

My heart skipped a beat, or ten, or twenty. Then I said, 'He sold a painting at the Wolverhampton's auction. I happen to like modern art. So I went to see him. I wanted to buy something from him.'

Miller started to laugh. 'Good. Very good.' Then he leaned his face into mine and grabbed my arm. 'Nice try, angel. Let's do that again. This time, let's be truthful, shall we?'

Yep, he could be trouble all right. Valery Yekimov had been correct.

'All right,' I said carefully. 'I'll tell you the truth. I thought he might know what had happened to Ian. I didn't even know anything about your painting at the time. Ian didn't die of liver failure in that hospital. Someone poisoned him.'

Miller didn't look surprised so I added recklessly, 'You, maybe.'

His face turned an unbecoming shade of aubergine. 'Why, you little ... I'll tell you who did it – that Russki artist, that's who. Nazarov. God knows he's got enough of a motive. He forged the Vermeer and buggered off with it. Now I reckon he's got the Bellini, too.'

'I don't believe you!'

He looked me up and down and said in a mocking voice, 'Oooh, angel. A bit touchy, aren't we? Awfully defensive. So tell me, is Nazarov your lover or something?'

I almost spat out the truth to this revolting toad, but figured I'd better keep my mouth shut. 'I don't know why Ian ever risked his neck for a low-life like you.'

'For the same reason we all do, lovey.' He rubbed the fingers of a gloved hand together in the universal sign for money.

'I doubt it.'

'Look, princess. He didn't turn the money down, okay? So

don't go getting all high and mighty with me.' He shifted his weight and folded his arms across his chest. He cocked his head to one side and the little pom-pom on his hat bounced and jiggled gaily. 'Tell me, where's Nazarov? I want my paintings back. I paid for them, you know.'

'You paid for one,' I said pointedly. 'Ian paid for the other.'

'Either way,' he said. 'I shouldn't have paid for them at all. Now I want them and Nazarov's got them.'

'I don't know why you're so sure,' I said. 'What would he do with them, for one thing? He can't possibly sell them. They're too hot. Whoever buys them is going to have to put them in a vault. Or hang them in their bathroom or some place where no one will *ever* see them.'

'I've been in his studio, angel. I found an extremely rough copy of the Vermeer. Unfinished, but there it was. A regular Han Van bleeding Meegeren. He even had some of the old pigments – colours they used in Vermeer's day. It's child's play, you know, to make a painting appear a few centuries older than it is if you're not overly concerned about authenticity.' He crossed his arms and smiled. 'Turn him over to me and there's something in it for you. You won't be sorry.'

He was lying, I knew.

'Who's Han Van Meegeren?' I asked.

'Dutchman. His specialty was forging Vermeers. He was so good some of his paintings were hung in museums as the real thing. He finally got caught selling a Vermeer to Hermann Goering who was buying it for Hitler. Ironic, isn't it?'

Sure. Real ironic.

If all this were true . . . although why would Harold Miller lie about finding the copy of the forged Vermeer? . . . then Sasha was the one who'd betrayed Ian.

And now I was supposed to turn him in to this . . . munchkin with the Santa hat for thirty pieces of silver.

Turn in my own brother?

I felt like throwing up.

'Listen, my angel,' Miller was saying in a voice that me think of slimy things that crawl out of rivers, 'if you see Nazarov, I want you to get in touch with me immediately. As

282

I said, they're my paintings. They've always been mine. Stalin wanted them for that revolting art museum he was planning to build. Then Zhukov stole them from Stalin, so to speak. Now it's time they were returned to their rightful owner.'

He stripped off a glove and reached into the pocket of his parka. He pulled out a card and handed it to me. His address in London and, on the back, a local phone number. He pointed to the hulking Ukraine. 'I'm staying here,' he said. 'That's my number. Call me if he gets in touch with you. It will be well worth your while, I assure you.' He pulled on his glove and adjusted the pom-pom hat. I think he thought he had the whole deal wrapped up.

'You mean, you're going to tell me what happened to the Amber Room?' I asked.

He looked vaguely surprised. 'Angel, do you honestly think I *know* what happened to the Amber Room? My God, if the Russkis thought I had that information, do you think I'd be standing here with you right now?' He laughed like he'd just said something incredibly witty. It sounded like an animal snorting. 'I have some ideas, of course, but can you imagine me actually keeping it a secret for all these years?'

What a pig. 'You deliberately misled Ian into thinking you'd tell him where the Amber Room was. You let him take risks to get your paintings out of the Soviet Union and you never planned to make good on your end of the deal. How *could* you?'

He held up his hand. 'Shut up, you little fool. Do you want to attract attention?' He took a step toward me and hissed, 'I never said anything of the kind. What I said to Ian was that I'd tell him what I knew. It's not my fault he misunderstood me. I also told him I'd pay him for his trouble in getting out the paintings, and that I did.'

'Well, aren't you a prince?' I said coldly. 'And now he's dead and so is Nick Ivory.'

'Good God!' He seemed honestly shocked at this. 'Not Nick, too? How awful. He came to me in London last week with Ian's roll of film. It's because of those photographs that I'm here now. What happened?'

'He wrapped his car around a lamp post two nights ago after leaving the bar at the National Hotel. Supposedly he was blind drunk, but I was with him just before it happened and he was as sober as you and me.'

'Good God!' Miller said again. He made a hasty sign of the cross and bowed his head.

At least he had a bit of humanity, however microscopic. 'I don't think it was an accident,' I said quietly.

He looked thoughtful. 'Well it's not Nazarov, if someone slipped something in Nick's vodka while he was at the National. No Russian could get in the place unless a Westerner was paying the bar bill in *valuta*, could they?'

'No.' I hadn't thought of that. Thank God, I suppose, for small mercies. I still couldn't buy his accusation that my brother was a thief and a forger, much less the thought that he might be a murderer, too. That he might have killed Nick in cold blood.

And Ian's death?

Who was responsible for that?

'So it's not too likely Nazarov popped into the National for a quick one, which puts him out of the picture so far as Nick is concerned,' Miller was saying. He rubbed his chin with a gloved hand. 'He must have a partner. I didn't think a Russski could be smart enough to pull this off alone.'

I let that pass, under the circumstances. 'You mean a Westerner?'

He shrugged. 'Ian never told me how he got the Vermeer out of this country. All he said was he had a safe way to get it out of the Soviet Union without its being searched, but he couldn't get it directly to England. It went to the States first, and then he had someone drop it in the post. I nearly had a cardiac arrest when he told me what he was doing but he said it was the safest way to go. The US Postal Service and the Royal Mail. Two venerable institutions. The package I got even had a customs declaration: 'Posters: Value, nil'. That's it. Ian made it look like he was sending me Communist propaganda posters.' He snorted with laughter again.

'Where was it postmarked from in the US?' I asked.

'Washington, D.C.'

'I guess that sounds right. Nick said something about Ian using diplomatic channels to get the painting out. But he also said whoever acted as courier had no idea what was in that package.'

'Well, somewhere in this chain there's a rotten link. Nazarov's part of it, but there's someone else.'

'Who?'

'Someone in your little circle of friends, perhaps?' Miller suggested. 'Maybe Ian had a vodka or two at the National, just like Nick, and spilled the beans about his great find.' He shrugged again. 'Who knows? Too bad dead men can't talk.'

I shivered. 'Yes,' I said, 'what a pity.'

'Well, I believe this concludes our little chat, angel. I do hope you'll give me a bell when you find Nazarov. I'll make you the same cash deal I made Ian. I'm prepared to be very generous, you know.'

Oh, sure. Philanthropist of the year.

'What makes you so convinced I'll find him and turn him over to you?'

'I've seen people sell their own mothers for the right price. You'll find Nazarov, if you can. Just don't be stupid and protect him.'

'Don't bet on it.'

'Okay, I won't,' he said shrewdly. 'Now I'm sure he's your lover.'

'You don't know what you're . . .'

'Which has me wondering why,' he continued as though I'd said nothing, 'you would defend him when Ian, who was also your lover, is dead? And Mr Nazarov may not have an alibi for that. So I don't think loyalty's such a big deal for you, angel.'

Harold Miller may have been just above pond scum in the genetic order of living things, but his words hit home like poisoned darts. 'Then you can just keep wondering,' I snapped, 'because I'm telling you for the last time – he's *not* my lover. And he didn't have anything to do with Ian's death, either.'

'Well, then, you'd better hope you find him before I do because after I leave you, I'm going to see a chap who visited me in London recently. At the time I wasn't interested in his little business deal. He wants me to, shall we say, help him get his merchandise into England . . . and I want Nazarov. I think I'm ready to deal with him now.'

'Anyone I know? Someone else in my circle of friends?' It

was quite clear we weren't going to be buddies, so I was a bit free with the sarcasm.

Anyway, I knew what he was going to say. Why I wanted to hear it, I'm not sure.

Harold Miller smiled like he'd read my thoughts perfectly and it struck me for the first time that he had entirely too many teeth in that crocodile mouth of his. 'I have no idea what his Christian name is,' he said. 'I just know him as "the Gypsy". Ta, angel.'

He left me standing by the Embankment, watching his retreating back and that stupid red pom-pom which bounced up and down as he lumbered over toward the group of rogue cab drivers who haunted the Ukraine and preyed on its guests.

Chapter Twenty

I didn't get back to the office before Manning did.

He was sitting at his desk when I walked in. Well, if looks could kill.

'Where were you?' He was furious.

'I'm back,' I said, 'so stop worrying. Nothing happened.' No way was I going to tell him about Harold Miller, which, in turn, would lead to Sasha.

'You didn't answer my question.'

'Lydia called,' I said calmly, 'the *dejournaya* from the Ukraine. She asked me to come over. She said it was something to do with Kisya.'

'The cat? And you went?'

'Oh, come on, David. What was I supposed to do? I can't live under a glass jar like some captive bug. How am I going to do my job?'

'What happened to Kisya?' he asked unexpectedly.

'I don't know,' I said. 'I didn't find either Lydia or Kisya. Maybe she went to lunch or something. Lydia, I mean. So what happened at the Embassy?'

He pulled a paper clip off a pile of papers on his desk. He started bending and unbending it. 'Not much,' he said. 'I talked to some guy who probably reports to a janitor. The Vice-President's flying in with a congressional delegation tomorrow, so they didn't have a lot of time for me. They told me to come back after the holiday and the Vice-President's visit.' The paper clip snapped in two and he threw it in the trash.

'Oh.'

'I want you to stick around here for the rest of the day and write the setup piece for the military parade tomorrow.' He got up and reached for his gloves which were on his desk.

'Where are you going?'

'Out. I'll be back later.'

I didn't see him for the rest of the afternoon so I drove out to Nick and Rebecca's apartment with Annabel.

Hugh answered the door of their apartment. I nearly didn't recognize him, he looked so old. He kissed Annabel and me and I smelled Scotch heavy on his breath. 'They're in the kitchen,' he said.

Rebecca Ivory was tiny and waif-like, with long blonde hair that came halfway down her back and the kind of ethereal, patrician beauty that seems to be inextricably linked with class and wealth and privilege. She was stubbing out a cigarette in an overfull ashtray when we walked into the kitchen. Her eyes were swollen and blotchy, but she seemed in control.

She looked up as we came in to the room and she and Paula took turns hugging Annabel and me. No one spoke until Hugh said, 'Why don't I fix you two a drink?'

So I figured seeing Nick would be rough ... rougher than I'd expected, or Hugh wouldn't have made that suggestion about the drink. I asked for a Scotch, which I almost never drink, and Annabel did the same.

'Thank you so much for coming,' Rebecca said. Her voice was quiet and breathy, the way I remembered it from our phone conversation. She lit up another cigarette and blew out a cloud of smoke. 'I don't know how I would have managed this on my own.'

We made small talk about her flight, the weather, everything but what had happened at the hospital and the coffin in the next room. Then there was silence, so painful it drilled into me, until Rebecca said, 'If you'd like to see him ...'

Hugh spoke up immediately. 'I'll take them.'

She nodded.

Annabel said, 'Could you give me a minute?' She walked over to the large picture window and stared outside. I went over and stood next to her. No stars, but stripes of winking white lights in the distance, some remote part of Moscow,

288

unreachable across a desolate expanse of dark snow and crystallized night air.

'I'll go with Hugh,' I told her. 'Take your time.'

After we left the kitchen, I murmured to him, 'She doesn't want to do it.'

He reached for my hand. 'I know. Do you?'

We stopped outside the partially open door to Nick's and Rebecca's bedroom. A wedge of pale gold light, the reflected light of candles, fell on Hugh and me. I held his hand with both of mine. 'I did it for Ian,' I said, 'this can't be any worse.'

Then we walked into the bedroom.

I do not remember how I got to the edge of Nick's coffin. Hugh must have let go of my hand, or maybe I let go of his, because I think I was standing there by myself. But I do remember . . . in fact, I will never forget . . . Nick's face. A blood-black gash down one cheek, beginning next to his eye socket and ending at his jawline, tidily cleaned up, but all the more brutal and shocking against his nearly transparent white, waxy skin. And his eyelids and lips, lurid purplish blue, like they were painted with ghoulish Hallowe'en face paint.

I closed my eyes and tried to pray for him, but all I could think of was the other night on Red Square, when he'd stood talking to me with his back to the powerful searchlights of the Kremlin and Lenin's tomb, and how the light-shot snow in his hair and on his clothes silhouetted him, making him seem like some kind of shimmering earth-angel. So I stood there for I don't know how long, until Hugh finally came and put his arm around me.

'Okay?' he whispered.

I nodded and he led me out of the room.

Victoria had arrived while Hugh and I were in with Nick. She had just got back from Armenia, after spending thirty-six hours at the airport in Yerevan waiting for a flight to Moscow. She didn't know about Nick until the Russian CBS driver who picked her up at Sheremetyvo told her and then she'd made him bring her straight here. It was the first time I'd seen her without makeup and with her hair slicked back into a ponytail instead of the high-glamour television way she usually wore it, but I thought I had never seen her look so beautiful. Hugh saw it, too, and every time I caught sight of him for the rest of the evening his eyes danced over her until it was obvious how he felt and it was equally obvious that she noticed him about as much as she noticed the paint on the wall.

Then the doorbell began ringing steadily. Word had gotten out and soon the apartment was flooded with people and it was nothing like the intimate gathering Rebecca had wanted. Dishes of food and bottles of wine started appearing in the kitchen, so Annabel, Victoria, Paula and I began setting out plates and silverware and glasses while Hugh stayed with Rebecca who leaned heavily on his arm, introducing her to Nick's friends, getting her a drink when she wanted one, lighting her an endless chain of cigarettes.

I didn't happen to notice when Simon got there but I heard his laughter, startlingly out of place, and then, as though he realized it too, he dropped his voice and I didn't hear him again. I finally caught sight of him, standing in a corner bent over some ravishing redhead, drink and cigarette in one hand, the other on her shoulder. I looked around the room hoping Annabel might be in the kitchen, but of course she just so happened to step into a little hole in the crowd at precisely the wrong moment and got the full impact of the scene in front of her. I saw the hurt, more anguished and raw than she'd ever let on, before she hid it, quick as a flash, behind indifference and a double Scotch, so I knew she was a long way from being over him and, Barbara Walters notwithstanding, he was a major reason she was quitting Moscow.

Not like he cared, either. I wanted to go over and dump my drink on him.

Then Philip showed up, which was as awkward for me as Simon's presence was for Annabel. I tried that nifty cocktail party trick of pretending I didn't see him, but actually it wasn't necessary.

He scarcely paid any attention to me. But, more surprisingly, he totally ignored Victoria too. I will say this, though, he did spend a long time alone in the bedroom by Nick's coffin. I passed by the doorway once and saw him on his knees, his head bowed. When he came out, his face was the colour of ashes.

'That poor kid,' he murmured to me. 'So unnecessary.'

'I know,' I said, 'it's awful.'

We were alone outside Nick's bedroom door. I was leaning against the wall and Philip was bent over me, one hand on the wall above my shoulder. Then he started to say something and I had to move closer to him because I couldn't hear him. He seemed almost incoherent. That's when I looked into his eyes and saw . . . emptiness.

It was the moment in the revisionist version of the fairy tale when the princess discovers the handsome prince really is a toad, after all, and she's glad she isn't stuck marrying him. Philip was a lonely old man. He had no one, no life, no one to love him. Just his work and whatever babe *du jour* he managed to shimmy into bed with. Although after the other night, I sensed his days of being the dashing, devastating, sexy *professeur* on the prowl were closing in on him and he was realizing it, too.

Pretty soon he was going to be just a dirty old man chasing little girls.

But right now he was mumbling something about needing to talk to me, something about the other night.

Just what I didn't want to talk about.

'Darling.'

Her voice was sharp with irritation. We both turned. It was Victoria, hands on hips, looking less than pleased to find Philip draped over me in a corner.

Behind her was David Manning, who'd seen everything and was clearly making something out of nothing. You'd think they'd caught Philip and me having sex. David turned and disappeared into the living room, but Victoria marched right over and glared at both of us.

'I've been looking everywhere for you, darling,' she said, somehow managing to elbow me out of the way and park herself in front of Philip. 'I'm absolutely exhausted. Let's go home now.'

Philip looked at her, like she was an alien who'd just landed from another planet. 'Do whatever you want, Vic,' he said. 'I'm going back to the university. I'll see you both later.' He turned on his heel and left her standing there. Well, both of us, actually.

I didn't think people flounced any more, but that's what

Victoria did. Straight over to the stash of liquor. As for Philip, a minute or so later I saw him shaking Rebecca's hand and she was nodding at him. Then he was gone.

I escaped to the kitchen where there was a small mountain of dirty dishes to hide behind.

I was making a dent in washing the mountain when Hugh came in. He leaned against the counter and watched me. 'Will you do something for me?' he asked.

I dried my hands on a dishtowel and turned to him. 'Anything.' The way he asked I had a feeling I'd just agreed to something I wouldn't be too thrilled about.

'Rebecca wants to sleep here tonight,' he said. He looked at me and added, 'In the bedroom. With Nick.'

'Oh, God. Hugh, she *can't*.' I had a nightmare vision of Rebecca climbing into that makeshift coffin to sleep on top of her dead husband, in a room full of flickering candlelight and the overpowering scent of flowers that now filled the flat like a shrine.

'I know,' he said. He walked over to the table and poured himself another Scotch. I saw that his hand shook a bit. 'We've persuaded her to sleep at Paula's instead. But she insists Nick shouldn't be alone. So ... we told her you and Victoria would ... stay ...with him for the night. I don't think Annabel can handle it and I'm going to the airport at something like five in the morning to pick up Nick's brother when he gets in on the flight from London.'

'Victoria? She's staying?'

He nodded. 'She's on her way to tying one on, unfortunately. She's really beat from her trip and completely shattered over Nick. Poor baby. That's why I want you here, too.'

Right. Mrs Common Sense. 'Sure. I'll stay.'

He smiled tiredly and said, 'Thanks, sweetheart,' and patted my arm. Then he picked up his Scotch and said, 'I'll go back to Victoria. Try to keep her off the booze.'

I stayed in the kitchen. My mountain of dishes grew again and there was more food to put out as new people arrived, and what seemed like hundreds of empty bottles to clear away.

I was drying plates with my back to the door when he came into the room. 'I'll help you with that.' I nearly dropped a plate, but Manning rescued it before it hit the ceramic tile floor. 'Watch it.' He picked up another dishtowel and began drying the plate, just like we'd done last night.

Well, not exactly like last night. The tension was pretty thick between us.

'I was beginning to think you got stuck at work,' I said as casually as I could. 'You got here so late.'

He set his dry plate on top of a stack of clean ones. 'I told Hugh I'd take care of making the arrangements for Nick and Rebecca and his brother to fly to London. It took a while to get through to the airline, what with the holiday tomorrow and all.'

'Oh.' I didn't know he and Hugh knew each other that well.

He walked over to the table and, without asking, poured two glasses of red wine. His fingers brushed mine as he gave a glass to me. 'They leave tomorrow at noon.'

I stared into my wineglass. 'Tomorrow! That was fast.'

'Well,' he said, 'I already knew who to call at the airport for something like this.'

I almost choked on my wine. 'I suppose you would.'

We drank in silence, then he said, like it was an afterthought, 'I'll drive you back to ... my place when you're finished here.'

'Um ...'

'What?'

'Actually, it's Annabel who could use the ride. We came in my car and I'm staying the night.'

His eyes flashed and I think there was anger in them as well as surprise. 'You're staying here?'

'Rebecca wants someone to keep a vigil,' I said. 'Hugh asked Victoria and me to stay.'

'Oh.' He set down the dishtowel and I heard the almost audible click of things shutting down between us. 'I saw you talking to Philip Robinson.'

'That's right,' I said evenly. 'We were talking.'

'I guess I'll go see about Annabel. Good night, Claire.'

'Good night.'

And I went back to my stack of dishes.

The general exodus started soon after that and the apartment cleared out so quickly it was as though everyone evaporated

293

into the heavy fog of cigarette smoke that hung in the air. Paula took Rebecca, now visibly in shock and glassy-eyed from alcohol and grief, back to her place. Hugh left to catch a few hours' sleep before making his second pre-dawn trip to Sheremetyevo in two days, this time to get Nick's brother Sean. Someone from Reuters had called him while we were contacting Rebecca. So now Sean was coming to Moscow for approximately two hours. Manning was leaving with Annabel.

He came over to me just before he walked out the door. 'There's something I should have told you.'

'What is it?' My heart was hammering. What now? Sasha? Harold Miller?

'It's Kisya.' He reached over and took my hand. 'I stopped by the Ukraine to see if I could get her and bring her back to ... my apartment ... now that you're not living at the hotel any more. I ran into Lydia. She told me Kisya had died. She figures she got into some of the exterminator's rat poison. I'm so sorry.'

I hadn't cried about Nick at all this evening, so it seemed absolutely appalling to cry for a little cat. Manning pulled me into his arms and held me and stroked my hair until I managed to stop. 'You going to be all right here tonight?' he asked. 'I can stay, if you want.'

'I'll be fine.' I bit my lip. 'Anyway, you've got to take Annabel home. She needs someone to be with her. She was too upset to go in and see Nick.'

'Sure.' He opened the front door slowly. 'I'll be at Red Square first thing tomorrow. I want you to go straight to the office and stay there, okay? After ... everything's taken care of here.'

I nodded. For a moment, I thought maybe things were all right between us again and he might kiss me.

But he didn't.

After he was gone, I walked back into the living room. Victoria was lying on the sofa on her back, one hand shielding her eyes. I figured she'd fallen asleep.

There were still dishes in the kitchen. I'd clean up there and maybe try to sleep in one of the chairs, or even on the floor.

'How about a drink?'

'You're awake,' I said.

'Um-hmm.'

'A drink would be fine.'

She got up and walked over to a table with several half-full bottles of red wine. She poured two huge glasses and handed one to me. She went back to the sofa and sat in the middle of it, crosslegged. In the pale lamp light she looked exotically hollow-eyed and bewitching.

'I think I'm going to get very drunk tonight,' she said serenely. 'Otherwise I'll never get through this.'

'I know.' I sat sideways in an overstuffed chair across the room, my legs dangling over one arm, and stared out of the picture window at the inky blackness and our mirrored reflections.

'Do you want to sleep?' I asked.

'Do you?'

'I can't.'

'Me neither.'

We drank in silence.

After a while, every little noise made us jump and the silence grew spooky.

'They've got a tape deck,' Victoria said. Her voice sounded unnecessarily loud. She said more quietly, 'We could listen to some music, I suppose.'

I looked at her.

'I know,' she said. 'Bad idea.'

She got up and got the wine bottle again. She divided what was left between our glasses. Then she picked up another bottle. 'Here,' she said. 'Have a little Chianti with your Beaujolais.' She was starting to slur her words.

'I'm going to check on . . . things.'

I got up and walked around and peeked into all the quiet, dark rooms, in that same scared way I used to check for monsters under my bed when I was a kid.

The silence was eerie.

God knows, Nick had a million reasons to come back and haunt us.

Maybe his murderer had been here tonight. Just checking, making sure he'd really done it. Maybe he was one of us, as Harold Miller had implied. Maybe I had given him a glass of wine and he had smiled at me and . . .

I used to do this to myself when I was a kid, terrify myself into near hysteria.

I practically ran back to the living room where Victoria was still sitting – well, actually listing to the right – on the couch. She raised one eyebrow. 'What is it?'

There was another bottle of wine next to her on the coffee table. She was drunk.

'Checking for poltergeists,' I said.

'Find any?'

'No.'

'You slept with him, didn't you?'

The courage and directness of alcohol. Rotten timing for this conversation.

'Victoria.'

'You did.' She sounded challenging.

'Look, I used to work for him years ago. I was one of his research assistants. He thought women were as disposable as ... chewing gum, for God's sake.'

She was watching me with a glassy-eyed look of acute concentration like this was a lecture on thermodynamics or Boolean logic.

Meaning it hadn't sunk in.

'Victoria.' I said, slowly and precisely, 'listen to me. Philip has dumped every woman he's ever been with. You've probably set the record for the longest sustained relationship he's ever had in his life. Six weeks. As brilliant as he is, he's only out for one thing. When he gets tired of a woman ... any woman ... he moves on. He doesn't care about the wreckage he leaves behind.'

'I don't believe you,' she said weakly. 'He told me he cared about me.'

'Open your eyes. The guy would say the moon is made of green cheese if he thought it would get you to go to bed with him.'

'I need a drink,' she said.

'You don't need a drink. You need a cup of coffee.' I levered myself from my chair. 'I'm going to see if there's any left in the pot in the kitchen. Stay there and don't fall over.'

Surprisingly she did and when I came back a few minutes

296

later with two cups of coffee, she took hers obediently and sipped it.

She made a face. 'It's boiling. I can't drink this. Besides, it tastes like paint stripper.' She set it down. 'I'll kill him. That will solve everything.'

'Take a number,' I said. 'I'm sure every woman he's ever jilted feels just like you do. And that's every woman he's ever been with.'

After a moment she said moodily, 'I'm a jerk.'

'No, you're not. You're just dumb. Hugh adores you and you won't even give him the time of day.'

She pulled back in surprise, eyes bright and angry, and I thought she was going to make some sharp retort. But instead she pressed her lips together tightly and stared into the depths of her coffee cup.

When she looked up again, she was clear-eyed and calm.

'I never saw Ian before he left Moscow,' she said, 'to say goodbye. Like ... this.'

We were really blazing a trail through the minefield of hot topics tonight, weren't we?

I managed to say steadily, 'You're lucky. You can remember him as he was.'

'I heard a weird rumour,' she said. 'I heard that some people think maybe his death was ... not because of liver failure.'

I didn't say anything.

She flopped on to her back and folded her arms across her eyes. I thought she had fallen asleep. Then I heard a long, slow breath. 'He never got over you, Claire.'

I said, after a moment, 'It was liver failure. But it was because he ate something that was highly toxic, not because he drank like a fish.'

'What?' She sat bolt upright and put a hand on the coffee table to deal with the vertigo. 'You mean, like food poisoning? Oh, God, poor Ian! I had that once. They had to med-evac me to Helsinki. I was sick as a dog. Do they know what he ate?'

'Mushrooms,' I said. 'He ate wild mushrooms. He obviously didn't realize they were poisonous.'

There was a moment of silence, sickening silence, while all

the blood drained from her face. 'Oh, no,' she whispered. '*I* did it. I picked them. The mushrooms. We were at Peredelkino on a picnic right before his last trip to Smolensk . . . I don't actually like them – they're a bit squishy for me, so I never eat them, but I thought, you know, it seemed so, you know, really kind of neat and back-to-nature to . . .I made an omelette . . . he was fine. He left for Smolensk the next morning and everything was . . . fine . . .' Her voice trailed off.

I wetted my lips and tried to say something, but everything died in my throat.

'Oh my God, Claire,' she said, her voice rising. 'I killed him, didn't I? I murdered him.' She buried her face in her hands. 'I don't believe I did it! I killed him.'

She was sobbing now, a kind of loud, hysterical wailing that was almost like screaming. The neighbours would be banging on the door in minutes, wondering who was being strangled. I ran to her and knelt beside her. I put my arms around her. 'Hush, now. It was an accident,' I said, but I felt sick myself. 'You didn't know.'

No one could fake this reaction, least of all if they'd downed a few gallons of wine, which she had. Ian, who thought all food originated in tin cans or frozen packages, wouldn't have known a good mushroom from a bad one, any more than she did. So he'd been on a picnic with her to Peredelkino Woods, the writer's retreat outside of Moscow.

His death really was an accident. Self-inflicted, almost.

Sasha couldn't . . .

Victoria uncovered her face. 'I probably need to go to the police, don't I? Oh my God, I'm going to jail!' She put her hands down on the table, blindly, and one of them knocked against the coffee cup. She was shaking so badly that when she tried to right it, it flipped over instead, so that both hands were doused with boiling coffee.

She jumped up and moaned, holding them away from the rest of her body. She looked at me and I thought she was going to crumple at my feet from the pain.

'Come on.' I dragged her towards the kitchen. 'Is it just your hands?'

She could hardly speak. 'Yes.'

I opened the freezer and prised out the last of the ice cube trays that was welded inside. I smacked it on the counter and ice cubes clattered out. I found a kitchen towel in one of the drawers and dampened it. Then I put the ice cubes in it and wrapped it into a long, narrow tube.

'My hands,' she whimpered, 'my hands. I need to go to the hospital. It hurts so much.'

Hospital. The place where Nick and Ian had died. 'We've got to deal with this right now,' I said, 'so it's probably best if we stay here. We'll be fine.'

Sure, me, the original Florence Nightingale. Nick in a coffin in the next room, and Victoria with second- or third-degree burns on both hands.

Real fine.

I held the cold pack against the burned flesh and she screamed and practically hit the ceiling.

'Let's get you back to the other room,' I said, 'so you can lie down. Maybe Nick and Rebecca have some aspirin or something for the pain.'

I put her back on the sofa, and fixed the compress on her hands again. She was nearly incoherent.

The bathroom was on the other side of Nick's bedroom. I took a deep breath and walked in once again where he lay amid the guttering wax-puddles of candles and the bouquets of flowers that had been heaped around his coffin. When I'd been with him earlier I'd felt his presence. Now the room felt spiritless and empty as though he'd left, too, when Rebecca and everyone else did.

There was aspirin in the medicine cabinet. I grabbed the bottle and ran back to Victoria. I managed to get two aspirins into her, then miraculously she fell asleep, although it was more like she'd passed out. After a while she started talking, muttering, actually, and was so restless I was afraid she was going to fall off the sofa.

So I sat with her again until she seemed to calm down.

Maybe she wouldn't wake up until morning. It would be easier, in the cold flat light of day, to deal with the dreadful bombshell she'd dropped. Maybe Hugh would be here by then ... Hugh would know what to do.

I couldn't ... wouldn't ... decide.

It was a relief to know the truth. In a twisted way, it was even good news. Ian's death had nothing to do with my brother, or with the painting either.

So for the next few hours I paced the hushed, darkened apartment, bizarrely relieved, and once or twice I went in to say a prayer at Nick's coffin. Around five in the morning Paula came back with Rebecca, both of them looking about as wrecked as I felt. We made a huge pot of coffee and sat in the kitchen drinking endless cups.

Victoria didn't stir, so we left her semi-comatose on the sofa.

Just after six o'clock Hugh arrived with Sean Ivory, which completely unnerved me because Sean was absolutely the portrait of Nick in ten years' time, when the babyish looks had matured into someone devastatingly, incredibly good-looking.

I pulled Hugh aside and told him what had happened last night with Victoria. All of it. He went even paler, if that was possible, and said he'd take her back to his place this morning and see if he could track down a doctor somewhere.

'Just take her to the Embassy,' I said.

'Sweetheart, this city's shut up tighter than a drum. Did you forget it's November the seventh?'

'Oh.'

So then he woke Victoria and when I happened to walk through the living room a minute later, I saw him sitting on the edge of the sofa holding her in his arms, murmuring tenderly into her hair. She was crying.

Poor Hugh. Maybe she'd finally give him a chance.

He found me in the kitchen drinking yet more coffee. 'I think I'm going to take her to my place. One of our drivers will take Rebecca and Sean and ... Nick to the airport. But Victoria needs a doctor.'

'I'm sure Paula and I can cope. You go along.'

I never got to say anything to Victoria, though, because just then the construction workers arrived with the lid for Nick's coffin and, by default, I was the one who took them into the bedroom. Rebecca refused to leave the apartment, but at least Paula and Sean persuaded her to remain in the kitchen while they nailed it in place. I stayed in the bedroom with my eyes closed, gritting my teeth until it was over.

I'm sure Rebecca could hear it. I'm sure the whole building could hear it.

Then Sean and the two construction workers carried Nick's coffin out of the apartment and into the elevator and brought it downstairs, outside to where the AP driver waited with a station wagon. Paula, Rebecca and I took the next elevator. By the time we got outside, the coffin was already in the car. There was only room for Sean, Rebecca and the driver. Rebecca clung to Paula and me just before she got in and then she started crying like the world was coming to an end.

Sean finally got her into the car and when they drove off, Paula raised her hand to wave goodbye. But neither of them saw her because Sean was bent over Rebecca who was sobbing hysterically on his shoulder. So Paula and I stood there, long after the car had vanished down the slip road, while the wind howled and whipped our hair and flung stinging splinters of snow in our faces. I looked around at the bleak, desolate landscape, the crummy tenement buildings and the grime of the dirty sky, and wondered what in the hell I was doing here.

'Let's get out of here,' Paula said.

'I've got to go to work,' I said.

'I'm going to Red Square for the parade,' she said. 'You want a lift?'

'Actually, I'm going to the office,' I said, 'but thanks, anyway.'

I drove back to Kutuzovsky through the deserted, snowy streets of Moscow. The office was empty when I got there. Both Manning and Annabel were probably at Red Square, along with every other journalist in the city. I was too restless to stay. The phone was silent. The place echoed. I packed my equipment.

The Kalinina Bridge was decked with red flags for the holiday. There was more traffic in this part of town than there had been out by Rublevskoye Shosse, all of it headed toward the Kremlin and Red Square. By the time I got to Dom Knigi, the bookstore, the GAI were waving to all cars either to turn around or get off the road. I drove past two of them, figuring my correspondent's licence plates gave me special dispensation, but today I was just like everyone else. The next GAI flapped his magic wand up and down at me, like an irritated band leader, the signal for me to pull over. I looked ahead down Kalinina Prospekt. No traffic was getting beyond the Arbat metro station. That meant going the rest of the way on foot.

Dammit.

If I had to stop here, it was at least another half-hour walk through the slow-moving crowds that milled along Kalinina Prospekt. The streets would be jammed all the way to the Manezh and the Alexander Gardens. Red Square would be packed full of people like a tin of sardines. I pretended not to see the GAI who was now furiously gesturing for me to pull over for a little chat. Instead I turned into Arbatskiy Pereulok and drove down the street towards Sasha's studio.

Long before I got there I saw the midnight blue Volvo station wagon with the yellow and black 'K' plate parked in front of Sasha's building.

Manning's car.

Maybe he was looking for a place to park, off Kalinina Prospekt, and just happened to leave his car here.

Sure he did. A real coincidence.

I parked directly behind the Volvo and headed for Sasha's building. If they were in this together . . . if they'd been using me all this time . . .

I ran up the stairs. The door was ajar. I saw the beam of light in the hallway as soon as I reached the top of the stairs. They were in the studio talking, their voices rising and falling.

I don't know how they missed the clattering of my boots on the marble stairs, but the talking continued. I tried to tiptoe down the hall until I got near enough to hear what they were saying.

'. . . can't keep it here,' Manning was saying.

'Do you think he knows where it is?' Sasha.

'I don't know. But we'd better not take any chances.'

'I know where to put it.' Sasha again. 'Where no one will ever think to look.'

'How are we going to get it out of here?' Manning sounded worried.

'We'll take it tonight. It'll be easier when it's dark. Can we use your car?'

'We haven't got that much time. What if he shows up?'

302

'All right. We'll do it now. Let's get . . .'

I would make a lousy spy. Spies don't sneeze, especially when they're eavesdropping. It ruins things.

It was an implosion, more than an explosion, but a sneeze is a sneeze.

They were out the door in milliseconds.

'What are you doing here?' Manning asked sharply. 'You're not supposed to be here.'

'Neither are you,' I said. I looked at Sasha whose pale eyes had narrowed to wolf-like slits. His face was opaque and impassive. The Welcome Wagon they weren't. 'You've got the paintings, haven't you?' I asked. 'You've had them all this time.'

He didn't need to answer. Neither of them did. The expression on their faces was enough.

I wanted to scream at them: for using me, betraying me, betraying Ian. My own brother whose innocence I would have staked my life on. And Manning. God, what a fool I'd been. He'd used me in bed, just like Philip had. Worse, even. I'd actually believed he meant some of what he'd said. Been stupid enough to care . . .

'You can both go straight to hell,' I said.

Then I turned and started walking back down the hall.

There was a moment of silence then Sasha said, 'We can't let her leave. It's too dangerous.'

That's when I ran.

'Claire!' It was Manning's voice.

Then footsteps behind me. Running. I skidded to the stairway. Later I realized it must have been Manning who took off after me because Sasha never would have grabbed the rotten rail. I heard the crack of wood and a thumping noise.

He was still cursing as I slipped sideways through the one-hinged door. I had no idea where Sasha was. For all I knew, there was a back exit and he'd be out the rear door right behind me. So I kept running, as fast as I could on the snow- and ice-rutted street, back to Kalinina Prospekt where there were crowds. I could lose them there, if only I could outrun them.

By the time I got to Kalinina Prospekt, winded and panting, I had a feeling no one was chasing me any more. I turned around.

No sign of them.

Now what? My car was at Sasha's studio. I couldn't go back and get it.

My things were at Manning's apartment.

'Hey!'

I looked up.

Philip Robinson pulled up to the kerb beside me in his Lada.

'Philip!'

'Need a ride?' he asked.

The answer to my prayers.

I nodded.

'Get in,' he said, so I did.

Chapter Twenty-One

'What are you doing here?' he asked. 'I thought you'd be at Red Square.'

'Uh ... there was a last-minute change of plans,' I said. 'I need to go back to the office on Kutuzovsky. Can you take me there?'

'What's wrong?' he said. 'You look upset.'

He started the engine. He signalled right and all of a sudden we were driving back down Arbatskiy Pereulok.

'Philip, this is the wrong way!' I said sharply.

'I'm taking a different route.'

'All you had to do was go straight down Kalinina Prospekt and over the bridge to Kutuzovsky.'

What was he doing?

'Relax,' he said. 'Don't worry. I'll get you there.'

He started whistling 'Moscow Nights' under his breath.

In just about thirty seconds, at the speed he was going, we were going to be in front of Sasha's building again. Right back to the place I'd just fled.

'Philip.' I said it through gritted teeth. 'Please take me to my office ... right ... now! I'm late.'

We drove by the fire-gutted building and Philip slowed down. The midnight blue Volvo was gone, but there, large as life, was my car.

'Isn't that yours?' he asked.

'Uh. Yes.'

'What's it doing here?'

'It ... stalled. I think I flooded the engine. It might be okay now. Maybe I should give it another try, since we're right here.'

'Why did you park here?' He spoke softly, but there was something dangerous in his voice.

'Because they were diverting traffic off Kalinina Prospekt,' I said, looking out the window so he couldn't see my face.

'But you were running from this direction when I picked you up. Why were you running?'

'I ... wasn't.' I put my hand on the door handle. 'Thanks for the ride.'

He reached over and yanked my hand away from the door. 'Please. It's probably still flooded. Let me take you. I'd like the company.' He reversed and made a sharp U-turn, taking us back the way we came. 'I insist.'

'I'd rather not.'

'It's no problem at all.'

The GAI waved us through the intersection of Kalinina Prospekt and Arbatskiy Pereulok but he wouldn't let Philip turn right toward the Kremlin.

'Damn.' He turned left, since he was forced to, which took us in the direction I wanted to go. I don't think he intended to drop me at the office, though.

'Where are we going?'

'I'm not sure,' he said. 'I've had a last-minute change of plans, too.'

'I don't want to inconvenience you, then.'

He stared grimly at the road and said nothing.

'You can just drop me ...'

'Don't be stupid. You're going with me.'

I said, with slow dread, 'Where are we really going?'

'Where's the Bellini, Claire?' He said it so nonchalantly I thought I'd misheard him.

'I don't know,' I lied. 'How do you know about it?'

The tyres squealed as Philip made a left on to Ulitsa Chaykovskogo. Today he didn't seem too bothered by trifling matters like illegal turns.

He accelerated again as we drove past the turning for the American ambassador's residence. 'From Ian, of course,' he said. 'Who else could have told me?'

Plenty of people could have told him. I knew most of the list.

He was the wild card.

Why would Ian ...?

What an idiot!

Smolensk.

Ian had gone there for his research on World War II. Philip had followed Napoleon there. Different century, same place. How dumb not to connect them. Although Philip's name had never, ever come up in any conversation with anyone. Not Nick, not Harold Miller, not anybody.

'You were coming from Nazarov's just now,' he said. 'That Russian artist. Don't tell me Ian gave the painting to him. Or did *you* do that?'

'I don't know what you're talking about,' I said, and wondered why I was protecting Sasha any more. Or Manning.

'You're lying,' he said.

'You have a vivid imagination, Philip,' I replied coldly. He made another illegal left on to Ulitsa Kropotkinskaya and kept up our speed. Where were the GAI when you needed them? The city was absolutely deserted. 'Where are we going?'

'I don't know,' he said. 'I'm thinking.'

'Let me out.'

We passed the UPDK building. He pulled over to the kerb and stopped.

'Okay,' he said. 'Get out.'

'You're mad,' I said, and reached for the door handle.

'Not so fast.' He turned towards me and smiled. I stopped breathing.

If the devil were sitting next to me, that's exactly how he'd smile.

He yanked my hand off the door handle. 'I didn't mean by yourself.'

I looked out of the car window and saw the cloud of steam rising from the outdoor swimming pool.

Then he leaned across to unlock my door and I could see, where his coat fell open, that he was wearing some kind of leather shoulder strap.

And I thought, although I couldn't be sure, that I caught a flash of dark metal. Something that looked very much like a gun.

'Get out. We need to talk.'

'I don't want to talk.'

'Do you remember that first night I saw you at Victoria's party?' he asked, pleasantly. He wasn't expecting an answer. 'I recognized your face, but quite honestly, my dear, I'd forgotten about you entirely. You weren't terribly memorable.'

I didn't think, under the circumstances, he could bruise my ego over my sex appeal or lack of it, but he still managed to stick the knife in.

'Probably because I didn't go to bed with you,' I snapped, 'although that's no criterion since you're probably up in the millions by now. I guess it gets hard to remember. At your age.'

'Some women just aren't worth the effort,' he said, ignoring my little gibe entirely, 'and you obviously weren't. But I digress. Now get out of the car.' He opened my door. Then he got out and came around to my side. He grabbed my arm and pulled me out. 'Move.' We started walking toward the swimming pool.

'I finally remembered you because of one peculiar trait,' he continued. 'The night we had dinner and I brought you here, to Stalin's swimming pool, it came back to me how utterly terrified you are of water. I finally remembered that pool party I gave when you wouldn't even change into a bathing suit.' He smiled happily. 'And you still don't know how to swim, do you.'

He wasn't asking.

'Philip,' I said, 'please don't do this.'

But he was doing it. And there was no one around to stop him. The streets were deserted. Empty. We were in a business district and it was a holiday. Absolutely no one would be here today.

No one.

We bypassed the main entrance to the swimming pool and headed toward another doorway. The service entrance. A child could have broken in.

If we'd really come here for a proper swim, then after we'd changed into our bathing suits we would swim through a small tunnel that fed from the changing area into the outdoor pool. I knew that because the short Yuri told me once when we drove by on the way to do some errand at UPDK. He said that's why

308

you could use the pool all year round since you never had to walk outside in subzero temperatures and freeze to death in your bathing suit.

Philip, however, knew a dry land route that bypassed the water tunnel. We walked out to the main deck of the swimming pool.

I knew it would be terrifyingly huge.

It was.

You couldn't see to the other side, especially through the cloud of steam. It was like being at the edge of the ocean when the fog rolled in. Sometimes there were gaps in the mist, but the only thing I could see was water and more water. A never-ending concrete coastline and all that water.

My heart was slamming so loudly against my chest I was sure he could hear it.

We were walking around the perimeter of the pool.

'What do you want to know about the Bellini?' I said. I looked over at the edge of the water, probably the way a first-time parachutist peeks out of the open door of the airplane.

'Where it is, you fool. Now tell me because I need it by tomorrow.' He was using his nobody-thwarts-me voice, the one dripping with arrogance.

'What's so special about tomorrow?' I said.

'I leave.'

'With the Bellini? On what, a broomstick?' I asked. 'You're not leaving.' Sometimes I should keep my mouth shut. Particularly when dealing with someone with a gun and a bad temper.

'Ah, but I am.' He touched his shoulder and it looked like he was brushing off a speck of dust. But that wasn't what he was doing. He was checking the gun. 'Now be a good girl and tell me where it is.'

'I already told you, I don't know where it is. Anyway, you couldn't get that painting out of the country unless you know Houdini and he makes it disappear for you.'

He laughed. 'What a little wit you are,' he said, but it wasn't a compliment. 'I'm going to do better than that. I've got a first-class seat on Air Force 2 as a personal guest of the Vice-President. I could probably get the iconostasis from one of the Kremlin churches out of the country tomorrow if I wanted to. The luggage on that flight won't be touched, unless it's with kid gloves. The Bellini will be there, of course. And the Vermeer.'

'The Vermeer? *You've* got it?' 'The original? God, Philip, you're despicable.'

'Thank you.'

I wanted to slap his face. Instead I said, 'Who painted the fake?'

He looked mildly startled, but then he said, in his didactic professor's voice, 'I found an artist on the Arbat who was painting the Mona Lisa. I had to buy it from him, of course, and then he showed me his other fakes. Pretty decent work. I hired him. I had a photograph of the Vermeer, ironically, in a book on the history of the Amber Room. There was a chapter on von Müller and his lost art collection.'

'And your friend, the pilot on Air Force 2, is going to keep his mouth shut about that?'

'He won't have a clue what he's taking. I told him I'd bought a few souvenir paintings on the Arbat. He said it's fine. Half the delegation will probably leave with icons or other works of art that fall under the category of 'national treasures', so what's one more package? Everybody sneaks things out if they've got the chance.'

'Well, you're just rolling in good luck, aren't you?'

'Don't antagonize me,' he said suddenly, 'I'm not in the mood.'

I saw him go for the gun. It was in my face in a flash. I stepped back and almost fell over. I don't know guns at all. It was a little one. A revolver, I suppose. Who cares? It was a gun.

'I don't want to do this,' Philip said.

'Then don't.' My voice cracked.

He didn't answer, just leaned down and kissed me, another of his bruising, tongue-in-my-mouth kisses. I guess the gun gave him a real erotic thrill, all that macho power and phallic symbolism. I kissed him back with all the passion I could manage, hoping he'd think I, too, was aroused by the danger and sexual tension between us. I think it's what he wanted. Maybe it would appease him.

I wanted to wipe the taste of him off my mouth when we were done kissing, but I didn't.

'You know, I think you're right,' he said. He sounded pleasantly conversational, all of a sudden. Maybe the kiss had changed his mind. Maybe he decided he'd rather bed me again than kill me.

'Right about what?' It was just above a whisper.

'I don't want to shoot you.'

'Okay.'

'I want to show you something.'

This didn't sound good. He took my arm, the perfect gentleman this time, and we started toward two concrete walkways that led out to the centre of the pool where the diving tower was. I'd seen it earlier, when we were out on the street, like the summit of a mountain poking through clouds. Now it was lost in the mist but I knew it was out there.

The two walkways formed the borders of a long rectangular swimming pool within the larger pool. It was a lap pool. There were half a dozen roped off lanes.

We were going out to the diving tower.

We started down the walkway on the right. By now, I was reasonably sure the water to either side of us was deep enough to go over my head. We passed a short walkway that connected the two longer ones. It also separated the lap pool from yet another interior pool. The one you used if you were going to dive off that multi-tiered Mount Everest diving tower.

I'll bet it was deep, that diving pool. It had to be.

'There are four diving platforms on the tower,' Philip said. 'Why don't we start climbing? You'll love the view.'

I looked up. The ladder disappeared into the mist.

'I forgot my camera,' I said, but my voice, dammit, was shaking. I don't know why I was making wisecracks now that I knew what he was going to do. Shove me off the tower. If I survived the impact of the fall, I'd drown. Less messy that way. Save him using up a perfectly good bullet.

'Start climbing,' he said. 'You won't be needing your camera.'

So up I went, like Jack climbing the beanstalk, obeying the orders of the man with the gun. He was right behind me.

311

At least the pool was heated. At least I wasn't going to die of hypothermia unless I tried to get out of the water ... if that was still an option. Minus ten Celsius. That's pretty damn' cold.

Higher up the ladders had a coating of snow on them and there were even some patches of ice. Mid-way up the second ladder my right foot, clumsy in its heavy boot, slipped out from under me. The only reason I didn't fall was because of my death grip on the sides of the ladder. I went as slowly as I could, but it wasn't like I had a choice. All I was doing was stalling for time. 'Keep climbing.'

We had reached the second platform. Two to go. I turned around and said, 'You won't get away with killing me. They'll know it's you.'

God, what an incredibly corny line. It's what they say in every bad movie you've ever seen. What was I doing provoking him like that? I couldn't back it up.

'I almost succeeded once,' he said, 'except for that stupid cat of yours.'

'My *what*? What are you talking about?'

'The caviare. I added a little something to it. You'd never have known. I expect your cat's dead.' He said it like it was nothing. 'But anyway, my darling, this time I'm not going to kill you. You're going to do it yourself.' He waved the gun in my face. 'You've been so depressed lately, haven't you? The death of your lover ... Moscow, such a bleak city ... it's all become too much for you, hasn't it? No one thought you were suicidal, little Mary Sunshine, but you never know ...'

He leaned over and kissed me again, another of his deep throat kisses. 'I'll miss you,' he whispered.

One thing about Philip, when he got involved in a kiss, he got involved in a kiss.

I'd never get another chance like this.

I brought my knee up into his groin and then shoved him away from me, with both hands, as hard as I could. He stumbled backward, a look of incredulous surprise and hurt betrayal on his face.

As though he were shocked I minded that he needed to kill me because I'd got in the way of his plans. After all these years he still thought he was entitled to have whatever he

312

wanted because he was so brilliant, so superior . . . and everyone else was utterly disposable.

Maybe the gods did favour him because just in the nick of time, he reached out with the hand without the gun and caught one of the rungs of the ladder. He nearly dropped the gun as he swayed precariously over the steamy water below. But he didn't fall, dammit.

He regained his balance. Then he raised the gun and pointed it at me.

'I've got the painting!' I screamed.

'What?' He lowered the gun a few millimetres, then reconsidered and raised it again. 'You're lying.'

'Fine. Kill me now. You'll never know, will you? You'll leave tomorrow without it.'

'Where is it?' He moved closer. 'Tell me.' His eyes glittered. He seemed . . . on the edge of sanity.

'I'll have to take you to it.'

'Don't be an idiot. I'm not going to fall for that.'

'You've still got the gun, Philip,' I said steadily. 'What have you got to lose?'

'I don't know. You tell me.'

'I'll take you to it. In return, you won't kill me. Just take the painting and get out of the country tomorrow.'

'Of course. And you'll keep your mouth shut, won't you? You won't say a word.' He was pretty heavy with the sarcasm.

'I won't if you'll pay me something for my trouble.'

'What?' He looked stunned. 'Why should I pay you?'

'Because I need the money,' I said flatly. 'I'm in debt so deep I'll never dig myself out. My grandmother died last summer. She spent months in the hospital so I won't burden you with how many zeroes there are after the first number on the bottom line of the hospital bill. Anyway, there's something else.'

I had his attention. He lowered the gun.

'What?'

'When Ian and I were still living together he asked me to promise I'd take care of his sister and her daughter if anything happened to him. His niece has cerebral palsy. She needs another operation. Their medical bills are worse than mine. If

I give you the painting and I get something for my trouble, it would solve all my problems. I don't have any way of getting it out of the country and you do.' It was amazing how convincing I sounded, but it was actually the truth.

All but the part about having the Bellini in my possession.

'Why should I give you anything?' he snapped.

'Because you're about to get away with the perfect crime,' I said. 'The whole world thinks those paintings were destroyed in the fire in von Müller's castle. What are the Russians going to say? Give us back the paintings we stole? Doesn't sound too likely, does it?'

'I don't know,' he said, 'I still don't know why I have to give you anything.'

At least I'd distracted him. He'd dropped the arm with the gun down by his side. I glanced briefly at the gun and happened to notice the pale sheen on the diving platform, just in front of where he stood. Ice.

'Will you kiss me again?' I asked.

'What?'

'Please.' I tried to look flirty. 'To seal our deal?'

He moved forward and his foot slipped sideways on the patch of ice. This time, he wasn't close enough to grab the ladder.

But he was near enough to entangle me with him. He fell on to me, the hand with the gun wrapped around my back in something between an embrace and a death grip. I tried to push him off me like I had the last time.

'You bitch,' he said as we stumbled together. 'You're going with me.'

He shoved the gun in my face. I fought him and then there was a loud crack and we stumbled backward off the diving platform, me more or less on top of him, in free-fall.

It was one of those horrible scenes, where your mind is moving in slow motion sequences but the reality is so swift you are powerless to change what's going to happen. I hit the water with such force it felt like I'd hit the concrete deck. My neck snapped backward like a dry twig and my breath got sucked out of me as though I'd fallen into a vacuum. I'm sure if Philip's body hadn't been under me to take the brunt of that thwacking fall, like a blistering belly flop, the impact could have knocked me out and I would have drowned. Thank God it was only the second tower.

I gagged and choked and inhaled a mouthful of water. Then I went under.

I clawed the water and sank deeper.

The swimming lessons I'd taken decades ago hadn't progressed very far, but the instructor had been compassionate enough to try to help me deal with my terror of the water. Drown-proofing, she'd called it.

Whatever you do, don't panic, she'd said, or you'll drown for sure. Use your arms and legs and keep your mouth shut. Don't keep swallowing water. I looked up and saw watery light above my head.

Then I kicked my feet, which were lead-heavy in snow boots, in a slow rhythm, while I pulled with my arms and kept my mouth clamped shut. The light got closer.

I exploded out of the water, like a sodden cork, weeping and coughing like my guts were going to spill out. And looked around for Philip.

Where was he in the mist? Did waterlogged guns still work? The silence, except for water slapping the edges of the pool and my own splashing to keep afloat, was eerie.

I heard him moan and call my name. 'Claire,' he said, 'I'm hurt.'

I thrashed around in my best doggy paddle away from the direction of his voice. The weight of my clothing pulled me down with the gravity force of Jupiter.

What about the gun? What if he still had it?

I had to get rid of my waterlogged clothes. First to go were the gloves. I gagged on more water as I bobbed under, then fumbled with the buttons of Victoria's cashmere coat. I finally shrugged out of it. It dropped away from me and I stopped sinking.

'Claire.' His voice broke. 'Answer me. I'm bleeding. I know you're there. You have to help me.'

The mist was so thick we still couldn't see each other. I kept silent and grimly got on with the business of finding the edge of the pool. Now I know how desperate Columbus must have felt when he was looking for land.

I saw the ledge ahead of me, a dark grey shadow, and

reached for it. I missed and tried again. This time I got it.

Now what?

'I'm coming to you.' His voice sounded weaker. 'Please help me.'

What if he was lying? Except he really did sound hurt. That crack when we'd gone off the diving board ... I thought he fired into the air.

'Where's the gun?' I said sharply.

'Bottom of ... the ... pool.' He was struggling to speak.

'How am I going to get help? If I get out of the water, I'll freeze in no time. Besides,' I said, 'in case you forgot, you picked a place that's completely deserted. No one will be here until tomorrow, at the earliest.'

I could hear him splashing faintly in the water. He was making his way around the perimeter of the pool. So I moved, too. Away from him.

Our little real-life game of water tag.

'Claire, dammit. I haven't ... got ... long. *Please* ...' He was really pleading. I'd never heard him sound scared like this.

What if he was dying? Could I let him bleed to death and do nothing to help him? And then what? Wait in the water with a corpse, until the lifeguard or whoever strolled in tomorrow when the pool opened again? Or maybe it wouldn't even be tomorrow. How did I know the pool wasn't closed tomorrow, too? Russian holidays could go on for more than one day.

'Your car,' I said. 'Maybe I can make it to your car. Do you still have the keys?'

A long pause. 'Yes.'

I changed direction and now moved, hand over hand, along the ledge towards his voice. Finally I saw him through the mist. His face was a death mask and the water around him was red. I thought I was going to throw up.

'Where are you hurt?'

'My ... chest.' His voice was rasping and his eyes were wild and terrified.

'Give me the keys.' If I'd moved closer, I could have got them from his pocket myself. But to move into that bloody water ...

He fumbled for a long time. Then he moved his hand toward mine. It was shaking. I reached to take the keys from

316

him but he was weaker than I realized because he let go before he connected with my hand.

I tried to grab them as they sank into the pink water. And missed.

I ducked below the surface, but it was too late. I came back up, sputtering. 'What did you do that for, dammit?' I shouted. 'They're sinking to the bottom of the pool!'

'Get . . . them.'

Oh, sure. Easy for him to say. He hadn't taken a header off that diving board with Esther Williams. He was talking to me.

'I . . . can't.'

'Have . . . to.'

'Philip!'

'Get . . . them.'

This was hopeless. He was going to bleed to death from that gunshot wound. And by the time somebody found us, I'd have hypothermia. Or worse.

For someone who could swim, diving to the bottom to retrieve the keys was surely no big deal. But for me, it was like contemplating diving for the wreckage of the *Titanic* without an oxygen tank.

But if I didn't do something . . . now . . . whatever chance he had would be finished.

'All right,' I said. 'I'll try.' I pulled off my boots and set them on the edge of the pool. I was hyperventilating. This was no good. Calm. I must stay calm. 'Just give me a minute . . .'

'Hurry.'

'Damn it, Philip. Leave me alone!' I shouted. 'I'll do it, I'll do it. Next time you do this, pick someone who can swim.'

'Very . . . funny.'

'Stop talking. You're making me nervous.'

Given my limited expertise, there was no way I was going to dive head-first and swim to the bottom. Instead, I'd try to position myself over where the keys had fallen and sink, feet first. But after three tries it was clear I couldn't make it down fast enough before running out of breath. I really needed to propel myself to the bottom and then push off and rocket back to the surface because, let me tell you, a pool with a four-tier diving tower is very, very deep.

I made half a dozen sorties, each one seemingly closer to

317

the bottom than the one before, but still I never made it. Then my lungs began aching so badly, I had to rest. Philip, alarmingly, was no longer speaking. He hung on to the ledge, barely, with his eyes closed.

I dived again, two more tries. It was hopeless. We were running out of time.

'Philip,' I said urgently, 'can you hear me?'

His eyelids fluttered briefly.

'Listen, the keys are gone. I can't find them. You have to hold on. I'm going to swim to the changing area. Do you know if there's a phone there? I'll call for help. I'll get David to come. Or someone.'

'Phone,' he whispered. 'Don't . . . know.'

It occurred to me that this would probably be easier if I got rid of more clothes. I mean, when people swim here, even at this time of year, they're only wearing a bathing suit. No thermal rubber diving suit or anything. So I stripped down to my bra and panties and groped around the perimeter of the pool until I came to the side that abutted the main pool nearest to the changing room. Or so I hoped.

It was like trying to look through thick clouds when you're on an airplane.

But I did see the metal railing.

Damn.

It probably surrounded the entire diving pool, separating it from the main swimming pool. If I touched that frigid metal trying to get from one pool to another when I was wet, a couple of layers of skin would instantly bond to it and there would be bloody pulp where flesh used to be.

I'd have to find a break in the railing somewhere.

So I went exploring, hand over hand, around the edge of the pool. I was probably halfway around the perimeter once again before I saw the place where the railing wasn't properly joined together. There wasn't going to be an optimum time to do this, especially as I was becoming stiffer and sorer by the minute. I hauled myself out of the warmth of the water and sprinted the few steps across the deck to the hole in the railing. I had to turn sideways to pass through it, but because I was already shaking in the arctic air, I bumped it with my arm and felt the skin rip as I pulled away. It panicked me and I jumped into the other pool, instead of lowering myself in, like I'd intended to.

I went under water again, but this time I was ready. I bobbed up and attached myself to the ledge. Surely that was the worst part.

Then I started to doggy paddle. My feet brushed the bottom before I'd gone twenty yards. Who would have believed it? I was in the world's biggest wading pool, not the middle of the Atlantic Ocean.

So I waded through the shallow water, searching in the mist for one of the portals that led into the changing area and, finally, I found one. The tunnel was dark and I wondered if the bottom, which I hopped along, was slimy or full of crawling creatures that I couldn't see.

Then I was inside the building and there was a phone.

It was in a cubicle by the main door. There was even a small heater that the ticket taker probably used to keep warm. I turned it on with blue hands that shook.

I sat down at someone's desk and picked up the phone.

No dial tone. Nothing.

Dead.

I banged it on the desk so hard I cracked the receiver.

Now what?

The changing room was bleak concrete, like someone's mildewed basement. The only things in it were half a dozen rough wooden benches and a row of rusty coat hooks along the walls. No one had left so much as a towel there.

I could stay here, in my little toasty cocoon, and wait until someone rescued me. I was warm, I could hold out. Why should I go for help for Philip, that murdering, heartless . . .? My muscles ached, my head throbbed. I stretched and my feet hit something under the desk.

Boots.

Someone's boots.

I yanked open the desk drawers. The dirty blue worker's uniform was underneath a stash of porno magazines. I threw the magazines on the floor and pulled out the uniform. It was heavy rough cotton and miles too big. I put it on and then slid my feet into the boots. I do mean 'slid' because they were also miles too big which, I suppose, since this wasn't Cinderella fitting her foot in the glass slipper, was better than five sizes too small.

How far was I going to get, though, dressed like this? A cotton jump-suit? No overcoat?

I'd freeze before anyone . . .

I warmed myself for another minute in front of the heater. Then I left through the nearest door, which happened to be the front entrance and, thank God, wasn't secured by a lock and key but merely by a deadbolt.

The neighbourhood was as bleakly deserted as it had been before. A siren wailed in the distance, like it had the first time I'd been here with Philip, an eternity ago, when he'd told me the story of Stalin's horrible, doomed swimming pool.

I ran toward the sound.

What warmth I'd accumulated in front of that heater lasted minutes. The cold penetrated the cotton fabric until I felt like I was being stabbed by thousands of tiny needles. I flapped my arms against my ribs to keep warm, and kept running, sliding around like some circus clown in my oversized boots. Once I fell, hard, on my hands and knees.

I thought I was running directly toward the river, but I'm as dyslexically oriented on the ground as I am when I read a map. There was a chance I was going in the opposite direction from where I wanted to go, probably taking the long way around the pool to the river. A street sign on a building said Ulitsa Volkhonka.

I tried to reconstruct the page of the CIA street map in my mind, because there was something familiar . . . I was near . . . the Kremlin?

Then I saw the huge building with its semi-circular drive and elegant colonnaded loggia.

The Pushkin Museum of Fine Arts.

It would be closed today, too.

Except for two visitors.

The midnight blue Volvo was still parked on the street.

They were here. Probably hiding the Bellini. What a brilliant idea. Who would think to look for a missing Old Master painting in an art museum?

I ran to the car. Not much chance Manning had left the keys in it.

320

He hadn't.

'Hey! Get away from that car!' he shouted at me, in Russian. It was Sasha and life was repeating itself. Dressed as I was, he thought I was Russian and that I was stealing the car.

I turned and they both stopped dead in their tracks.

'My God,' Manning said, 'it's you.'

Then he ran to me and pulled me, shivering from the cold, into his arms.

'Philip . . .' I said weakly.

'Where is he?' Manning's voice was harsh. 'Were you with him?'

Oh, God. He still thought I was having a fling with Philip.

'The swimming pool,' I mumbled. 'He's been shot.'

Then I passed out.

When I came to, I was at the clinic at the American Embassy. Manning was there, along with the doctor and four or five people from the security office, including a couple of Marines. It was the beginning of the end.

I was in trouble.

Big trouble.

Chapter Twenty-Two

They expelled me.

It was, I suppose, inevitable given the way things turned out.

Philip was dead. By the time the police got to the swimming pool, he was at the bottom of it. I don't know whether he died from the gunshot wound or passed out and let go of the ledge and drowned.

There was no way the Foreign Ministry could overlook such a grisly death and the scandal that went with it. I was the logical choice when it came to a scapegoat. I was formally accused of being an accomplice in the conspiracy to remove national treasures from the Union of Soviet Socialist Republics. That was a little too much, if you ask me. They'd stolen the paintings to begin with.

That I didn't end up having a personal tour of Lubyanka was thanks to Barry, the sharp-talking lawyer from the American Embassy, who kept me from a worse fate than expulsion. I owed him big time. I think he called in some markers for me. We had a few blunt, private conversations in the secure room on the top floor of the crumbling Old Embassy building on Ulitsa Chaykovskogo. I didn't get off without a lecture about what an idiotic thing I'd got myself involved in, but I bit my tongue and took it. When the KGB questioned me, though, Barry was my best friend.

I told them where they could find the Vermeer, which was duly reclaimed from Philip's room at the university.

As for the Bellini, I said nothing.

Hey, no one asked.

David told me later, in a conversation we typed out on our laptops and then deleted, that Sasha had put it in the basement of the Pushkin as I'd guessed, along with crates of plundered trophy art that were already jammed in there. If I said anything, he would be in some gulag in the space of a heart-beat.

By default, my silence about Sasha's involvement meant David's fleeting role in helping to move the painting to the Pushkin had to be hushed up. It made him squirm, but, really, what choice was there? I was adamant about keeping Sasha out of this and David understood that. Besides, Harold Miller had bolted from Moscow and was back in London, according to Nigel's minions.

And curiously there was no reaction from London when the Soviet Ministry of Culture issued a press release announcing the surprise discovery of a priceless work of art, a rare paint-ing by Jan Vermeer. They called it a 'lost treasure recently rediscovered', which would hang, in due course, in the Pushkin Museum of Fine Arts.

It's a funny old world, isn't it?

For whatever reason, Miller never uttered a word of protest. David guessed that maybe he hadn't told me the truth about not knowing the fate of the Amber Room. Reclaiming his paintings via Ian was one thing. Asking the KGB to give them back was another.

Which was even better for Sasha.

Those last days in Moscow, I was like a sleepwalker. Barry guiding me through the grilling sessions with the KGB, then at night, in David's arms, in his bed, trying to forget what happened during the day.

We finally had the conversation about what they'd been doing when I found them at Sasha's studio, in whispers so soft it was like breathing. He said he hadn't known anything about either Sasha or Philip until the morning of the Revolution Day parade. First Sasha called the office, asking for me.

'You were still at Nick's,' he said, 'so he asked if I'd tell you to meet him at his studio. I asked for the address but he said you knew it.'

'How did you find it?'

There was a pause, then David said, 'I went through your

323

things. You'd written it down. I found the paper in your bag. You'd left it in the bedroom.'

'Pretty nervy,' I said.

'Lucky for you,' he said, and leaned over and kissed me. 'Then I ran into Hugh and Fiona in Red Square, waiting for the parade to start. Hugh told me about Victoria. The whole thing with the mushrooms. He said it had been Philip Robinson's idea to pick them when he took her out to Peredelkino. He took her to see Boris Pasternak's grave, then they had a picnic. He told her they were great in an omelette. He knew she was seeing Ian that night, so he figured maybe, if he suggested it, she'd be dumb enough actually to use them.'

'I didn't know she was with Philip,' I said. 'She never said she was with *him* at Peredelkino. She said 'we' but I assumed she was talking about Ian.'

'After Hugh said that, Fiona said she'd seen Philip with Nick at the bar at the National the night he supposedly drove his car off the road. She said they were really knocking back the vodka. Maybe Philip slipped something in his drink.' He stroked my hair. 'I went to Sasha's studio as soon as I heard that. It was a wild guess that he was connected to the missing painting since he was an artist, though by that time I'd figured out that Philip Robinson was dirty.'

'You never liked him.'

'Nope.' He brushed my nose with his finger. 'So I found Sasha in his studio. We were talking about what to do with the Bellini when you barged in, looking like Queen Boadicea ready to take on the Romans.'

I made a face. 'I know, bloodied but unbowed. Then I left.'

'You really thought it was us, didn't you?'

'Of course not. I knew Philip Robinson was on his way to the studio. I knew he did it.'

David pulled me on top of him. 'That is one huge lie. You didn't have a clue.'

'No. Yes. I didn't know what to think.' I kissed him. 'But if I hadn't left, he would have found the two of you with the Bellini. Him and his little revolver. Lucky for you he ran into me instead on the way there.'

'And decided he needed to kill you. Yeah, that was a stroke

of luck all right.' David buried his face in my hair. 'Don't. I don't want to think about it.'

He kissed me again and we forgot about everything but each other for the rest of the night.

The next day the KGB was finished with me and I was told I had twenty-four hours to leave the country. By one of life's supreme ironies, my shipment got liberated from its warehouse in Morocco and was arriving in Moscow the following week. You had to laugh.

The night before I left, David came downstairs to the apartment where I was fixing us dinner. He walked into the kitchen and put a finger against his lips. He had his laptop with him.

He set it on the kitchen table and flipped it open. When the little cursor started to blink on the screen he typed: YOUR BROTHER WANTS TO SEE YOU BEFORE YOU GO.

I moved the keyboard so it was facing me. IMPOSSIBLE!! TOO DANGEROUS!!

ALREADY ARRANGED.

WHAT ARE YOU TALKING ABOUT?

WHITE ZHIG WITH A DENTED FENDER IN THE PARKING LOT OF THE UKRAINE. IN AN HOUR. BY THE STATUE OF SCHEVCHENKO. HE'LL BE DRIVING. BE CAREFUL.

Then, while I stared at the screen, he hit delete.

I was there before the white Zhiguli showed up. I knew it was a Russian car since only the parking lights were on. As soon as he drove close to the park, near the statue of Taras Schevchenko, I slipped out of the shadows. He opened the door and I got in.

We drove for a few minutes without speaking. I studied his profile, when I could see it, in the pale light cast by the occasional streetlight. We weren't keeping to main roads.

Finally I said, 'This is very dangerous for you.'

Sasha turned and looked at me. 'It is more dangerous for you.'

I shrugged. 'It's finished for me.'

'I know. I'm sorry.'

I had to ask. 'How long have you known about the paintings?'

325

He said gently, 'Ian brought them both to me to authenticate. The Bellini just before he died.'

'Harold Miller said he found a copy of the Vermeer in your studio. He said you were the forger.'

Even in the dim light I could see the surprised look on Sasha's face. Then he laughed, but there was no humour in it. 'So. That explains many things.'

'Why did you paint the fake?'

'I did not "paint a fake", Clara,' he said. 'Vermeer was a genius in manipulating light and shadow ...the expressions on the faces of his subjects are painted with such power, such mastery ... the purity of his work transcends time. He is as much of a genius today as he was in the seventeenth century. Of course I tried to copy his technique. Who wouldn't, in my place? You see people doing it all the time in museums.'

We left the city behind. I hadn't been paying attention to the route he was taking, but now there was nothing but woods on either side of the road. It was pitch black all around us, except for the pale swath cut by our watery parking lights.

He stopped the car and switched off the lights. We were in the middle of nowhere. He turned to me.

'Why did you hide it?' I asked. 'Why did you move it to the Pushkin?'

He leaned back against his seat and stared at the ceiling of the Zhig.

'Those paintings, the Bellini and the Vermeer, are responsible for the deaths of three people. And the expulsion of my sister.' I winced when he said that but he continued as though he hadn't noticed. 'They have the Vermeer. The Bellini has been lost for more than forty years. Let them find it again when they decide to excavate the stolen art in the basement of the Pushkin. It has done enough damage.' He started the engine and we drove slowly back to where there were street lamps and buildings and sidewalks again.

Sasha let me off where he'd found me. By the statue of Taras Schevchenko.

'I'll miss you,' he said.

I could hardly speak. 'I'll miss you, too.'

'Nina sends her love.'

326

I nearly lost it then. 'I'll try to stay in touch. I don't want to cause any trouble for you.'

'I know.' Then he kissed me on the forehead and said softly, '*S'bogom*, Clara.'

I got out of the car and he pulled away immediately. The parking lot of the Ukraine was dark and quiet. Only a few lights winked from the darker hulk of the Ukraine itself.

I walked slowly back to David's apartment. The miliman wasn't in his booth in the Kutuzovsky parking lot. I slipped into the building out of the shadows. I don't think anyone saw me.

I cried that night in bed, until finally, I wore myself out and fell asleep wrapped in David's arms. He said nothing, just stroked my hair and held me.

When I woke up, it was still dark. I lifted my head off the pillow so I could see the luminescent wrist watch on his arm, which was lying across my chest.

'It's four-thirty,' he said softly.

'Why aren't you sleeping?'

'For the same reason you're not.'

We made love again until daylight. For the last time.

Tanya fixed all my favourite things for lunch on my last day. Borscht. *Pelmeni*. I couldn't imagine how I was going to get through this day without more tears. Larisa, Tanya, and the Yuris surprised me with farewell gifts and that really undid me. From Tanya I got an exquisite shawl she'd crocheted for me herself. She'd stayed up all night to finish it in time. She looked exhausted when she kissed me and pressed it into my hand. From the short Yuri I got a collection of Chekov's plays. English on one side of the page, Russian on the other. The tall Yuri gave me music, of course. A cassette of piano music played by the winners of the last International Tchaikovsky Competition and another of *a cappella* music sung by male choirs from several Russian monasteries. He said they had voices like the angels.

'It's not Old Blue Eyes,' he said, winking at me, 'but I think you will remember me anyway.'

Larisa gave me a book of Pushkin's poetry. Only in Russian. 'Your Russian is good, Claire,' she said. 'You must keep working at it.'

I nodded mutely, unable to speak.

327

David took me to the airport himself. Just the two of us.

We didn't talk during the entire journey. But I devoured the bleak scenery as though I could tattoo the memories to the lining of my brain.

I clung to him at the security checkpoint.

'As soon as I get some leave,' he said, 'let's go away some place together and figure out what we're going to do.'

I nodded. 'Anywhere. I'll meet you anywhere. They're probably going to fire me when I get to New York,' I said, 'so I expect I'll have a lot of free time on my hands.'

'Nonsense,' he said, but I knew he'd talked to Stan and Mark and it hadn't gone well. 'I'll quit if they fire you.'

'Don't you dare. What good will it do if both of us are unemployed? Anyway, I'm going to sell my house. I want to bring Sasha and Nina to the States. I'll need the money.'

He took my hands in his. 'Don't you worry about money,' he said. 'Or them.'

Then they called my flight to New York and there was no way, no cajoling, bribes, anything, that the uniformed guards hovering near us would relent and let him go all the way to the gate with me.

David kissed me for the longest time. So sweet I wanted it to last forever.

'I'll call you,' I said, 'when I get to New York. I'll try not to wake you up.'

'You won't wake me. I won't sleep until I hear from you,' he said. 'Call me the minute you arrive.'

Then he turned and walked away. I knew he wouldn't look back.

When the plane took off, I could hardly bear to look out of the window.

I did, of course. I watched the frostbitten landscape below disappear almost immediately under a heavy bank of clouds. The next time the clouds went away and I could see land again, we were over Poland.

The plane continued steadily west and I closed my eyes and remembered the colours and smells and sounds of Russia.

A SELECTION OF NOVELS AVAILABLE FROM JUDY PIATKUS (PUBLISHERS) LIMITED

0 7499 3215 5	Carolina Moon	Nora Roberts	£5.99
0 7499 3214 7	Blind Fear	Hilary Norman	£5.99
0 7499 3185 X	Endgame	James Elliott	£5.99
0 7499 3225 2	Special Circumstances	Sheldon Siegel	£5.99
0 7499 3211 2	A Study In Death	Iain McDowall	£5.99
0 7499 3216 3	The Funeral Boat	Kate Ellis	£5.99
0 7499 3234 1	The Confession	Janet Bettle	£5.99
0 7499 3213 7	Grave Concerns	Rebecca Tope	£5.99

All Piatkus titles are avaialble by post from:

**Bookpost PLC, P.O. Box 29, Douglas,
Isle of Man IM99 1BQ**

Credit Cards accepted. Please telephone 01624 836000
Fax 01624 837033, Internet http://www.bookpost.co.uk
Or e-mail: bookshop@enterprise.net for details.

Free postage and packing in the UK. Overseas customers: allow
£1 per book (paperback) and £3 per book (hardbacks).